She was im[...] been no las[...] hidden dee[...] admitted, that even a handshake would arouse in her that unbidden flash of desire she had felt for him, a desire that she knew would be fatal. Fatal in the most literal sense. There was no doubt in her mind that she could not go on living if she ever committed the ultimate treachery. She would not wish to live. She should not be allowed to live.

BLACK SUMMER

Julian Hale

Hamlyn Paperbacks

A Hamlyn Paperback
Published by Arrow Books Limited
17–21 Conway Street, London W1P 6JD

A division of the Hutchinson Publishing Group

London Melbourne Sydney Auckland
Johannesburg and agencies throughout the world

First published in Great Britain by Hamish Hamilton Ltd 1982
Hamlyn Paperbacks edition 1983
Reprinted 1985
© Julian Hale 1982

This book is sold subject to the condition that it shall not, by way of trade or otherwise, be lent, resold, hired out, or otherwise circulated without the publisher's prior consent in any form of binding or cover other than that in which it is published and without a similar condition including this condition being imposed on the subsequent purchaser.

Printed and bound in Great Britain by
Cox & Wyman Ltd, Reading

ISBN 0 09 937130 8

CONTENTS

★

Prologue 1

Part One: Black Summer 5
Part Two: Under the Wave 59
Part Three: Oaths and Promises 135
Part Four: Liberation 255

Epilogue 295

For Markie and Laura

I love my work and my children. God
Is distant, difficult. Things happen.
Too near the ancient troughs of blood
Innocence is no earthly weapon.

I have learned one thing: not to look down
So much upon the damned. They, in their sphere,
Harmonize strangely with the divine
Love. I, in mine, celebrate the love-choir.

Geoffrey Hill, *Ovid in the Third Reich*
(Reprinted by courtesy of Andre Deutsch Ltd)

PROLOGUE

When they kissed for the first time, Boris had to bend to reach Nadia's face. They were both fourteen in that summer of 1932, he very tall and thin, she small but already a woman. She wanted him to touch her breasts – gently, through the brown cotton of her Pioneer shirt – but instead his hands pressed her shoulder-blades. Her breasts were new and firm, and she was proud of them. But the disappointment she felt was not deep. She knew she would marry Boris when the right time came.

As it turned out, the wedding took place earlier than she had imagined – when she was nineteen and pregnant with Darya, and he just twenty. Boris had to take special leave from military service. After only four days he returned to duty. A month later, under the threat of a European war, he entered Military Academy to train as a regular officer in the Red Army.

And now, on the last day of June 1942, the Great Patriotic War was a year old. And Nadia Surkova stood alone on the side of a steeply-sloping street in the South Russian town of Pyatigorsk and watched her soldier husband go away – again.

All the way from Nalchik, their home town, Boris had travelled in the back of the Red Army truck with Nadia and her father and the ten partisan recruits. Now he sat up front in the cab, as the vehicle rattled down the dusty street, until the wild cherry trees smothered it under their fresh green foliage.

A moment of silence followed the truck's disappearance, and gradually the smell of its exhaust drifted away on the cool breeze off the mountains. Nadia sighed deeply and turned back into the sanitarium where her father still lay in a blanket on the stone floor of the entrance hall.

A doctor – elderly, unshaven – was bending over him, peering through steel-rimmed spectacles and shaking his head. A long, soft groan rose from the blanket heaped so casually on the floor. Hurriedly, Nadia knelt down, reaching out her hand to clutch her father's. He was only semi-conscious. All through the journey across the rich plain, smelling of hot wet earth and the sweat of the peasant partisans, Sergei Ivanovich had slept. Now, as Nadia rubbed his cold hand, he opened his eyes.

'Go back, darling,' he whispered. 'They need you. Your own child needs you. Please. Go home.'

But Nadia Surkova was a woman with no instinct for turning back – and absolutely no intention of doing so now.

Part One

BLACK SUMMER

ONE

First came the Red Army. Fifty stubble-bearded men, the detritus of the 295th Rifle Division, straggled in the midday heat eastward across the treeless Kuban plain. The peasants of Leninskoye, a small collective farm settlement, locked themselves in their houses and watched the retreat through chinks in their shuttered windows. One soldier bent to scoop a melon from a vine-shaded patch of garden by the roadside. Another tried to catch a squawking chicken, but the bird was too nimble. A young wife – knowing her husband, somewhere, fared no better than these men – ran out to offer the village's last fly-ridden horse to pull the wounded soldiers' single cart. Cut free, the mule which had stayed between its shafts ever since the Ukraine stretched out voluptuously in the dust – and died.

The soldiers passed through Leninskoye softly. The only noise was the creaking of the cartwheels, the rattling of mess-tins, the wheezing and spitting of men.

In the silence that followed the retreating soldiers, the earth seemed to be vibrating. Very gently at first, as if a faint heartbeat strained to announce life deep inside a corpse.

Minutes went by. Then suddenly the thin shriek of a hunting-horn pierced the sunbaked air. Fragments of shrill sound burst into the barricaded cottages.

A dog yelped.

Children clutched their mothers' skirts. The old men and women mumbled prayers and trembled with ancestral memories of Tatar hordes.

The distant horn grew louder.

The vibrating earth began to shake so violently that plates rattled and candles flickered in front of the icons. The flames' reflections shimmered in the gold leaf like sunflowers behind a heat haze.

The rumbling turned into a roar. Through their slatted shutters the peasants watched the slits of sun-bleached road. Suddenly the brilliance blacked out, flared up again, blacked out – a bewilderingly rapid quivering of light that matched their frantic heartbeats. Their gaping eyes glimpsed slabs of brown and gray metal, soldiers' chins and noses, helmets, guns, jagged black crosses, white-painted animals and flowers and numbers and letters in strange script, all rushing past, sparkling with dust. Praying and whining in anticipation of death, the peasants waited for the tanks to crush them and their cottages like wheat-grains on a threshing floor.

But as if by a miracle the Panzers touched no-one, nothing. Nor did they slow. They came through the settlement like transcontinental locomotives through a wayside halt. Columns of jeeps and armoured troop carriers followed in tight formation like coupled freight cars.

Then, as suddenly as they had come, they were gone.

It grew quiet again. The eddies of dust swirled up and away off the street, spreading out over the houses and gardens and the fields beyond. The sunlight settled back into its constant glare. The earth's vibrations became fainter.

The peasants understood. They were not to be murdered, raped, tortured. The Germans had not stopped to steal or burn, had not even jumped down from their iron horses. Was that progress? The Tatars had never left a cowering peasant alive or a house unplundered.

They moved closer to the windows, reluctant to believe. They opened the shutters. Yes, it was all over. Their heartbeats slowed. Children escaped from their mothers and rushed outside to see the duststorm retreat and listen to the last fading whoops and echoes of the hunting-horn.

Rostov had fallen. Then Krasnodar, Armavir, Stavropol. Now another settlement, a tiny element in one of so many hundreds of State farms called by the name of Lenin, was in 'occupied' territory. Way back, toward the west, the black smoke of the burning Maikop oilfields polluted the blue sky. The fires had been burning for two days.

*

The tankmen of the III Panzer Corps were intoxicated. Drunk with the exhilaration they remembered from the first heady days of Blitzkrieg in the West, they scarcely noticed the hamlet they had just conquered. They were stampeding. Dust pluming from clanking tracks, the tanks led the pack across the unresisting Russian plain.

The Ivans had cracked.

The hunt was on. The chase was faster and faster.

Behind the Panzers came mobile units of the 7th Mountain Division.

In the lead jeep stood Colonel Siegfried Brandt. Goggles protected his pale blue eyes. The skin of his face and hands was bronzed. Zeiss binoculars were slung around the neck of his field-gray uniform streaked with the fine grit of the steppe.

He raised an arm and pointed.

The column swung off right. Far ahead a dustcloud betrayed some small detachment of the Red Army.

The Colonel turned. He checked that the whole column was with him. He signalled the Panzers that his men were splitting from them. His own vehicles fanned out in a V formation, then into line abreast.

After the grim campaign of the winter and spring, after the slow destruction of the Russian 'super-hedgehogs' – city strongpoints which had to be battered to defeat – this hectic, full-throttle, thrilling dash across empty spaces was a liberation, a glorious release.

Besides, as Brandt knew well, you couldn't stop. The heat would have burned you up. It would have grasped you by the throat, choked you to death. The only way to go was fast, creating your own fresh wind.

He peered into the dustcloud ahead. It seemed to be approaching him instead of the other way round. Again the hunting-horn sounded, over to his left. Soldiers riding shotgun on the back of Panzers had been blowing away on every full-tilt charge since the Ukraine.

Suddenly, fifty ragged genies appeared out of the dust. Many of them were bandaged and supported themselves on sticks and crutches. They turned sluggishly and watched the Germans coming at them. A few with a remnant of energy began scattering like disoriented bees from an overturned hive. Any who still had weapons threw them away. Some collapsed onto the ground. Others put their hands above their heads. Still others simply continued to stare. The horse from Leninskoye tried to bolt for home, but only succeeded in spilling the cart over onto its side. The wounded slid out into the dust.

In the German personnel carriers gray-denimed troops brandished their guns.

'*Ni shagu nazad*, Ivan! Hey, stop! You heard what Uncle Joe told you? *Ni shagu nazad!*'

They threw back at the Russians the Soviet Generalissimo's instructions, issued after the fall of Rostov. 'Not a step back!'

How Stalin would weep at this, Brandt thought.

'Hey, Russki, *ni shagu nazad!*' his driver repeated beside him.

But already the column had raced on past, on further toward the mountains.

Brandt didn't bother to take such men prisoners. Other more sedate units would do the mopping up.

Yes, by Christ, it was exhilarating. No man could resist. Even a desk-officer, even a pacifist, would get caught up in the enthusiasm. Everything was forgotten in these moments of high-speed thrust, everything except the thrill of being the spearhead of the most brilliant, disciplined, energetic troops in the world.

No-one, now, could stop what had been set in such heady motion.

Just then Brandt's eyes picked up for the first time the sight he had really been waiting for. The land was rising.

Steadying himself with one hand on the metal bar fixed to the dashboard of his jeep, with the other hand he clamped the binoculars to his eyes. Yes – there it was. The first hazy outline of a hill. Just a small hill, jagged with trees. But this was a start, the first bump in the land that, rising and falling, then rising still more and yet more, eventually soared up to the eternal snows of the Caucasus, where Europe came to an end in one final surge at the continent's very highest peak, Mount Elbrus.

He took off his forage cap and stood bare-headed, staring ahead.

The Caucasus mountains.

For Colonel Brandt they were the real, the only, justification of the frantic pace. And now, now at last he was here. Behind the shimmering wall of dust and heat waited the ice-cool loneliness of the mountains he would claim as his own.

*

Monday, August 10, 1942.

A fine summer morning in the northern foothills of the Caucasus, midway between the Black and Caspian seas. Hot, yet agreeably fresh after the blazing chase across the Kuban plain.

Overhead, a lone Stormovik assault bomber flew out of the cloudbank over Elbrus and into the blue air above the plain. Its fuselage gleamed clean and silvery like the underbelly of a leaping salmon.

Colonel Siegfried Brandt turned on his heel and walked briskly to his tent, a custom-built artefact of gray parachute silk which had already done peacetime duty on climbing expeditions in the Alps, Dolomites and Cairngorms.

At the age of thirty-five, he commanded three battalions of the 7th Mountain Division, part of the 17th Army spearheading the thrust toward the Black Sea, Tiflis and the Caspian oil port of Baku.

With the summer campaign just half-way through, the master plan was succeeding. The signs now were that the entire Caucasus region – and the Caspian oil – would be in Nazi control before winter could come and seize the attackers in its paralysing grip.

'Breakfast, Herr Oberst.'

Hans Guggenbühl's round head appeared in the tent opening. An Austrian, Hans had drifted into the German army on account of his noodles. In 1939, disconsolate as second under-cook in the Kitzbühel hotel frequented by Brandt and his fellow Alpenjäger officers, nearing forty years of age, suffering from unrequited love for the manager's daughter, Hans needed little persuasion from the noodle-appreciative officers to return with them to Bavaria when their spell of training ended. Two months later Colonel Brandt obtained the Austrian cook's personal services as batman. The Divisional Commander, Lieutenant-General von Kreuss, coveted these services, however. Von Kreuss made Brandt promise that, if anything happened, he would have them for himself.

In a quiet spot shaded by a walnut tree Hans had laid out a folding table covered by a clean white cloth. On it were set a plate of ham and eggs. For lack of tea or coffee, an infusion of requisitioned herbs was served. The ham was from a can. The eggs had been the property of a Circassian woman in whose 'abandoned' hen-run, the night before, Hans detected traces of fresh footmarks.

'Excellent breakfast.' Brandt sat on his folding wicker chair. 'Compliments.'

'*Mahlzeit*, Herr Oberst,' replied the batman, sweating with pleasure. '*Mahlzeit*.' His mood was inclined toward satisfaction. He himself had just consumed a gargantuan breakfast.

The haze began to clear as Colonel Brandt ate. A small corner of Pyatigorsk revealed itself through a fold in the Besh Tau hills. White houses, several large and pillared, peeped out from among the trees and sloping gardens. A century ago the Russian poet and novelist Mikhail Lermontov had also marvelled at the emerging view of this pretty spa town. From the lower slopes of Mount Mashuk, the conical hill that dominated the town, Lermontov, like Brandt today, had admired the fresh bright watering-place with its sanitaria and villas and medicinal fountains and tree-filled parks bathed in brilliant air. The poet too had fought in the surrounding mountains, battling with Circassian and Kabardinian and Chechen tribesmen, all the motley Muslim array that the Tsar's army, with the aid of Cossack henchmen, resolved to subdue. Brandt was well aware of this past. Since the first order to join the Caucasus campaign, he had dreamed of following in the footsteps of Lermontov, Pushkin, Tolstoy . . . but, even more, of their magnificent enemies, men like Imam Shamyl and Hadji Murad. He romanticized this struggle – he knew that Germans were given to romanticism, but so had the great Russian soldier-writers. The Caucasus bred characters larger than life, heroic, implacable, generous, free.

He finished his meal and stood up. Today and tomorrow would take his Regiment into Pyatigorsk. He would try, he decided, to set up his headquarters in the Pushkin Baths. Brigade HQ would surely occupy the Stalin Hotel. But the hotel was not likely to be as comfortable as the rooms the doctors reserved for themselves in the town's plushest sanitarium.

A young officer, Lieutenant Fabian Lauterbach, accosted the Colonel outside his tent with the news that a meeting of senior officers from front-line Divisions was scheduled for 08.30 hours.

*

Brandt's good mood soured at the sight of SS Major Fritz Stegl's jeep parked beside General Konrad's command post, a solid square whitewashed cottage protected by a low cliff. He dismissed his driver with more of a curt wave than a salute.

Stegl had been wished on Colonel Brandt and his regiment. On attachment – like glue. As bad – Brandt once said to Major Ott – as having a commissar on one's back. He believed firmly that Stegl's natural home was the Gestapo.

Inside the small farmhouse the officers sat round the white-painted kitchen table. There were no refreshments.

General Konrad cleared his throat. 'There's something I want to get out of the way first. The plan has been put to me that the flag of the Third Reich be planted on Mount Elbrus, the highest mountain in Europe. The propaganda people support the idea, good for morale. I agree. Indeed, preparations are already under way. The only question is: can it be done? Major von Hirschfeld, they tell me, says yes, it can be done. I would expect him to say yes, having been selected to plan the expedition.' Only Stegl smiled. 'Now, von Grabenhofen, you've been closest to the route they'll have to take to Elbrus by all accounts. Is it secure yet?'

'At that height, Herr General, it will never be entirely secure,' von Grabenhofen – Colonel in the 4th 'Edelweiss' Mountain Division – answered evenly. 'But reconnaissance suggests that with strong back-up there would be no apparent reason for failure. Apart from the weather, of course, which even in August is unpredictable over twelve thousand feet. This peak is more than sixteen thousand.'

'Siegfried?'

'Let them try for the top, Herr General. I'd go myself if –'

'If you weren't needed down here. You'll have time enough to be reunited with your beloved mountains, Colonel.' Then Konrad added with sudden urgency: 'This is a joint expedition. No jealousy among Divisions. And a strong signals party. Taken care of? Fine. I suggest a final briefing with you, Major, in five days' time. Dismissed. Heil Hitler!'

'Heil Hitler!'

Von Hirschfeld saluted, heel-clicked and backed out quickly.

Konrad led the remaining group of men over to a large map pinned on the best-lit wall, made lumpy by the rough edges of stone.

'Speed, gentlemen, is of the essence. Fuel supplies are not without limits. The line of attack, I suggest, remains the one some of us discussed on Saturday. You all have copies of that briefing? Fine. . . .'

His fingers flitted over the big Russian 1:50,000 map with its German over-printing, pointing out the arrows, crosses and other symbols that represented the agreed lines of attack. Pyatigorsk was to be penetrated from the north and west. At the same time a Battalion of Pioneers and two Battalions of Colonel Brandt's 21st Regiment were to conduct a diversionary pincer move from the south. If resistance was weak, so much the better. All groups would enter the town simultaneously.

'Do we know any more about what opposition to expect?' Brandt asked at the end of the General's exposition, when they were all seated again.

Konrad laughed. 'Women! I mean it. I just had in an Intelligence report of a female Battalion in the city. But never underestimate women.'

'I don't,' Brandt said soberly. 'I saw what they did in the defense of Sevastopol.'

'There is also in Pyatigorsk an NKVD Division. Plus God knows what other kind of riff-raff. The big Battalions have pulled back. By all accounts they'll start to get serious along the Baksan River. Fine. We'll find that out for ourselves. It shouldn't be too hard, gentlemen, Pyatigorsk. I repeat, however, never, never, underestimate the enemy.'

'May I suggest, Herr General,' interposed von Grabenhofen, 'the quicker our forces take Stalingrad and cut off the Volga supply route to Moscow, the quicker the enemy will collapse on this front too. I hear,' he added smugly, 'the Ivans are already referring to their "Black Summer". It's a comfort to know they recognize the full extent of their desperate plight.'

Brandt said nothing. In his judgment the transfer of the 4th Panzer Army to Stalingrad was a sign that things were getting tough up there on the Volga, not a prelude to a spectacular breakthrough. Besides, there wasn't much summer left, and winter would be a very different matter. His silence on this was tactical. 'Defeatist' talk was not only useless but, in front of Stegl, dangerous.

'Questions, gentlemen?'

'Weather problems, Herr General?' asked an artillery Colonel.

'Certainly not. A beautiful day. Quite beautiful. We should go outside and enjoy it while we can.'

Wooden chairs scraped on the rough boards as the men stood up. There was an immediate buzz of chatter.

At the door the artillery Colonel took Brandt's arm.

'Tell me,' he said. 'This mood of wildness, is it infecting your men too?'

'Wildness?'

'No stopping them. I'd have thought those hills would give them pause for sober thought. Cavalry as well as gunners. But it's this mad zest for advance, for attack –'

'Soldiers with no high-altitude training,' Brandt said with a shrug, 'cannot know the challenge of the mountains.'

Major Stegl, immaculate in the black uniform of the Nazi 'Guards', came up behind Brandt.

'Yes, the mountains.' A curl of cigarette smoke escaped his mouth as he spoke. 'Glorious, are they not?'

'Quite so, Herr Sturmbannführer,' Brandt said neutrally, ignoring Stegl's irony. 'Glorious.' Then he added, 'I do not you see our mountain goat, however, painted on your jeep.'

'It was Schweppenburg, I think, Colonel – an excellent Panzer commander, by the way – who pointed out what a gift to enemy Intelligence these divisional emblems are.'

Stegl stamped his cigarette butt into the worm-eaten floor of the porch and walked on out into the courtyard, brushing Brandt's shoulder as he passed.

Brandt stood rigidly a few seconds, then followed.

Outside the HQ, the sound of gunfire was breaking into the still morning, drowning the chirruping of birds. A sharp hoarse cry from a mountain turkey was the only birdsound to penetrate the mounting roar of anti-aircraft guns. Then once again, abruptly, the guns stopped, and the background of buzzing and chirping returned.

General Konrad came out into the courtyard. There were final salutes, handshakes. The briefing was over. Brandt looked around, blinking, waiting for the greens and browns and blues to emerge from the brilliant monochrome with which the sun at first had blinded him. Under the trees Corporal Beutner started the engine of the jeep in anticipation. Brandt walked over slowly.

'Sir?'

'Take it gently, Klaus. Let's enjoy the place while we can.'

'Sir!'

The engine idled.

'It'll be down into the town then, Herr Oberst,' the driver said, half-inquiringly, half-prophesying.

'Soon enough,' Brandt said with a sigh. 'Let's find the regiment first.'

Screwing up his eyes and sitting low in his seat, supporting the back of his head with cupped hands, Colonel Brandt directed their slow return along a criss-cross of paths and fields and orchards. Apples, pears and quinces were bursting with succulence. The hedgerows were heavy with bilberries and scarlet poppies, and the smell of wild daphne and oleander filled the air. It was ten past nine. Through the freshness, the full stifling heat of summer was just beginning to rise.

TWO

A Junior Lieutenant of the Red Army looked out toward the hills from the central boulevard in Pyatigorsk, where Lermontov and the fashionable drinkers of the spa waters, a century before, had wandered up and down, up and down, bowing and gossiping. The possession of a pair of field glasses marked him out as special. His uniform was clean. He'd shaved only six hours ago with a new safety razor purchased from Voyentorg, the Red Army shop. Tall, with a wide forehead and a narrow chin, a short narrow mouth and prominent cheekbones, Lieutenant Boris Surkov was chastely handsome in the manner of recruiting posters and propaganda films.

Watching, he began to tremble. The signs of German presence – glinting metal, smoke, flashes of gunfire – made the muscles in his jaw twitch and sweat burst out in beads all over his body. When the lenses began to fog, he dropped the binoculars on his chest. The cord jabbed into the back of his close-cropped neck like the whiplash of a feudal prince.

Fascist monsters!

Assyrians!

For days the noise of approaching battle had grown louder while Boris waited for the Germans like a once-defeated challenger impatient for the return fight. Their previous engagement had taken place the summer before when, on the very first day of battle, a bullet had grazed the membrane surrounding his left lung. He had returned to the Caucasus, his home. Today he was as fit as before the war, desperate for revenge, confident that now the war had come to him, to his own native territory, the Fritzes had come too far.

At twenty-four, Boris Surkov was the precise twin of the

Revolution. It marked him as someone special – or so he had always believed – this fact of being born on October 26, 1917. Though now they had changed the calendar and called it November 7.

An orphan, his only parents were the Red Army and the Party. At times – this was one of them – he felt they were his only family, despite his wife and child.

Almost at the top of the wide tree-lined street that ended above him in a steep garden and flights of white stone steps, he stared up impatiently at the Elizabeth Gallery beyond. In this spindly arcade, before it was clogged with sandbags, the sick and the hypochondriacs (in Boris's view entirely the latter) used to take the mineral waters and discuss their ailments. Turning, he saw the town below sparkling among the many trees, each whitewashed villa and house and official building like a rich lady wrapped around the shoulders with a green fur stole. Boris preferred his native city of Nalchik, dustier and dirtier, but more serious.

Furious with impatience, he strode back down the boulevard.

What, he wondered for the nineteenth time, made his wife so obstinate? What made her want to throw away her life like this, the life he'd planned for her, marching forward arm in arm to a New Society? It was a crime against reason. An anti-Soviet act.

Once more he turned, walked up toward the decadent drinking gallery, turned again, and walked down the boulevard.

Finally an elderly nurse came to the doorway of the dumpy, pale-brown edifice of the Pushkin Baths and called for Lieutenant Surkov to come inside.

'Hurry, Comrade,' she said curtly as he ran in. 'The patients are being got ready for transfer.'

He stopped. 'Transfer? Out of town?'

'What d'you think, Comrade blockhead? To a secure room at the back. If you want to see Nadia Sergeevna, you'll have to move a sight quicker.'

Boris, anxious to get it over and done with, ran in. He found his wife at once in a bleak, stone-flagged corridor. It was six weeks since he had brought her, and her father, over from Nalchik in the back of that truck. She seemed smaller than he remembered her, haggard, very tired. In the dank, sweat-filled air, her auburn curls clung to her forehead and temples. Dark rims ringed her large oval eyes. Appalled, because despite his impatience with her he loved her, he stopped for a second and stared. But only for a second. The matter was urgent. He hurried on, his heavy boots making echoes down the grim passage. When she raised her face for him to kiss, he ignored her gesture. He stood in front of her formally.

'Aren't you ready?'

Nadia sighed. Her features steadied, and her eyes hardened. 'I wrote to you. I can't leave father. There are no nurses to look after the civilians anymore. He has only me. I wrote to you all this. Please Boris. You shouldn't have come.'

'Of course I came. You're my wife. I love you. You're my responsibility.'

'I can look after myself, Boris Alexandrovich.'

Boris sat stiffly, 'I respect your independence. You have always insisted I should. All the same you must come.'

'No, Boris.' She folded her arms and tilted her head. One of the curls came unstuck and flopped onto her shoulder. 'Thank you for trying. But, believe me, please, I can't. Now, before you leave, I've been so cut off here, tell me how the battle is going. Tell me about you.' She put out a hand and touched his arm. 'Can you get out before the town is taken? The sick here, we —'

'Why should the town be taken?' Boris said angrily.

His chin was above the level of the top of her head. He said gently: 'I'd fight better knowing you were safe.'

'I can't take father. You know that, you understand that. Please. A move would kill him.' Again she touched the arm of his uniform. 'How is our Dasha?'

Boris relaxed. He had seen Dasha only a week before. 'She's well. Teasing your mother. Making Ilya laugh.'

'Ilya. My poor darling.'

'Your brother's fine, Nadia. I just wish he had come here with the old man, not you. He would have taken my advice now the Fritzes have got so close.'

'Ilya is only sixteen,' she reminded him. 'And he has been sick. Very sick.'

'Nadia, Nadia. I love you. I'll always love you. But this is war.'

'Not between us.'

Boris began to laugh, but then said abruptly: 'Nadia Sergeevna, I command you to leave.'

'Boris!' She snatched her hand away. Her cheeks flamed red. 'I'm not your Muslim whore. My father won't survive without me.'

'He won't survive even with you, you fool. He's dying.'

'Yes, he is dying. But he's not dead. I won't abandon him. Not even for your sake – yet I love you. Now go.' She glared at him. 'Yes, go.'

He was confused. Did he want her to be a soldier herself? Or a nurse? But caring for the war wounded, not the civilian sick. A teacher again? But there were no classes now. Or at home, minding Darya, their precious darling, just five years old? They had always had shared ideals, a shared love. Or so he had thought. Perhaps he had never come to terms with her Circassian blood . . .

Boris drew in a deep breath. 'The truck is arranged. There's room for your father. For the sake of the Soviet Union, come.'

'Please, please,' Nadia said softly.

'This is an order!'

'Then I disobey it.'

'Traitor!'

She slapped him, stinging his cheek with the whipping cut of her fingers.

A man on crutches and a bloodstained orderly, witnesses just yards away, shouted abuse at Boris. Boris, too angry and upset to speak, stalked off, then began to run. He ran through the big doors at the far end of the hall and vaulted onto his waiting motorcycle. Stabbing it into action with the ball of his foot, he dive-bombed down into the town like a Stuka, screaming through the dusty paths between shacks and twisted trees into which the main road west degenerated.

At the railway station he stopped, cutting the engine and hauling the bike up onto its stand as if lifting a wild goat by its horns. He stood beside it a moment, letting his heartbeats settle. Here he had another rendezvous, with the local partisan chief, Tembot Kochan. Here he was back in the real business of war. There was no time – and he was glad of this – for his anger to turn to remorse. All the same, picking his way slowly down the railroad track littered with garbage and pieces of brick, he began rubbing his cheek, still tender from Nadia's slap.

Ten minutes later, leaning against a concrete tank-trap shaped like a dragon's tooth, Boris raised his field glasses to his eyes again for the third time. Could the town really be defended? he wondered. He scanned the jagged horizon, the three visible peaks of Besh Tau's five in front of him, then the long descent to the flat ground on his left. 'We'll damn well try,' he murmured to himself. Already he was feeling stronger, a soldier again.

But a Junior Lieutenant attached to the staff of General Ivan Ivanovich Maslennikov, to perform liaison duties with the partisans in the central seetor of the north Caucasus front, had no way of knowing that the Supreme Commander in Moscow had already taken the decision to stabilize the main line of Russian defense along the Baksan River, thirty-five miles further east. Senior Red Army officers knew this. The Germans had a suspicion. Militarily the decision was logical. But to Boris each square yard of Soviet soil was sacred. Not a step back! The *Stavka*, Soviet General Headquarters, encouraged his kind of obduracy and devotion. It had also learned the lesson that to defend everywhere meant overstretching your defence line.

For six months Boris Surkov had prepared for this moment. For six months, every day of each month, he had been forming and training and supplying the embryo partisan groups between Pyatigorsk and the capital of the Kabardin-Balkar Autonomous Region, Nalchik, fifty miles east.

Now, he was sure, the partisans and the Red Army would stand firm.

Yet even as Boris formed these thoughts, his head moved slowly from side to side. He recalled images of the work he had done, of the struggle. He saw in his mind the guide and the shepherd who had fought with knives over a woman –

until he had fired into the ground by their feet and they fled, surely to fight on to the death in the forest. Neither had returned. He saw the horse lacerated by a collision with a supply truck, still standing in the centre of the road, its flesh in bloody ribbons, and heard the ghoulish laughter from the black-toothed faces all around. He recalled the time when he had tried to teach young Marko's platoon how to handle grenades. Ugh! The memory of an old man blown to pieces and the hand that flew off and hung by its twisted fingers in the topmost branches of a poplar. The men had used it for target practice.

Partisans! Gangs of kids and tottery tribesmen.

Boris found it hard not to succumb to a guilty but persistent feeling of contempt. He was a hundred percent Russian boy. His mother was a Russian schoolteacher from Nalchik, and his father was a Red Army officer born in Moscow. Both had been killed, heroically, in the Civil War. The partisans were peasants. Many were Kabardinians and Balkars. Some were from other tribes. So many tribes. Like Africa. Boris often wondered if they had ever accepted the fact that they were Soviet Russians now. Did they even know that Islam was dead, abolished?

But they were fighters. Some of them good fighters. Yes, he decided, he was proud to have the job of integrating these men into the grand strategy of the Red Army. Fine men, in many cases. And he was personally responsible for them. General Maslennikov had selected him.

He stared up at the hills again, one foot balanced on a steel track like a hunter on the corpse of a bear.

Kochan was late.

Eventually, he turned and strode back toward the blue-and-white station building with its gleaming walls and domes.

All around was bustle, noise. On many faces were obvious signs of panic. A platoon of infantry, nimblest elements of the 37th Army who less than three weeks ago were watching the quiet Don flow by, had taken up defensive positions at key points in and around the station. Their faces showed bewilderment from the constant battering, the chaotic retreat, the horror of being in so short a time among the few survivors. They were in Pyatigorsk now because they just happened to have retreated this far and were too tired to go any further. Their job, they knew by the instinct of beaten soldiers, wasn't a crucial one. Unlike Boris, they knew they were there to sacrifice their lives in exchange for a very small slice of time. They knew the officers and commissars told them lies. The station didn't even have tactical importance. The last wagon had pulled out twenty-four hours ago. Rolling stock – unlike men – was too scarce to risk capture.

In the forecourt, a few inveterate peasants, would-be kulaks, champions of outdated private enterprise, were hawking their wares. All they had to sell were such staples as sunflower seeds, bruised apples, pears and squashy peppers. But there were takers among the soldiers and those townsmen and townswomen too old or too obstinate or simply too frightened to join the streams of refugees pushing and fighting and weeping their way east. Mostly they bartered – old clothes or knick-knacks or even canned army rations against the fresh food. Boris had a communist soldier's contempt for peasant profiteers. And for refugees. Escapers. Who could possibly not be fit enough to fight the Nazis? The old folk, just as much as the kids, could all do something, run errands, help carry stretchers, something. Besides, it was useless, this crowd milling around the station. How many times did they have to be told – there would *be* no more trains?

'Boris Alexandrovich!'

The roar of his name was like a gunshot.

'Boris Alexandrovich!'

Boris spun round. In front of him appeared an enormous, broad-shouldered man with the deeply lined and white-mustached face of a Kabardinian mountain shepherd dressed in a dirty quilted jacket, home-made felt shoes and, despite the heat, a flat round fur hat. A Moisin 7.62-mm rifle was slung over one shoulder and a full cartridge belt over the other – arms and ammunition supplied by Boris himself. He advanced toward the young Lieutenant with hands outstretched.

'Boris Alexandrovich! Boris Alexandrovich! A pleasure,

dear young Comrade. So they finally got here, the bastard Fritzes.'

Tembot Kochan spoke Kabardinian to Boris though his Russian was equally fluent. Tembot in fact had spoken Russian for most of a long career, as first (indeed) a mountain shepherd, then a cement factory worker before the Revolution, then a Civil War soldier, and finally, during the twenty years of uncertain peace and reconstruction, the leaven of humanity in the Nalchik force of the NKVD – 'one Old Bolshevik forgotten, thank God, by Moscow'. In August 1939, on his sixtieth birthday, Tembot had retired as the local chief of secret police. Now he was a partisan. Leader of the Nalchik sector by rank and by right.

'I expected you at ten hundred hours,' Boris said flatly, in Russian, letting himself, however, be grabbed by the shoulders and embraced.

'When you issue us partisans with watches like yours that work, I'll be on time, my boy,' Tembot said with a deep-throated laugh. Then he himself switched to Russian, which he knew Boris understood better. The Russian population of the Caucasus – the conquerors – seldom mastered any of the hundreds of languages and dialects of their 'brother peoples'. 'So, when are you expecting the Fritzes down here?'

'Tonight. That's what the General thinks. Maybe a diversion or two today. But we're ready.'

'Nadia and the old man. Both out safely?'

Boris looked at the older man. 'No. She won't leave.'

'What? You're a damn fool, Boris.'

'That's enough of that, Comrade. I've orders for you. Orders from General Maslennikov.'

'Orders?' Tembot sighed. 'Let's have 'em.'

Boris was opening his mouth to issue the instructions he'd so carefully rehearsed when a shell from a German 75-mm Howitzer landed in the station forecourt. It smashed to a pulp a barrow of peppers, onions and grapes . . . and the flesh of the peasant who had brought them to town, braving his life for a profit. A bowl of sunflower seeds burst like tiny fragments of shrapnel. People and animals scattered. Only Tembot remained where he was in the centre of the track, waiting for his orders. Boris, who had run for cover behind a sandbagged position in the ticket office, came back with a sheepish grin on his face.

'I know,' he said. 'If it missed you once, it'll not come back and try again.'

'That what I always say?'

The young man relaxed at last. 'So long as there's you, Tembot Batazarovich –'

'Yes, yes, come on lad, you had orders for me.'

Boris recollected himself, embarrassed.

'Well, HQ thinks they'll try and encircle the town first. So –'

'They already have. All except the Nalchik road and a strip on each side.'

'The point is the road itself must be kept open. Now, look. There's a point here . . .' Boris at this moment tugging out a creased map and stabbing it with his index finger, 'where the Germans will try a probe for sure, down this valley here. The General instructs your group to prepare an ambush right here . . . by the bridge. To be in position by sunset tonight.'

Tembot considered, raised his eyebrows, then nodded. 'Difficult. I know the peasants in that sector. Hard to tell if they'll give you protection or give you away. Word's going round the Fritzes'll hand 'em back their land. Some hope. The bastards don't even consider 'em people!' Tembot gave a loud laugh. 'All the same –'

'All the same, the people are with us.'

'Ah yes, my boy. Yes. The people. Well, as I say, it's difficult. But possible. In fact we'll do it.' Tembot paused, then looked into Boris's eyes. 'How long are you going to try and hold the town?'

'There's a whole NKVD Division here. The Party has organized ten new detachments. Pyatigorsk can be defended.'

Boris saluted, formally. But when he felt his face brushed by the stiff white whiskers again, he clasped the old man to him, the companion of his father and now his own friend and comrade in arms.

'May God be on our side,' Tembot murmured, then turned away. 'As they used to say, the people. You'll know where to find me.'

He strode off, passing by the mess of fruit and blood in the forecourt as if he'd seen worse, which, as Boris well knew, he had. Tembot's Shaloukh stallion was grazing in the garden of the mud baths. Seeing him, it whinnied with pleasure.

Watching the old partisan mount and ride off, Boris broke out into a cold sweat. Suddenly the stench of blood and fruit and home-boiled potato alcohol and rough tobacco and excrement and hot paving-stones and dust overwhelmed him. He felt small and helpless, caught – just as Nadia was – in the clash of steel-hard forces of destruction. But the moment passed. He had more work to do. There was a cache of small arms the police had unearthed in a construction materials store in the south of town. The store manager claimed they were put there ready for the partisans. Boris had been ordered to go meet Captain Nazir Bekirbi of the NKVD and verify the claim . . . else prove the manager was lying, a traitor ready to hand over the guns to the Germans. It was going to be awkward. Boris needed the weapons. He could probably get them by saying they were indeed part of the supplies under his control. And a traitor would go free. Or he could tell what seemed likely to be the truth, that the manager had kept them, not for the partisans, but for himself – or the Germans. In that case Boris would lose the guns. He decided he would just have to judge from their quality.

But the real awkwardness was the fact that this same Captain Bekirbi was having an affair with Luda, Boris's sister. An affair of which Nadia openly disapproved. Boris, but only to himself, was inclined to agree with her, despite Bekirbi's eminence in the People's Commissariat for Internal Affairs.

Where Tembot had his stallion, Boris had his motorcycle: another perk of his job. The shell-blast had knocked it over but not caused any serious damage to its frame.

The iron-heavy 350 cc machine roared into life first time, and Boris guided it carefully through the messy station court and out along the sidestreets. Since yesterday they had emptied fast. Only military vehicles and soldiers were on the move now. He had to manoeuvre, using all his skill, to pass a line of trucks requisitioned from the cement factory, 3-ton army lorries and donkey-carts. This convoy was supposed to be taking valuables, including Party documents and food, out of town. In fact it was chock full of last-minute refugees – and hopelessly stalled by a breakdown of the lead truck. Boris looked in all the cabs for the driver who had said he would take Nadia out, but couldn't see him.

Boris rode phlegmatically, pulling out of his pocket a hunk of stale bread and chewing it. He could manipulate the machine one-handed despite the pot-holes and shell-holes.

*

The store was a miserable shack, whitewashed on the front but not at the sides or back. It looked onto a dusty street on which the only life was a small flock of geese that seemed from their lack of feathers to be ready-plucked for the oven while still alive. When Captain Bekirbi arrived, there was no sign of Boris. He was relieved. He turned to the Sergeant of the Militia who doubled as his driver.

'Get in there and do the bastard.'

Bekirbi – round-bellied but thin-faced, with dark crinkly hair – waited, trembling, in his Zim automobile while the Sergeant went inside the store.

Five minutes later the job was done, and Bekirbi had helped load the guns onto the rear seat. He and the Sergeant were already back inside the store when the distant throb of a heavy motorcycle was heard outside.

'Sergeant!'

'At your service, Comrade Captain.'

'Take this piece of garbage and dump it.' Bekirbi kicked the battered corpse of the manager disdainfully, though he had to hold his hands behind his back to prevent the Sergeant seeing how they shook.

The Sergeant had already begun to drag the body through the doorway when the throb in the street grew louder then abruptly died.

Bekirbi appeared behind the corpse as if indicating to Boris that he was merely supervising its removal. 'At last, Comrade,' he shouted. He treated Boris as an inferior officer, not as the brother of his girl. 'Two rusty hunting rifles, that's all the shitty traitor had,' he added over-loudly, emerging onto the street.

'Your message said a dozen weapons at least,' Boris replied, hauling the cycle onto its stand and ignoring the body being dragged along the edge of the street. 'If I'd known –'

'Correct. My information was a dozen at least.' Bekirbi's voice lowered as the two men approached each other. 'The traitor had distributed the valuable weapons, so much is clear. I have occupied you unnecessarily. I knew you would understand.' He spoke with exaggerated courtesy.

Boris glanced at the black Packard-style saloon hunched like a gangster's getaway car outside the store. Bekirbi's eyes followed. The windows were open. There was no disguising the fact that more than just two hunting rifles were piled in the back. And they certainly weren't rusty. Bekirbi hoped that Boris's respect for rank would make him keep his observations to himself.

'So you've nothing for me, Nazir Kerimovich? Nothing for my partisans?'

'Nothing. In any case, your partisans are more skillful with knives and pitchforks than modern firearms.'

Boris saluted.

'Till next time, Comrade Captain,' he said coldly.

It was Bekirbi's turn to salute.

His right hand was still raised to his forehead when he suddenly froze.

An expression of terror sucked in his lips, cupping his badly-shaven cheeks. His arm jerked forward, pointing. His fingers shook like a drunkard's.

His voice made a kind of gurgling sound.

'*Tanks!*'

At the end of the street, where it tailed off into a track snaking through fields of corn and sunflowers, first one, then a second German tank came into view, squeaking and rumbling round the wall of the furthest house like a pair of huge iron-clad rats.

They were a quarter of a mile away but looked close enough to touch.

A spurt of flame and smoke erupted from the leading tank.

At the same moment a handful of infantrymen fanned out from behind its protection and darted for cover – a line of single-storey cottages on the edge of the fields. The first shell whined over the store, then more in quick succession. A machine-gun opened fire from the Russian forward positions.

It was this that caught the Sergeant – though he had dropped the corpse and was sprinting to the shelter of the store. His body pirouetted and fell, raising a cloud of dust.

The same moment, Bekirbi ran for the Zim, and Boris for his motorcycle.

The gunners of the leading tanks – three already had crossed the road and were grinding forward over vegetable plots and fruit-trees and frail garden walls – marked down the store as the front line of the Russian defence perimeter. Pausing, wheeling, the front tank aimed its 37-mm cannon at the mud-and-plaster walls. The gunner's aim was as precise as if competing in the Division's annual shooting competition. With a bellow of hot air and smoke and splintered fragments of wall and tin roof, the shack disintegrated.

Debris spattered down. Paint barrels exploded. A shard of wood shattered the Zim's windshield. Bekirbi screamed. He felt a jet of hot urine on his thighs. He tried to croak an order to Boris. Then, to his relief, he saw Boris straddle his bike, fire its engine and gun it toward the automobile.

The tanks clanked forward.

Of the citizens cowering in the houses further up toward the fields only one was foolish enough to offer resistance. An old tribesman poked an even more ancient musket through the rear window of his cottage and picked off a German rifleman riding shotgun on the leading tank. The soldier fell sideways into the road. The tracks of the following tank ground his head into a red smear.

At once the cottage was obliterated with a shower of grenades. But the tribesman's brave, suicidal action diverted attention for a few vital seconds.

'Get on the back!' Boris yelled.

Bekirbi, half-paralysed with fright, fumbled with the Zim's door handle, cursing its inaccessibility, its cheapness, its sharp tinplate finish.

'Leave it!' Boris shouted.

The tanks were two hundred yards away. Less.

At last Bekirbi gave up trying to get into the Zim. He clambered on the pillion and clamped his arms tight round Boris's stomach.

Boris swivelled his heavy machine, raising spurts of dust like dragon's breath. Accelerating past the blazing ruin of the store, he zigzagged at top speed toward the centre of town, negotiating the tank barriers as if riding a Lippizaner stallion.

Just before the Podkumok River, Bekirbi peered round Boris's back. That very moment dead ahead – a second column of tanks appeared. He was about to cheer . . . when he saw – again – they were Panzers!

He buried his head in Boris's shoulder, and screwed his eyes shut. By the junction with the main road east – the only road still open – Boris made another sharp right. Bekirbi held on as tight as an infant sloth to its mother. He could smell his urine. His thighs were sore from it. If he hadn't been so full of fear, he'd have felt shame. He comforted himself with the steady roar of the motor. At last he opened his eyes, noticed the route they were taking, and shivered with relief. Already they were on the road to Nalchik, the road to safety.

THREE

Inside the Pushkin Baths, at the back of the building, was a scullery with a single small window. Minutes after Boris had gone to the station to meet Tembot Kochan, a dozen terminally sick patients – together with all the relations, friends and neighbours nursing them – were pushed and carried and shooed into this dark, dank room. Nadia and her father were among them.

A hose was improvised to run into the scullery from a natural spring inside the Baths. The acrid mineral water dripped into a metal bucket. As soon as the tinny trickle became a deeper, plopping noise, someone – often several at a time – rushed to tip it into a cup. Fights broke out. Soon a rota would have to be arranged. The bad temper and squabbling over the best positions, the least lumpy beds, the space to be occupied by each group of sick and healthy festered like an untreated wound. For food there were several large loaves of black bread – enough of that at least to avoid either hunger or fighting.

Nadia, having struggled for her place, listened with stubborn patience to the discontents and to the sounds of distant but approaching battle. She didn't move from beside the cot on which her father lay still and dying.

Nothing more could be done for him except give what comfort she could.

She thought of Boris. A quick anger flared in her then, not shame, but a sadness. She glanced down at her father, who had groaned faintly.

He, more than her husband, needed her attention and care.

They hadn't seen a doctor for a week. The doctors were too

busy with the wounded. Only occasionally could they be spared for the less urgent task of killing the pain suffered by the diseased and the old.

And it was pain that was killing her father as much as the cancer causing it. At times Nadia was tempted to beg for a drug to put him out of his agony. But she couldn't do it, not while there was any hope. She was a modern woman, with none of the religious prejudices of her Muslim relations. A Soviet woman, wife of a Soviet man. All the same she could not kill her father, any more than she could desert him, not for any 'theory'.

Besides, she had chosen her role, insisted she, not her mother, make a last attempt in Pyatigorsk to rewrite the drama of the cancer's headlong gallop toward death through her father's wasted body. Now she was having to live the part – however unrewarding it might be. Ever since she had been aware of her father, he had suffered physically, first from war wounds and then in recent years from illness. That made him a hero, victim of the State's enemies and of fate. Yet he was a passive figure.

He was not old, barely fifty-nine. He looked ninety, emaciated and parchment-skinned. Stirring on the narrow cot, he moaned so quietly that only Nadia heard the sound in this cramped scullery full of old men and women stertorously dying. She dabbed his forehead with a wet handkerchief. The water and thin sweat made new stains on the soiled blanket and watered the drab flowers printed on her smock.

'Go back, darling,' he whispered. 'Go back.'

She stroked his hand and smiled at him. Those were the only words he uttered now. But the Fritzes had advanced too far, too quickly. It was too late to go back, even if the loyalty of a daughter had not prevented her absolutely. What if she herself were old and sick, and little Darya, grown-up Darya, were beside her . . . ? No, it was too painful to think about a five-year-old threatened by this barbaric war. At least – so far – her child was safe.

Surreptitiously, Nadia spat over her left shoulder three times, for luck.

Then quickly she began cooling her father's forehead again with the rag in her hand. When he smiled at her, she got up and wrung out the rag, rinsed it under the hose-pipe still dripping water that smelled of stale breath, then took breadcrumbs from the pocket of her smock and softened them with the water for him to eat.

Night fell. There was little sleep to be had. No-one came in or out. The door remained locked.

From outside there came more frequent noises, but they seemed random, incoherent. The room stank worse than ever with the slops bucket overflowing.

Nothing changed in the morning except the light of the sun filtering brighter through the dust-streaked window. At nine o'clock, an old syphilitic woman died in a corner of the scullery – at least it was then that the others realized she was dead.

'Why the hell ain't it me?' an old man muttered in a sulky voice. The look in her father's eyes told Nadia that his own wishes were no different. Others in the ward mumbled prayers, fragments of prayers remembered from burials in days gone by. The very oldest patient's lips palpitated like a dying fish's as she went through elaborate, silent rituals.

The water dripped, dripped, dripped into the bucket. It sounded to Nadia as if someone were plucking a dirge from a badly-tuned guitar.

*

Outside in the town, the artillery battle and the street-fighting were becoming more intense. Four hundred yards from the Pushkin Baths, all around the iron structure of the 'Lermontov' Gallery and the vine-covered Stalin Hotel, German shock troops and Russian sharpshooters met in hand-to-hand, house-to-house battle.

The German losses were as heavy as the Russian. In the town centre they came under the heavy fire of a Russian 15-cm gun battery positioned in a rocky hollow behind the Aeolian Harp – erected inside a kind of stone-pillared summer-house by a nineteenth-century German doctor in an attempt to make Nature play Bach. A detachment of Grenadiers was deployed to attack it now from the rear. At eleven o'clock both battery and wind-blown music were silenced.

At five past eleven, in the boulevard in front of the Pushkin Baths, two light tanks made a dash forward, churning the central flowerbeds into kaleidoscopic confetti. One stalled in a small fish-pond ornamented with crumbling copies of Greek urns, was picked off by a volley of anti-tank rockets and finally set on fire by a Molotov cocktail. While it burned, the other tank cranked round in a half-circle. Its machine-gun raked the facade of the Baths and the scrub behind, where a platoon of the Women's Rifle Battalion was dug in. Seeing finally he had no support, the tank commander directed his machine in an even tighter circle, then raced for cover, trailing black smoke. At the same moment, an attack party of Brandt's 21st Regiment rode up on the deck of a brand-new Model G Panther tank. The soldiers sprang out from behind the cover of the billowing smoke and, hurling egg grenades, charged up the slope behind the Baths, killing all twelve women hidden in the scrub.

The attackers had no way of knowing it, but these were the last of the Russian troops defending positions in and around the old centre of the spa. Taking no chances, they launched ferocious new assaults. A party with a flame gun and machine pistols burst in through the main door of the theatre, built sideways on to the boulevard, more like a warehouse than a home of dramatic art. Inside, a nine-year-old boy, who had run there for shelter and collapsed inside the foyer from a mixture of terror and exhaustion, was instantly incinerated.

One by one, the buildings on both sides of the boulevard were smashed into and raked with fire.

The scullery at the back of the Pushkin Baths was not discovered for half an hour after the first German soldier entered the building. At exactly ten minutes past noon, a hobnailed boot burst open the locked door, and a Corporal and two Grenadier Privates flung themselves inside.

'Shitting hell! What's this?'

The Corporal held his nose, searching the gloom with disbelieving eyes. He stood still, as if considering whether to put this whole wailing crew out of their misery for ever. But then he made out Nadia and a sturdy Kuban girl, the only two standing upright. His rifle lowered.

'Fetch those two lovelies out of here,' he shouted.

Two Privates shouldered their guns, kicked aside the old and the sick and pulled at the Kuban girl, who suddenly switched from petrified passivity to wildcat action, and swung her fist at the man who grabbed her, at the same time kicking out with flailing fat legs. In a second she was free. But instead of retreating – or pressing the attack – she jumped across a cot and shoved Nadia from behind.

'What d'you want with me?' she screamed. 'Take *her*.'

Nadia shot forward and was grabbed by the Corporal, then hauled across the room. She tried to wrench herself out of his grip. The German backhanded her across the face.

But he had also hit her hard enough to jerk her free.

She spun against the wall, ripping a notice on drug abuse, buckled her knee against a wooden chair, righted herself, and ran.

'Get that bitch!' the Corporal yelled.

The thump of all three soldiers' boots sounded in pursuit. But Nadia knew the layout of the building. She sidestepped into a narrow passage leading to the washrooms. From there down a wide corridor toward the entrance hall. If no-one was there to stop her she would be safe. She had to get out – out in the gardens, in the streets.

Nadia ran fast, barefoot, her legs flying free in her light smock of Tashkent cotton, noiseless on the stone floors. Across the hall she saw flowers and trees through the big front windows shattered by gunfire – but also German soldiers. Armed men in field-gray out on the boulevard, everywhere. She must still go out, she knew that at once. The shouts behind were getting louder. But she mustn't run. She mustn't give anyone outside the idea she was being pursued.

At the door she paused for a second to see which way to go. To the left, a column of armoured cars clattered into view, coming up from the town centre. To the right, up the hill by the Elizabeth Gallery, all was clear. She could go – free!

But just as she was running to the door, it burst inward. Nadia gasped as the heavy wood hit her shoulder, slamming her against the stone wall. Germans ran in. Five of them. At the same moment, from the far end of the hall, the Corporal and the two Grenadier Privates hurtled out at her. In the first instant of confusion, Nadia tried to slip out of the door. But the Corporal saw her, shouted. Running up, he seized her arm. This time his grip was like a vise.

'What's the hurry, Comrade?'

In a swift movement he grabbed a handful of her thickly-curled hair in his free hand, bending her face back and up, forcing her to look into his eyes. He was a stocky man, not much taller than Nadia, with a broad ill-shaven face.

'What've you got there, Corporal, spy or summat?' said a young spectacled soldier, one of the five who had run in from the boulevard.

'Don't look like one,' said another.

'Anyone speak Russki round here?'

There was a chorus of laughter.

'Good-looker for a Bolshie,' said the Corporal. 'Touch of the romantic East we've got here.'

'Yeah. Big black eyes.'

'Tits and ass like a skinny Chinee.'

'Keep your milkmaids. Give me tits you can get your hands round.'

'She's a present,' said the Corporal. 'To me. That fat friend of hers gave her to me. You guys remember that.'

'To us, you mean,' said a Grenadier Private oafishly. 'Gave her to us.'

'What – all of us?'

'Christ, I'm busting.' One of the soldiers unbuttoned his fly and exposed an enormous bulge in his dingy gray underpants.

There were whistles and catcalls.

'Get her out of here,' someone said. 'They'll see us through the window.'

'Yeah, then the whole Regiment will want to get his dick in.'

The Corporal said, 'Mine first. Afterward I don't give a damn.'

'Couldn't if you wanted to.'

One or two men laughed, others – too excited – helped the Corporal drag Nadia toward a door in the back of the hall.

Nadia made no sound. She didn't understand the words, but she got their meaning. When the Corporal again dragged her face to his, she did what she'd been too surprised and shocked to do the first time. She spat.

He didn't seem to notice the spittle, or care. They all began pulling her. She twisted impotently. Greasy, battle-soiled hands pulled the smock off her shoulder and broke the strap of her bra, exposing her breasts. Another hand reached up between her thighs, fumbling in the fleshy slippery parts behind her cotton panties. In a small anteroom off the hall they flung her onto a floor of grimy green linoleum.

Nadia gritted her teeth to remain silent, not to cry out. But the shock of hitting the floor expelled from her all the fury she felt. She screamed a stream of vicious, rageful insults, using every limb of her body to writhe and kick and flail. But her own violence drove the soldiers on. They tore at her clothes, her flesh, her hair. Shouted insults back at her in German. Taunted her and spread her legs. A hand seized her pubic hair and wrenched a tuft free. The pain made Nadia gasp. The Corporal's gunbutt pushed the hand aside, tearing the flesh on her inner thigh. His chin was wet with saliva, hers and his own. He spat a jet at another soldier getting too close, fumbling with his fly.

Then suddenly his body jackknifed.

The Corporal, naked from his huge erect penis to his knees, slewed round, spun away from Nadia and slammed into the craning leering form of a soldier behind him. The other soldiers scrambled for their guns, but stopped rigid.

A German Colonel stood in the doorway. His machine pistol was levelled at them.

New soldiers entered the room at a run, deployed round the walls, neat and quick in their movements.

Nadia lay where she was, barely aware of the trickle of blood warming the inside of her thighs and creeping slowly and stickily between her buttocks. She couldn't move, couldn't scream.

There were two or three seconds of icy silent tension.

The Colonel broke it with a curt order. 'Get back to your units!'

The two Grenadiers and the five other soldiers picked up their weapons, adjusted their clothing and without a word fled back out of the room and into the open air. The

Corporal's body, blood bubbling from a gaping hole in the left side of his chest, lay motionless in the corner, in the foetal position.

The Colonel looked round at his own men.

'You two get the girl dressed. Find new clothes, shoes. Sergeant, see that that rapist gets buried somewhere. The rest carry on making this building secure.'

Nadia's eyes opened a crack. No thoughts, but an image registered in her brain, a picture of a German officer's hand trembling, holding a gun. Then of the same man, flinging the pistol angrily down on a bare table beside him and burying his head in his hands. Gradually the image turned into mere splashes of colour . . . then nothing, black nothing.

FOUR

At midnight, Colonel Brandt returned to the Pushkin Baths. He had spent more time than necessary, in strictly military terms, checking out the rape attempt, still more time in a futile effort to trace the other inmates of the 'terminal ward'. Every investigation so far had failed to come up with hard information. The most likely rumour was that an SS detachment had been in the Baths soon after he had left them. And he knew the SS habitually executed 'unfit' citizens. Unfortunately details of these matters were officially 'unavailable'. The fact was, however, all the people in the ward had disappeared. All, that is, except for the girl – and a dead old woman riddled with syphilis from her scalp to the soles of her feet. Brandt had ordered the scullery to be thoroughly fumigated.

Sitting heavily in a decaying stuffed chair, a relic from Tsarist days, he turned to his batman, who had just come in.

'How is she?'

Hans Guggenbühl shook his big round head and shrugged.

'*So lala*, Herr Oberst. Sleeping still.'

'Good.'

Hans coughed lightly. 'When the lady wakes, Herr Oberst . . .'

'No, Hans, no. You look after her if she needs anything. Look after her with great care.'

Hans cleared his throat. 'Your camp bed in the corridor, Herr Oberst,' he said pointing. 'I thought maybe you'd want –'

'Thank you, Hans. Good night.'

'Good night, Herr Oberst.'

Hans squeezed his pudgy legs together, bowed stiffly and went out through a door to the waiting-room – between his own and the Colonel's room – where Nadia was sleeping. He looked in, raised an eyebrow, pulled his head back out, shut the door and locked it again.

Colonel Brandt reached for the bottle of wine and the bottle of mineral water that Hans was enjoined to leave every evening, as cool as possible, within reach of his bed. As always, Hans had remembered. Brandt mixed a spritzer and swallowed. Already he was getting a taste for the light Georgian white wines.

For the first time since the battle started, he was alone. The image of the girl began to fill his mind, pushing out those of the fighting, the smells of burning flesh and gunsmoke, the memories of men wounded and dying. He shut his eyes and fixed that image inside his brain, imprinting it there as if on a camera's sensitive compound. Not the image of her on the floor, shamed and humiliated by German soldiers – that he wasn't ready to deal with – but of the girl as he had just seen her, sleeping with a hand curled beside her face, her cheeks as pink as those of a small child. She slept as if she knew someone was watching over her. Or so he liked to think. German sentimentality, perhaps – but it was what he believed, despite the fact that he knew, from what she had said to Lieutenant Lauterbach earlier, that she would refuse his protection. She reminded him of a deer he had seen once, in the Alps. It had thrown its head up and looked at him across a meadow. Then, instead of leaping away, it had continued to stand, its big eyes studying him. He had been motionless too, and so they had remained – how long? A minute? And when the deer had moved away, it had done so not in fear, but peacefully and slowly.

He refilled his glass.

Lauterbach had found out a few basic facts about the girl. Her name was Nadia. Nadia Sergeevna Surkova, nee Dobroliubova. He preferred the maiden name – 'Goodlove!'

She had taken the news about her father's disappearance well. Lauterbach, however, on instructions, had omitted to mention the visit of the SS detachment. It was, after all, an unconfirmed rumour.

Of course she was refusing his offer of protection. But he didn't plan to keep her longer than necessary. The problem was a military one. The Red Army was putting up a stiffer fight now the Germans had reached the towns in the Caucasian foothills. Pyatigorsk itself was not yet a hundred percent secure. The Russians had their backs up against the wall – the last mountain wall, the final bastion. Every house, every field, every river gorge would be defended. It wasn't going to be a picnic any more. The exercise, the cross-country run, was over. She would have to wait a little longer before he would let her return.

Inside the Baths, with its thick walls, the sounds of night battle were faint. Here, he thought with a feeling of satisfaction, she will be safe . . .

*

Colonel Brandt snapped so fast out of his sleep next morning that by the time he thought to recreate his dreams they had vanished. Yet he woke with the image of the girl still in his mind, as clear as if she'd never left him, that much he knew.

It was mid-morning before he had the chance to see her again. After knocking on her door, he entered at her curt 'Yes!'

She was standing, arms folded. She reminded Brandt of the actress who had played the fiery colleen in an Irish drama – Synge's *Playboy* – that he had seen in London on his way to a climbing holiday in Scotland. He noticed the same freckles, the same ebullient copper curls and eyes the colour of beechleaves in spring, the same large mouth with tilting corners, however angry she was – or pretended to be.

'Why do you still hold me prisoner?'

The reality of her anger splintered his romantic daydream. He looked at her almost timidly.

'I hope you slept well.'

'At least you understand my language. None of the others know so much as to say good morning.'

'They are not here out of choice,' he said, still trying to create a calm atmosphere.

'Please don't try any crude apologies,' she said, looking

squarely at her captor . . . her rescuer, standing awkward and stiff in front of her. 'I asked you a question.'

'The answer is the same one my Lieutenant gave you yesterday.' He came further into the room. 'For your own safety you will have to stay. When the fighting stops –'

'The fighting will never stop. Not until you're all, every one, out of my country and back where you came from. Else dead. I'm not so stupid as to think you'll go on your own.'

'Nadia Sergeevna,' Brandt said urgently, 'forgive me using just your name and patronymic, but you. . . .' He stopped, then went on with a faint smile. 'Could we make a pact? Could we agree that wars should never be fought? Perhaps neither of us will survive this one. Meanwhile, maybe we could treat each other as –'

'Rape me, Colonel, if you dare try. Don't seduce me. Better, treat me like a human being and release me. Let me go and find my father. At least let me return to my daughter and my mother.' Furious tears glistened across the surface of her eyes.

Brandt turned round a wooden chair, the only other piece of furniture in the tiny room apart from the cot where Nadia had slept, and straddled it. She stood with her back to the wall, arms folded, hair unkempt, lips trembling, bruises apparent on her neck and her thin calves. The smock – mended by Hans's fat seamstress's fingers – barely hid other bruises and welts. She was still barefoot, though a pair of sandals with wooden soles had been found for her. In the room with its peeling, stained walls and sparse furniture, she looked to Brandt uncomfortably like a woman under interrogation by the Gestapo.

'They are in Nalchik,' he said. 'Your family. That's fifty miles further east, isn't it?'

'A short distance for me. Not so easy for you, Colonel.'

'Yes, of course I shall let you return,' he said. 'As soon as Pyatigorsk is secure. I don't mean to interrogate you,' he added.

For the first time the hardness left her face.

'The Lieutenant you sent did that.'

And probably, he thought, I shall find out very little more than she told Lauterbach. Interesting, her being half-

Kabardinian. He had wondered about such people, but never seen one before. The Kabardinians – this he had checked in the reference book issued by the army – had once been a Christian tribe, converted by the Georgians, but a couple of hundred years ago they had reverted to the Muslim faith of their nearest neighbours, the Balkars. Like most of the several hundred small Caucasian groups, they had their own language. In fact, Kabardinian itself was subdivided into four dialects. The Kabardinians, he had also discovered, were traditionally more co-operative with the Russians than were the more warlike and fanatically Muslim Chechen people, for instance, of the Ingush....

Hard to remember sometimes he was not an explorer, an anthropologist. That was certainly how he would have preferred to come to these mountains.

He looked up at her over the back of the chair. Now that she had calmed down, she reminded him of those woodcuts of idealized oriental beauty printed in the early editions of the great Russian romantic novelists and poets. Dark, mysterious, dangerous. The Caucasus had been their frontier, their Wild West, and the women of the Caucasus – they had made the Moscow and Petersburg beauties seem as tame as the German girls back home had seemed to him.

'I always dreamed of coming to the Caucasus,' the Colonel said after an awkward silence, adding with an embarrassed smile: 'Not as a soldier. Do you believe in the legends, the monstrous birds of prey, the hoards of treasure buried up there, the invincible giants? What are they called? Narts? I was born within sight of the Alps,' he finished lamely.

'Adolf Hitler too is fond of mountains, Colonel.'

Brandt gave a dry laugh.

'The free air of the mountains.' He stood up. 'I am a professional soldier. Unlike you, I remember the Great War, the First World War we must now call it. I was a child of course. But Germans believed, after that war – I was taught to believe – that only if we could defend ourselves, would we have a chance of living in peace. That was my reason for becoming a soldier. Russians, too, believed that, or so I'm told. That was the reason for the creation of the Red Army, as for the existence of all other armies.'

Nadia said sharply, unable, it seemed, to stop herself, 'Yet here you are in our country. We are not in yours.'

'We should talk more about this. I want to understand –' Brandt stopped. 'No, that is wrong. I do understand. I know how you feel about our presence here. But – I am going to ask you something that I have no right to ask. I want you to help me understand how I feel about it. Perhaps tonight you will have dinner with me?'

'Dinner?' Nadia laughed contemptuously.

He said as lightly as he could, 'It is more of an order than an invitation. You need food and rest, and I am responsible for you.'

She said, without looking at him, 'Yes. I am your prisoner and I have to eat.'

'Then I will tell Hans to do his best.'

Colonel Brandt left the cell-like room quickly, without formal gesture.

Once outside, he leaned against the wall and shut his eyes, the misery of the war sweeping over him for what he realized, incredibly, was the first time. He was paying, finally, for the elation of that rush across the plains, for his pride, his exhilaration at the first sight of the mountains. His nerves were raw. What was he going to say to this half-Kabardinian woman? What, after all, was he doing?

*

Nadia lay on the bed. She was hungry, but she had been hungry for so long that the ache had become something she didn't notice or had trained herself to ignore.

She opened her eyes.

A tray of cold food, tinned meat of some sort, a slice – not a lump, a slice – of *white* bread, two small tomatoes and a glass of water, lay on the floor by the wall.

The door opened, and Nadia glanced up.

It was only Hans.

Only Hans?

Furious with herself for feeling a slight sense of letdown, Nadia looked away. Not hearing him move, she turned again and glared.

The servant had small moist rapist's eyes. She shuddered, and wondered if she would always be afraid, now, because of what had almost happened to her. The women she had always despised, the women who hadn't shaken off the bad old ways, had been saying to her all her life: Be careful, Nadia Sergeevna. Don't go out of the house dressed like that. Don't go alone at night. Don't talk to men in that bold way, cover your head, your legs, stay at home, keep quiet.

And that had been what they were warning her against, when you came right down to it, hadn't it? She had ridiculed them. Now would she listen?

But it had been a man who had rescued her. And it had only happened because of the war. You couldn't draw any conclusions from that, could you?

What was his name, that German colonel? Wolfgang? Eberhard . . . Helmuth . . . Rudolf . . . Siegfried. Middle-class, maybe even aristocratic in a small-town way. He had shot that raping soldier the way he would have shot a worker ogling his own daughter.

Nadia was too tired to think it through. Her brain wouldn't work. She shook her head and chewed another mouthful of the bread.

Tell the truth, now. Boris used to say anything was valid as long as it formed the right attitudes. All right for him, but for her, a teacher? Didn't you have a duty to the truth? And the truth was that Boris had left her alone, and this German colonel had saved her life.

No, that was unjust. She had told Boris to go, pushed him out. And the idea of leaning on a man, being protected by a man – that had gone for good, that notion which had never appealed to her in the first place. But, she thought, chewing the bread and meat with a certain voluptuousness, just for once to lay down the duty of partnership, of standing up all the time and showing them that you were just as strong as they were –

She felt so weak, so tired. She let her eyes wander.

'Get out!' she snapped suddenly. She hadn't realized that the big lout of a servant was still standing there, all that time, watching her eat . . . watching her think!

Hans went out, expressionless.

*

At eight in the evening Pyatigorsk was in German hands. Not without casualties. At the very end of the fighting, Lieutenant Lauterbach had been dismembered like a crudely butchered calf by a random volley from a 'Stalin organ' multiple mortar.

For Brandt, depressed by the young officer's death, only one good thing had happened. Major Fritz Stegl was being transferred to 'Intelligence' duties with the Gestapo. At last where he belonged. Stegl had been seconded to the 7th Mountain Division only because . . . well, God alone knew why. There were times when Brandt believed it was simply and solely to spy on himself.

Over the radio in his new quarters was coming the first muddled news of the American offensive in the paradise islands of the South Pacific.

Brandt yawned, stretched his arms over his head, undid the buttons of his uniform jacket. He thought of the pictures one always saw of those islands, green palm trees bending over a lagoon or a rock pool, a brown-skinned girl with long, long silky black hair. The girl smiled at him. A flash of white teeth in what he realized was Nadia's face.

The door opened, and he started. 'Ah! Hans. Did you locate a worthy bottle? Or two?'

The batman smiled. 'Georgian, Herr Oberst. I made them let me taste it. It will go tolerably well with the liver sausage.'

'Liver sausage?'

'I regret deeply, Herr Oberst, I . . . the best I –'

'Liver sausage, then. And Georgian wine. In fifteen minutes. I'm hungry, I expect she is too. Fetch her.'

Five minutes later, she walked into the Colonel's room with her head held high. She had made use of the comb Hans had given her, but she looked at him fiercely, as if to indicate that it was more from self-respect than from any desire to appear attractive to him. Still, she was beautiful, that was something she couldn't conceal and he couldn't deny.

Brandt wondered how long he had been standing at attention, watching her. He took a hesitant step forward, bent and kissed her hand.

The gesture obviously surprised her, because she smiled. The smile of the girl in the rock pool.

But when she spoke, she said grimly, 'So you have our town under your control. You have killed our last heroic resisters.'

'Yes,' he said, pulling himself out of his trance. 'There will be no more bloodshed, please God, in Pyatigorsk.'

'God!' she said. 'Perhaps a German god. Thor, is it called? A god who demands sacrifices.'

'I have no belief in a god myself.'

She folded her arms, still standing erect.

'No, you believe only in – what? – the superior German people who have the right to crush all the others? Is that what you believe?'

Anger briefly restricted his throat. Then he said: 'I shall arrange for your return to Nalchik as soon as possible, as I've already promised you. That at least I can do. But now, let's eat. Please sit down. Hans has some wine outside which he's attempting to cool. Hans!'

'You brought elegant things, Colonel,' Nadia said, picking up a silver goblet with a long slender stem.

'A privilege of rank.'

'And of class.'

'Hans! Where is he? Yes, please, sit. Of course, of class as well. Did you expect me to deny that?' He smiled at her. 'My grandfather, a timber merchant, was presented these goblets by his grateful employees – grateful, I expect, because he was retiring. He had made, however, a modest fortune dealing in Black Forest, and later Baltic, timber. Part of his trade was with Russia. You know how, in the novels of Russian families, there is always an efficient German merchant? He is very clumsy and they despise him. That was my grandfather.'

'There's always a German governess, too,' added Nadia, with the beginning of a laugh that Brandt himself – nervously – finished for her.

Hans came in with the wine, and Brandt poured it out. He went on, 'When I was a child, the family was less prosperous. The business declined. My father became a soldier, and it was natural for me to follow him into the army.'

'Hitler's army.'

'No.' Brandt's abrupt reply made her blink. 'I was a

soldier before Hitler. I'm sorry, I didn't mean to shout. Yes, the wine is a pleasant one, Hans. But . . . ice?'

'No ice, Herr Oberst. I put in the bucket the coldest water I could find.'

'Thank you, Hans.'

He dismissed the batman with a quick wave and picked up his goblet, noticing the alert expression with which Nadia had been watching the exchange in rapid German. Afraid of the conclusions she might draw – did she think he was imperious with his servant, or that he and Hans had some agreement about her? – he raised the silver goblet, said quietly, in Russian again, 'To peace!' and drank.

She drank too.

Encouraged, he said, 'Tell me about your life. Your life before the war.'

Nadia took another sip. She already had colour in her cheeks, as if in spite of herself the wine was reviving her, giving her strength.

'It was another person living then,' she said at last. 'My life hasn't been like yours, Colonel. For example, I have never . . . never travelled in a foreign country.'

'Did you go walking, climbing, in the mountains?'

'The mountains are not a playground. To us they are – beautiful, yes. But more than anything, frightening. No-one goes up there who doesn't have to. We have seen what the mountains can do. The people who climb them – they come from outside. They have guides from among us, because there's always someone who needs the money, but –' She made a gesture with her hands.

The Colonel's batman came in again, bringing liver sausage, fried onions and peppers, white bread. Then another trip, carrying a basket of fresh fruit and another bottle of wine.

Brandt served them both. When Nadia had started eating, he looked away, not wanting to embarrass her by observing the way she tried to slow down, not to eat as fast as her hunger forced her to.

He said, 'I was born in the province of Baden-Württemberg, in a small town called Waldshut. On the Rhine. Very pretty but dull. To the north is the Black Forest.

To the south, across the river, you can see the first northern peaks of the Alps. I spent my youth in the mountains.' He paused. 'I shall probably die in the mountains.' He glanced as Nadia, but she didn't look up. 'I understand what you say about being afraid of them; the Alpine people are the same way. They go to the high pastures in the summer, and always there are one or two who don't come back. Avalanches, rockfalls – but, you see, every man is living close to death always. It's just that a mountain man knows how close it is. Like a soldier. I prefer – not to hide it from myself.'

Finally Nadia looked at him, her face sombre. 'And that is how you justify war. A way for a man to prove himself. To kill the innocent so that he can call himself a man.'

Brandt said nothing for a while. He wanted to talk about himself as a boy, in the mountains. But it seemed unreal now, even to himself. He was aware also of the image she must have of German youth, so many pictures in magazines, on newsreels, images of boys in Hitlerjugend uniform stretching out their hands in a fascist salute, faces radiant with insane adoration of the Führer. How could a German boy be anything else? He tried to imagine her own very different childhood, the day-to-day struggles, the chaos of Revolution and Civil War – but among family and neighbours, a life of warmth. Suddenly he felt jealousy toward her, the envy of a lonely boy striding tight-lipped and intense along high rocky crests in the pure thin air of the Alps for a person who had the confidence of having been loved.

For the first time he caught her looking at him, studying him. Physically, he was sure of himself. He felt at ease in his own skin. But in his mind?

What does she see, he wondered? A man? An Aryan monster?

He had lost his appetite, but he took another swallow of wine. 'My father was one of the old guard who fought in the Great War, and he accepted to the end of his life the warrior view. As you say, Nadia Sergeevna, to be a man. After that terrible war, even after he'd seen so much death, he was still eager to fight it out, to revenge what Germans thought was the treachery of 1918. There were many like him. My father wasn't able to continue for very long; he had been wounded, and he died of those wounds. But even before that, he had been invalided out of the army, and that was his great disappointment. Perhaps you know that Germany was permitted only a small army at that time, and there was no room in it for a wounded man. So my father became, well, militarist as only a frustrated ex-soldier can be. He was sympathetic to the brownshirts, he employed many of them in the business.'

Nadia seemed about to say something, but Brandt held up his hand. 'No. I know. But, you see, my mother died of influenza after the war. My father was alone, except for me. What would you have done?' Remembering what she had done, that her presence there was a result of her care for her father, he hurried on. 'Perhaps I . . . but Nadia, let me say this. You believe that the attitudes people have come from the class they belong to, from their origin. Do you believe this? If you're a communist, you have to believe it. Even if you're not, it seems probable, doesn't it? And what do you think? In the 1920s, in my town, being my father's son – well, I joined the German army. In 1929. At that time we still lived in a republic, the Weimar Republic. It was hardly my father's kind of army. I remember, as one of the hundred thousand soldiers, in the early days, I used to do shooting practice using rifles from the 1870 campaign in France. The targets were toy balloons.'

'Even toy balloons were useful when you had the real enemy in your sights at last, the Russian people. Or had you already done proper shooting practice on the Poles or the French?'

Brandt was reluctant to admit that all his training had been geared to a Russian campaign, including an intensive course in the Russian language. And yet he had never considered resigning his commission. It would have been a useless gesture. When war, inevitably, came, he would have been called up – and been condemned to remain for ever in the ranks.

Nadia interrupted his thoughts, with an insistence he found increasingly uncomfortable, 'So you joined the army, Colonel, to escape the warrior class of your father. And later you swore an oath to Hitler. A personal oath, sworn by every German soldier. True?'

Brandt drew in a deep breath. 'Many Germans have come to believe that in our world, the world we both unfortunately live in, you must be strong and, if your opponent is strong, you must be stronger still. Aren't there men in your country who believe the same? That nothing is too inhuman – too desperate – if it succeeds against the enemy.'

She stood up abruptly. 'Colonel, do you really believe that? That every country is the same and all men defend themselves in the same way? It's you who are attacking us. Why? It wasn't the Russians who defeated poor little Germany and forced the Gestapo to learn their torture methods.' She swallowed tears. 'The Russians are the first to try – perhaps we are wrong, I don't know – but we are the first in all of history to try socialism, and that means no more war, not between countries, not between classes.'

'In the 1920s, you too had a war, a civil war that lasted for a very long time.' He pleaded with her, as much with his eyes as with his voice. 'Sit down, Nadia, please. You are a patriot. I like that. It's a good thing. You must allow me, in my way, to be a patriot too. It's not just the Germans who are in arms. Today, in the world, it's everybody.'

He waited till she sat down, then refilled her plate and glass. 'Nadia, what can I say? I am in your country. I confess that until you forced me to think about what I was doing, I was glad to be here. I'm still glad.' He glanced at her, but she didn't meet his gaze. 'When I first saw the mountains, I felt – I felt, if only I'd come here in peacetime, as a friend, to know this country as it deserves to be known.'

'I suppose,' she said abruptly, 'your men all love you. Their dashing, handsome, liberal Colonel.'

Brandt flushed.

She stood up again, and her chair fell back with a crack.

Colonel Brandt got to his feet quickly and came round the table. 'I'm sorry.'

'Don't be sorry. For someone like me who has lived all her life in a remote, provincial, ignorant country, it's a real education to be in the company of a member of the master race, a hero from the land of Goethe and Beethoven and . . .

Rosa Luxemburg. It's useful to understand those who come to a foreign country, my country, to kill us and rape us and take our food and –'

'If I –'

'I know. But you *are* here. You and your army. It's impossible to forget that fact.'

'I understand, Nadia Sergeevna. Of course I understand.' He stopped and looked into her eyes. 'Forgive me.'

'It was wrong of me to come here. Good night, Colonel.'

He put out a hand to hold her back, but let it drop to his side before he touched her. He felt through his own body the *frisson* she would feel to be touched by him – like a shudder of horror, like the climax of a nightmare in the split second before the mind can bear it no longer and jerks the body awake. He pulled the door open, shouting for his batman, and watched as she walked across the small connecting room to where she had her bed. Her prison bed. Nadia, when he had given up hope, turned in the doorway. She smiled sadly, but not, as he saw it, without sympathy.

'Good night, Colonel Brandt. I wish to leave tomorrow. Please. Let me go.'

*

At four-thirty in the morning a loud knock woke the Colonel.

'Herr Oberst – the Russian girl!' A young Corporal's head appeared round the door. His voice was edged with panic. 'She's escaping.'

Brandt swore and leaped out of bed. Pulling on his uniform over the underpants he wore in bed, he ran out.

'On the roof, Herr Oberst,' the Corporal said over his shoulder. 'I'd never have noticed if the stupid bitch hadn't knocked a tile off.'

Brandt snapped: 'How did she get out?'

'Hans was sleeping a bit heavy. She picked the lock. So he says.'

Brandt grunted. 'Up there?' He pointed through an open skylight guarded by another young soldier.

'Yes, Herr Oberst.'

'Anyone else looking for her?'

'No, Herr Oberst. I thought you –'

'Very good, Corporal. Stay here.'

Colonel Brandt levered himself easily through the skylight, as if through the narrow exit of a rock chimney. The roof, or roofs, formed an incomplete square with funnel-shaped turrets on the front corners, a separate cone just out of jumping distance in the centre of the inner courtyard and a jumble of chimneys, the tallest, itself roofed, on the south-west corner. He waited for his eyes to grow accustomed to the starlight. His feet were bare. After a few seconds he set off as silently as a cat. A sudden flash of fire from the mountains followed by a deep reverberating growl was the only reminder of the war all around, the only false note in the stillness of imminent dawn.

'Nadia!'

His soft call went unanswered. He padded rapidly to the furthest part of the roof near the tall chimney at the back of the building. No-one. Not even a bird. He called her name again.

There was no need, however, to call a third time, for he saw her huddled in the gutter that ran along the east side of the building, staring at a hole cut through the low balustrade like a ship's scupper. Below her dropped a sheer thirty-foot wall. He came close, but for a moment just stood behind her. When he looked up again a tiny pink light had appeared on the horizon. He stared at it, fascinated, not yet sure whether man with his guns, or Nature, had created this strange glow. It grew, changing from the faintest pink to an eery shade of orange purple. At the same time the whole sky became streaked with colour, like a series of mirrors multiplying into a vast brilliance the compressed energy of a single fire opal.

'Dykh Tau,' she said in a whisper. She was shivering.

Brandt gazed at the mountain peak she had named, hypnotized by the dawn expanding all around it. His eyes moved along the high crest of the horizon until another focus of light in the shape of a double-headed cone fixed his attention. This was Elbrus. The mountain so seldom free from mist and cloud that people called it 'Shy Elbrus'; but this morning daring to show its twin summits, unearthly pink, floating in the dawn sky.

He knelt down beside Nadia.

She turned to face him, and the light from the sky was reflected in her eyes.

Instinctively Brandt took her face in his hands and kissed her gently on the lips.

For a long while she didn't move, not returning the pressure of his kiss, not even letting, it seemed to him, her lashes flick across the glinting surface of her eyes.

Then abruptly she stood up. 'I am sorry,' she said. Her voice was under tight control.

Brandt, trembling as if he had cut himself by accident and was waiting for the first intense pain to strike, began saying, 'No, I'm the one who . . . ,' then fell silent.

He felt as if he were on fire, that the sun-red mountains had set him alight. Yet he couldn't move.

He stood absolutely still watching Elbrus, not a mirage now but a solid mountain.

Nadia too continued to stare resolutely out toward the peaks.

At last Brandt's paralysis began to wear off. But his mouth had no words to deliver. His tongue felt languid, useless. Had she been a German girl, any one of the many he had known, daughters of fellow officers, civil servants and landowners – even wives of fellow officers, civil servants and landowners – he would have known what to say. He would have told her how it was from Elbrus that the dove came to fetch the olive leaf and flew back with it to Noah on the ark. He would have talked of Prometheus bound by indestructible chains to Kazbek, where 'an eagle with outstretched wings, sent by Zeus, fed upon his immortal liver; as much as the winged monster devoured during the day, that much grew again during the night.' He would, as the charm worked, have compared her to the famously beautiful Circassian slave-women, and she would have lifted her limp face for him to kiss, again and again, each time more passionately. But with Nadia such romance was – impossible.

Unconscious even of forming the words, he said at last softly, 'Nadia, what have you done? What are you doing?'

She said simply, 'Perhaps I am asking you to change, Colonel.'

'In Nalchik –' he began, but stopped, aware instantly that any hint of his setting foot in her home town implied its capture by the German army.

The spell of the dawn light was breaking.

Suddenly Brandt became aware of a figure behind him in deep shadow. He turned, half-crouching, like a deer scenting a hunter.

But it was only Hans Guggenbühl, waiting, quivering, not a hunter but a cowardly dog expecting the whip. He had been pushed forward by the Corporal, who stood, grinning, in the edge of a shadow on the other side of the roof.

Brandt let out a sigh and began to smile, then to laugh.

Nadia looked at him with his uniform and bare feet, then at the monstrous spaniel of a servant, then again at the half of a shirt-tail hanging out of Brandt's jacket.

'You are coming apart, Colonel. Perhaps that is a beginning.'

*

The day had begun early. Brandt threw himself into his military duties. By eight o'clock, when he went to the first staff officers' conference, he knew where every man under his command was quartered. He attended to the sick and wounded. At eleven, he discussed with his Majors and Captains the possibility of effective action in the high mountains.

He also confirmed to himself, talking to senior officers, hearing reports and studying the maps, that the real Russian resistance was only just beginning. The Red Army and the partisans were preparing for the big battle to turn the tide of the war. His colleagues, aware of the same facts, persisted in their optimistic predictions. They didn't seem to Brandt to understand that the gallop had ended, that from now on the advance would be yard by yard, not mile by mile. And very likely there would be no advance at all.

But then they had noticed no change in himself either.

In the evening he walked into the temporary mess, the main bar of the Stalin Hotel, rechristened the Bayerhof.

'Ott!' he called, seeing the lanky figure of the officer who commanded his 3rd Battalion propped against the counter, alone. 'Champagne.'

Heads turned. There was laughter from a corner where a group of young officers were drinking beer from their personal steins. Someone's hand putting on a record of *Lili Marlene* slipped, so the first bars of the tune sounded like a passage of Stravinsky.

'Welcome to Pyatigorsk,' Brandt said, clapping the Major on the shoulder. 'Welcome back to active duty.'

Ott clicked his heels.

'You wonder what's come over me,' Brandt said loudly, so everyone could hear even above the raucous music. 'Gentlemen, it's . . . the mountain air.' He signalled to the Corporal serving the drinks. 'Well? For everyone, of course.'

'Right away, Herr Oberst.'

The young officers started singing along. Even Ott's rigid features relaxed. The sound of popping corks and laughter came from the pantry behind the bar. In seconds, trays of frothing glasses appeared in the mess, hands seizing them as they were passed around. Brandt took a glass and waved for silence. Someone lifted the thorn off the whirling disc.

'Gentlemen,' said the Colonel. 'Fellow men of the mountains. Before you, you have the most beautiful sight in the world, the Caucasus. Nothing is more precious than finding what we set our hearts on. But remember. The great peaks are our gods, our children, our women. They are what we live for.' He was aware of sounding pompous. He didn't care. 'Gentlemen, let us drink a toast. Let us drink to the nearest we mortals can get to heaven.'

'To the Caucasus!' Voices echoed round the bar. No-one saw that Brandt's lips formed different words.

*

Next morning a German escort brought Nadia to an assembly point in the south-east quarter of town where she joined a party of other women, old people and children who had been stranded in Pyatigorsk and were now permitted to find their own way home.

In her pocket was a paper. She hadn't seen the Colonel

again, but a junior officer pointed it out to her when he returned her personal documents. It was an authorization to pass through the front line, now stabilized beyond the Malka River. She took it silently, intending at first to tear it up. Then she thrust it into the pocket of her smock.

She was immensely relieved there had been no last meeting, aware of a terror hidden deep within her, only half-admitted, that even a handshake would arouse in her that unbidden flash of desire she had felt for him, a desire that she knew would be fatal. Fatal in the most literal sense. There was no doubt in her mind that she could not go on living if she ever committed the ultimate treachery. She would not wish to live. She should not be allowed to live.

Nadia left Pyatigorsk aboard a creaky cart at eleven in the morning of Friday, August 14, 1942.

The heat was intense. The temperature had passed 100 degrees by the time the overloaded wagon, pulled by a recalcitrant mule teamed with a thin black mare, joined the shell-pocked road across the plain to Nalchik. She rocked and jolted with the uneven rhythm of the cart and deliberately fixed in her mind, to the exclusion of all else, the image of her little daughter's face. She smiled, happy at the thought of seeing Darya again. It seemed – at last – that her own Black Summer was over.

Part Two

UNDER THE WAVE

FIVE

Captain Nazir Bekirbi's left eye blinked shut, his left cheek screwed itself painfully into a wrinkled ball, then sprang back. That hurt too. He cursed inwardly, afraid this tic of his – it had come on only in the last few days, since that hideous escape from Pyatigorsk – would make him look unreliable. Not that anyone could see him clearly at the moment. He and five Muslim elders were in a dark room, hung on all four walls with thick rugs. The smell of tea seemed to increase the gloom, like a sickly-sweet fog.

The People's Commissariat for Internal Affairs needed to know the intentions of the 'traditionalist elements' in Nalchik. Bekirbi found he had returned to a hornets' nest. The NKVD had ordered him to feign sympathy with Muslim treachery in order to sniff out collaborators. A shitty job. But – in some ways – useful. He himself was anxious to know where people stood.

To Bekirbi, only one fact was certain: the Germans were winning the war. Any day they could cross the baksan River and enter Nalchik. Captain Bekirbi had no confidence at all in the Soviet capacity to resist. Everything so far confirmed the most extreme of his inner doubts. The memory of those tanks, like armoured rats, haunted him.

And if – when – the Nazis entered the town? Bekirbi was no ordinary citizen. He was a Captain in the secret police. State-registered butcher, communist. They'd stick red-hot needles under his nails and red-hot pokers up his ass. They'd make him eat his own shit and drink his own piss. He knew the sort of thing they were capable of. He had been told what happened – what was still happening – in the Ukraine. He had heard about the Gestapo. Above all others they hated their Soviet 'counterparts'.

His eye grimaced shut, snapped open. Damn it! All he needed to know was what was going to happen next – and when.

In wars, he believed, the simple-minded, the obstinately 'faithful', died first. War was a matter of survival or death. In his case a hideously contrived death.

At forty, he had been through the Civil War – on both sides – and through three nationalist uprisings, and still ended up with the winners. But he knew he had succeeded through luck and – frankly – opportunism, not because he had understood the 'iron laws' of progress.

Meanwhile the damn Muslims were sipping their tea and telling him very little. Probably they were even more suspicious of him than he was of them.

The meeting had, however, established one fact. They weren't just rumours, these reports he'd been getting of German agents inside the city making extravagant offers of 'friendship'. Hundreds, maybe thousands, of citizens – mostly devout Muslims – had already fled, not east, but west. Into welcoming German arms, even into German uniform. There were firm Intelligence reports of both Muslim and Cossack detachments in the German 17th Army.

But the real question was: had the ones who chose the Fritzes made the right – the reasonable – decision? It wasn't going to be easy in Nalchik for anyone who misjudged the tide of history. Nor was judging a simple matter. When the tide was high, how could anyone tell if it had further to go, or if it was on the turn?

He yawned. It was late.

The Muslim spokesman at the meeting had been speaking for fifteen minutes without stopping. The language was Balkar, with which Bekirbi was less familiar than with Russian. Yet behind the flowery phrases the message was simple enough: these were troubled times and all men had to examine their consciences, see where their primary duty lay, to Allah or to the Soviet state.

For Allah, read Adolf Hitler.

Clearly now they were waiting for a move from him. They

wanted a commitment. But why should he give them anything, even a hint? It was still just possible that Baksan would be the final limit of the German advance. The high tide mark. They knew that. That was why they spelled out nothing – except of course they never came clean about anything, those devious old tribesmen.

He knew them, he knew their culture. By blood he was one of them – half-Balkar, at any rate, on his dead father's side. But younger – a different generation. A product of atheist Soviet culture.

The spokesman fell silent. No-one else said a word. The silence was getting oppressive, certainly to Bekirbi. His face hurt. He got to his feet. He wasn't going to give them any satisfaction, not yet.

Then he hesitated. The curt goodbye he had planned stuck just before it escaped his lips. His left eye gave another, more violent, twitch. Curse it, he couldn't afford to leave them like this. Either way, whatever he did, they would take it as his decision. He turned toward them, outlines in the dark room.

'Allah be with us,' he said. 'With all of us.'

There was a murmur of approval and of reciprocated farewells. But Bekirbi had gone.

*

He emerged quickly from the peeling pale-blue stucco house, one of the oldest in the city, built more than a hundred years ago. The dark wood supporting the roof was pitted by years of exposure to intense heat and intense cold; nevertheless it was solid – and soundproof. Bekirbi looked up at it from the corner of the street. No light was showing. Even without the blackout, no light would have been visible from outside. From the thatched roof a grapevine trailed down over the two balconies, one above the other, obscuring the already shuttered windows. The house itself seemed a live organism, as if the sap came up through its roughly painted stucco, through its wooden beams, to feed the fruit hanging against the walls.

Just before he turned into the main street, Bekirbi was aware of a man falling into step beside him. He didn't need to look to know it was Yusef Tsagov. He didn't want to look. Even on this dark night, the man's swarthy, stubbled face was an uncomfortable reminder of why he was so . . . so useful.

'Well?'

Tsagov remained silent long enough to force Bekirbi to glance in his direction. He smiled, revealing a row of striped front teeth. Split years before by the glancing blow of a knifeblade, they had been repaired with thin strips of silver, now tarnished.

'Well?' Bekirbi repeated impatiently.

'No, Captain. No-one saw you go in. No-one saw you come out. No-one was watching the house.'

Except you, Tsagov, Bekirbi thought to himself. Except you.

They separated without another word.

*

Luda Surkova was in bed. For four years she had lived in this room above a State shoe-repair shop. The stop itself closed down within hours of the German invasion, when the manager volunteered for military service. It was never a thriving concern. But there had always been a pair of tooled leather boots in the window. Luda had the idea she would break in one day and get the boots – but they were several sizes too small. Even before the war the only way to get a good pair was to join the army or the police, or winkle out one of the old-fashioned 'private' cobblers and have him fix you up.

What the shut-down meant to Luda was peace and quiet. No more noise of doors slamming, nails hammering, people complaining loudly. She had to go round the back to get to her room, but that too was good. Only people who really wanted to see her pushed their way past the dustbins and latrine as far as the rickety wooden staircase to the first floor.

And – one man who wanted her body.

She heard Nazir Bekirbi come up. He always slammed his boots on the stairs, a little bang then a big bang, as if he were hobbling.

She didn't want to see him. More and more strongly she

had been feeling Nadia's disapproval. It was a kind of telepathy – because Nadia had been all this time in Pyatigorsk, and there was no news from her.

Perhaps, if Nazir had proposed marriage, she might have accepted. In bed sometimes he gave her the kind of pleasure she had never dreamed of before she knew him. When she had first met him, he had looked so – sleek, like a film star. But her brother Boris had persuaded her that love in the Soviet Union was not constrained by old-fashioned institutions. And Nazir had never even mentioned marriage.

Yet Boris had married Nadia.

If only, Luda thought, I had Nadia's looks, Nadia's brains, Nadia's way of making up her own mind, Nadia's self-control.

The tramping on the stairs reached her door. Before he had a chance to beat on it with his fist, she had slipped on a calico robe, lit a candle and opened up for him.

Without a word, he seized her and kissed her hard on the mouth. She struggled free, laughing uneasily, hiding the anger his kiss had aroused in her, hiding too, from herself, the quick unasked-for thrill.

'I – I'd fallen asleep,' she lied. 'What time is it?'

Bekirbi grabbed the carafe of vodka off the single small table in the room and put it to his lips. He took a gulp, then wiped his mouth with his sleeve. It was he who supplied the stuff – just as he supplied for her the tall bottle of Red Moscow perfume on the shelf by her bed.

She sat down while he remained standing. He looked at her, then glanced out the small window at the mess of outhouses and the backs of low cottages, no more than silhouettes in the moonless night.

'Where've you been?' she asked.

He wheeled round.

'What's that supposed to mean?'

She sighed. He was in one of those moods. 'Look,' she said. 'I told you I was asleep. I've been working all day. Come tomorrow, if you like, earlier.'

'Tomorrow! There's a war on, woman. Tomorrow we may all be dead.'

'Why? Are they –?'

'Don't be a fool. We're safe enough. What's the matter with you? Frightened?'

The one thing Luda was not was frightened. Perhaps this in itself was a sign she wasn't too intelligent. He was always telling her she was a fool.

'When the Fritzes get here,' Bekirbi insisted, his voice thickening with the vodka, 'I tell you all hell'll break loose. I know.'

She said nothing.

'How do I know?' he shouted. 'Because I was in Pyatigorsk the day the Fritzes came in. Because I had to get your brother out of there as well as myself.'

He sat down clumsily beside her and pulled drunkenly at his long leather boots, first the right, then the left. They were tall shiny leather boots, new, too tight at the calves and ankles.

'Goddamn these –'

'Keep them on,' Luda said. 'Go back to your barracks tonight. I'm too tired.'

He stopped what he was doing, sat up straight and turned slowly toward her.

Suddenly her anger burst out.

She pushed him so he overbalanced and fell off the bed onto the floor. Scrambling up, roaring, he hit her on the head and forearms, blow after blow. It wasn't the first time they'd fought, but this attack was the most vicious. She kept cool, however. As soon as he tired, Luda, as tall as her lover, sprang up at him, bringing her right knee up, hard and swift, into his crotch. He screamed and buckled. He fell writhing to the floor, clutching his bruised balls.

'I'll arrest you,' he gasped as soon as he could utter a word.

Luda laughed, this time uproariously. 'For beating up a man! You wouldn't dare. You're a coward, Captain Bekirbi. A twitching coward. What'll you do when the Fritzes come, eh? Grovel like you're doing now?' She burst into another shriek of laughter, seeing his angry, horrified expression. 'That's what happened in Pyatigorsk! Wasn't it? Wasn't it?' Then she saw his eyes. It was eerie in the dim light. But the message was unmistakable. She'd said something to mock him. And it was the truth. The truth! He had panicked back there in Pyatigorsk much worse – he was planning to grovel before the Nazis. He was not just a coward. The planning to be a traitor. She knew it. He had no need to tell her, to confess. She didn't even need Nadia to spell it out for her.

She sat down quickly on the bed – her legs had gone weak under her.

'Get out, coward,' she whispered. 'Never never come back.'

Captain Bekirbi averted his face. For a long time he looked out into the night. When he turned round again, his features were set. It was an expression Luda felt sure he adopted in the interrogation cells, an expression of cold indifference. The tic had gone, though the strain of controlling it was apparent.

He picked up his peaked cap with its gold braid and red star and put it firmly on his head. Then he strode to the door, pulled it open. Framed by the night, he turned in her direction, but failed to catch her eyes.

'Woman,' he said quietly but fiercely, as if in imitation of her own low fury. 'Don't ever forget who I am. I am an officer in the most powerful organization in this entire godforsaken country. One word out of place from you and –'

He left the threat hanging in the air, but still didn't go out through the door. He wanted a reaction from her. He wanted to know where she stood – and thus where *he* stood, to know just how safe he was from her. She could read his mind.

But Luda gave nothing away, turning her face from him so he couldn't even judge from her expression what she might feel.

'You're not a fool,' he insisted, with the hint of a whine in his voice. 'When trouble comes, you'll stick with me. You'll need me.'

She still said nothing, still didn't move a muscle. At last he stepped out into the black night and slammed the rickety door behind him.

*

Yusef Tsagov, when he split from Bekirbi in Red Army Street, made three quick left turns, bringing him in minutes back to the house in which the NKVD Captain had held the meeting with the Muslim elders. Tsagov entered by the back way. The elders were waiting for him. They wasted no time in greetings – this was not his first visit that day.

'Berlin's new batch of princes,' Tsagov said, not without a trace of sourness, because no-one appreciated the return of the émigré Muslim aristocrats who had sat out the hard times of Revolution and Civil War and Bolshevism on a cushion of German money. 'The first made contact less than an hour ago.' He mentioned a name.

'The émigrés,' one elder said, 'are marinated in arrogance and luxury.'

There was a murmur of agreement. 'They expect to take over the administration,' one said, 'as if there has been a vacuum of leadership during these years of so-called established Revolution.'

Tsagov needed to use all his skill, all his fleetness of mind, to keep from getting too closely identified with the anti-émigré faction, or any other faction, while still retaining the confidence of at least some sections of the Party and the NKVD. If anything of what he said here found its way back to such quarters, he would need more than good luck on his side.

As well, he reflected, to be the one man ready to undertake the less pleasant tasks – and have a reputation for discretion.

The six men discussed the latest arrival, concluding that some position of honour but little substance would have to be found for him. So few of those coming back were satisfactory; either too fundamentalist, or else they had neglected their religion – and their friends – in the flattering fleshpots of the West. Too naively pure, or too bent on personal revenge – and reward. The dark room buzzed with hushed voices until far into the morning.

'And Bekirbi?' one of the elders asked toward the end of their long discussion.

Tsagov shrugged. 'A man guided by fear. Without faith. Useful to us now. Later . . . ?'

'Kill him,' said the chief elder, 'whenever you should judge it necessary.'

SIX

At eight-thirty that morning Boris Surkov waited for General Maslennikov to be free. The anteroom at headquarters was dark; empty now, but still reeking of acrid smoke and littered with long cardboard butts of *papirosi* cigarettes.

'Boris Alexandrovich! They told me you were in here.'

Boris looked up, nodded, said nothing. Typical of that bastard Bekirbi to come into a room without any noise.

'Nothing but news this morning,' Bekirbi went on cheerfully, as if oblivious to Boris's sullenness. 'You know who's come down to the front from Moscow? How could you? Lavrenti Parlovich.' He paused, looked around, saw that they were alone. 'Beria himself.'

'And Stalingrad? We're beating them back up there?'

'Oh sure, the Great Leader'll have something to say if his own town gets knocked out.'

'Stalingrad is the key to the Volga, the nation's lifeline.'

'What good's a lifeline – without lifeblood? The Fritzes get our oil and . . .' Bekirbi drew the side of his hand across his throat.

Boris clenched and unclenched his fists fiercely.

An aide entered and called for Lieutenant Surkov to see the General.

'Your big moment, young man,' Bekirbi said mockingly.

Boris entered the office at the double, slammed his feet to attention.

General Ivan Ivanovich Maslennikov sat stiffly behind a table, a bull-necked, bullet-headed man with a fearsome scowl. Still a few weeks short of his forty-second birthday, he looked a solid fifty. An aide once claimed that if the entire Red Army were issued with Maslennikov masks and rushed to the front lines, the Germans would run right back to Berlin – those who weren't paralysed by fear.

Lieutenant Surkov delivered his report of partisan activities quickly and efficiently. It was on the optimistic side, but not false. Not flattering. 'The partisans, Comrade General, are fulfilling their vital role of harassing the enemy and protecting the main body of our glorious Red Army,' he concluded.

'Tonight,' said the General firmly, 'I leave for the northern sector. We must hold the line at the Baksan. The Germans are short of fuel. We must use the opportunity to reinforce every valley, every gorge, every stream and hillock, to prepare for the winter counter-offensive.'

'Understood, Comrade General.'

Maslennikov's expression softened. He got up and came round the table to put his arm across Boris's shoulders.

'You're doing fine, young Comrade. Young men like you will save Russia.'

General Maslennikov turned and walked quickly out to where his staff car and his aides were waiting.

Boris stood for a moment, savouring the brief instant of privilege. Then he too left the building, showing his military pass to three separate guards. Bekirbi had gone. A good omen.

Outside, Boris's motorcycle was ready.

*

The small town of Baksan, fifteen miles back up the road toward Pyatigorsk, was beyond the Baksan River, the Red Army defence line, and therefore in German – and Romanian – hands. In fact the Germans had already crossed the river further north, establishing a precarious bridgehead.'

Boris had no direct route to the partisans' new position on the loosely defined front line up in the foothills south of Baksan town. The only way to reach them was to turn off the main road and take a stony track, then foot it over the crest. Meanwhile he observed that the main road had more peasant carts than military vehicles travelling on it, despite the good opportunity for moving up men and material provided by the lull in bombing.

This lull was encouraging. Maybe the Germans *had* run out of fuel. Many of the faces Boris saw seemed cheerful, as if the people too had sensed the tide was turning.

Even the flowers and the wild cherry and walnut trees along the roadside seemed to be basking, not wilting, in the heat. Up on Boris's left the mountains were veiled by a shimmering haze, a haze that stretched right down from the peaks to Boris himself, caressing him like warm lapping waves. He felt good. He was travelling light, his only weapon a new Shpagin sub-machine gun slung downward-pointing across his back. He wore his field cap with its double line of red piping and its red star on the front tipped sideways, like a Yank.

At the first junction he turned left toward the mountains, as if about to breast the swell. To start with, the dirt road along the winding course of the Chegem was flat, but in less than a mile, at the first hill, the road got narrower, more rutted. Boris drove his machine on, making it buck and rear like a mule. He hated mules. He was a machine man, a modern man. You didn't have to persuade a motorbike to go in the direction you wanted, you ordered it.

Flushed and still full of energy, he climbed on up into the foothills. The road was flanked by tall forests, then by steep-sided meadows, bare and brown. Then more forests. He passed quickly through villages with their green-painted gates of solid iron fronting the road – solid because tradition had demanded that the women in the courtyards be invisible from the street. He had to swerve to avoid a donkey that came trotting out between two houses. A couple of boys, aged about seven or eight and sitting on a double saddle facing each other, whistled and waved their flat caps. Boris waved back.

The new front was getting closer. Now too the mountains began to squeeze close; but then, abruptly, they would open out again, then squeeze close, then open, like a concertina. Finally he clattered into Kyshto Sirt, the village that huddled in the very last of the open spaces along the road. From here on the gorge narrowed dramatically, and waterfalls splashed down from soaring cliffs on each side.

But Boris didn't have to run the gauntlet of German snipers, who had already killed three travellers braving the winding track and the rickety wooden bridges between the gorge's sheer limestone walls. Here was where he would turn off and begin his walk over to the next valley, the approach to the Baksan gorge. In Kyshto Sirt, smelling sharply of chicken shit and horse droppings – Boris noticed the stench as soon as he switched off his motor – a company of regular soldiers, mountain troops, had their headquarters. They would care for his bike. A soldier with a bandaged head told him that few men were left in the village apart from the cooks, the sick and senior officers. The others were in forward positions, constructing defences or on high patrol.

Boris shrugged. He had no-one to report to.

In ten minutes he was out again and on the mountain trail, his bike locked in a compound behind the cookhouse, the bandaged soldier richer by two roubles. The air Boris breathed was beautifully refreshing after the hot and smelly village. His boots fitted well and gripped the rocky surface of the path.

On the top of the crest he sat on a flat rock and rested for two minutes. Way down in front were craggy artificial-looking shapes in the limestone cliffs – the Baksan gorge. Far to his right tumbled the rolling wooded and scrubby country toward the front where traces of black smoke and a distant rumble told of spasmodic engagements. Up to his left, huge stands of oak and beech and hornbeam and maple and ash – with rhododendron, daphne, jasmine, juneberry, honeysuckle and saxifrage entwined at their feet – hid the ice and snow-covered rocks and glaciers of the great peaks behind, down from which tinkled hundreds of cool streams. He had been up in these hills in all weathers; they filled him with vigour.

Tembot Kochan was waiting with some of his men in a natural cave above a stretch of tumbling rapids in the Baksan River.

'Welcome, welcome, Boris Alexandrovich,' he roared, squeezing out of the cave and clasping Boris by the shoulders, pressing him to his huge body.

Boris recalled the time at the railway station in Pyatigorsk, the last occasion he had been embraced by Tembot. His immediate reaction was to remember Nadia, how she had looked in the sanitarium. Since that moment he had had no news of her. Sometimes he woke terrified, as much by the realization that a day or more had gone by without his thinking of her as by the fate he imagined she could have suffered.

'I guess you've no news – no news of Nadia?' he asked. He had little hope of a satisfactory answer.

Tembot shook his head. 'But that's no bad sign.'

Boris winced. His military service, and now the war, had given them such a short time together, really together. They had such wonderful plans. It was almost unbearable to think how differently everything had turned out.

'No,' he said, his throat catching. 'No bad news – that's a good sign.'

'All right, all right. What's your good friend the General got on his mind for us, huh? A quick thrust back to the Ukraine?'

As Tembot spoke, he urged Boris into the cave, then he squatted on the floor. Taking out a plug of home-cured tobacco and rolling it in a leaf, which lasted longer and tasted better than newspaper, he lit it by setting a spark to an impregnated string and inhaled deeply.

'What about equipment?' Boris asked. 'How many Maxims do you still have?'

'Aha, so that's it! We still have the two of 'em. But those Maxims, you know how much they weigh? Stripped? Fifty kilos. Of course you know.' His voice rose to a boom that echoed round the small cave. 'What can we do with guns that heavy up here? All right, they're still effective at this height. But when we go back up? Right up?' He jerked his thumb to his left and upward.

'We'll hold the line here,' Boris said firmly.

Tembot Kochan slapped Boris cheerfully on the shoulder. 'We got our hands on some German MP 40's, four-kilo beauties. So I'm not complaining. We keep our knives sharp too. Let's go get something to eat. Killa! Marko! Hadju! Shaliman! Hey, Osman! What d'you think you're at? A

Marxism-Leninism lecture?' He roared with laughter, at the same time planting a heavy boot in all the backsides he could reach. The men hardly stirred.

Boris and Tembot climbed up to a small clearing in the forest where an old man in a tattered camelskin cloak, the *burka*, with a dagger stuck in his belt, was doling out chunks of iron-hard black bread, pieces of dried fish and, from a two-kilo army-issue can, a mush of eggplant.

Boris chose one of the larger pieces of dried fish and jammed it into his mouth.

At that moment a shot rang out.

Tembot turned like a startled lion.

His huge frame vanished out of the clearing in the direction of the shots, upstream. A pair of buzzards took off from the top of a tall silver fire, screeching.

Boris, spitting fish, followed in the old man's tracks.

Somehow Tembot knew exactly who'd fired the shot and from where – as if he could personally identify by their sound each of the fifty rifles in his detachment's possession. He flung himself down beside two young guards, barely teenagers, on a rocky promontory with a good view across to the woods on the far bank.

'Well?'

'Half a dozen, Comrade. Between those two big rocks.'

'Weapons?'

The smaller of the two baby-faced partisans shrugged, jerking his shoulders awkwardly in his prone position.

'Saw their helmets,' said the second. The two boys looked and sounded alike.

Then a voice came loud and clear from beyond the river, on the opposite cliff. Russian, with the accent of a local Balkar tribesman. 'Hey, Comrades, it's us, friends. Hold it. Hey! What the hell're you doing? Where are you?'

The boy raised his head to shout back, ashamed of having fired at his own people.

The bullet hit him square between the eyes.

Tembot, who'd dived to save him, a cry of warning choking in his throat, rolled behind cover, cursing. Boris ducked, but the rock already gave protection.

'Keep your heads down. Wait,' Tembot hissed. He ran

into the forest to alert the others in his command and co-ordinate their defence.

The second youth cradled the dead partisan in his arms. There was the sound of loud laughter and catcalls from across the river. Then another voice, German-accented. 'Hey, Ivan, get the message?' Tears welled in the young guard's eyes, then fell unchecked on the hole in his comrade's forehead. The bleeding victim and the weeping soldier were more than comrades. They were brothers.

Boris, who knew them well, looked away. He saw clearly, in his mind's eye, Nadia, his wife. She was dead, drilled through the head by an enemy bullet. Tears pricked his eyes too. But curiously this made him feel happier, relieved. With Nadia dead, he was free to fight the war like a gladiator proudly facing the prospect of his own heroic death.

Immediately he felt ashamed, and put his arm around the crying boy's shoulder.

He knew, deep inside himself, he needed Nadia's strength now more than ever.

SEVEN

On August 28, two and a half weeks after the fall of Pyatigorsk, at the height of a furiously hot afternoon, Nadia's mother and five-year-old Darya were sorting a heap of rotting vegetables in the main room of their Nalchik house. Darya, who didn't like sticky hands, was complaining more than working. The old woman kept rasping her own fingers with the blunt peeling knife. Excising the good parts of the vegetables demanded close attention rather than skill, but her mind was elsewhere.

'Yeukh,' moaned Darya. 'I hate this mouldy stuff.'

'The devil!' exclaimed her grandmother. 'Not you, darling. My hands.' She muttered something in Kabardinian, the language of her parents. Russian was the language she used with her own family. 'But it's better cut out,' she went on coaxingly. 'You don't want to eat it, do you?'

The little girl shivered in the heat. Despite the war and her ragged smock and the long summer and all the worries in the family about mother and grandfather – gone almost two months already – she looked as plump and sleek as a pampered maharani. With her mother's dark copper hair and her father's long-jawed face, she had a serious, but contented, look when in repose. Which meant to all intents and purposes, asleep.

Mariana Dobroliubova's fingers paused, and she looked tenderly at her granddaughter. She sighed. Thank God at least they had a roof over their heads, the same roof for twenty-five years, shelter and continuity.

Mariana loved her shabby city. It altered little over the years. One or two developments, shoddy and built at the pace of a cart pulled by an obstinate donkey. She had her own old-fashioned place, and it suited her; a typical cottage, built of plaster slapped over a criss-cross of sticks, then painted in pastel blue. It was part of a small complex of single-storey houses, the most important of the three. The only neighbour, in the shack at the end of the yard, hardly bigger than an outhouse, was Hassan Pachev, a grumpy Kabardinian who drank and feuded with Mariana over trifles. The other neighbours, like so many people in Nalchik, had fled across the Caspian Sea or over the mountains into Georgia or Armenia.

Nalchik. The name meant 'horseshoe', the shape of the mountains that came down and enfolded it on three sides, leaving the town open to the great gray-brown steppe only to the north-east. A practical city. Its only remarkable buildings were the fat palaces of the bureaucrats. Even the mosques were just like ordinary houses – no elegant minarets. There were factories too, many half-built or just begun. But most of these were on the edge of town. A city of a hundred thousand people. Mariana remembered it smaller. But there had been a constant stream into town since the Revolution, shepherds and farmers from the hills and plains seeking the protection of wages and steady work.

Now they were leaving again or had already left. The Germans were at the city gates. How could life ever be the same again?

And yet, in a stupid homely kind of way, nothing had changed. Here she was, in the same old house. The windows shuttered and the curtains drawn to keep out the heat and the dust, just the door left open a crack to let in the faint draught from the courtyard shaded by the old poplar shedding white fluff like cotton balls. Like every summer. And Darya beside her by the kitchen table.

Mariana was more and more often brought to the brink of tears – she had reason in plenty. But she almost always succeeded in not crying, restraining herself by the thought that she could still hope – and by the knowledge that every time her tears came Darya cried too. Not softly, in quiet despair, like her grandmother, but loud and angry.

And when that happened Old Rags would start his chesty laments.

'Old Rags', now as always in the corner by the stove, came to the family one November night in 1937. He said he was from the Donbass, that he'd been a miner there for twenty years. But principally he maintained his name was Oleg Pavlovich Tryapichnik and hence, by a logic that escaped every other member of the Dobroliubov family, their cousin. Nadia and Boris – only Darya accepted his claim unconditionally – were sure this wheezy old miner was playing a confidence trick. He had full confidence, that is, in the tradition of Caucasian hospitality triumphing over any rational doubts as to the precise truth of his story. Old Rags was fond of quoting proverbs, particularly the proverb *Neither a mountain of gold nor a prince's stallion is worth so much as a guest in the home*. At least he claimed it was a proverb. No-one else had heard it before, though the words expressed a real Caucasian truth.

The only certainty was that Old Rags was sick. 'Good for nothing,' Mariana described him as a rule, though she admitted the physical symptoms, as who could not, so loud was his breathing. She would point out that Old Rags's name – which resembled the Russian word *tryapka*, meaning 'rag' – was the aptest thing she'd ever heard.

To Boris's constant fury, the old man would blame the communists for his plight, for their mismanagement of the mines, in fact for everything. It was all the communists' fault, down to the mud and hailstorms and the overflowing latrine. Everything was a punishment from God. Old Rags recited endless details of 'Red terrorism'. His memory, he said, was 'faultless'. Only when asked to talk about his family connections would his brain start to tire and his chest play up, and he would plead old age.

It wasn't easy for a cheerful five-year-old in this atmosphere of back-biting and moral infection spread by the all-pervasive war. Yet Darya made a good attempt. Though she did burst into tears every time granny cried, for the most part it was granny who followed her burst of happy laughter.

'Nearly through, darling,' said Mariana.

Finally, at ten minutes to five, just as they were finishing with the pile of vegetables and throwing the rotten parts into the garbage bucket, Luda arrived.

Boris's sister brought pork fat in the reed basket she carried on her arm, but really she'd come to see if there were news of Nadia.

'Where did you find *that*, darling?' Mariana exclaimed, giving Luda a hug and kiss, thinking as she always thought how much Luda looked like Boris, then holding up the pork fat to examine it. 'My meat ration's finished. Did you –?'

'They started a field kitchen in the garden,' Luda explained, bending to kiss Darya. 'I pinched a bit that fell out.'

'Aren't they all going to leave, dear?' said Mariana, putting the fat away in a cupboard.

'The City Executive Committee? What for?' Luda replied, stretching. 'We've burned all the documents we don't want the Fritzes to find, town records, Party records. Don't worry, mother.'

'Of course I worry. So they *are* expecting the . . . that they'll. . . .'

'No,' Luda said impatiently. 'I mean everything's ready *if* they come in.' She paused, glancing at Mariana, at Dasha and finally at Old Rags, snoring uneasily. 'None of you looks any happier.'

'No, no news,' Mariana said with a sigh. 'Nothing for over three weeks now.'

'News?' grumbled Old Rags, waking, more or less, from his stupor. 'We've got news enough already and to spare, all the news we want.'

'Where's Ilya?' Luda asked, looking again round the small room.

'Oh darling!' Mariana cried. 'Don't you –?'

Darya interrupted, 'He's gone to the mountains. He's gone to the mountains to fight the Fritzes.'

Luda's hand shot up to cover her gaping mouth.

'Yes, yes,' Mariana said quietly, sitting down at the table, not noticing that her elbow made a thick streak in the smear of pulp. 'Ilya's gone to join the partisans. If my mind wasn't so confused I'd have told you as soon as . . . as soon as. . . .' Tears choked her words off.

'Oh, God, and I had no idea he was thinking of that.' Luda took Darya onto her knees.

'You couldn't have known, darling,' Mariana said. 'It was so sudden. Yesterday.'

'I suppose he's –'

'He'd been thinking of it for weeks, though he never told anyone. Ever since Nadia left with Sergei. You know how they love each other, my two darling children. They have always been so close – and he so much the younger. Ilya is still only sixteen. He has been out of his mind with worry. I know it, though he has been the one to comfort all of us. Oh, Luda, he's not well enough, so soon after his lung collapsed. I know they say it's all mended, and a lung collapsing like that is just something that happens to thin nervous boys like him, but all the same. His friends put him up to it. Ilya's so sensitive with their being on the road gangs and things.'

Darya said, 'When he said goodbye he shook my hand and there was a squashed spider in it. I want to go too. Everyone's going away. Why should I –'

'So where's he gone?' Luda interrupted, shushing the little girl.

The old woman shrugged. 'And now *he*'ll be worse than ever.' She pointed toward Pachev's shack. 'There isn't a reliable man left. Perhaps your . . . oh! But you've broken with that Captain of yours, darling. I'd glad. But who on earth's left to . . . to . . . ?'

Her lips were trembling, but seeing Darya's rapidly puckering face, she pulled herself together.

'It'll be all right, little mother,' Luda said as firmly as she could. 'He'll be safer in the mountains. Let us hope so.'

Luda stretched across the table and patted Mariana's arm. Darya stirred on her lap; the heat had sent the little girl into a sudden dream-filled doze.

Mariana sighed again. Seeing Darya's eyes shut, she allowed a tear or two to seep out of her own.

A long silence followed. Then Mariana stood up. 'I cannot understand,' she muttered, retying the scarf around her head, 'why nothing, in three weeks not the smallest message. . . .'

She stopped, shrugged. She found it impossible to envision life behind the German front, in 'occupied' Russia. Her mental picture of Nadia – her wonderful exotic bird, her pet, her enchantress whom she still scarcely believed she had herself conceived and carried in her womb – in a cage, a foreign cage, was so fragmentary, so confused, she refused to accept it. Her mental image of her husband had merely faded. Now, quite calmly, she had accepted his death. It was better so. But Nadia was absolutely living . . . somewhere, somewhere.

'Let me give you a hand with something,' Luda said. 'Come on, Dasha, wake up, sweetheart. Wake up, little niece.'

Darya grumbled incomprehensibly. Her aunt began tickling her cheeks and pinching her, till the little girl came back to life and announced she was hungry.

Outside there was a distant burst of firing, the first for some hours.

'All right, let's see what we can do,' Mariana said quickly, as if determined to ignore the war and all its consequences.

So Luda helped squeeze the mishmash of usable vegetables into a tin saucepan . . . then transfer it all to a larger pan because they had forgotten about the pork fat. This made both the women laugh. Of course they should be cheerful! The soup that evening wouldn't be the worst they had ever tasted.

Luda gave no hint of the emotional turbulence she had been through because of her split with Nazir Bekirbi. It was all over now. Whether her suspicions about him were right or wrong – and she was almost a hundred percent sure – he now revolted her. If only he would accept it was all over. But men, especially local men, Balkars and Kabardinians, were like that. They felt personally insulted if *they* were the ones to be jilted. But then, of course, she reflected sadly, Caucasian men assumed that any woman ready to sleep with them as a lover but not as a wife was, even in her heart, a whore.

Luda was no less reticent about her fears for Nadia. She saw clearly in her mind's eye what Mariana so desperately tried to avoid seeing. Sleeping or waking, Luda was tormented by images of Nadia tortured. But none of this did she even hint at to the family.

'Hey, Old Rags,' she said, when the silence was beginning to weigh again, and the women had sat down at the table, their tasks completed. 'What about a moan? What's the matter with you?'

'It's all going to bad,' came a mumble out of the heap of clothes in the corner. 'A real piece of bad and that's all there is to it. You leave me be.'

Luda laughed and turned to Mariana. 'Do you need anything? Oil for the lamps?'

Darya, squatting under the table and chewing a hunk of black bread, piped up, 'I like candles better.'

'The devil blind me!' Luda suddenly exclaimed, startling the little girl so she bumped her head on the underside of the table though she didn't cry. 'That reminds me what I brought you, darling. Look. Look at this I've got you.'

She pulled from inside her cotton smock something small enough to conceal in her hand. Darya crawled out and tried to pull her aunt's fingers open. Only when Ludá had teased her to the point when Darya was beginning to feel frustrated did she open her fingers and reveal the present. It was a single pink candle, three inches high, stuck into a holder that ended in a sharp pin. The tip of its wick was black, but the candle itself showed no sign of having been burned.

Darya's eyes opened in wonder.

'A birthday candle,' Mariana declared, almost as astonished as Darya. '*How* did you find it?'

'It's mine!' said Darya very loudly.

'Yes of course, darling. Keep it safe till it's your next birthday,' Luda said. 'It was in the back of a drawer in the office. I found it when we were turning out papers to burn.'

Old Rags began saying, 'I remember the candles we had when I was a –'

Then the door flew open.

A figure stood motionless in the doorway.

'Mummy!'

Darya's shriek of delight electrified everyone.

'Mummy! Mummy! Mummy!'

The little girl flung herself into her mother's arms.

'Mummy, you're all dirty!'

Nadia buried her head in her daughter's hair, her warm little body, her soft sunburnt cheeks.

She was still holding Darya in her arms when her legs gave

way beneath her, and she sank onto the floor. Her mother and Luda rushed to pick her up and sit her on a chair. With a strong arm around her shoulder, Luda kept Nadia upright.

'Darling, my darling!' Mariana put her lips to her daughter's forehead. As she did so Darya thrust one arm round her grandmother's neck and the other round her mother's and drew them all into a mix of hair and soft faces and kisses. Then Luda knelt on the floor and hugged and embraced her sister-in-law and Darya and Mariana until they could all scarcely breathe.

Mariana pulled herself away first. 'Nadia, darling. Nadia, darling Nadia!'

'Look at my candle, Mummy!' Darya shouted, thrusting it into her mother's face. 'Look at it. It's pink. Luda gave it to me. Luda found it. I'm going to keep it for ever.'

'It's beautiful, darling,' Nadia said softly. 'Beautiful.' She looked up at her own mother and tried to smile. 'I was with father until . . . ,' she began, faltered, then started again, controlling the shrillness. 'The Germans came and . . . no, no, I didn't see him again. I –'

'Did they kill him?' Mariana said, her voice suddenly sharp in her desperate eagerness to know. Her fingers reached out and clutched Nadia's arm.

Nadia sighed. 'I don't know, Mother. I don't know. We were separated and . . . I did everything I could, but no, there was no trace afterward. I –'

Luda put her finger on her sister-in-law's lips. 'Slowly, darling, we've so much to hear. But first you must eat. We have some soup. It'll be ready soon. Meanwhile there's bread. You look so thin, so tired.'

Mariana turned and looked at the wall . . . at nothing.

'And . . . Ilya?' Nadia said, suddenly looking round as if he'd been hiding somewhere.

Luda told her.

'Oh . . . God!' Nadia took a deep laborious breath. 'My poor darling boy.'

She burst into tears, as if they had been restrained for too long and suddenly overflowed. Darya flung her arms back around her mother's neck and howled as well. Mariana sat now at the kitchen table, the shock retaining her own tears.

Then Luda said, 'If only we could tell Boris you're safe.'

Nadia stared at her sister-in-law. She drew in a deep breath. 'Boris!' she said, like a conjuror calling for the person just cut in half with a saw to step out of his box and show himself intact.

Luda told her how he had escaped from Pyatigorsk. 'We've had no recent news,' she added uneasily. 'But I'm sure he's well.'

'Yes, yes, I'm sure he's well. That's good. Boris is so – so brave.'

There was a long silence.

Old Rags suggested testily that someone should bring up hot water and make an infusion. 'There's still some dried camomile in the house. That'll help Nadia pull herself together, help everyone.'

Luda got to her feet at once, the practical one, and went out into the yard to pump water.

By the time she returned, Nadia was recovering and talking to Darya, finding out everything her daughter had been doing since she went away. Then she nibbled black bread and drank cup after cup of camomile tea while she listened to Darya and to Luda and heard Old Rags utter a few unexpectedly kind sentences. They all talked again about Ilya's decision to join the partisans . . . and cried again, then dried their eyes. At last, at a quarter to nine, Darya was persuaded to go to bed, though it was obvious she wouldn't sleep, not while her mother was in the room.

So Nadia and Luda went outside.

The two women linked arms and walked slowly along the dim road and into Kabardinskaya Street, at the end of which stood the school where Nadia taught. Before they reached it they stopped outside the pink-and-white cinema, its walls shabby with tattered posters of heroes and heroines in uniform. The street was deserted. A forlorn iron bench stood beneath a lime tree, dirty with bird-droppings and dust. Neither of them paid attention to the dirt or to the rumble of distant firing or the flashes, like lightning, eerie without the storm. They sat down, absorbed in their reunion.

As Nadia began to relate her story, the red glow on the western horizon slowly yielded to a plump yellow harvest moon.

*

The cart on which she had set out from Pyatigorsk – that fiery morning exactly two weeks before – rolled fast along the ragged edge of the asphalt road. There were ten people aboard. Timidly at first, then noisily, they shared pieces of bread, a length of slimy sausage and some red peppers.

Night fell as they reached the Malka River, two-thirds of the way to Nalchik. German engineers were repairing the broken bridge. Trucks, jeeps, armoured cars, tank transporters and heavy guns littered the road and the surrounding fields and gardens like toys after a rowdy children's party. Mixed up among the military vehicles and equipment were the horses and carts, the barrows and bundles of several hundred Russians and Caucasians. But refugees were low priority. The German soldiers themselves bickered through the night, establishing their own priority for early passage, sweltering, jostling in the dust like animals in cramped lairage pens outside an abattoir.

At first light Russian planes made a lightning strike.

In seconds, human screams, the bellowing of horses and the roar of engines drowned the howl of the dive-bombing YAKs. Explosions crescendoed into one huge background of sound. Nadia grabbed two handfuls of children and pulled them under the cart.

The raid lasted just three minutes.

The anti-aircraft guns took almost a minute to open fire; firing went on for another minute after the aircraft had disappeared.

When Nadia finally looked out from beneath the cart, the faint dawn light revealed a bloody battlefield that made real for the first time the painted scenes of medieval massacre in her history textbooks. At the edge of a cucumber patch in front of her a man was lying cut almost in half, but still with enough life to send out a hissing scream like a boiling kettle. Suddenly, as if the flame had been turned off, he died. A child, a boy, was beside him, his right foot missing. He was sitting in stunned silence, looking at the end of his leg. Crawling out, Nadia was met by sights no less horrific. To her left, the charred remains of a tank . . . and its crew. Beyond, a truck had overturned. Two men in uniform were crushed beneath it, screaming for their fellow-soldiers to lift the agonizing weight off their bodies.

Nadia had no time to react, even to register shock, before a detachment of German military police moved to where the refugee carts were camped.

'*Raus! Alle Russen geradewegs hinausfahren!*'

The MPs began herding the refugees – those who could walk or hobble – back onto their carts and barrows. A Sergeant pointed north and south, his arms outstretched like a crucifix.

'Anywhere. Just move. Move! Out of the way.'

Slowly the people began to reassemble. Soldiers goaded them with voice and boot. The mule and the mare strained and chafed in the shafts of Nadia's cart.

Several people she hadn't seen before began to clamber onto it, shouting that their cart had been blown to pieces.

'Wait! Wait!' Nadia shouted as the cart jolted forward. 'There's more of us. Wait for us!'

By now, reliving those terrible scenes with Luda on the bench in Kabardinskaya Street, Nadia had so completely transported herself back in time that she was shouting, gesticulating, playing all the parts of the drama. Her heart pounded, and her voice had grown hoarse. Suddenly aware of Luda's caressing hand on her cheek and her arm around her shoulder, Nadia stopped, panting.

'Slowly, darling, slowly,' Luda murmured, and gradually Nadia picked up the story more calmly.

After thirty-six hours the overloaded cart, several times repaired, finally disintegrated in the boiling waters of the Malka River, twenty miles up into the hills. Nadia, who had earlier waded across, pulling a panic-struck twelve-year-old, Olga, by the hand, could only look back from the bank.

Next day she found herself alone with Olga. The others had gone back, dispirited, or attempted the high passes. A shepherd gave Nadia and Olga some goat's milk and bread.

He guided them to the Baksan River, but warned that enemy troops – Romanians – were digging in along the river, while raiding parties had penetrated into the high mountains. Indeed the faint sound of shots, howitzers or light artillery, reverberated from way up on the crest.

'I kept thinking,' Nadia said, 'I kept dreaming – if only Boris was in the mountains, close. He would know I was there too. I was sure of it. Somewhere in those hills were the partisans. Perhaps, I kept hoping, they would find me. Was Boris – was Boris thinking of me? Luda, was he?'

'Of course, of course.'

'But you don't know. He tried to make me leave father. I refused.'

'Leave?'

'It was for my sake. Perhaps he was right. Yes, none of this would have happened if I had done what he said. But, Luda, we quarrelled. It was the last time I saw him. If he – if he were to die –'

'No!'

'You look so alike, you and Boris. Brother and sister – I sometimes think you must be twins.'

Nadia put her hand on Luda's thigh. Suddenly she laughed and raised her head – she had been talking to her feet, not looking up at all into her sister-in-law's face. She saw Luda clearly now, pale in the ochreous moonlight.

'What happened next was so silly, if it hadn't been so tragic,' she said, tears forming behind her dying laughter.

Luda put her hand on Nadia's, but Nadia didn't feel it. Space and time had ceased to have any present meaning for her; she had returned totally to there – and then.

The shepherd, stabbing the ground with a staff, his long gray summer coat flowing out behind him, tugging constantly at his stubby black moustache, took Nadia and Olga to a valley just short of the Baksan River. They stopped to eat their bread and fruit. Olga was sleepy afterward and lay down and closed her eyes. The guide took Nadia to the top of a low crest from which they could survey the river. Below them was flat water between two sandy beaches, a place where they could wade across at night without the risk of being dragged downstream by the current. On the banks snowy-blossomed rhododendrons, with which Nature each summer supplanted the whiteness of winter, sparkled in the sunlight.

The guide had just finished pointing out the precise spot where she should cross when Nadia happened to turn her head toward the valley where Olga was sleeping. At that moment, out of the edge of an oakwood only twenty yards from the girl, something came into view. Nadia's heart gave a leap. But it was only a herd of small pale-brown deer, pushing their way cautiously into the clearing. Olga, who could only have been dozing, saw them too. She sat up and pointed. The deer, startled, dug in their tiny feet, twisted their thin agile bodies and bounded back into the cover of the forest. The girl – her laughter audible to Nadia up on the crest – jumped to her feet. With scarcely less agility than the deer, she ran down to the dense cover and disappeared. Seconds later the firing started – a series of staccato rifle shots that whistled and thudded into the trees. Nadia heard the crashing of the frightened deer – then a thin high human scream. She flew down the slope toward the clearing, raced across it ... then clung to a sturdy oak, suddenly disoriented. 'Olga! Olga!' Where had the girl disappeared? It all looked so different. But the sound of voices came suddenly very close. Then anguished shouts. A man appeared in the clearing, a man in dark green uniform, a rifle slung over his back. He saw Nadia at the same moment she saw him. His shout was in a language she didn't recognize.

'*Ei vezi, frumoasa! Asa. Inca una.*'

He yelled again to the soldiers still in the forest, in the same language.

A group of men streamed out from the trees, talking animatedly to each other, confused.

Nadia shouted at them in Russian. 'Where is Olga? What did you do to the girl?'

But she had her answer at once, unspoken. The last of the soldiers came out of the oak forest bearing in his arms the body of the young Russian. A bullet had penetrated her chest, leaving only a neat hole, with just a rim of blood. She still had on her face the excited expression of a child who'd just seen something wild and beautiful.

The soldier – a young ordinary soldier in the Romanian 2nd Mountain Division – laid her gently on the grass.

He was crying.

Nadia walked silently to where she lay and, not for the first time, cradled in her arms a victim of the war. She remained like that until an officer arrived. He took her away, guiding her by the arm along a winding path until they came to his jeep. He helped her in, and they drove off in the back seat, side by side. She never uttered a word.

Nadia was taken twenty miles back toward the north-east, down again onto the Pyatigorsk to Nalchik road. In the village of Malka, in a building that once had housed the Party offices and the local administration, she was held for ten days.

The Romanians treated her well. She was fed regularly and given a room to herself, as if in compensation for Olga. The welts disappeared from her feet, chafed by the straps of her wood-soled sandals. A female secretary-interpreter, like a nurse in the Romanian spinach-coloured army uniform, looked after her tenderly. But Nadia fretted the whole time, furious to be back almost at the point she'd reached after the first day of her journey from Pyatigorsk, still in a state of shock over the death of Olga. Every day her 'nurse' explained that the officer in charge was too busy to deal with her case right now, he had more 'dangerous' elements to control, but nothing was amiss, her freedom would be granted in due course.

Now – on the bench – she paused, uncertain how, whether at all, to explain what happened next.

But at last, tensely, Nadia told Luda about the paper Colonel Brandt had given her, how she used it and then – many days later – she was free to leave Malka.

'Colonel Brandt?' Luda interposed in a puzzled voice.

Nadia stared silently at her feet, chapped again from the leather straps of her sandals.

'A German officer. He looked for father when he couldn't be found in the sanitarium. He was –'

The tears began to fall.

'Later, darling,' Luda murmured. 'You must try to forget that horrible time. You're home now.'

'Home!' said Nadia grimly. 'Home. How long before the murdering Hitlerites come here too? It won't be just father who suffers. It'll be Dasha and mother and you and everyone.' She bent forward and rested her head in her hands. 'But let me finish.'

And she told Luda how she had walked back to the river, taken off her dress and waded across naked, holding the dress above her head. A gaping partisan met her on the far bank.

Nadia laughed at last. 'Venus rising from the water! I got a lift in a Red Army truck for the last ten miles. That's it. That's how I came home.'

Luda paused a long while before murmuring, 'But you've said nothing about Pyatigorsk, darling, nothing about your father. Did –?'

'I don't know. I don't know. I'm sure he must be dead. They snatched me away. I never knew.'

'But what happened? Why –?'

Nadia knew she should tell Luda everything now – or never.

Yes – she looked so like – so like Boris, so like her husband.

But she said nothing, and both women remained silent on the bench.

A minute passed.

At last Luda said solemnly, 'You've learned what it's really like, darling. Here we just wait.' She paused, then went on. 'But there is danger here too. I'm sorry, but it's true. I am sure.'

'That the Germans will come?'

'No. I mean there are traitors.'

And it was Luda's turn to pour out her heart. She told Nadia her suspicions of Nazir Bekirbi; not just of him, but how she had begun to see all around her, to sense, to feel, to overhear, that not everyone in the town anticipated with dread the *Neue Ordnung*, the New Order the Germans promised to bring.

'You know I always hated your Captain,' Nadia exclaimed. 'But Luda. Listen to me a moment longer,' she went on urgently, leaning so that her head was almost touching the other woman's. 'Everything. I'll do everything to fight the Hitlerites. They believe we're animals, they believe we have no feelings, we're not real human beings. But it's they, they are the animals. Let's promise to fight them. Together. I prefer for all of us to die than let Darya live in the power of the Hitlerites. She'll never be their whore. You understand?'

'Whore?' Luda whispered, frightened by Nadia's intensity.

'Hitlerites! I mean every single German,' Nadia whispered, her voice husky with the effort – because, for her, perhaps one German, one alone, should be spared. 'There are no good Germans. None belong here. We must support Boris and Ilya and Tembot Batazarovich and all the other partisans and soldiers. We must be as brave as the fighting women of the Red Army, Luda my darling. To the death. I swear it. Swear it with me.'

'To the death,' Luda said softly. She took Nadia in her arms and held her tight. Then they walked gently, linked together, back to the small cramped room where Darya was sleeping and Mariana was waiting up for them, white-faced, tearful, but half-consoled by the return of one, at least, of her darling family.

*

But Nadia hadn't held back only what happened in Pyatigorsk. She had censored more than that from her account.

He had come!

She had seen him again – in Malka.

She was in that bare room – just a mattress and a wooden chair. The heat was hammering pain into her skull. Suddenly he had come bursting in, clutching a bottle of Georgian wine in one hand, a smaller bottle of Nartan mineral water in the other.

'You're free!' he said. His eyes were brilliant and volatile. Was he drunk, Nadia wondered, or had he gone mad?

From his jacket pocket he produced two glasses. Clumsily he filled both with a mix of wine and water. 'Drink, and we'll go.' He was trembling. He placed her drink on the floor near her hand. The glass rattled like a drum.

'Go? Go where?' she managed to gasp out.

The Colonel paced up and down, not looking at her. 'Nadia, I had to see you again. I love you. No, don't say anything. You know it already, if you've thought of me at all. I will take you to safety. Come.'

'With you, Colonel? You saved my life, I know that, but you must be –'

'No, not mad. Drink, please. You are thirsty in this terrible heat. All right.' He twirled the single wooden chair round like a lion-tamer and straddled it, leaning forward against the thin struts of the back. 'Nadia, I am grateful to you for turning me back into a human being. Why didn't you ask for my help earlier? You know I would have come.'

She made a helpless gesture with her hands.

He stared at her. His face was smeared with dust and sweat. Then he reached out and took her hand, holding it in both of his, turning it over, examining it, finally clasping it between his hands in a firm grip and looking at her with a kind of sad defiance. 'Nadia, I'm going to find you again. There is something between us, whatever you say, and it's not finished yet. You know that as well as I do. For now, I will give instructions to the local commander. He will let you go – alone. But you will see me again and then we can say everything we have to say.'

'No!' Nadia pulled her hand away. 'Please, Colonel. If you look for me, I will be branded as a traitor. My own people will turn against me, and they would be justified.'

'I will never put you in danger, Nadia. Trust me. Don't be afraid.'

'Colonel, it's not possible.' Hating herself, she felt tears start from her eyes. 'Go now. Leave me.'

Brandt stood up, looked down at her for a long moment, and said softly, 'I love you.'

Then he was gone.

When she looked up again, she saw the wine and water he had left by her bed. She drank it in a single swallow.

EIGHT

There was no moment when things began to go wrong for the Germans, when the hectic, daredevil advance suddenly broke down, when the prospect of not achieving their aims entered their heads suddenly as a possibility. Brandt remembered the month of September 1942 as a time of gradually increasing frustration. A time of rumours. Rumours which, as the days and weeks went by, became increasingly dangerous to repeat.

He tried to get some confirmation of what was happening from his divisional commander, von Kreuss, a mild-mannered, sober professional soldier from the Austrian border country. Von Kreuss had just returned from Berlin.

'Read your report,' he said as Brandt entered his dug-out in the centre of a collective farm complex. 'First class. Bloody useless. Sit down.'

Von Kreuss got a bottle of scotch whisky out of a desk drawer, poured out two glasses and pushed one over to Brandt.

'Will to fight. Have they got it? Answer, best bet, is yes. You agree. Said so in your report. This is it, the critical moment. Their Great Patriotic War. That's their name for it. Win or bust. Now or never. Every bloody Russian, soldier, civilian, old, young, I don't care, knows that. What they think is this. We penetrate their lines now, they fetch up dead or slaves. Colony of serfs from Atlantic to Urals. Well, that's as may be. Not my job to know. But they think it. We break through now, that's it, end of Soviet Union. No wonder the Russians call it their Black Summer, '42. If they get a black winter after it, it's all over. Nothing. Death. Better death. You agree.'

Brandt nodded. He liked his commanding officer's bluntness. But could he accept what was happening in the same detached way? He had up to now – well, up to the time he had seen Nadia again in Malka.

'What about the next Russian move, eh?' von Kreuss asked.

Brandt drained his glass. Von Kreuss immediately refilled it.

'I wish I could be sure. I guess they are wondering the same as we are – which weighs more in the balance, our fire-power or their capacity to absorb punishment and still retain enough strength to fight back? They have a few encouraging signs, which must cheer them up. They got the flag down from Elbrus. A Red Army detachment crossed the highest pass in the whole Caucasian crest. By night. That's a spectacular achievement too. It shows what they are capable of. But, more important, we have stopped advancing. Do they know we are as short of fuel as we really are? How can we guess? In any case they must be glad of the breathing space we are giving them. I don't think they'll counter-attack yet. Their best chance is still to let us grind ourselves to pieces, and counter-attack then.'

They talked on for hours.

Throughout the 17th Army, October was a month of intense planning.

On the nineteenth, details of the plan for the new offensive were finalised. The date for action was set – October 25.

The first, vital, target at the centre of the German advance was – Nalchik.

Hitler's edict came through on the eve of the attack. This, he declared, would be the final thrust. The decisive action. The attack on Nalchik would signal the final proof that he had been right, had always been right. The Bolsheviks were a spent force. The oilfields were within the grasp of the Third Reich. The breakthrough to Nalchik was the key to this whole, brilliant, personal Caucasus strategy.

The key to total victory.

*

At nine fifty-five a.m., October 25, Colonel Siegfried Brandt waited moodily on a scrubby knoll a hundred yards back from the west bank of the Baksan and two miles south of the Pyatigorsk to Nalchik road. Beside him stood the commanding officers of his three Battalions. All were waiting for the signal. All showed signs of impatience, stamping their feet, folding and unfolding their arms. It was a long time since they'd seen large-scale action.

But for Colonel Brandt there was a difference. He would never again be caught up in the fury and excitement of successful action. It had been intoxicating once. Who could not have felt it, been swept up by the collective, virile excitement? But now he was going into *her* town. He would do it, yes; he would protect his men, support them, fight professionally, correctly. He would minimize the killing by doing it quicker, more efficiently, than anyone else. That, perhaps, was the only way he could help her now.

And then . . . then he would have to decide.

Always later. He shook his head and stared grimly ahead.

The Indian summer had broken suddenly three days before. Now, after heavy rain, there was an uncertain pause. The clouds were still darkly ominous, however, and a bitter wind buffeted the men's backs, cracking the hems of their olive duck wind-jackets like whips. The same wind blew away eastward the steady roar of Luftwaffe bombing and heavy artillery bombardment, both of which had been going on since dawn.

A lone 3-ton Opel Blitz truck ground along a muddy track fifty yards to Brandt's right. This was the truck that refused to start last night. The Colonel was relieved to note all his equipment was now in working order. It was the kind of satisfaction he needed now. Suddenly a red flare lit the gloom-gray morning. The lurid light hung beneath the low clouds like emanations from a blood-red moon.

It was 10.00 hours. Precisely.

At once tanks coughed into life. Engines roared. Tracks creaked and wheels spun in the mud. Brandt ran down the knoll to his jeep. Major Ott stayed put. His Battalion was part of the rear formation. Ahead, two columns moved forward, twin lines of tanks, jeeps, trucks, armoured cars, motorcycles with machine guns in their sidecars, troop carriers hauling light artillery and, in the rear, mules and donkeys laden with ammunition boxes.

The battle of Nalchik was under way.

*

For five days a cold drizzle fell over the town. The drab brown leaves in the parks and along the sides of the broad streets dripped and quivered. A lurid light flickered day and night. The roar of firing and collapsing buildings made a non-stop percussion. Steadily the town was surrounded . . . then squeezed like an old, dry lemon; men and women were prised from their hiding places, like pips, and discarded. The squat, pastel-washed, pink and blue and yellow houses flaked and crumbled. The big E-shaped hotel guarding the Nalchik end of the long park that stretched down to the sanitaria of Dolinsk village lost first one, then another, of its wings. Two gaping holes appeared in its balconied facade. Beyond, a cement factory burned for thirty-six hours.

In the early morning of October 30, Colonel Brandt was in his jeep near the shattered Party headquarters. Nalchik was all but taken, virtually 'tidy'. Flags with the swastika – and some with a red crescent – were flying or being erected on public buildings.

Brandt was slumped on the front seat, deep in thought, awed and at the same time elated at the prospect of searching for Nadia. For the first time the logistical problems of locating her without arousing suspicion could be seen against the background of 'her' city.

He was turning to tell his driver to move on toward the Town Hall when he heard a shout. A man in the yellowish-khaki uniform and long sleek boots of an NKVD officer was running toward the jeep. In the man's right hand was a piece of white cloth. Two or three times he stopped and raised the cloth above his head. Brandt beckoned him to advance.

When the man came up to the jeep, Brandt saw he had no markings on his uniform, no tabs of rank. He was bare-headed, and his short dark hair was plastered to his skull with mist and sweat. His chin and cheeks were covered with a dense stubble of beard that seemed to ripple strangely like scurrying snakes.

The figure stopped and bowed awkwardly.

'*Willkommen auf Nalchik,*' he said, accenting strangely his attempt at German. '*Nicht mehr scheissen. Willkommen, meine Herrn.*'

Brandt's driver laughed. But the message was understood by everyone who heard it. 'No more shitting,' he'd said. What he meant was '*Nicht mehr schiessen*' – no more shooting.

'Good,' Brandt replied, in Russian. 'Now let's see how welcome we really are.'

The man bowed again. 'Ex-Captain Nazir Kerimovich Bekirbi,' he said as formally as circumstances permitted. 'At your service.'

NINE

For Nadia, the seven weeks between her home-coming and the German capture of Nalchik passed like seven days. The role of heroine was short-lived. She needed action – a new, positive role.

The cue had been the arrival, on the first day of September, of a message from Ilya.

The messenger interested Nadia more than the note – which said only that Ilya was with 'friends' and they weren't to worry. She didn't know the name of the boy who brought it, but his face was familiar as a classmate of Ilya's – though now it was smeared with mud, almost as if he had plastered it on like make-up to disguise a pimply skin.

Nadia had to hold his arm to stop him darting off. 'I want to help,' she said. 'If you're with the partisans, maybe you know someone here I could contact – here in Nalchik.'

The boy told her – reluctantly, only because she was Ilya's sister – to see 'Auntie' if she wanted to volunteer for 'special duties'. Auntie worked as a sweeper at the railway station.

Nadia went that afternoon. Despite the lack of trains the station was full of noise. Stalls had been set up. Beggars were plying their illicit but tolerated trade. Gypsies – 'Romanians', people called them – lugged their babies around and held out their dark palms fretted with pink lines. Men in loose leather jackets and thin cotton trousers met in clusters to smoke and spit and discuss the new rationing regulations. Auntie, a woman of impeccable ugliness, easily recognizable from the boy's description, was deep in conversation with another woman. Both were bending forward, waving their hands. Nadia waited for ten minutes before the woman left, mumbling and shaking her head.

Auntie at last became aware of Nadia's presence and looked up, staring with rheumy, gloomy eyes. Despite the late-summer heat she wore moth-eaten ear muffs. Her hair was thin and short, and her dirty headscarf was slipping off – it was only on her head at all because it was snagged in the muffs. Her body was square.

'I want to help,' Nadia said simply. 'I'm Nadia Sergeevna, Lieutenant Boris Surkov's wife.'

Auntie continued to look at her coldly. 'You want to help. Half of 'em are ready to help one side and half the other. What are you asking an old fool like me for? But I know you, Nadia Sergeevna. Damn me for the old hag I am, but I know who you are.'

The dumpy scarecrow wagged her head slowly, as if the knowledge weighed heavy on her. But when Nadia saw her old eyes, she detected more than a trace of warmth, of compassion.

She was puzzled, however. 'Did the boy –?'

'Maybe he did.'

'What should I do?' Nadia asked, wondering if Auntie could really be the key to a new role in the underground.

'Shift! Standing here too damn long.'

She picked up her besom and began scratching the dusty ground with it, working her way slowly back toward the station hall with its white columns and silver dome, like a secular mosque.

'They couldn't use the miserable Party,' she said, as if in explanation to Nadia's thoughts. 'The Party will all have to fuck off when the Fritzes come. Regular system now. We're learning the lesson. Anyone's welcome so long as they hate the bloody Fritzes.' She stopped an instant and looked straight at Nadia. 'Me, I hate 'em like the beasts they are. Three granddaughters, and I'm not standing doing nothing while they come and give 'em a dose of hussar's catarrh. Oh no . . . yes, that's better. It's not so we'll be noticed here.' Suddenly her voice softened. 'So you want to do something, my little dove?'

Nadia said, 'I have a daughter myself.'

Auntie stood leaning a moment on her broom. All around, people pushed and gesticulated and shouted. A drop of sweat fell into Nadia's right eye. She rubbed it so the eye smarted.

'Go fuck your mother!'

Nadia looked at the old woman, startled. Then she laughed. Auntie was swearing at a boy of about ten who'd just run into her and who now darted away, alarmed at the dour old woman's ferocity.

'You have a word with Nina Petrovna,' she said at last. 'She knows the score.'

'Who? Where can I – ?'

'Reckon she'll be needing someone like you to get a bit friendly with 'em maybe. Beauty like you.' Auntie winked at her, bashfully, as if any reference to Nadia as a sexually attractive woman, however modestly expressed, was more obscene than her routine cursing.

Nadia looked away, silent.

Auntie went on, 'I wouldn't touch 'em myself. Fat chance!'

'Who is Nina Petrovna?' Nadia asked again, her heart already beating fast, stimulated by a growing unease ... even fear. 'Where is she?'

'Don't you worry, my little darling,' Auntie said. 'She'll come along and see you. One day.'

'Soon. She must come soon. They could be here any day, the Germans. I don't want –'

'She'll come. She'll be in time. Eh, you see that man, no, don't stare. One of the others. Allah-loving bastards. They think they'll be on top, they do, when the bloody Fritzes get here.'

*

Three days later a big peasant woman, in her mid-forties and smelling of home-boiled soap, knocked at Nadia's door and stayed an hour, chewing sunflower seeds and talking in a corner of the kitchen with Nadia, while Mariana and Darya went out, and Old Rags was picked up and banished to the back room. Nadia and Nina Petrovna sat on the edge of the double bed which, curtained off, had been the scene of Darya's embarrassed conception.

The following morning, in a sparsely furnished room at

the north end of town, Nadia finished reading out loud words typed on a grimy card: '. . . if from weakness, cowardice or ill-will I fail to keep the oath and commit treason, contrary to the interests of the people, then I will die a damned death from the hands of my comrades. On these conditions I sign.'

Nina Petrovna spat out the husk of a sunflower seed and handed Nadia the stub of a pencil.

Nadia signed.

The two women sat opposite each other at a small table. Four other women sat on chairs along one wall. Nadia found it hard to focus on them because of the flu she'd contracted – the flu Old Rags had passed on to her. For a week it had seemed likely to kill him, and the family hovered, uncertain how big an effort to make to cure him. Then he'd begun to shake it off . . . for Nadia to catch. She felt guilty at doing nothing for Old Rags, but also furious. Her eyes were now red and streaming, and her sinuses were sore. The ceremony wasn't the dramatic occasion she had hoped for.

'So, Nadia Sergeevna,' said Nina Petrovna. She looked and dressed like a washerwoman. She was one. Her face was large and round and beaded with sweat, and tufts of hair grew from warts that dotted the folds of flesh hanging on the bone structure of her face like blobs of half-melted wax. 'So. You're one of us.' Still chewing, she looked around at the other women in the room and gave a deep bass laugh. 'Now when they catch you they'll hang you.' She shoved a photograph across the table.

Nadia took it and paled. It showed a line of women, all of them young. All of them were hanging by their necks. In a Ukrainian village, a scaffold had been set up in the hen-run of one of the wooden huts. A group of old women were in the background, gaping, weeping, huddled. Around the stretched neck of each of the hanged women was a string holding a crudely printed placard, every placard with the same message: *'This is a partisan woman who did* not *give herself up.'*

The image appalled yet fascinated Nadia. These women weren't just dead. They would hang there in their misery for ever, for as long as the photograph existed – for as long as anyone who'd seen it existed.

But, for herself, the image wasn't frightening. She had

seen enough in Pyatigorsk and on her journey back to Nalchik to know that war meant death – revolting, humiliating death. The photograph Nina Petrovna showed her cauterized her fear. A flame flared up inside her – lit by a flint-sharp desire for revenge.

Nadia looked up at Nina Petrovna and handed back the photograph.

'They died believing in what they did,' she said.

Nina Petrovna added grimly, 'So may we all.' Then she relaxed. 'Now, some names.'

At once the four women who had been sitting along the edge of the room began clapping and moving forward to kiss Nadia, introducing themselves and shaking her hand. Before, they had affected not to notice her. Nadia had ignored them. Now she was one of them. She was a member of the Nalchik Women's Anti-Nazi Opposition Group.

Two of the women she already knew. One was a teacher at No 4 School, the other a cleaning woman at the Kabardinskaya Street school where she herself taught. The cleaning woman produced from a goatskin bag a bottle of beer, and the women passed it from one to the other. Before drinking, they raised the bottle in a toast to their success.

Nina Petrovna was the last to drink. When she lifted the almost-empty bottle, she spat and said in her loud hoarse voice, 'To the best swimmers – they'll be the ones to survive.'

When the others looked at her curiously, Nina Petrovna drank and went on, 'The Fritzes, they're like a wave. What do you do when you see a wave coming? You dive under it. The bigger the wave, the better the swimmer you've got to be to come up on the other side. It's what we'll do, when that tide of Fritzy filth reaches us. All right, finish. There's too much danger already, us all being here so long. Remember. Don't try and be heroines. Don't do anything by yourselves. Everything from me and through me. Our Group isn't the Party. But it's Party discipline we've got to have if we're not going to be drowned, the whole lot of us.'

Over the following weeks Nadia had several meetings with Nina Petrovna, always the two of them alone. They met in different places, usually in the streets or in the park or some other public place, sometimes in Nadia's own house.

Darya was curious at first about the 'ugly lady', as she called Nina Petrovna. But soon the little girl accepted the newcomer as part of their comings and goings.

Nadia also met the others, less frequently, and with less pleasure.

'I expect you miss your husband, dear,' the cleaning woman said one night, as if it were a question to which the answer was in doubt.

Nadia's instinct – which surprised and shocked her – was to feel a stab of desire for – that German Colonel. Damn anyone who pried! For days Nadia hadn't even though of him, had suppressed that horrible nagging memory. Why *had* she never told anyone, not even Nina Petrovna, who *ought* to know, about Colonel Siegfried Brandt? It's no use, she said to herself, it's my secret. My secret for ever and ever. What happened in Pyatigorsk and in Malka was a training for discretion – why not look at it like that? It was a hypocritical way of rationalizing her guilt, and she knew it.

She stabbed a fork into the potato stew to see if the eye-ridden spuds had completely disintegrated.

'Soup's as ready as it'll ever be,' she said cheerlessly, and the cleaning woman sat down to dinner with the rest of them.

*

That same night – a week before the capture of Nalchik, the imminence of it already, somehow, in the air – Luda woke Nadia, shaking her shoulder roughly. Luda, the money-winner with her few roubles earned from the City Executive Committee, had her own key and frequently spent nights at Nadia's house.

'Wake up, darling,' she whispered urgently.

Nadia needed little prompting.

'Let's go out into the yard,' Luda said.

With the watery moon shimmering behind the fluttering poplar leaves, the women sat on a wooden bench side by side, as they had seven weeks earlier, in Kabardinskaya Street. They both shivered, though it was one of the last warm nights of the autumn.

'I saw Boris,' Luda said immediately.

Nadia gasped. 'Where? How?'

'Today at Party headquarters. He came for a briefing.'

'Didn't he have time to see me, to see Dasha?'

Luda said impatiently, 'Darling, of course not. What are you thinking of?'

'We have never seen each other – not since that terrible time. I know, he has duties. But he is close by. If only he would come.'

'He would, darling. I know he would if it were possible.'

'Yes. I'm sorry. How was he?'

Luda's lips clamped tightly together. Her brother was a hero to her, but she was confused. Boris seemed to have such a strange attitude now to Nadia, whom she herself loved no less than she loved her brother. He seemed puzzled – as though he had only just met her and wanted Luda's opinion.

'How was he?' Nadia repeated.

'Angry – with me. I don't know why. Darling, he loves you so. Perhaps – he feels guilty.'

'*He?*' Nadia turned and took Luda's hand. 'I think – I think. . . .' She broke off. 'Luda. Luda. You know what I'm doing here, the work I'm doing? You remember how we swore to fight? I am fighting. No less than you. No less than Boris.'

'Yes, darling, yes, I know.'

'I'm sorry. Now, tell me. What did he say?'

'He sent you his love,' Luda lied. 'He was optimistic. I saw Boris only for a few minutes, a few seconds, as he was leaving. He's with Tembot now. He worships the old man.'

'Thank God for that at least.'

'Yes, he has a father in Tembot. And he's so brave, my brother. We should be proud of him.'

'I am proud of him, of what he's doing,' Nadia said. 'I'm proud of all of us who resist. I wish Boris realized there are others who make sacrifices.'

'He does! I told him. I told him how you were engaged in the struggle, darling, as much as I knew, because it's all so secret, and it must be secret, but. . . .' Luda remembered Boris's puzzled reaction – 'Why is she so intent on risking her own life?' Perhaps, she thought, my brother is right. A sacrifice wasn't always a useful gesture. It hadn't saved Nadia's father.

'I think I understand,' she said tentatively. 'He wants to own you, but you are free. I wanted to tell him. But there was no time. How can we solve such problems in the middle of a war?'

Nadia said fiercely, 'War has no point if it kills love.' She paused. 'But thank you.' She squeezed Luda's hand. 'I'm happy that Boris is so well, so active. I truly am. When this war is over, you'll see. Things may never be the same – but they'll be better. If we are true, true to what we believe in, the new life will be better, I promise you.'

Luda smiled, feeling the warmth of Nadia's passion like a ray of summer heat. 'If you promise something, darling, then that's how it'll be.'

*

A week later, in the early, blustery morning of October 25, Nadia took Darya to the doctor. Not precisely a doctor, because anyone fully trained was at the front or in military hospitals well behind the lines, but a woman whose skills with traditional herbal remedies, plus a smattering of science gleaned from her son's medical textbooks, gave her a reputation as a healer – and who accepted 'spare' ration coupons or face powder or even home-brewed vodka as payment.

Darya's fever had already gone on for a week, a variation of Old Rags's original. Nadia herself was better, but only, she thought with exasperation, in time to see Dasha succumb. Finally Nadia was forced to sacrifice her last pair of cotton stockings and seek advice.

Still being carried the short distance down Kabardinskaya Street, Darya asked a question that lately came less and less frequently from her lips.

'Where's Daddy?'

Reluctantly Nadia counted the days since she herself had seen Boris, in Pyatigorsk. More than two months ago.

'Where's Daddy?'

'In the mountains,' Nadia answered abstractedly.

'Can I go too? When's he coming back?' Darya insisted, whining from the fever.

'Soon, darling,' her mother said. But Dasha was not soothed.

'Why won't he –?'

'Come along! We're here.'

Then Darya screamed.

Not because of her mother's sharp tone – or the imminent prospect of seeing the doctor. Her scream was from real, immediate fear. At the very moment Nadai knocked on the doctor's door, the first bomb fell on Nalchik.

Mother and daughter turned and fled. Nadia carried Darya rigid in her arms like a corpse. Reaching their house in less than a minute, she ran to the cellar beneath the main room, the shelter they'd stocked and reinforced – just in case; the Dobroliubovs and Hassan Pachev too, for he had no cellar of his own in the single-roomed house across the yard. Mariana, Old Rags and Luda, who'd been visiting, were already inside.

Only Pachev, mysteriously, was missing.

'The Mohammedan's gone to take his chance,' muttered Mariana.

They stayed in the cellar four days.

For Nadia this was the period under the wave. She held her breath. Just occasionally she thought, with sadness, not with rancour, 'Damn him! Can he do nothing to stop this? What's it worth, his so-called love?'

It was Hassan Pachev who brought them news that the fighting was over, only minutes, in fact, before the time that Nadia had set herself as a deadline for their incarceration. Against her mother's wishes, she was going to put her head out and see.

Instead, the trapdoor opened above them, and Pachev's grizzled face poked through.

'Fritzes are the bosses now,' he announced.

Nadia looked up at him intently. He didn't seem perturbed either by her scrutiny or by the news he'd brought.

Next day Pachev tried to be 'kind'. He came across – something he rarely did – and 'advised' Nadia to lie low. The Germans, he said as if with some authority, didn't like 'indoctrinators'. And apart from being a teacher she was also the wife of a notoriously ardent Bolshevik. This self-confidence, this new vocabulary, this gratuitous giving of advice, was deeply suspicious to Nadia.

She said nothing. But she watched him. The second morning of the occupation, she trailed him as far as the top of Nogmov Prospect, where she saw him talking to a German SS officer.

She walked back quickly, so he wouldn't notice her.

It was eerie, always now, in the streets of her own – occupied – town, spectrally quiet, deserted by everyone except the Germans – and their friends. The water on the far side of the German breaker was deceptively calm. But she felt an exhilaration all the same, now the Fritzes were actually here, like when the curtain was going up on the first night. She felt nervous, but prepared. She knew her role. She knew the exits and entrances and the cues. Nina Petrovna had coached her well. She had signs, she knew the addresses of safe houses, she had learned coded signals and passwords. It was all in her head, nothing written down. No prompter.

But there would also be no applause. Not even, the Nalchik Women's Anti-Nazi Opposition Group hoped, an audience.

Forty-eight hours into the occupation, on November 1, Nadia met Nina Petrovna on the sidewalk of Nogmov Prospect. To a background of thunder and lightning from a storm gathering in the mountains, they discussed two scenarios for action.

One was Nadia's first assignment. Nina Petrovna had been informed the Germans were looking for clerks and secretaries. 'We can be the eyes and ears, Nadia Sergeevna. We've got to know what they're doing, get close to them every moment, make contact – and then pass everything on to the army and the partisans. Every day we must do this till the mother-rapers are chased out. You know your letters. I'll try and fix something soon.'

Nadia's courage seemed to evaporate. If she were actually to work for the Germans, all kinds of pretences would have to be kept up – that she hated her communist husband, for instance, that she had been living a clandestine life as a communist-hater, that the New Order was the hope of the frustrated intellectual class. All this she would have to tell the Germans. It would be also what her own people were bound to believe. An ungrateful, dangerous role.

At the same time Nadia burned the last bridge of her own innocence. She betrayed to Nina Petrovna her suspicions regarding her neighbour, Hassan Pachev.

Nina Petrovna said nothing, but had Pachev put under observation. Next day, early on a murky evening, with thunder again in the air, a trap was sprung.

On the Baksan Chaussee, out beyond the railway station, a woman with a broom and shaggy goat's-wool ear muffs stopped Hassan Pachev and asked him for the time. Pachev obliged, holding up a wrist that displayed a steel-cased watch. He consulted it with a proud flourish. It was, after all, new. A present. A second later a felt-cloaked tribesman stabbed him in the back, three times, with a well-honed steel dagger.

A German patrol, appearing unexpectedly, saw the incident. Auntie slipped away. But they chased the tribesman and shot him dead.

Nadia had blood on her hands. From now on she would have to live a totally secret life, a prisoner as much as a soldier of the underground. During the night she kissed her family goodbye, slipped out into the drumming rain and disappeared.

TEN

On that same night of November 2, winter hit the high mountains like a blare of brass blotting out a solo flute. Blizzards, chasing each other like rival wolf-packs, howled and snarled over peaks and valleys, scaring the wild animals no less than men into numb submission. Tembot Kochan, however, was ready. His partisans were encamped in the shadow and protection of a wall of sheer rock and ice nine miles long and more than a mile from foundation to crest – the Bezengi Ice Wall. Their base was an abandoned, now resurrected, village. The houses were mere heaps of stone, but palaces compared to the shallow caves that provided the only alternative shelter. With branches, canvas, skins and sheets of waste metal artfully beaten and arranged, the village was home and fortress for two hundred and fifty partisans and hangers-on. It was a strong base, strategically positioned high on the right bank of the Cherek River where it gushed from an ice grotto in the Bezengi glacier.

Taking to the mountains was the traditional response to danger for the Caucasians. But it was still a defeat, hard on morale.

Tembot came nearest to despair when he lost his stallion. During the retreat from the Baksan, a Captain in the 63rd Division commandeered the magnificent shaloukh for service in the Red Army. New regular units, he said, were being formed in the west. 'Hold the mountains, Comrade, and with luck you'll see him again.' 'Let's hope so,' said Tembot. He kissed the stallion's nose.

There were tears in his eyes at that moment.

Not now. What was past was past.

In a hut in the bleak mountains Tembot chewed on a hunk

of black bread and looked impassively at Boris. The young Junior Lieutenant was screwing up his eyes to read an old copy of *Defender of the Homeland* by the light of a flickering oil lamp.

Boris threw the newspaper down and looked up at Tembot. 'It's crazy,' he said angrily, 'rotting here in this rubble.'

Tembot chewed on regardless, then swallowed. 'You shouldn't read out-of-date propaganda,' he said at last. 'Just for now, we've lost. Losing a battle has its own lessons.'

'But we can't lose any more.'

'With a bit of care we don't need to.'

'Care!'

Tembot yawned loudly. 'Defeat gives you shock, like an automobile accident. Another thing that rag of yours never prints.' He paused. 'You know what happened to our great Generalissimo when the Fritzes came barging in last year? How could you? He went crazy. Vinegar on the brain.'

'That's a lie!'

'Why d'you think nobody heard from Old Joe the first couple of months, eh? He was lucky Beria never locked him up.'

'How do you know?'

Tembot laughed uproariously. 'You forget I was Chief of police in these parts. Chief of *secret* police. But that's not the point. The point is, in the end, Josef Vissarionovich learned the lesson. He learned you can lose battles and still win wars.'

'That's the first time I've ever heard you say we'll win.'

'The thin air. Softens the brain.'

A swish of sleety wind rushed by outside, brushing the patched-up huts and curling away up the rock face behind. Darkness enclosed them like ice-cold armour.

'But why?' Boris burst out again. 'I mean, cutting their supply lines, sabotage, ambushes, why can't we –?'

'We've just fought a hard defensive battle, Boris,' Tembot said gently. He was happy to repeat the lesson. There wasn't much else to do. 'Now we're busy surviving. There'll be enough time for rolling bits of dynamite in coal dust and sticking them in Fritzy train tenders. We'll bury them under avalanches and toss Molotov cocktails in the backs of trucks and dig holes in the snow so their patrols don't see us till too late and put sugar in their gasoline tanks. But to do all that you don't just need the dynamite – and the sugar. You need men. Men and women with their strength intact and all their toes and fingers. Or most of 'em,' he added, thinking of Killa whose hand had been mutilated by a German anti-personnel mine. 'You'll be seeing action soon enough.'

'You know, Tembot Batazarovich,' said Boris eagerly, 'the whole world, the whole future of the world, it depends on us here, if we win or not.'

To Boris's evident surprise Tembot didn't mock him. Instead he said soberly, 'You are damn right, my lad. You are damn right.'

There was a pause. Then Boris spoke again. 'They'll really come this high, you reckon?'

'They've been higher. But not where I've been waiting for 'em.' Tembot chuckled. The idea amused him, foreigners coming to fight him up in his very own mountains. But right now, the last crust of bread eaten, he pulled the folds of his felt cloak round his large frame, tugged at his fur earflaps, tilted himself for comfort and dropped off to sleep.

*

Boris lay awake, fretting. He was hungry again, hungry as a bear in spring, but there would be nothing to eat till morning.

At midnight, the wind's wild keening finally stupefying him into sleep, he dreamed of a school classroom. The teacher, good Party man, was saying how he should grow up to be like Josef Vissarionovich. The children were all clapping. Boris didn't know if he was meant to say something, give a speech, or if he should just sit there displaying comradely modesty. What had he done that was so praiseworthy? Why was he chosen? Should he speak or shouldn't he? Suddenly this dilemma assumed frightening proportions. Everybody was watching him to see what he would do. His blood froze with fear. He felt an overwhelming impotence. It was cold. They were looking at him now with cold expressions on their faces. The face in the Great Leader's portrait behind the teacher's desk began to leer – or was he angry, shouting something, a death sentence . . . ?

'Wake up and shut up. Else dream of your Nadia.'

Tembot was shaking him by the shoulder. Boris saw the old man's lips moving but heard him indistinctly. . . . Just the name 'Nadia' was clear. He struggled toward consciousness. But the effort started to warm his blood, inducing a new sleepiness.

Boris lapsed into dreams again. Nadia was trapped somewhere. He had told her he would rescue her. But he couldn't remember where she was. Or who or what was threatening her life. He asked people, but they laughed at him. An old woman slapped his face. Her fingers came away drenched in his blood. He was weak from lack of blood, but he didn't mind dying. He deserved to die. He had failed her, he said he would rescue her but he couldn't find where she was . . . Soon his sleep grew deeper. His dreams became insipid, shapeless. For another hour he slept peacefully.

When Boris woke again Tembot was no longer in the hut. Boris poked his head through the canvas flap strung across the entrance, where part of the wall had fallen down. His bladder urged him to go out and get it emptied. But the early-morning wind, though calmer than overnight, carried another message. He could see a number of men moving around. One was stripped to the waist – a middle-aged Russian, not a Caucasian – doing exercises, touching his toes and stretching and swinging his shoulders from side to side. It was a challenge Boris couldn't resist. He crawled out, ignoring the snow that fell off the canvas and down the back of his neck, and jogged toward the open-air latrine in a circle of wind-bent birches. At least the cold cuts the stink, he thought, fumbling through layers of rough material and taking his penis carefully in his hand so that only the very tip was exposed. Others squatted nearby. Boris was grateful for the constipation which had solved that problem for the last three days.

Back inside the hut, Tembot and two men Boris didn't know were conferring. One of the two had walked overnight to bring a report of a German advance upward of Kashka Tau. The village of Kashka Tau – 'Bald Hill' in the Mountain Turk language of the Balkars – was half-way between Nalchik and the Ice Wall.

'In what strength?' Tembot asked, his expression neutral.

The man shrugged. He fingered the sharp-bladed *kindjal* at his waist. His body was totally wrapped in furs. 'Women saw 'em.'

Outside a dog snarled. It thrust its thin yellowish snout through the entrance to the hut, then, as quickly, snapped it out of view.

'Bastards. Fucking bastard Fritzes,' the second man whispered, nodding his head, communicating with a memory. 'I hope they keep coming. Just let 'em keep coming. It'll be fried Fritz I'll be eating every day.' He spat voluminously. Not for the first time Boris sensed that blood-curdling hatred of the Germans which churned in the hearts of so many Russians and Caucasians.

He felt it himself – whenever he imagined what they might have done to Nadia.

A louder snarling outside interrupted his thoughts. Four or five dogs this time were snapping and yelping. Men began to shout. Tembot ducked outside, Boris right behind him. A string of mules was being led up into the village, the front two carrying on their backs metal boxes with chimneys on each side. Men cheered. The camp kitchens had arrived! Three more mules carried boxes of ammunition and a supply of that commodity Tembot prized above all the others, the 'winter grease' which kept the guns from jamming even in the most extreme cold. Tembot saw this grease as the key to the winter's fighting, giving him twice the efficiency of the Germans – equalizing in effect the two sides' firepower.

The last two of the seven mules carried the pieces of a 45-mm anti-tank gun.

'The devil!' Tembot exclaimed. 'Is this your doing, Boris?'

Boris was tempted to take the credit, but didn't dare in case the person really responsible had arrived with the gun. He shook his head, but compensated with a knowing smile.

It was as well he hadn't told a lie. At that moment a figure enveloped in a greasy quilted jacket ran up – Marko, the seventeen-year-old Chechen whom Boris had last seen asleep in a cave beside the Baksan.

Marko shouted: 'A big one, huh? *I* got it. You want to know where? Of course you want to know!' He looked all around, enticing his audience closer. Tembot put his hands on his hips and chuckled. 'I'll tell you,' Marko continued, satisfied. 'From the Fritzes!' Again he swivelled his head from left to right. 'I tell you, I got the gun from the Fritzes.' Marko stopped to spit. 'Idiots left it last night with just two of 'em guarding it.'

'Where?' Tembot boomed.

Marko turned to face the old man. 'Half an hour's march this side of Kashka Tau.'

'Ha! *This* side. So you saw 'em? Come on in here.'

Tembot took Marko by the arm and hustled him into the largest of the huts. At that very moment Boris felt his bowels loosen. He cursed and ran – the pressure was suddenly grotesquely urgent – toward the copse of stubby birches. As he fled, crouching from the pain, the thought worked its way upward from his bowels to his brain: The Germans are coming – they'll be here, right here, in less time than it takes me to shit.

*

Lower down the valley trail that led up to the Bezengi glacier and the massive Ice Wall behind it, Colonel Brandt stood, round-shouldered, beside his tent, unsure about advancing higher.

He had stayed precisely twelve hours inside Nalchik before being ordered into the mountains. Twelve frustrating hours of intensive military activity and planning. He had even argued, against his professional judgement, the futility of pushing the enemy back up higher, of attempting to chase them over the top of the 800-mile crest. He had been overruled, and now he was doing just that, searching for partisans in the mountains with a team selected from the three Battalions of the 21st Regiment, with no choice but to keep moving, keep climbing – when his mind, every moment, was pulled the other way, back to Nalchik, back to her.

A dark young Lieutenant approached at a brisk walk. Lieutenant Dibelius couldn't fail to notice the redness about his superior officer's eyes, a rare lack of early-morning freshness. He saluted neatly and reported the loss of an anti-tank gun captured during the night.

'Why wasn't I informed at once?' Brandt said angrily, standing stiffly in front of his tent.

'It was only discovered a few minutes ago, Herr Oberst. Two guards had their throats cut.'

'Which two?'

The Lieutenant told him. 'They waited for the relief and hit them together so the alarm wouldn't be raised too soon.'

'Any chance of getting after them?'

'No, Herr Oberst. They took the gun on mules.'

Brandt cursed under his breath. That was what happened when his mind wasn't on the job. He felt as if he himself had killed the two men.

The Lieutenant coughed to attract the Colonel's attention. 'One of the NSU caterpillar motorcycles won't start. Carburettor trouble.'

'We need a new part?'

'Sergeant Baumann says he can fix it.'

'Then carry on. The order remains. We move at 09.00 hours.'

*

In the oak and beech forest outside Kashka Tau, the fading leaves oozed moisture like sodden wool hung out to dry.

Higher up, among the slick-barked birches, the air was crisper and colder.

Tembot Kochan paced round the ruined village, stopping to observe the valley, the forests, the crags and hollows, then striding to another position.

The defence of the high mountains depended on observation of the enemy's movements. Heavy guns were too cumbersome to move around with speed – a single rifle with plenty of ammunition was more valuable than a whole battery of 99-pounders. Even laying mines was a waste of time, because the snow covered them and the ice shifted their position. The key was good reconnaissance, sharp eyes, quick, clear signals and the instinct that senses where a trap has been laid.

At midday the German advance was spotted by a partisan scout on a trail parallel to the Cherek River. He flagged the news to a colleague higher up the valley, who got through at once to Tembot Kochan on the field telephone.

But the excitement at this news turned by early afternoon into frustration. The Germans never emerged higher up the trail.

Tembot sent out three more patrols. Impatiently he waited for reports, but none came in.

He knew that, if the Fritzes managed to keep out of sight to a point as high as the staging hut at Mishirgi Kosh, at the foot of the Bezengi glacier, they then could penetrate the parallel Mishirgi glacier and climb the ridge separating the two glaciers . . .

Then they would occupy the key position, the dominating peak with 360-degree visibility. It would be a bold move on their part. But a sound one.

If Tembot was right, it involved a complete change of plan for the partisans. The German manoeuvre could be countered. The ridge at this point reached 12,000 feet, at the very end of the great horseshoe-shaped Ice Wall. The west face was steeper but no harder than the east face of the ridge which the Germans would have to take.

On the other hand . . . if the German move were a feint? Again, it all depended on observation. His men *couldn't* have lost them between Kashka Tau and the partisans' camp. Yet they had. He had to decide – now.

Yes. Yes. He would take his men to the very top.

But Boris would have to stay to co-ordinate the main force – just in case the German disappearance was a trick. The partisans' rear had to be protected.

In ten minutes, thirty selected men prepared to move off. This was the test, the first battle in the high mountains. It had to be won. The Fritzes *had* to learn that they couldn't break through.

*

On the far side of the ridge between the Bezengi and Mishirgi glaciers, Colonel Brandt was leading an advance column of seventy-five men.

While the main body spread out lower down, sealing off the trails that connected mountain and foothills between the several tributaries of the Cherek, he led a group of his most experienced climbers, including Sergeant Baumann, an Alpine guide before the war. The maps he had were excellent. He was able to follow the very trails pioneered by German and Austrian expeditions in the thirties.

They kept on the Mishirgi glacier for less than a mile, picking their way over chunks of ice as tall as three-storey buildings and round crevasses deep as canyons. Then they made a ninety-degree turn to the right and, with the aid of ropes and crampons and ice-axes, began the task of scaling the cliffs. To their left was the 15,000-foot peak of Dykh Tau; behind them Koshtan Tau. But those great peaks, the goals of peacetime mountaineers, were neither practical nor tactically important.

Brandt's decision personally to lead the high assault party was a deliberate, almost bloody-minded decision. It was a curse of professional life: as soon as you became expert, you were promoted to a rank that prevented you from using your skills. You became an instructor, an administrator, a bureaucrat. Now, the higher he climbed, the freer he felt. His listlessness dropped away. Even the siren song in his ears grew fainter.

Brandt dug his ice-axe through a thin layer of half-melted ice and guided his feet confidently, almost ecstatically, round a huge, sparkling overhang.

When darkness fell, both the German mountain troops and the partisans were short of their common goal – the single 'pass' on top of the ridge. Little more than a V-shaped scar, this irregular depression was the key to a long jagged spine, the one position on the Ice Wall dominating the glaciers below.

The partisans' advantage was: they knew the terrain. For Brandt and his men, despite the theoretical knowledge gleaned from maps, each step was a step into the unknown.

Both teams climbed for about four hours after darkness. Both then bivouacked. The Germans found a protected gully. The partisans, on the sheerer side, located a ledge just ten foot deep, virtually a cave. They stamped the loose snow to make themselves a secure platform, then dug shallow-snow-boats and fitted their bodies in. The only noises were the distant howl of wolves, the tinkling of small rocks bouncing down the cliff faces and the hissing of wind-blown snow.

*

At nine-thirty on the morning of November 4, Tembot Kochan advanced to lift his head over the ridge, lay for a moment on the soft snow. Ahead, in a huge 180-degree panorama, tilting in a series of plunging gradients from the eternal snows of Dykh Tau and Koshtan Tau to his right as far as the forested foothills below the Mishirgi glacier on his left, way over to Kazbek, glittered a cloud-free mountainscape.

Marko flung himself down by Tembot's side.

'If I'm right,' whispered Tembot, 'the old crocks and the kids won the race.'

Slowly and thoroughly they surveyed the terrain below them through their field glasses. There was no human movement; only swirls of dancing snow as the wind blew the light powder from crest to crest.

There was, however, a large area hidden behind a shoulder of rock at a 45-degree angle to their left.

'If they're up here at all, they have to be on the ice slope behind that shoulder,' Tembot went on softly, fearful of his voice being picked up by the wind and hurled through the cold thin air as far as the enemy. 'Marko, take five men and get behind that rock up there that looks like a cudweed flower. You should be able to see 'em from that position . . . *if* by any remote chance they're up there. Keep in sight of me and raise your rifle if you spot 'em.' He waved up the other two section leaders. 'Osman, Killa, fan out right behind those small rocks and keep me covered.'

Quickly the partisans moved to their positions.

At first Marko made no sign. Tembot saw him train his binoculars on the lower slopes. Marko's sweep became wider. He was looking up to his left, he appeared to be concentrating on something. Up *there?* Tembot's heart skipped a beat. Suddenly Marko began signalling. Urgently. His

Moisin rifle shot up in the air, down again, up again. And with his free hand he pointed – upward.

'Higher?'

Tembot's eyes followed the line of the crest. Could it be possible? If so, the Germans had really stolen a march on him. By taking an almost impossible route, they would have gained the height advantage. *Almost* impossible. That was the point. Only the literally impossible was out of their power – and even then? Tembot swore. Keeping out of sight below the snow ridge, he ploughed through the soft white powder to where Marko had positioned himself.

Yes, there was movement up and to the left – Tembot could see it through his field glasses. A rope of three men – three at least – tackling an overhang. How many more had reached the top? Or were these the advance guard? If so, there was still a chance. The route up the north-west face of the ridge, the partisans' side, was fast and straightforward, protected from German observation. But he would have to move now, and in strength. He stood up and curved his arm in a great sweep that left his finger pointing in the direction they'd have to go.

Tembot set off up the ridge as nearly at a run as the altitude and powdery snow and his sixty-three-year-old heart permitted.

The sound of the men's breath as they pushed and heaved themselves higher grew harsher and quicker. Gusts of steam poured from their lips. Their stomachs tightened with nausea. Lungs prickled with pain. Brains began to sing tuneless, wordless songs. Their rifles and submachine guns now began to chafe.

After forty minutes Tembot reckoned they must be almost level with the men he had glimpsed through the binoculars. There was a big rounded rock up here, a kind of dome. If the Germans had stayed over on the eastern slope, all would be well. If they had climbed to the very top, then within minutes, maybe seconds, they would spot the partisans.

'Marko,' Tembot whispered, his breath coming in gasps. 'Take ten men. Go down to that gully there. Keep out of sight. If you hear shots, move quick. We've got to . . . we've *got* to keep 'em off the dome.'

He himself chose three – Osman, in his fifties, an underworld informer in Tembot's days as NKVD chief; Hadju, a squat, barrel-chested man of the mountains, nearing sixty; and Shaliman, a tough sixteen-year-old Balkar, famous as the youngest-ever goalkeeper of the Nalchik football team.

Between the ridge and the top of the dome there was no cover. The muddy browns and grays of the partisans' quilted jackets and long flowing coats stood out against the pure white snow. Tembot knew it. 'Let's go,' he snapped.

*

The four partisans were spotted by a single German Private, when they were a hundred yards from the round top of the dome. He flung himself to the ground, yelled for support. Heart pounding, he watched the partisans approach, their legs sinking into the soft snow up to their knees. Then came a hard patch where the wind had exposed sheets of smooth rock. They seemed to gallop forward. Only yards later a snowdrift slowed them down again like sheep rushing into a dip.

But on the dome the Private was alone. His two companions had gone back two hundred yards to belay, to secure the ropes for the final ascent of the men following. Hearing the yell, one of them set off back immediately toward the agitated figure on top of the dome. The senior NCO, Sergeant Baumann, continued to pull at a knot, fumbling and cursing in the cold, finishing the essential job he had begun. With the rope at last secured round a mushroom-shaped boulder, he too began to run up to the dome.

The Private lay with his heartbeats going like a drum crescendo, his gun aiming first at one then at another of the four men advancing up toward him from the eastern side. He waited – to be sure. Soon, he knew, he must force them to crawl. Even if he didn't hit one, they must be slowed down. Sweat dripped into his eyes, and he shook his head like a dog bounding out of a river. Then suddenly he could see only three. He aimed at the one in the centre, pulled the trigger. The submachine gun roared fire in his ear. The figure fell. He switched aim to the right. The other two had dropped to the snow. But he could see them, brown against the white, like crouching bears. Easy. He aimed again, pulled the trigger. Silence. He swore, shook the gun, stared at it, then thought to check it carefully. Nothing seemed wrong. There they were, crawling closer. He aimed quickly, fired. Silence. He looked around. Help was still a hundred yards away. The soldier seemed to be climbing with lead in his boots. Sergeant Baumann was nowhere. The Private yelled again for them to hurry.

*

Fifty yards from the top, Hadju lay dead. Osman and Shaliman, flanking him, wasted no time mourning. The yells from the German sounded to them like shrieks of fear, giving them heart. Like lizards they slightered up the slope. To them it seemed they were making faster progress than on their feet. It was an illusion. They were waiting, waiting for the next burst of fire, and their minds were operating on two time scales.

Tembot was twenty-five yards to their right, where the contour of the slope made it more difficult to be spotted. The dome here was more convex, like a beetling brow on an otherwise smoothly-rounded skull.

The others were dangerously exposed. He could see Osman and Shaliman crawling upward. Tembot decided he could risk a burst of speed with a semi-upright stance. Crablike, he sprinted for the top.

The protection he'd enjoyed from the bulging ice-nose ended twenty yards from the summit. To hell with cover! He straightened up, running, his Shpagin submachine gun at the ready. The German was lying in the snow, pulling at something in the breech of his gun. Suddenly he spotted Tembot. He reached his hand round for the knife at his belt. Tembot shot him in the chest with a single round. Simultaneously the partisan leader shouted at Osman and Shaliman to join him.

Flinging himself in the snow, Tembot peered over the steeper slope on the far side of the dome. A single figure was scrambling up fifty . . . sixty yards below. Tembot took careful aim, fired a rapid burst. The figure slumped to the ground. Snatching his field glasses up to his eyes, Tembot checked for wounds. Yes, the telltale red smear was seeping into the snow. Wasting no more time on the body, he scanned the entire slope. There had been *three* men on that rope.

Suddenly a burst of fire broke out on his left. Then more firing, rifles and submachine guns. Marko's men had encountered another German unit.

Osman and Shaliman arrived together.

'There's at least one more of 'em,' Tembot hissed. 'Osman, go round the left. Shaliman the right. Watch out, Osman, for anyone coming at you from up Marko's direction.' Then he added as an afterthought, 'Any chance for Hadju?'

'None,' Osman said flatly. 'Through the head.'

'Get going.'

Tembot slithered his great bulk forward, down the steep incline. He had to stop himself tumbling down and yet be ready to fire at any moment. This third Fritz knew the art of taking cover.

In fact Sergeant Baumann had hidden on a ledge nearer than Tembot imagined.

The partisan leader, suddenly, slid right on top of him.

The German swivelled, tried to get his machine pistol into a firing position, couldn't. The two men collided, rolled off the ledge and like a couple of enormous circus clowns went on rolling over and over, plunging down the slope.

It was the mushroom-shaped rock which the belaying rope was fixed to that saved them both from hurtling over the sheer drop down onto the glacier. The shock, however, drove the wind out of both bodies. It was several seconds before either began fumbling for their weapons. They were three yards apart.

Sergeant Baumann had lost his machine pistol in the fall, but still had a Luger semi-automatic beneath his mountain parka. Tembot had only his hunting knife.

Their weapons were never tested. Instead, Tembot suddenly saw the big German gape and clutch his stomach. Squatting... he began to topple. Another volley struck him and the Sergeant's body pirouetted like a top. It skidded, spinning, away from the rock, hit a patch of ice and in a sudden spurt flipped over into the void.

Tembot lay back for a moment, gasping on the snow. Only for a moment. Then he pulled himself to his feet and began brushing the clots of snow off his rough clothing. As he did so he felt suddenly the huge weight that his body was carrying. His legs buckled, and he was forced to sit down again, just as Shaliman came bounding down and dropped on his haunches at Tembot's side. The boy was smiling.

'You dropped this, Comrade.' He held out Tembot's gun. The curved magazine and the barrel of the Shpagin were clogged with snow.

Tembot smiled but said nothing. He had to let his heart settle. For the time being he needed all his concentration to control its wild beat and to catch his breath. His lungs were keeping up a clashing accompaniment to his heart, like cymbals and bass drum in a Turkish band.

A minute later, the tempo slowed, and he was able to move. He patted young Shaliman gratefully on the shoulder, then slung his submachine gun over his back and started up the slope again, where Osman was waiting for them.

Intermittent firing still came from further up the crest, and it was toward these sounds the three men trudged. After the sheer hard slog of getting back over the ridge, the going became easier.

'So far we've kept above 'em,' Tembot said, speaking slowly in between breaths. Everything seemed to him to be moving at half pace, after the violent action on the dome. 'Above Marko there's only one more peak. I'll take ten men with me.' Tembot pointed toward a cleft between two sharp rocks. 'Bastards. They came straight up!'

*

Colonel Brandt made a fine calculation. The main body of his men had not yet scaled the sheer cliff which led up to the crest. Twenty were engaged, a quarter of a mile to his left, in a sniping battle with a smaller but effective body of partisans. The question was: how many partisans – or Red Army soldiers – were up this high?

They had matched him trick for trick. Now the decision was whether to disengage, or try to eliminate the enemy. The only hope of beating them lay in circling the peak at the northernmost end of the Ice Wall and attacking them from their rear. It would be a gamble. But no mountaineer worth the name gave up just before the final peak. Brandt consulted his Lufft altimeter. The reading was just above the 3400-metre mark, by no means the maximum height at which his soldiers were trained to operate.

Fifty minutes later, at a quarter past one, Brandt himself, plus a party of five, were within sight of that final peak.

At 13.22 hours they hauled themselves to the end of the last rock-strewn shoulder. Brandt, in the lead, strode over the top.

Suddenly he confronted a bear-like man in a dirty quilted jacket. Their eyes met.

For an age, in fact no more than a second, they stared at each other. Brandt, fascinated by the sight of his rival, felt hypnotized by admiration that the other had seen so precisely the advantage of being just there, just then. Had he been alone with this man, he would have advanced, shaken him by the hand, sealing the bond of sympathy he knew must exist between rival climbers arriving simultaneously on the unconquered summit.

Then their trance snapped.

Both men leaped for cover. Their shouted orders combined in a bellow that echoed round the boulders and crevices on the narrow shoulder.

It was only then that Brandt really understood what had happened. Unlike the partisan, he had been holding his gun – at the ready. His machine pistol had been pointed straight at the man's chest. All he'd had to do was pull the trigger. Instead, he had locked his gaze onto the massive, fur-clad figure with the face smothered in the human fur of a gray mustache and the eyes peering from a weatherbeaten skin, and – just as he had fixed the image of Nadia – imprinted this man's image on his brain. A second permanent record. The recognition that instinctively he had spared the partisan's life was as instantaneous as the mental snapshot he had taken of him.

But now he had to get away – get his men away.

Using a group of three to cover, the other trio – which included himself – pulled back to a new defensive position. The two groups then leapfrogged each other till they had rejoined the main body. Finally, employing the same technique to counter the fire from a lower detachment of partisans, the men of the 21st Regiment abseiled hand over hand down to the glacier below.

Brandt was content. Content to leave the Ice Wall to the people of the Caucasus.

ELEVEN

On November 5, in the early afternoon, Brandt's jeep slithered to a halt in front of his billet in Nalchik. He got out, stretched and looked wistfully at the drab city huddled in the mist.

'Herr Oberst? Ah, Herr Oberst!'

Hans Guggenbühl came to attention sloppily. He had not expected his master back so soon from the mountains. He walked gingerly down the slippery steps of the verandah.

'Welcome back, Herr Oberst.'

The fat Austrian pulled the Colonel's kitbag off the back seat of the jeep and stumbled back up the steps.

Brandt gave instructions to his driver, dismissed him, then stood for a moment alone outside the squat, blue-washed house. He had returned to this deserted house, abandoned by the widow of a Red Army officer, almost as if to home, though he'd scarcely had time to approve it in principle before the expedition to the mountains.

Inside, a door slammed. Brandt turned once more and looked down the alley that connected his billet with the town.

He sighed, and went inside.

For all Hans's faults, he had excelled himself finding this particular house – clean, spacious, furnished in a comfortable old-fashioned style, more Great Russian than Caucasian. The two windows in the principal room were curtained in maroon damask, a flaky icon was propped on a stand in one corner, and a pale birchwood screen, in the opposite corner, hid the tattered red plush of an ottoman. In the centre of the room a faded-pink shawl fringed with heavy gold thread hung heavily over a big round table. The walls were almost invisible behind banks of ornately framed pictures of lush Crimean and Caucasian landscapes, cyclamens and lilies, swans, autumn leaves, toga'd figures in classi ruins – and one immense canvas, signed 'N. Sverchkov', o troika in a snowstorm; the driver, toppled off the sled, w; being dragged through the snow clutching the reins of ; terrified trio of Siberian horses. As for sleeping arrangements, Brandt preferred stretching out his sleeping bag on a motheaten bearskin to testing the strength of the ottoman's bandy legs.

Through the window was a magnificent view, framed in the curtains' maroon damask, of the foaming Nalchik River and the line of poplars along its south bank, out to the Urvan Forest of gaunt oaks beyond, then, to the right, the higher and higher folds of the foothills rising to the superb backdrop of the white Caucasian crest. In the other direction, only half a mile away, was the railway station. The bus station, which his regiment had converted into their barracks, was also close by. Looking south, he had a direct communication with the mountains. Turn around, and he was in instant touch with his men.

The billet, however, was also close to the old NKVD building now occupied by the Gestapo. It was here he had to go first of all. Everywhere Brandt had the same sense of being tracked remorselessly by Major Fritz Stegl.

His right ankle hurt. He had twisted it in the mountains, but only now, faced with a virtual summons to present himself at Gestapo headquarters at 16.00 hours, did it begin to throb painfully.

Hans made amends by cooking a copious late lunch of eggs, goat's cheese, semolina and ersatz coffee. As a result, Brandt's anger was under control when he presented himself to Stegl at precisely four o'clock.

He waited ten minutes before Major Stegl received him.

'Heil Hitler! Sit down, Herr Oberst.'

'You wanted to see me about this man Bekirbi? That was the message.'

'A successful expedition, Herr Oberst?'

'Very,' Brandt replied firmly, smiling inwardly at the thought of how shocked Stegl would be to learn that Brandt's measure of success was the continuing existence of the magnificent partisan confronted on Mishirgi peak. His first act of homage to Nadia.

'How is your ankle, Herr Oberst?'

Brandt frowned, taken aback that Stegl even knew about it. 'Better. It was only twisted.' He sat on the chair next to Stegl's desk.

'Ah! But it might have been much worse, mightn't it? It would have been a pity for such a distinguished Colonel to be injured while clambering about in the mountains, would it not? It is so easy to die there.'

'All too easy, Herr Sturmbannführer. Perhaps you will come to the point. I have a great deal to do.'

Stegl began shuffling some papers abstractedly. Brandt lost patience – though he had made every effort not to. 'Look, this Bekirbi's your man, your opposite number. I've no time to waste with him myself. So what is the problem?'

Stegl didn't react to Brandt's implicit identification of the Gestapo with the NKVD. 'Problem, Herr Oberst? No, no. But I am sure you understand no security matter is entirely simple. There are a great number of men and women in this town who have suddenly become converts to the New Order, as you must know. A handful will be infiltrators. It is my job to ascertain which is the true article, which the false.'

'I can tell you nothing about this one.'

'He came to you alone, did he not?'

'Yes.'

'What were his precise words when he approached you, Herr Oberst?'

Brandt remembered the linguistic error the man had made, decided it would be wasted on Stegl. He merely said, 'He was hardly coherent. Lieutenant Dibelius took charge of the matter. My first duty was to capture the city with the minimum loss of life, not to debate in the middle of the street with a Russian traitor.'

'Traitor?' Stegl shot an icy look at the Colonel.

'Potential collaborator, if you prefer, Herr Sturmbannführer,' Brandt amended. 'If that answers your question, I must –'

'A moment more, Herr Oberst. In your venture into the

mountains, you had with you a number of trusted local guides – *Vertrauensleute?*'

'VT's? Of course. Though none in good enough shape to scale the cliffs. They were useful when we had to avoid detection in the earlier stages of the operation along the Cherek River.'

'How did you recruit these men? Who were they?'

Brandt felt a surge of anger. 'My tactical decisions are my own, Herr Sturmbannführer. Besides, I have no personal knowledge of the men involved. I have competent junior officers responsible for these decisions. I would be grateful if they are left to operate exactly as they see fit in this matter. The 7th Mountain Division cannot be accountable to the Gestapo for every tactical initiative simply because it might involve the use of local sources of information.'

Stegl left a moment's silence when Brandt had finished, then said, 'Thank you, Herr Oberst. Most helpful.' He stared at Brandt. 'Perhaps I could return the compliment – be helpful to you.'

Brandt said nothing.

Stegl went on, 'The town records. You were interested in something? Something I could help you find perhaps?'

Brandt's heart missed a beat. 'Nothing which could concern you, Herr Sturmbannführer.'

'Everything concerns me, Herr Oberst. You knew someone already, here in Nalchik?'

Commissar Stegl. The label was ominously apt.

Brandt said coldly, 'You fight your war, Herr Sturmbannführer. Leave me to fight mine.'

*

At half past four, Brandt walked angrily out onto the windswept street. He limped slightly. His ankle was playing up – but his head was clear. In the slowly fading light, shapeless lumps of dark cloud were scudding high overhead. The wind brought with it fragments of hard sound, sometimes like distant thunder, sometimes more like the cracking of cosmic whips. The German armoured thrust was advancing. But painfully. Every heap of Russian stones became a defensive blockhaus.

He stopped abruptly in the street and folded his arms.

Somewhere she was here, near where he stood, almost within touching distance. To hell with Stegl. At last he had some *time*. Before the expedition to the mountains, Nalchik had been just a momentary staging post. Now he could use every possible means at his disposal to find her.

He thought, I won't move until I decide what to do first. Looking all around, he could see few people out on the streets, just desolate little queues at shops or street-corner stalls where there was rumoured to be food, old women standing in line, wrapped from head to toe in shawls and formless garments stitched together from every kind of material. Was Nadia among them? Or was she over there, on the corner of Tolstoy Street, where a detachment from a German anti-terrorist *Einsatzgruppe* was marshalling unwary citizens to form lines and cheer as a column of tanks and Panzer Grenadiers headed up toward the railway station and then presumably, to the front?

No, no, of course not. It was no good standing in the street shivering, expecting to see her among the hundred thousand people who lived in, or occupied, the city. Yet if she did appear, he knew he would notice her, even if she were shrouded in a bundle of rags like the old women. She would walk purposefully, stand straight. Her city might be defeated, but she would be –

An old couple caught his eye, supporting each other as they picked a slow course along the sidewalk. They looked so German. As they came closer, he heard them in fact whispering German to each other, with some kind of antique rural accent. He remembered there had indeed been a German colony in Nalchik before the Revolution, Alexandersdorf out in the north-west part of town. For a moment he entertained the idea that Nadia herself might be partly German. He would approach the couple, question them.

But the plan was absurd. Not just because it would be such a remote coincidence, should they know her. Not just because it would terrify the old couple – what must they be enduring already, branded with the invader's tongue? But because he didn't *want* Nadia to have German blood in her veins. He didn't want her to be one of the passive Gretchens he had never been satisfied with. He wanted her to belong to the race of partisans he'd confronted up there on the high peaks. She was his Caucasian goddess. There should be in her no taint of – Stegl.

How ironic to be rooted to the spot, unable to make a decision, when he was here as the conqueror with all the resources and power of a senior officer in the occupying army. Yet it was precisely this role, this uniform of his, that prevented him from making the enquiries that would lead him to her.

It was galling to realize he had no-one, no-one at all, German or Russian or Caucasian, in whom he could confide, whom he could trust.

That was the penalty of a lifetime of loneliness; the penalty of being a German, trained to stoicism. It was the penalty, too, of falling in love with the enemy.

A blast of wind made him shudder. He walked on.

*

Colonel Brandt was struggling with the lock of a trunk that Hans had found in the attic of his new billet when the telephone rang. Von Kreuss was on the line, anxious to discuss the possibility of setting up a cordon sanitaire in the foothills at the 3000-foot mark. Brandt replied listlessly.

'Town living,' von Kreuss barked. 'Bad for you. Evidently. Have to get you out into the mountains again. That's what you like.'

Brandt thought, No, I must stay here. I must find Nadia again. I must have time. She is here, close to me, so close I'm afraid sometimes I shall go mad, go out into the streets and shout her name, turn my three battalions into one huge search party.

'Sleep on it, Colonel. Sleep on it. Then come and discuss with me how we're going to set about it. 07.00 hours. Early start. Lot to be done.'

'Good night, Herr General.'

Brandt gave up trying to open the trunk and lay down, still

in his uniform. No point in undressing. No energy. No time. His ankle hurt again.

He went to sleep forcing himself to consider the details of his troop dispositions in the foothills beyond his window. But the dreams he remembered on waking were about Nadia. At three in the morning, something occurred that he'd almost forgotten could happen to him – a wet dream. Nadia, naked, was pressing herself against him, moving her hips, inciting him. He was dressed in his uniform, in his dream as well as in reality, seized by frustration that he couldn't free himself to penetrate her. Even so, waking, he tried to hold on to the dream, moving his body gently as he lay on his stomach. But the image disappeared, and he felt as he had as an embarrassed schoolboy. Yet he also welcomed the dream, frankly but at the same time guiltily revelling in the pleasure. It took him half an hour to drop back off to sleep.

*

By dawn that same morning, the wind had increased to a gale, cutting through the wide streets of Nalchik like a scythe through hay. Nadia struggled along, observing nervously all around her, but at the same time deep in thought.

In the first few frantic days of occupation, nothing had gone right for the Group, nothing except that very first strike, the killing of Hassan Pachev.

It turned out that there were no jobs for the Group members as clerks or cleaning women. The Fritzes made that tactic impossible by using imported émigrés or local sympathizers. When the Group discussed the practicality of whoring, laughing coarsely at the idea of Nina Petrovna tarted up to raise a German prick, they decided in the end it was too risky. Not just when soliciting; there was always a strong chance of getting paid with a bullet or a knife if a 'client' suspected it was information his pick-up wanted, not cash or silk stockings or scent.

'Anyway, Nadia's the only one of us with the looks,' Nina Petrovna said bluntly. 'And the dumbest Fritz would see she hated him.'

Yet Nadia had had a target in mind – ever since Auntie had first mentioned the idea at the railway station. Could she serve the cause – *and* see . . . him?

But she hadn't dared suggest it, after the occupation any more than before, either to Nina Petrovna or to any of the others.

She hadn't spoken, though at times her heartbeats bored into her ribcage like blows from a sledgehammer, and the blood filled her cheeks so close to bursting she felt scared to touch herself in case she scratched the surface of her skin with her nail and the blood spurted through.

She wished more and more there was something active to do. Something pure and positive to concentrate on. Soon – Nina Petrovna was always promising action soon.

Meanwhile, today, she was on her way to see her mother and her darling, her Dasha, for the first time since going underground. Nina Petrovna hadn't given her approval at first. But Nadia insisted, fiercely. She *had* to do it. Seeing Darya became a compulsion. The future belonged to the child, a bright future – *if* the war was won. That was why Nadia had to fight. Why she also needed to *see* that Dasha was alive, to touch her, to fan into flames her own clear, clean motive for risking her own life in the active resistance.

Because, in the matter of Porandt, Nadia knew her motives were confused and humiliatingly weak.

She ducked her head into the gale, and in another two minutes she reached the rendezvous point.

There!

Was that Dasha there? In front? Nariana should be holding her hand. No, it was another child, much bigger, ten or eleven at least. Perhaps in the gray dawn light the girl appeared smaller, from a distance. Or perhaps, Nadia felt, she was losing the instinctive faculty of recognition. Already that telepathic sense of remote control, the magnetic mother-child attraction, was beginning to weaken.

But there she was!

Yes, really. Nadia flushed. Her heart began to pound, more violently even than after making love.

Darya broke free of her grandmother's hand and threw herself silently into her mother's embrace – silently, because she'd been told, over and over, not to make a noise, not to shout with joy.

They met and whispered and hugged in the big recessed doorway where, before the Germans came, trucks with offal and tough scraps of meat scraped off carcasses backed in to unload at a line of bays, at the side of the meat cannery.

Now the factory was silent. There was no more meat.

All too soon came the last hugs, tears, nonsense words, and the final kisses.

Then Nadia went quickly, just once again, over the plan for next meeting, in case . . . in case she had to stay underground.

'I mean *underground*, Mother,' she added with a laugh. 'Like a mole.'

Part Three

OATHS AND PROMISES

TWELVE

Tembot Kochan was suspicious of the calm in his sector. The Fritzes had pulled right back. Now – ten days later – none were reported higher than Kashka Tau. That raiding party they had sent to the top of the Ice Wall had disappeared like rooks at the sight of a gun – except the Fritzes made no noise about it. Instead of raucous cawing, an eerie silence. An unnatural peace had settled in. Worse, so had a thaw. The danger of new sorties was growing. In Nalchik, reports said, the snow had already melted.

The partisan leader, like a bull walrus with his long white tusks of hair and his large body wrapped in fur, looked fretfully up at the sky. Patches of pale blue shone obstinately between the irregular white and gray clouds.

All the same, it was far from warm, with the sun going down fast below the pine-spiked horizon. A thin whistle from the radio aerial, strung between two of the tallest trees, added to the chill, seeming to tilt the precarious mid-November balance between autumn and winter in favour of winter again.

Tembot stamped his feet wrapped in thick felt boots, his precious *valenki*, but more from vexation than from cold.

His men were impatient. Offensive operations could only be launched when the Fritzes were held tight in their positions by the fierceness of winter. But the frost had lost its grip. Meanwhile Tembot wasn't about to lose men just so the madcap elements could find a substitute for a café brawl.

Then he heard Killa's voice: 'Hey! Look who's coming. The lad himself. In his tropical plumage.'

From the centre of the clearing, Tembot watched Boris walk out of the forest. Two brand new red and white badges of excellence, visible through the front of his flowing cape, gave point to Killa's image.

Boris came nearer and saluted. A smile spread over his face, and he pointed behind the two partisans. 'Look, Comrades.' High up in the mountains a thin ray of slanting sunlight struck the tip of a distant mile-high cliff of rust-red porphyry. A red star appeared to shine from the summit of the Bezengi Ice Wall. 'A good omen,' Boris went on. 'It means the attack'll be successful.'

'Attack?' Tembot said, shaking his head.

'Sure, sure. It's going to snow tonight,' Boris insisted confidently. 'When it does, we move.'

'Killa, old friend,' said Tembot wearily, 'see that Lieutenant Surkov, our Caucasian oracle, gets something to refresh himself with.'

Tembot ducked inside the small square hut in which he and a dozen others shared their body warmth and their sweat. Boris wrinkled his nose.

As he followed Tembot in, however, the rancid odour of the hut felt comforting, a mark of warmth and shelter and companionship after twenty miles of forest trails. From the top of a pile, he took a small flat loaf wrapped round dried yogurt and sank his teeth into it. Water was simmering in a kettle dumped down on some ashes. Boris took a lump of chocolate from his pocket, pushed it into a mess-tin and poured on some of the water.

High up along the Chegem gorge, a wolf howled. Marko gave a perfect imitation of its heartrending wail.

'Tomorrow,' said Boris loudly. 'Red Army command wants action. And I guess you know,' he added archly, 'what day went by a week ago without the victory to mark it. Well, now we –'

A sarcastic voice – Killa's – came from behind him. 'We're too young to remember the Revolution.'

'Too old to care,' said another.

Tembot said gruffly to Boris. 'Don't forget we're risking our lives too, lad. For the same causes as you. So there was no magic victory on the anniversary of the Revolution. *I* also happen to know that makes you an old man too – a quarter of a century old.'

Boris looked at his feet, ashamed. He gulped his bitter – and cooling – chocolate. 'Tomorrow,' he repeated, but gently, 'we have to move. That's the order HQ instructed me to bring up here.'

'Okay, that's an order,' Tembot said with a sigh. 'Let's have the details.'

Boris described quickly the ammunition dump at Kashka Tau, the partisans' primary target. There was a prisoners' camp in the village too, where partisans were known to be held for use – temporarily – in constructing defences.

At the end, Tembot gave a quick nod. He was very tired. 'Killa, it's time for the Fritz-and-prisoner routine, eh? Listen, Boris, here's a rundown of how we'll do it. But let me tell you this right away. There's no way I go along with this operation against Kashka Tau if the weather's not right. If it's still warm and bright, I'll get a message through on the radio and to hell with interception. I'll call it off. We've got to have snow. A damn great blizzard.'

'It'll snow,' said Boris. 'I told you already. It'll snow.'

And that night it snowed.

*

Through the night and all next day the thick flakes fell. The wind steadily increased, sending swirls of fine crystals into every cranny of the men's furs and greatcoats, building up drifts against the huts and the trunks of the pines and oaks and birches, burying shrubs and the tangled, dying undergrowth. Even Tembot admitted it was turning into the sort of blizzard that would leave the Fritzes huddling beside any warm fire they could build. The temperature at midday plunged to minus fifteen degrees centigrade. In the village of Bagubent, five miles away, the wind ripped the roof off the brand-new Machine Tractor Station. The men slept, knowing that they would be marching all night. Later in the evening, they applied quantities of winter grease to their Moisin rifles and Shpagin submachine guns. At the same time the wind began to fall. But the snowflakes didn't stop. They grew fatter and heavier and began filling the hollows and crevasses created by the turbulence of the storm's first strike. By midnight there was nowhere left where snow didn't reach to a man's knees.

A special unit was assembled and kitted out in the four German uniforms the partisans had captured. These four 'Fritzes' took charge of a ragged brigade of Russian 'prisoners', hiding under their coats 'guerilla pistols', as they called their sawn-off versions of military and hunting rifles.

This was the assault squad Tembot had trained for dangerous missions – missions that involved getting as close as possible to the Germans before discovery. Killa, an experienced fighter, led the squad.

At 01.00 hours the partisans broke camp and began the march down to Kashka Tau.

Boris, elated, was among the first in the long file. This at last was *his* operation. Not like that so-called triumph on the Ice Wall where he had spent a frustrating day at Tembot's base camp ineffectually trying to keep the men from getting drunk.

Visibility was virtually nil. The thick snow would have rendered even daylight useless. Only swift swirls of an intermittent wind in the bare branches of the hardwood trees, and the soft puff of snowlumps landing in the thick drifts below, disturbed the silence. The men, capped and epauletted in white, dug a narrow sinuous trench through the forest. Theirs were the only prints.

After an hour's march, the men felt that pleasant lightheadedness which comes from exertion in an enclosed world without perspective; where the body drops or climbs with no guidance from the eyes; where even the sensation of having a man in front and a man behind dissolves into loneliness.

Much later, at a point in the forest that seemed to Boris no different from any other but which Tembot seemed to know well, the column halted. Guns were unslung and checked.

Tembot chuckled – a huge snowman in a forest clearing.

'Hey – Fritzes!'

His voice rang out but died quickly in the snow-heavy air. A bunch of men indistinguishable from the rest moved forward.

Four partisans beat their coats and in seconds reappeared as a German Captain and three Privates. Another group, ragged, half of them bearded, like wild men beside the shaven, greatcoated Germans, formed up. Subconsciously, they began playing their parts: the 'Germans' made a neat square – the dozen 'prisoners' milled about, shambling and shiftless.

'Boris, you go with 'em. Keep as far back as you can without losing contact. I go ahead with the saboteurs. When the dump goes up, we'll move back to the cowshed we earmarked half a mile from the dump on the edge of the village. If there's a problem at the camp, it's you I'm relying on to get back to me there. Questions?'

There were none.

'Listen to me, all of you. This operation may seem like letting off steam. Let me tell you it's more than that. Much, much more. It's our best chance of fixing the Fritzes for the winter – maybe for good. Right now, this moment, the Soviet forces are launching a whole series of attacks. At Maitamadag, Digora, Alagir. Everywhere between here and Ordzhonikidze. The radio's burning with 'em. But remember this.' The strong, confident tone of an old NKVD agitator came back into Tembot's voice, 'Nalchik's the last big town the bastards took. It's got to be the last they'll ever take – in this war or any other. What we're doing here in Kashka Tau is holding 'em up, driving 'em back to their last big operational centre. If ever the Fritzes feel free to relax here, they'll push on, winter or no winter. To Ordzhonikidze, Tbilisi, Baku, the oil. They'll outflank our defenders of Stalingrad. *This* is where we stop 'em. *Now*'s the time we're going to do it. Beat 'em at Kashka Tau, we'll win the war. And that's what we'll do, Comrades.'

The men gave a ragged cheer.

Only the four 'Germans' remained impassive.

*

The ground sloped down steeply toward Kashka Tau. A goat trail, though icy and strewn with awkward snow and rock falls, made the going fast. Tembot's saboteurs went ahead. Two of the partisans in German uniform, including 'Hauptmann' Killa, led the second group; the other two brought up the rear, with the prisoners in between. Boris, last of all, lagged as far behind as visibility permitted.

At 06.25 the first building came into view, an isolated cowshed where Tembot had arranged to re-group. The spiky tips of a wattle fence surrounding it thrust up through the smooth waves of snow like a breakwater half-immersed in a calm sea. Not dawn, but a preview of it behind a dark gray veil, made the men's hearts beat faster with its promise of action.

Keeping low behind the huge snowdrifts, the partisans advanced. Soon they glimpsed the floodlights and heard the deep low throb of a generator. A minute later they saw the edge of the perimeter fence.

The snow was still falling.

Fritz Captain Killa held up his right hand. The camp detail stopped.

Two men went up to the wire fence and cut a wide hole. No problem here; a token defence, more against wolves and bears than the human enemy.

Killa's unit ducked through, formed up and moved off right.

The last man in Tembot's assault party, loaded with dynamite and fuses and all the apparatus of demolition, disappeared left, outside the wire.

Boris followed the 'Germans' herding their ragged, rounded-up prisoners.

The sheds and the high fence around them became clearer in the yellowish lights. The main watchtower was a rickety wooden structure, built as a silo. The platform was low. By keeping behind the last of the sheds, the partisans were able to avoid observation until they were very close.

Boris stopped again, crouched low by a fence post in a small hollow. He was sweating. His heartbeats were the loudest sound in his ears, drowning out the noise of the generator. Then a cheerful shout from the direction of the dump pierced that flat throbbing. The partisans dropped to the ground. Somewhere a motor roared. Another shout, still cheerful, in German. It was only the Fritzes coming awake. The partisans stood up. The moment had come to bluff it.

Quickly the four 'Germans' led their prisoners out into view, striding along the track around the camp's high fence.

'*Gefangener!*' Killa shouted.

They marched, leading their raggle-taggle prisoners with sawn-off guns hidden in their tatty clothes, up to the watchtower. A guard sleepily approached, slid back a bolt in the wire door, held his hand out for papers.

Then, suddenly chaos.

But not, as Boris anticipated, from Killa and his men, liberating the partisan prisoners. The action came from far over to the right of the camp. Snowy figures were running out of the forest. Some opened fire while still running. Their guns sounded like pattering hail. Then shouts, shots, screams suddenly vanished beneath a roar of powerful motors, coming from Kashka Tau. Immediately, fifty yards from Boris, another group – Caucasians, bizarrely uniformed – careered out from their forest cover. One or two wielded long curved swords, with which they slashed the perimeter fence aside. Charging the camp, they yelled in a language Boris didn't understand. Another roar of motors. A lone armoured personnel carrier loomed into view from the left, the direction of the dump. Then it turned and lumbered back. In the camp compound a mass of shouting men milled and fought. The Germans, real and false, were outnumbered. Boris, huddling lower than ever, saw one clinging to the wire fence as he fell. Even from a hundred yards Boris saw his blood–smeared face. Then there was Killa, yelling loudest of all, waving his rifle. 'No, no! We're not Fritzes! We're –'

That desperate wail was the last sound he uttered.

In confusion, other partisans turned and tried to flee the camp through the single gate.

Two horsemen suddenly appeared right behind Boris.

He leaped up, scaring the horses, which shied. The riders swore. Again Boris didn't understand the language. One – tall, straightbacked in the saddle – swung his pistol round.

'You're killing our men!' Boris shouted in Russian, too furious to be afraid. 'We're partisans.'

The man with the pistol laughed. He galloped off, standing tall in his stirrups, firing at random into the melée in the camp. His squat companion stayed a moment to control his plunging horse.

'Then get out of our goddamn way – Comrade!'

'Who the hell are you?'

Boris's question wasn't even heard. The man had gone.

'Oh mother of. . . .'

Boris ran forward across the trampled snow. Inside the compound men were going mad. No German was left alive. No real German – or fake. Two of Tembot's 'prisoners' were also dead, another two wounded.

A fuck-up. A shambles.

'Who's the senior officer here?' Boris yelled. 'Who's in charge of this rabble?'

His uniform of a Red Army Lieutenant made no impact on the crowd of shouting men. Some were firing shots in the air for lack of German targets, others, linking arms, were dancing a few chaotic steps, others were pulling at German soldiers' uniforms, searching for watches or anything else of value. When one young man, hissing with pleasure, began tugging at the collar on Killa's corpse, Boris's anger burst open.

Grabbing a handful of quilted jacket, he hauled the boy to his feet.

'Robber!' He spat in the lad's face. 'Bandit! Peasant!'

And with each word he slapped him, left, right, left. Two men leaped on Boris. They fell in the snow, punching, kicking, yelling obscenities. Boris's fury gave him strength to shake off his assailants, scattering them over Killa's bloodstained body.

'Crazy murderers.' Boris lurched to his feet. His chest heaved with the violent intake of freezing air. 'We're Russians. All of us. Who's your commanding officer?'

'I am!'

The voice came from behind Boris – and above. He turned to look up into the face of the tall rider.

'Ali Aziz Mohammed, chief of the Ossetian Irregulars.' He smiled, baring his sleek teeth like an angry dog – or a matinee idol.

'Who sent you here?'

The smile vanished. 'Sent me? Boy, nobody sends Ali

Aziz. Even Dzugashvili knows Ali Aziz Mohammed.'

'Comrade Stalin would clap you in jail for killing my men. You've no right –'

'Boy, take your miserable peasants and go.' A shot zinging over his head made the tall rider swivel in his saddle. 'Nazi swine. They're returning.'

'You fucked up our plan!' Boris yelled. 'The prisoners haven't been freed yet. The partisans are still in the camp, for God's sake. If you're operating against the Fritzes in this sector, you must report to –'

The tall man's laughter drowned Boris's words. He flourished his pistol, a captured Luger.

'Infidel! Communist!'

But before Ali Aziz could act, the Germans counter-attacked.

There was a rush of tribesmen to the gate. The wooden posts fell in a tangle of barbed wire. The two horsemen led the retreat. As the first German rifleman stormed the camp, the last Ossetian was pulling himself free and running like a hare toward the forest.

A T-26 tank rumbled out from behind one of the sheds. Its long-barrelled cannon searched out a target like a teacher's cane picking out the boy who'd flicked the pellet from the back of the class. Then pop! A puff of blue smoke erupted from its tip. The shell screamed into the forest. Only one man was hit – by a pine splinter in the leg. He, and all the others, scurried away, bloody in many cases, but safe.

Boris stopped as soon as the trees enclosed him.

What a fuck-up. And what the hell was happening down by the ammunition –?

That instant a huge explosion ripped open the dawn gloom like a roaring lion plunging through a paper hoop. The blast followed the flash, tearing through the forest. In the village, roofs and walls flew into the air like paper flakes from a bonfire.

Another explosion came from the direction of the dump, followed by a series of smaller bangs in a chain reaction. Then small arms fire – cannon. At the same time the real light of dawn was coming up over the hills. But smoke obscured these first dim rays of the sun just as they were beginning to fight their way through the blanketing of snow. An eerie grayness settled over the village like a pall.

Boris crept to the very edge of the forest. Lumps of damp snow fell on him as he pushed his way through laden bushes. Finally he got a clear view. The camp was deserted – apart from the corpses. Not a soul moved there. The wire fence lay twisted and tangled on the ground. The Germans had abandoned the camp to meet the threat from the exploding dump.

Boris stared uneasily at the scene below him.

Should he go back down to the camp? After all, the prisoners they had come to liberate hadn't been freed because of the shambles caused by Ali Aziz. They would still be in those huts he could see clearly.

But, maybe, first, he should find Tembot?

It was crazy to go down there alone.

Besides, the plan was to rendezvous with the main body back at the cowshed. That was where any survivors from the raiding party would have gone.

Best obey orders.

Boris ducked back into the forest's protection. At times it was more like swimming, pulling through the snowdrifts with arms and legs. But he was fit. He got lost a couple of times, and turned a half-mile hike into a two-mile struggle, but there, finally, was the rendezvous point. He found the right shed, behind the wattle fence.

Except – no-one was there.

Boris sat in the snow and groaned. No-one was there to advise him what to do. No-one to receive his report. And now . . . now he was too far away to help the prisoners. Too far and too late.

*

Later the same night, back in the camp high above Bagubent, beyond the perilous Cherek gorge, a weary residue led by Tembot Kochan found Boris asleep.

Tembot was grim-faced. Half the operation had been a success. The dump had been blown, and tens, maybe scores, of Fritzes wouldn't fight anymore. Several vehicles had been put out of action. But at a cost. Six partisans dead, ten injured. As for the shambles at the prisoners' camp – that half of things was a straight failure. Seven-figured Killa, one of his best men, was dead. Tembot grieved for him.

He had mounted a last-minute raiding party. Too late. The Fritzes had already re-occupied the camp. The prisoners remained in German hands.

Tembot looked at the sleeping Boris. Where had *he* been then?

Too late now.

Too late as well to stop his men killing the Fritzes they had rounded up. Not just Germans, but an assortment of Caucasians and Cossacks and Muslim scum fighting on the German side, mercenaries and traitors. Tembot would have liked to have them alive. Though they filled his mouth with bile, the mere sight of them, they had a lot of useful information. Now they were dead, every last one.

Tembot sat a moment, exhausted, on a pile of furs inside the hut. Others with him – just half a dozen – sprawled out in corners, beards grimed with frost, eyes black with fatigue.

Boris hadn't stirred.

Tembot held his massive head in his hands, recalling the Civil War, the war he thought had taught him all he ever wanted to know about man's brutality to man, about brother killing brother. But still there were surprises.

THIRTEEN

Fritz Stegl saw only hollyhocks. Purple and pink, tall, erect, magnificent. Back home in his neat garden in a suburb of Cologne, they grew seven, ten – fifteen feet high, way above his head. He saw them now in his mind, just as they were. And Gisela down on her knees, weeding, churning the horse manure with a trowel. Stegl respected tall, straight flowers. Primroses, violets, pansies – for these he felt nothing but contempt.

'Yes?'

Someone had been speaking. Always interruptions. Heat. The office was brutally stuffy, like a top-floor interrogation cell in summer.

'What?' he said again.

'New prisoners, Herr Sturmbannführer.'

A bead of sweat made a sudden dash, overflowing from the small pools in the cup of his nostril, and streaked across the corner of his lips before hanging like a nervous diver on the point of his chin, then plunging to the desk top.

Well, Aristotle had approved, had he not? And the Romans and a whole string of Spanish bishops. Torture was not a matter of conscience. There was a war on.

'What?' Stegl repeated snappishly.

'Three new prisoners, Herr Sturmbannführer. One is a boy.'

Stegl spun to face the Gestapo Corporal. 'Boy? Old enough to fire a rifle perhaps? To throw a petrol bomb?'

The Corporal said nothing, stood straight.

'Later, later,' Stegl said at last with a sigh. 'Let him brood. Let them all brood. Look, there are so many damn papers. Where is my stenographer? Never mind. Put the boy – put the prisoners in a cell. Separate cells. If we have them. I'll deal with them tomorrow.'

'*Jawohl*, Herr Sturmbannführer. Heil Hitler!'

Stegl felt too damn hot and tired even to reply, let alone raise his arm. Inside, this pitiless heat, over which, maddeningly, he had no control. Outside, the snow was piling up, inch on inch, in absolute silence.

Papers.

Fine when they were orders, something to get on with. But half of them – just paper. Those digests of military progress, for example. He picked up two typed sheets from the top of one of the many heaps on his desk. Bad news, why did they always give the bad news? There – the 93rd Motorized Regiment – reading between the lines, but obvious enough – virtually destroyed. And Stalingrad. What did all these papers mean? Where was the good news? If there was none, for God's sake, let them be silent. Yes – the Army believed itself to be in charge in this sector of the war. That was just the trouble. 'Treat the Caucasian people as friends,' he read. He crumpled the paper, threw it to the floor. That wasn't the sort of thing that would be on his desk if only – as everywhere else in this damn desert of Slavs and subhumans – the Party insisted on direct control. Even the Bolsheviks had a better idea of discipline.

Impossible. Things were impossible.

The Mountain Jews, these so-called Tats, they were in many ways the worst of all. As soon as they were drawn to the attention of the Gestapo, he had identified them, isolated them, imposed the usual conditions, issued the yellow stars, made preliminary arrangements for their disposal. But what happened? The Jews dared send so-called representatives in Nalchik. To the Regional Committee, a body in theory totally subservient to the wishes and commands of the occupiers. The Regional Committee referred the matter – not to himself – but to the Army authorities. 'An exception is to be made in the case of the Mountain Jews as a demonstration of good will to the native populations of the Caucasian region. No action is to be taken.'

In black and white – right on the top of that heap there – on letterheaded paper – reference number A/42.OH/3965.2.

The Army had already opened the churches and the mosques. Next thing, Stegl said angrily to himself, they'll build a synagogue and present it as a Passover present to the Mountain Jews!

'Yes?'

Did the Army resent perhaps – not respect – a Waffen SS Major attached to them? Did even the Gestapo resent him?

Always attached. Why was he always on attachment, he wondered?

'Yes?'

Finally he looked up to see who had entered the room and was standing in front of his desk at attention. 'Ah, stenographer.' Stegl got to his feet and fine-tuned his features into a mocking smile. Sweat spurted again through the gaping pores on his face and in the small of his back. 'These communications – these papers. They – can wait. We have more important work to do. Below.'

*

Ilya Dobroliubov had been crying. Now his face was dry, though discoloured. The tears had swirled the crust of mud and dirt around his cheeks like a flash flood scoring an arid river-bed, then passing on, leaving only the patterns of its fierce passage.

His lung hurt. It had 'gone' again. But the pain didn't frighten him – only the knowledge of his weakness, his physical weakness. He felt, he knew, that the pain and the incapacity were making him mentally weak too, just when he needed all his strength.

Ilya was a thin boy, nervy and wiry. His small face, dark, tightly-curled hair and prominent nose had prompted one of the guards when they brought him in to aim a kick at the back of his legs and shout, 'Fucking Jew we've netted here!'

He had been captured in an ambush four weeks before, just about the time when Nalchik was taken. He had never had a chance to achieve anything as a partisan. A double humiliation followed. First, he had been made to work for the Fritzes, digging trenches and repairing roads in villages around Kashka Tau. Then, just after all that fighting – he'd heard it from his hut, but couldn't see a thing – his lung deflated, and they had moved him down to Nalchik.

Ilya was determined not to fail again. The Fritzes seemed to think he knew about the raid on the camp in Kashka Tau. He hadn't known of course. But he wasn't about to tell them anything anyway.

Ilya shivered. Seven others were in the cell – crammed together like those tins of tiny fishes he had seen before the war. Yet it felt even colder than in the mountains.

No-one talked. No-one had even asked him who he was when he was pushed inside, hardly looked at him.

Suspicion.

No-one trusted anybody.

There was no food, no bed, not even a bucket. One corner of the cell was greasy with stinking excrement. Why had the damn lung gone again? Why? Perhaps the air had been seeping out all the time, ever since, in the hospital, three months ago, the doctor had stuck that long thick needle through his ribs – he had felt the muscles as they were pierced, snapping like pieces of rubber cut under tension. Probably, he thought, that's what has been going on, a slow puncture. Now all the air was gone, and the raw pain was back, and his breathing rasped like a circular saw.

Who were these men with him in the cell, all craggy and bearded?

Ilya had only a thick black shadow on his upper lip. He had just had his sixteenth birthday.

He felt tears forming.

What were they going to do to him?

He thought, wildly, of his family. But the only one he could picture in his mind was that fraud, Old Rags.

Then the image of his sister Nadia came into his mind. She was alive – he knew that now. The message had got through before he was captured. Nadia was alive. She had escaped from Pyatigorsk. Though as for father. . . .'

Ilya's thoughts were like a whirlpool, sucking in random impressions, memories, fears, swirling them around and pushing them, crushing them, into a black hole in the centre of his mind. Nothing coherent came out again.

He let himself down into a squatting position on the damp

earth floor, hearing curses as legs moved a few inches to make room for him. He sat, wrapping his arms round his legs. His head fell on his knees. Finally, for a while, sleep overcame him, an automatic mechanism that tried to sort out in his brain the real from the unreal, the hopes from the ever-present pain and the fear of pain to come.

He hardly noticed when the guard pulled him to his feet and took him along a corridor to another room. It seemed to be night. Maybe very early morning.

Only when a powerful light was switched on above his head did reality come pulsing back.

He was sitting on a plain wooden chair. In front was a simple desk with nothing on it. Beyond, a door. Not a cell door, not barred, but an ordinary wooden door with a handle made of yellow ceramic. The walls were plastered and peeling, so close he could touch all four of them by taking a single pace in each direction.

The ceiling was low.

He was alone.

Ilya sat in this room for an hour. It seemed for ever.

At last the door opened, and a German officer entered. Ilya's throat tightened.

They've come for me – the torturers!

*

But, looking up, Ilya's first reaction on seeing Colonel Siegfried Brandt was one of relief. The man had no Gestapo markings on his uniform. He looked stern, completely German, so immaculately dressed that his neatness seemed calculated to point up Ilya's own misery. But a less threatening figure than Ilya had so vividly imagined.

For a long time the officer stared silently at him like an artist at a painting or a zoologist at an unfamiliar species of animal. But the man's eyes were not those of a critic – or a vivisectionist. He seemed rather to be searching for something.

After a while Ilya became uncomfortable, began blinking uncontrollably. The unrelenting stare was not cruel. Why was it so disturbing?

His chest began to grind, and he coughed. A spasm of pain shot through his lungs, like red-hot irons applied back and front to his ribs and his shoulder-blades. He gasped for breath.

The officer waited for him to recover, then asked, 'Ilya Dobroliubov?'

Ilya was again surprised, not so much by the friendly tone and the perfect Russian accent as by the use of his name.

He said nothing, however. Say nothing, risk nothing.

'I'm sorry,' the officer began again, 'about your father. The fighting in Pyatigorsk, the conditions of combat. . . .'

The skin on Ilya's forehead contracted. He found it hard to concentrate. Back in the camp he had overheard them talking one time, maybe several times, about the ways the Fritzes got things out of you. One gives you a cigarette, a light, another comes in and knocks the burning tobacco down your throat, the first comes back and apologizes for his colleague and so on and so on.

'I'm sure,' the officer said, 'German uniforms look alike to you. Unless,' he smiled, 'you've had an exceptionally thorough training. The men who transferred you to Nalchik were Alpine troops, men of the mountains. My men. I am their Colonel. I'm sorry – I was unaware myself until too late – when I saw the name. You should be in hospital.'

'Are you going to kill me?'

The words escaped Ilya's lips when he wasn't even trying to speak. He looked away, down at his knees, shut his eyes, anything to hide the shame.

Brandt sat on the corner of the empty desk.

'The pneumothorax. Is it hurting very much?'

'No,' Ilya growled. His lung gave another grating heave.

'When did it happen? How long ago exactly?'

Ilya kept silent. He was getting dangerously close to confidences. He wished it had been a wound. He wished he'd had the chance to get in a firefight.

Outside, there was a clatter of boots and shouting in German. Then a yell in the Balkar language, which Ilya recognized but didn't understand. The idea came into his head – involuntarily again – that the Fritzes must be having a hell of a problem with the crazy quilt of language that covered the whole Caucasian region. He knew one village, Hinalug, where they spoke one language in the upper part and another language lower down – and both were separate from any other language. His lips formed a kind of vacant smile.

'I will see you get proper treatment for your lung.'

The officer's voice stuck a barb into Ilya's thoughts and hauled them back into the room like a gaffed fish. He began to cough. The pain made him want to cry out.

'Your family,' the officer went on, 'you have family here, in Nalchik, able to take care of you?'

Ilya glared at him.

'I would like to assure them you . . . that everything is being done . . .'

Yes, I understand, Ilya thought. He was in the hands of the Gestapo. He knew what that meant. Even if this man here wasn't one of them – oh yes? Who said he wasn't? If only the pain would go away. Perhaps this officer would deliver a message. Now Nadia was back, maybe she could – help? Help him escape. Organize something. It was a feeble, fluttering hope that stole into his brain like a cat burglar on a dark night. But no. Involve his darling Nadia, his family? He had to be crazy even to think of it. Ilya tried to force himself to put everyone he loved out of his mind. In case he let something slip. If they – if the Gestapo got hold of his family because he gave them information that led to –

Tears came into his eyes again.

'What do you want?' he whispered. 'Who sent you here? There's nothing I'll tell you. Kill me if that's what you want. I'd die rather than tell you anything.'

The officer stood up.

'Is there nothing you'd like to tell me, Ilya?' He leaned forward, his knuckles on the table, and spoke with a low intensity. 'I understand you cannot trust me. Of course you can't. I have no business to be here at all, not in your country. I don't expect you to understand me or believe me. But you're old enough to know where you are, into whose hands you have fallen. You know what you did to cause you to be here. I can do very little, although I shall try. I admire your bravery, your patriotism. I sincerely regret you were caught, that it was you who were caught.'

Ilya looked up questioningly – the question remaining, however, in his eyes alone. He forced himself not to speak, not to show his curiosity.

'I never saw your father. But I believe him to be dead. That is why I asked you if you had family remaining. I don't need to know who or where they are,' he added quickly. 'But to be assured . . .'

Ilya wondered more and more who was this German who asked such questions, not an interrogation at all. He said such weird things about him being a patriot.

'Please understand, Ilya. The Gestapo know who you are. They can, if they wish, trace all the members of your family, in Nalchik or anywhere else in the zone of occupation. This they will not bother to do unless they judge the search to be of importance to their work. If your mother is not in hiding, she can easily be found. The town is not large. Not even with the Gestapo does she have any reason to fear, however. The same is true of your sister.'

'Nadia's like me,' Ilya whispered fiercely. 'She will fight, fight you all, till you leave our country, till you all die. Like me – except she's free. You'll never find her. She's gone underground.' He hissed the word like a challenge.

But then he stared into the officer's eyes – amazed.

There were tears in the German's eyes. Not enough to flow. But tears – glinting blue tears.

A long terrible cough formed in Ilya's lungs. He sat rigid on the hard chair, controlling it, fighting it down. His resistance was even more painful than the cough itself, had he let it escape. But it was a symbol. He would show no more weakness in front of this officer, give nothing else away. Already he'd said too much. But he'd proved he couldn't be broken, mind or body. God be thanked, the man was going. Quick! He was opening the door. The pain rose, spread, became a fire. He was turning. Go. Go! He was waiting there – what for, what for?

The burning air shot from every inflamed tissue in Ilya's damaged chest and throat, searing the membranes of the pleural cavities – one intact and one collapsed – with equal intensity. He bent over the table, forcing his hands over his ears as if by cutting the noise he could take away the pain – and the shame of failing.

Gradually his lung returned to normal, working hard to bring in new air, resisting the pressure of its burdensome, useless neighbour.

Slowly Ilya raised his head.

The German officer had gone. The room was eerily silent.

But almost at once there was tramping and voices outside. Two guards clattered in, each to one side of the desk. Laughing, they picked him up by putting a hand under each armpit and lifted him up over the desk. His knees and shins scraped its sharp edge, but he hardly noticed. Still finding fun in their handling of the boy like a limp doll, the guards – young men, hardly older than Ilya – carried him down a wide concrete staircase along an underground corridor and dumped him into a brightly lit room. The walls of the room were covered with white tiles. White, but flecked with stains, fresh red and stale reddish-brown.

*

It was evening. The boy had been dead an hour. Stegl was alone, back in his office.

What puzzled him more than the Dobroliubov boy's refusal to provide information to his interrogators – perhaps, after all, he had none to give – was the curious interest in him shown by Brandt. Certainly the Colonel had every right of access. As commanding officer of the troops who brought the prisoners in when Kashka Tau had been evacuated, as the officer in charge of mountain operations against the terrorist forces, Brandt was correct to make the attempt to gather whatever information he could. Stegl himself had encouraged such enterprise.

But, to Stegl, nothing happened randomly. Every action was part of a nexus, a single thread in the woven cloth. You didn't need many threads spun together to observe the pattern. Two, three, four – with each thread the pattern began to emerge.

Brandt had appealed directly to General Konrad, urging

him to exercise clemency in the matter of young Dobroliubov. Too late, of course. The boy was already dead – an unusually fragile constitution, according to the interrogating team.

Stegl rifled the papers in Brandt's file, a file stamped with the seal of General Zeitzler himself. Stegl pulled a piece of blank paper out of the mess on his desk and jotted a few – speculations.

FOURTEEN

Bekirbi lifted his glass, clinked it against the other glass which remained on the table. 'Eh, Yusef, you know what Allah had to say about vodka!'

'The Prophet Mohammed,' said the small dark man, with a curl of the upper lip that revealed the black and white stripes of his top front teeth, 'said nothing but good of a little water.'

Bekirbi didn't laugh, not even smile. He drank down the milk-coloured, sickly-stinking vodka, poured another two fingers.

The two men were sitting in a miserable café in the oldest part of town, not an old building itself but a Soviet shack with greasy trestle tables and crude uncomfortable chairs and a cracked glass counter with two rows of bottles on rickety shelves behind. The stink of the inferior vodka reminded Bekirbi of a field hospital. They were the only ones there apart from the old man with a drip on the end of his nose who pulled out the corks and pretended to wash the stubby glasses. Cafés under the occupation had few customers.

Bekirbi said, as if making an announcement, 'Ali Aziz is dead. You heard that? The fool, he deserved to –'

'I know it,' Yusef Tsagov said softly but incisively. 'Murdered.'

Bekirbi's smile faded before it formed. He cursed under his breath. Damn Tsagov. It was impossible to surprise the little weasel. Perhaps, he thought, I should tell the Gestapo who really is this source of mine, my cutting arm. Except – I'm afraid of the bastard. What would Yusef do if he found out I'd betrayed his anonymity? Bekirbi's sweat ran cold. He had heard things . . .

'A dog's death awaits all bandits who kill friends as readily as enemies,' he added portentously, spoiling the effect by wiping his lips nervously with the back of his hand.

Tsagov said nothing.

Another five minutes went by before Bekirbi broached the real subject of his 'interview'.

'Maybe you know this too,' he began with strained sarcasm. 'I had this woman. Bitch. Know who I mean?'

Tsagov nodded.

Bekirbi scowled. 'But the bigger bitch is the sister-in-law. Surkov's wife. That kid Lieutenant who's such a big Soviet hero now, if rumours are right. One of Kochan's little boys.'

Bekirbi spat. Of all men, Tembot Kochan – his one-time chief – was the one he despised most, a secret policeman who had never, deep down, respected the peaked cap of authority.

Tsagov continued to nod slowly. A faint smile parted his lips again. His tongue licked languidly at the teeth with the zebra stripes.

'I've had a tip-off,' Bekirbi announced, leaning forward. He looked at Tsagov to see if he'd aroused interest. 'Something I thought maybe we could . . . get together about.' Hell, he thought, it's like talking to an alley-cat.

'No names,' Bekirbi went on. 'Someone – it seems – wants to find the girl. Nadia Sergeevna Surkova. The sister-in-law. There's a certain German Colonel . . . interested. Army, not Gestapo. But the other side wants to know. Get me?'

Bekirbi didn't name the Colonel to Tsagov, but he remembered him all right, the same supercilious bastard he had surrendered to. He realized now what his first words in German had been, why they'd all laughed.

'I shan't tell you everything,' Bekirbi said. He couldn't. He didn't know more. He knew damn little in fact, just what Stegl had told him.

'There's money in it,' he added.

That raised a full smile on Tsagov's face. Bekirbi nodded contentedly, seeing he'd struck a responsive chord. The mere mention of money obviously set the mercenary tribesman's heart beating.

'You think you can find her?'

Tsagov nodded.

'It's a big town.'

'It's a small town, Captain.'

'Then find her. But keep my name out of it. And I'm not a Captain.'

'Of course. Now, this Colonel?' Tsagov almost swallowed the word in a shot of vodka – the first time he'd touched the drink that Bekirbi had poured for him.

'Later. Later,' Bekirbi said impatiently. 'I'll tell you all you need to know. First find the bitch.'

*

When Bekirbi had gone, Tsagov remained sitting at the café table, turning his glass with the tips of his stained, jagged nails. The job Bekirbi had given him was easy as catching a wild pig in the snow. Easier. He didn't even have to look for Nadia Sergeevna Surkova. He already knew where she was. More exactly, he knew how to find her. It might take him twenty-four hours. But within a day he could locate any member of the 'underground' opposition. Every one of the groups was penetrated or spied on, if not by the Gestapo then by the 'independent' Muslim organizations. There was always the possibility of new, small, autonomous resistance groups springing up. For a while they would be difficult to trace. But those with communist support were far from being as discreet as they thought. Tsagov went through some of the possibilities in his mind.

One of them was the Nalchik Women's Anti-Nazi Group.

The problem was not finding the woman. The problem was finding out who wanted her, and why, and how this 'German Colonel' fitted into the picture. And then there was the secondary problem, to decide whether or not to pass on to Bekirbi the information obtained. Sometimes knowledge gained was of greater value when put to more direct, personal use.

Tsagov had not been raised in a mountain *aul* to be an easy victim of plainsmen's intrigues. He knew he was cleverer than they. He thought further ahead. Like everyone else he followed the fortunes of the war. But, unlike most, he did not believe that one success, however important, led inevitably to another. The plainsmen read maps as if they had no contours. Living in sight of the great peaks of Elbrus and Kazbek, they still didn't understand – the Caucasus was God's own Maginot Line. And though in theory the mountains could be outflanked, on one side was the desert, on the other a narrow, treacherous line along the Black Sea coast, like a thin lip beneath a craggy nose. There were no lush European plains for the Panzers to ride across as if they were on a racecourse.

Yusef Tsagov did not believe the Germans had come to the Caucasus to stay.

He twirled the glass, staring at the bare wall.

Of course Bekirbi would be grateful for the information on this woman Surkova. He would even steal the credit for it. Fine. But did Bekirbi's gratitude have value? Perhaps some, probably none. Tsagov shook his head and grinned. Bekirbi was so sure a purseful of money was like a nosebag to a hungry horse.

'What are you staring at?' Tsagov suddenly screamed.

The old man behind the counter blinked. A drop fell from his nose onto the greasy counter.

'Me?'

'You. Who else?' Tsagov got up, peering exaggeratedly into every corner of the café. 'Who am I? You know me?'

The old man stepped back against the shelves of vodka bottles, dislodging one. It splintered on the floor by his feet.

'You know who *he* was?' Tsagov jerked his thumb toward the door and moved another pace forward. The tip of a knifeblade appeared below his right sleeve.

The old man glanced down at the jagged glass.

Tsagov sprang, vaulting the counter and grabbing the man's collar in a single motion.

'Curious, are you? A few words of what we said reached your ears maybe? You wonder . . .'

'No!'

'Yes. You wonder, old man.'

'No!'

'How'll I help you forget? Eh?'

The knife was in Tsagov's hand now. A thin trickle of

saliva moistened the runnels at each corner of his mouth. His smile was broad, and his hands completely steady.

'You can't forget?' he went on, his voice getting softer each time he spoke. 'You'll never forget. Unless I kill you.'

The man ducked, desperately groping for the glass at his feet, but Tsagov's wiry strength was too great.

'Eh, old man? No, you keep your memory – and I'll keep a hostage. A tongue? An eye? To remind you. And then I'll know you, old man. I'll know who it was who talked if ever one day someone says to me, "That café meeting, that's where you slipped up."'

'I don't know you. I don't know the other one. How can I –?'

The knifeblade flashed. The old man's hands clutched at his face to protect it. A blubbering scream escaped his lips. On the cracked glass counter a red blotch appeared, then another and another. The old man slumped to the floor, crunching the broken bottle under him.

'A mark,' said Tsagov. 'So I shall know you.'

He walked pensively out of the café while the old man whimpered behind the counter, examining the crescent moon etched in red on the back of his right hand.

*

Six days later, on the evening of December 1, Yusef Tsagov was one of twenty men in cloaks and fur hats who sat or squatted in the same upstairs room which the 'dissident' Muslim elders had used before the Germans captured Nalchik. Some were conspicuously opulent, with silk-embroidered shirts and jewelled daggers at their waists. These were the émigrés, many with the title of Prince. Others, like Tsagov, were humbly dressed, even shabby, their black wool *burkas* stained and covered with ragged tufts like a moulting donkey. But the power lay with those who knew, not with those who lived elegantly on German money. Inside knowledge was the only solid currency.

Tsagov was meanly born, a poor Balkar peasant for whom formal respect to the princes was an obligation, but he was the one they wanted to hear. He and the handful of others like him who knew both sides. In certain cases they were tolerated intermediaries. But Tsagov kept his contacts separate.

The conversation moved slowly. There was a language difficulty, as always on such occasions. The Kabardinians who spoke their own language of mysterious origin understood imperfectly the Balkars with their Turkic dialect. Compromises were made, some mixing of words. Frequently the men turned to Russian to ensure clear understanding.

At the heart of their meeting was the need for new insight into the military situation. It was important to understand, not to judge. No-one in the room was present in order to celebrate German victories – or defeats. Equally, no-one expressed encouragement at the successes of Red Army resistance or delight in the Russian humiliations.

All they needed to know was: who were to be their masters? Rather, who in the years to come would set themselves up in authority over them and in the end – since neither German nor Russian, Nazi nor Soviet, respected Allah or the traditional rights of the Caucasian people – who would therefore have to be resisted?

All the men present, even Yusef Tsagov, had as their ambition, ultimately, the establishment in the northern Caucasus of an Islamic state.

The tone of the debate was unemotional. The enclosed room excluded the flashes and roars that were so much a feature of Nalchik, day and night. It was like talking in a padded cell – or in the headman's hut in a lonely village high in the mountains. The decisions, as Tsagov knew they had to, all amounted to the same thing: wait and see.

But, on the question of the partisans, for the first time acrimony rose in the men's voices.

'Their activity,' said one of the princes in the tone of decisive authority uncertainly acquired, 'must be actively discouraged. They are endangering the respect with which we are treated by the occupying authorities.'

'Respect!' sneered a Kabardinian councillor who had remained in the city in Soviet times and who resented the return of the supercilious but well-connected émigrés. 'Rule from Berlin no more implies respect than rule from Moscow.'

'Neither implies nor gives,' agreed a white-bearded man, the oldest present. 'All who resist, wisely or unwisely, provide us with a remnant of self-respect. History will show.'

'The partisans are mere bandits,' shouted a corpulent prince. 'We must issue instructions to the faithful that they are endangering their faith by consorting with the atheistical powers and darkness.'

'Perhaps,' said Tsagov mildly, 'we could agree that the partisans should be condemned for their anti-religious associations, while on the other hand we do our best to ensure that reprisals by the occupying authorities do not deprive us of the lives of our fellow nationals and . . . true believers. We would do well to remember that the permission we have been granted to reopen our mosques is in part designed to emphasize the divisions that so sadly exist among us.'

Tsagov's words were accepted with sympathetic nodding. They were in the true spirit of the meeting. Compromise. Cunning.

It was not long before the men began to leave the house discreetly, one by one, from back and front.

Tsagov was pleased with his own performance as he glided down the shadowy side of the street. There was a weak sun, had been for the last two or three days, and the snow was melting into a mess of slush and horse-manure and oil and shredded paper. He stepped lightly on the crusty edges of the pools.

All the same, too much talk and too little action made the blood in his veins as sluggish as buttermilk. Diplomacy, acting as other people's ferret, was necessary, surely. But an exclusive diet of false subservience would soon make him lose his appetite for real pleasure. The struggle for political power was a satisfaction. But pleasure came only from the fear in the eyes of the enemy, from the kids he had threatened in his village, so many years ago – oh, they knew how quick he was with a knife! They knew he wasn't pretending, that the cuts he made were deep. They *hurt*. Others had found out since. Time and again he had seen that fear in his enemies' eyes. But now – he was forty-three years old, in danger of winning a much more tepid kind of respect.

Who fears me now? he wondered.

Bartenders. Old men with dripping noses.
He spat.
Perhaps, he thought, cracking his heel into a thin sheet of ice that zinged like shivered glass, this Colonel will lead me into something more serious. Now that I've succeeded in tracking him down.
Colonel Siegfried Brandt. I have the name now. What is his weak spot?

FIFTEEN

That same dirty slush was beginning to crisp, and the pools of melted snow to crinkle with a thin topping of scummy ice, when Nadia emerged from the heap of rubble where she had been hiding.

As she walked, tufts of felt pushed through the holes in her goat-leather boots and stuck underfoot like the suction pads of a cautious salamander. The only light came from the distant flashes of gunfire, no brighter than starlight. Low clouds were scudding in from the north, sucked into the storms raging along the entire crest of the Caucasus mountains. She picked her way slowly, keeping to the rough sidewalk. A few other figures, mere shadows, stumbled by. An old man, slipping and sliding, breathing like a spent horse, overtook her, nudging her into the gutter. All were urgently seeking home or shelter in the premature dark before official night came, the dead hours of curfew.

All except Nadia.

The jumble of stones she had come out of, like a rat from its hole, was the ruin of a shed used by Number 4 School to store equipment and old files. There was barely room for two people to stretch out at the same time among the rubble and the rough wood beams, even after it had been 'emptied'. Yet for a week between four and seven women had lived there, the latest in a series of hide-outs. For heat they had their own bodies and a small oil-burning stove which they used only rarely because of the smoke.

A flurry of sleet wet Nadia's face like tears. But she wasn't crying. She was scared – but also elated.

Yet she wondered if the long-postponed plan of action was

the best one possible – trying to seize weapons for themselves. All seven had been present for the vote, and decided 'yes' by five to two. Nadia had been one of the dissenting two. Of course she now accepted the decision. 'Party' rules. But she felt they were acting less out of good sense than frustration at the long weeks of false alarms and waiting.

Another trouble was that they only had two watches between them. Nina Petrovna had one. The other was passed round to whoever needed it. Tonight the cleaning woman had it.

She walked on, keeping close to the walls, sheltering as far as possible from the gusting wind.

Perhaps, she thought, the Fritzes wouldn't mount a regular two-man guard tonight? No. That was one sure thing about these gentlemen of the New Order. They were consistent. They always did the same thing at the same time, once the order had gone out. Air raids at 15.00 hours. House searches at 05.00 hours. A double guard at the top end of Dolinsk Park from 21.30 to 05.30 hours. A hell of a long shift, Nadia said to herself. Maybe they chose only the semicompetent for it? Or the astute chose themselves – better to guard the park gates, even on a freezing cold night, than storm a machine-gun nest on some impregnable Circassian rock!

Nadia's job was look-out.

She approached the park along the low scrubby ground between the Nalchik River and the south end of town. Dense bushes and thick clumps of the native silver fir hid her as effectively as one of those famous London fogs. The most dangerous moment was crossing the road that curved down the hill from the town. Having chosen the sharpest point of the curve, watching and listening carefully, she slipped across, crouching, then darting like a lizard.

Up in the park a skeletal black bush seemed to beckon her into its shelter. Brushing its thin branches, trembling and damp, and sending a thousand droplets flying and tinkling into the muddy pool around its twisted trunk. Some drilled an icy tattoo on her cheeks. Evergreens to her left offered better shelter, and she crawled quickly over to them.

She was too early perhaps. Always there was too much

time. Too much time to think, think about things she'd rather forget.

Concentrate.

Did she have her whistle? Where was it? It couldn't have dropped out of her –? No, there it was, in her coat pocket. Nadia sighed. Her school whistle. She never imagined she would have to use it to warn her fellow partisans of German troops. Time perhaps to move now, was it? During the day there was generally a lot of coming and going between Dolinsk at one end of the park and Nalchik at the other. At night, the Group had observed, such movements were rare. But if a truck or a jeep or just a foot patrol were to come along at the very moment the guards were being – but Nadia didn't quite know how Nina Petrovna planned to get the weapons. 'That's not your job, Nadia Sergeevna. You listen for the first signal. When you hear it, wait for the next. If there's any sign of anything going on in the park between the two signals, blow. Once. Very loud. That's all there is to it. Very simple,' said Nina Petrovna.

The trouble with not having a watch was that Nadia had no clear idea when to expect Nina Petrovna's first alert.

A chill gust rustled the leaves above her head, bringing down another shower, not of water droplets but of ice crystals. At least, she thought, it's finally decided to freeze.

Waiting, waiting, waiting. That's what she'd heard men complain of. The incredible boredom of war. Even Boris – where was he now? – had told her how patient he sometimes had to be.

Yet the violence and the pain, when they came, would be so sudden, so dramatic – or was that true? How could she know before it happened to her?

She shifted position five or six times in the next thirty, forty minutes. The night gradually became calmer, except for sudden spasms of wind. Sometimes she could hear the gurgling of the Nalchik River. The noise had wonderful associations of summer. Afternoon, in a meadow, the breeze off the foothills . . . for a while Nadia's reverie almost turned to sleep.

She forced herself awake. It might be easier, she thought, if there was heavy firing tonight, or an air-raid nearby.

On the other hand, if there were a lot of noise, maybe she would miss Nina Petrovna's signal.

The signal! Devil take it – she couldn't have missed it when her mind was away, dreaming, just then? – Nadia crawled to the edge of the bush that hid her and looked this way and that down what she supposed to be long paths. She cocked an ear like a chicken listening out for a fox. Nothing but the wind. Then a very distant shout. A German word, perhaps. If it was Russian or Kabardinian or Balkar she didn't recognize it. A scream then – no, a laugh.

They couldn't have put traps in the park, could they? Man-traps? Mines?

Her heart gave a flutter.

No, no. She made herself answer logically. Everyone used the park. Well, less now in winter. But there would be no point in setting traps, even trip-wires, anything like that. The Germans would be as likely to trap themselves as anyone else.

Still, to the Germans there was a difference, wasn't there? Germans were human, the rest – animals, subhuman.

How did a subhuman look? Did they illustrate picture books for their own children with drawings of the terrifying subhumans, all black fur and drooling jaws, like monsters from Grimm's tales, the Black Forest? Or –?

A long low note like an owl's floated through the park like a wisp of thin smoke. Then a single shrill note.

Nina Petrovna's signal!

The operation had begun.

Nadia listened with every nerve.

She crept silently to a point at the north end of the park, a hundred and fifty yards from the open square beyond the twin towers, with their four white columns on concrete columns, that guarded the entrance gates. But, in the blackness, behind the low boughs of the trees, she still had no view of anything beyond the very closest objects – branches, an iron bench. Over to her right, also visible though black against the black sky, was the tip of the obelisk erected in memory of the victims of Civil War.

Suddenly a voice. A shout. *'Halt! Wer geht –?'*

A strangled cry. Running feet. Whistles.
Then a flare.
A scream.
What –?
A clatter of steely boots, running. Voices shouting. A burst of shooting. Loud, loud, like firecrackers. An engine fired. Another.

Nadia's heart pounded like an overloaded freight train.

This wasn't how it was supposed to –

More shooting. The whole square at the top of the park suddenly came alive. A verey light erupted like a multiple lightning flash. Between the pillared towers, Nadia could suddenly see the whole drama. Except – what drama? What *was* happening?

Just running figures. Germans, German soldiers everywhere. Voices. Lights. Tears were smarting her eyes, destroying her vision. She blinked them away angrily.

The glittering light faded.

The incident seemed . . . over.

What was going to happen now? It seemed confusion. Just shouts now, no more shots.

A searchlight suddenly came on behind her, from a derrick-like structure in the middle of the park, in the German camp where the children's funfair had been. The beam wavered in the air, hitting roofs and tall buildings in the city, then the treetops around her. It was coming down.

Nadia bolted.

She had to get out of the park.

What if they came after her with dogs?

Keeping low, Nadia ran toward the river. Branches whipped her face, but she didn't feel them, not as pain. Several times she stumbled. The ground dropped away sharply. Then the damn road again. Without waiting, looking or even thinking, she scuttled across. She ran toward the swampy ground near the river. Thin ice snapped like glass under her feet. Along the river bank the line of poplars seemed to bend toward her as she ran, sighing and shuddering, a frantic counterpoint to the rhythm of her feet. She ran and ran. Away – toward the outskirts of the town, toward the Free Village, where Balkars and Kabardinians traditionally sought shelter from the pursuit of their feudal princes. Now it would be her protection.

But she didn't stop in the Free Village. Immediately she began circling, over fences and through bleak, deserted vegetable plots and round, back again, in the direction of the city, vaulting walls that otherwise she would have regarded as impossibly high.

Had she got out fast enough? What had happened to Nina Petrovna and the others? Should she go straight to the hideout in the shed? What would they do? What should she do?

Questions made a drumbeat in her head, rhythmically following the rapid pounding of her feet on the frosty ground, just as the poplars had done back by the river.

By a square, whitewashed house perched on a slight rise, she turned down a narrow alley.

Yes, it had to be back to the ruined shed – even though, unknown to her, she'd passed within ten yards of Brandt's billet, where another kind of shelter would have awaited her.

The questions drummed on. Had they captured Nina Petrovna? Killed her? Would she, or any of the other women, talk if the Gestapo held them – tell the Germans about the hideout? – Nina would never talk – but the others?

Where else though? There'd be search parties, patrols all night. Already sirens were screaming in all quarters of the town, jeep engines roaring, and always those terrible orders shouted, shouted. Not home, either, not where Darya was. If they were looking for Nadia, found out who she was, home was impossible. If the neighbours saw anyone going in there – after curfew? No-one could be trusted. She wouldn't ever, ever, risk Dasha's life. Let them hunt her. Like a lapwing, she would trail her invented wounds for them to follow, away from the nest. She would entice them further, further, till they no longer suspected she had a vulnerable child.

At last, hiding in doorways, once with only a thin, inadequate tree to protect her, yet safe, unseen, she reached the shed door. Huddling low, catching her breath, noticing for the first time the streams of sweat that soaked her coarse cotton underwear, she leaned her shoulder against the rough planks. She panted, motionless, with relief. Then she put her ear to the wooden door. No sound from inside. She tapped the usual signal with her knuckles – a splinter pierced her skin, but she scarcely felt it. No, she was the first to return. She would have to get the emergency key. Despite its battering from German shells, the shed had no way in except the door.

Nadia tensed herself for one more risk.

Cautiously, she peered out along the valley. To her right was a blank brick wall. To her left the wide Red Army Street. No lights were playing on it. Those confused flashes and noises came from beyond, toward the park.

The key was some yards away in a hole scraped out of loose plaster in the wall of Number 4 School, then blocked up again with a stone.

Nadia crept along like a mouse making a night sortie for a piece of cheese – a mouse who could anticipate what the trap would feel like if it snapped shut.

But she found the key. No-one disturbed the dark.

She flitted back toward the shed.

Sirens blared. Shouts.

She tripped on a pile of stones and fell. Her right knee hit the door with a jarring shock, but she didn't pause. Raising herself on her left hand, she fitted the big iron key into its lock and wrenched it round. The door creaked open. Nadia fell in as if she had been leaning on it, eavesdropping. The key clattered out of her hand onto a pile of rubble inside.

With a deep sigh, she pushed the door shut and huddled there, pressing her back to the rough, raw, comfortable planks. Safety.

*

Nadia was tired, cold, hungry. No-one came, none of the women from the Group. After a long wait, she lit the oil lamp. The bare bundles of clothes and rags which served them for beds were as they had been left. They seemed to Nadia more than ever pathetic, useless.

Had they all, *all* the others, really been killed? Or – worse – captured?

After uncountable hours, she stopped worrying about the

answer to that question. She became obsessed with the more immediate problem: *how* was she to find the answer? Who could she go to if no-one came to her?

Where did the other women live? But even if she knew, she couldn't risk going there. The safe houses, whose addresses she had memorized, would be safe no longer. She shut off the feeble light of the lamp.

For a while in the late morning she dropped off to sleep, waking with no sense of passing time.

Another thought occurred to her: tomorrow she had arranged another meeting with her mother and Dasha. It had been her talisman of success, that new rendezvous of the day after the operation. But how could she see them now, after the débacle?

She needed help, advice. She needed them urgently.

After several more hours, she heard a voice call her name. It came from outside, softly. A man's voice. 'Nadia Sergeevna. Nadia Sergeevna.'

Who? She didn't recognize the tone, the accent. All the same, a flutter of hope stirred inside her. Or was it fear?

'Nadia Sergeevna.'

Just that, no more. No emphasis. No urgency in it nor even a sense of threat.

But if someone – a man – knew where she was, the shed was no longer her secret, the Group's secret. Hope vanished. Her blood chilled.

All the same, cautiously – there was no point pretending she wasn't in the shed; the man *knew* – she pulled back the wooden bar that held the door firm. Her head peered outside. The air felt warm after the icy shed. The late afternoon gloom seemed beacon-bright. Her eyes blinked. She sneezed – even the weak sun had that effect after her earthworm existence inside the shed.

Out on the street a man laughed softly.

Nadia felt exposed. Any second a sharp beak would swoop and tear her out of her hole.

A figure walked forward. She put her hand to her mouth, though there was no danger of her screaming. Training, became habitual, had suppressed instinct.

'Nadia Sergeevna,' the man said again. 'It's not safe where

you are.' His accent was mountain, not town. A Balkar.

'Who are you?' she asked without thinking, then quickly, 'How do you know my name – that I'm here?'

'Inside! Best shut the door. Is there light?'

Nadia obeyed. He didn't look like a man she could trust – small, dark-skinned, with a dirty felt cloak wrapped over most of his body. Only the black eyes and veined hands were visible.

'It's no use to you now, this place,' he said. 'You're lucky I found you as soon as they knew.'

'They – the Gestapo? Have they –?'

'Three of your women are dead, Nadia Sergeevna. Including Nina Petrovna. What foolishness,' he sighed.

Nadia could say nothing.

'The others are arrested. No hope for them. You've been lucky, Nadia Sergeevna. What foolishness,' he repeated. 'They had to tell about it – in the end. Besides, they guessed you'd be gone already, knowing the risk.'

The man smiled. The way the man's teeth were patched like that – a zebra, she thought. Not a man, a wild beast. She began to see him as one of a vast herd of small, swarthy, centaur-like animals with coats of shabby fur and striped teeth, hunting, hunting . . .

'Hnnh? Did you expect your colleagues to resist for ever the Gestapo?'

'No,' she whispered. 'No, no.'

He sighed again. 'You'll have to come with me. But very, very quickly.'

'With you? Who are you?'

He picked up a piece of rubble in his sinewy, calloused hand, tossed it up and caught it, repeating the action several times. Then he stood up. He was small enough to have no need to bend even in the low shed with its sagging beams.

'Come,' he said.

She felt unable to decide, to react, to think coherently. Shock at the horrifying failure of the Group's operation was spreading in her brain like ether. Wave-like images invaded her senses including nausea, like the first awareness of being seasick. She found she couldn't move. Her mental and physical coordination had gone.

'Quick,' the man insisted, more sharply. 'Each minute is dangerous here.'

He took her under the arms and dragged her to her feet. She stood groggily. He slapped her, once, back again, the knuckles of his hand raising small but vicious welts on her cheeks. Nadia reacted sluggishly, but gradually her catatonic state began to ease.

Nina Petrovna had asked her to take over the Group if anything happened. She mustn't be helpless. But what Group was there now to take over? Who *was* this man? She found herself stumbling out into the alley.

'You must walk now,' his voice sounded stern beside her. 'Walk.'

'Where? Where?'

'Just walk.'

I must have time, she thought. Before something happens, I must have time to think. I am in danger. Boris is gone. Perhaps he is dead? I am alone.

He was telling her something. An address – a street she was only half aware of, somewhere on the north-eastern edge of town, on the Baksan road.

'Too far, too far,' she murmured, not knowing what she was saying, what she ought to be saying.

The man grabbed her. She winced with pain. His fingers squeezed the flesh of her arm like claws. Sensation was returning. She was glad. Pain was better than that frightening numbness.

'Stay at that address. Someone will come. Be patient. There's food there. Don't leave the house. Repeat the address.'

She did so. 'But you are coming –?'

'No. Control yourself. Go carefully. Don't stop. Here, eat this.'

He thrust a piece of hard sausage into her hand. Another wave of nausea overtook her, and she stumbled, letting it fall onto the slushy ground.

He swore, leaned down and stuffed the sausage in her coat pocket.

'Go,' he whispered. 'Trust me. You have no choice.'

SIXTEEN

Boris Surkov penetrated the German defence perimeter easily, alone at night with a primitive pair of wirecutters. The Fritzes were disorganized, noisy, moving in and out of their own positions like ants when someone has kicked their nest over, some running out while those outside keep running in and colliding.

Relaxing behind the wattle fence of a cottage garden, the deserted railway line only a hundred yards away, Boris felt as buoyant as he had been in Pyatigorsk, the day he had waited on the station platform, scanning the infested hills. He had that same strong sense of invulnerability.

That day had no longer any memory in it of Nadia, of their quarrel. In the same way, the memory of Kashka Tau – that, perhaps, he had failed to do all he could to liberate the partisans held prisoner in the camp – this residue of shame was buried beneath a new sense of confidence.

This was now his most important mission. The partisans remaining in the hills had no reliable information about what was happening inside Nalchik – who was collaborating, who was resisting, even passively. Boris had been chosen to infiltrate and collect this information. He had a number of names he had to contact – in his mind, of course, nothing written down.

Immobile, he began to feel the cold. He would have to move on.

Not far. That was the first contact's house, over there. Boris envisioned it precisely. It was too dark for his eyes. In an hour Kafarov would be going to work on the railway gangs, trying, but not too hard, to get the smashed tracks open for use again. They would have a quick talk down by the sheds there, where they wouldn't be observed.

Just a little patience now.

Nadia! Where was Nadia now?

The question burst into his head like a bubble rising from the muddy bottom to break the surface of a pond.

Hadn't he promised he would look after her? It was his duty. One of his duties.

Boris's heart beat faster, but a fog settled on his mind. In reality now – not just in his dreams – he was unable to imagine where she was, what she was doing. Probably she was at home, with Dasha. But he couldn't go there. In that quarter of town he would be recognized for sure – even without his Red Army uniform.

After the war – yes, after it was over, they would get back together again.

Surely she wasn't really dead? That had been just a crazy idea – or was it a vision he had had by the Baksan gorge, when the partisan boy was shot?

A noise distracted him. A door creaked open . . . and shut. A dog barked, another. A cock crew, then fell silent with a hoarse choking noise as if unwilling to announce the break of day until the occupation was over. Boris observed the sounds, the lights, the first movements of animals and people, though still the black sky gave no hint of dawn.

At last the old worker, Kafarov, appeared. Boris crept forward and murmured the name. Kafarov stopped, then side-stepped beneath a tree by the roadside. A whispered conversation followed, becoming urgent at times, lapsing into short silences, then picking up again more urgently than before.

At the end Kafarov walked on to his work. Boris remained where he was for a few more moments. He cursed under his breath.

Nadia was alive – but in trouble. The old man couldn't tell him much. A rumour – a strong rumour, however. A fiasco! She exists to plague me – she should *know* I'm a soldier, he thought angrily. My first duty is to fight the enemy, not to be a nursemaid to a woman, wife or no wife. I told her so. Why does she persist in taking risks, endangering us all?

But then he thought – I love her. Now is my chance to prove it.

*

In her new hiding-place, a single-storey cottage just like the one her family lived in a mile away beyond the town centre – except that this one was half-destroyed by the shelling – Nadia slept deeper than a bear in hibernation. A sleep so like its twin, death, that a watcher could not have told them apart.

But there was no-one to see her. Only an old blind woman lived in the room, chairbound, though within reach of a small cooking stove. She had expected Nadia, fed her and let her sleep on the straw mattress. But grudgingly, Nadia felt, as she lost the last shred of failing consciousness.

Fourteen hours later, Nadia woke with just one thought in her mind. The rendezvous. Today was the day she had arranged to meet them again. Soon Mariana and Dasha would be walking along the canning factory wall, looking for her, as they had agreed, hoping desperately that nothing terrible had happened to prevent them meeting, hoping, perhaps, that the rumours they might have heard were untrue, that, after all, she was safe. She *had* to be there.

The man who had come to the shed had told her not to leave the shelter he provided. But to stop her he would have to lock her in.

Considerations of logic and safety had been driven out of her confused mind.

Nadia waited until the last moment, sipping some bitter, much-boiled tea and chewing black bread.

Through the window she watched the snow begin to fall again, not heavily but enough to soften the cruelly hard outlines of the dark, gaunt town. To Nadia it seemed as if a fresh carpet were being laid for her. She would glide over the snow, weightless as she felt herself to be, even inside the house, tipping forward on a hard chair with her elbows on the kitchen table. Her body seemed to have become hollow, insubstantial. Certainly she had lost weight. But more than that, she felt herself floating, mingling with the air, an essence, unreal.

As soon as the blind woman heard the door open she screamed at Nadia. 'Disobedient fool, we'll both pay for it!'

Nadia ignored the bleating woman, slipped out and through the solid iron gate, which creaked like a portcullis. She nearly fell, not noticing a deep pit in the road – no memory of it existed from the day before. But out in the snow she realized she had been right: she could glide along, with what seemed like incredible speed, as if she were a sledge pulled by a frisky team of invisible horses. Walking seemed to demand no physical effort from her.

She kept in a straight line, making no attempt to use side streets or avoid detection. Others were still about.

Suddenly the recess in the wall was there to welcome her. She leaned against the metal door, breathing in rapid, shallow gulps of air, expelling them in puffs of steam like a child exhaling cigarette smoke in imitation of a steam train.

A half-hour passed like two minutes. The darkness of evening closed around her, and it felt like a warm cloak. Images of childhood, standing under a waterfall smothered by the soft bouncing drops, the first kiss with Boris, her teenage boyfriend, the time when the newsreel ran backwards and her friends had laughed, but to her it seemed so sad that time could so easily reverse, that occasion in infant school when the teacher fainted – all these images comforted her like a warm drink. Curious – a whole life passed in this town where now she crept like a criminal.

The thin snow fell mesmerically, tumbling down and drifting in the curls of wind against her felt-wrapped feet.

Figures passed her, not glancing in her direction.

Now, suddenly, one was in front of her. At once she knew her family had come.

A smile spread over her frozen lips. She knew she had been right to keep the rendezvous. They too would never have missed the precious meeting.

'Nadia,' said a voice.

She felt faint. With joy, relief – then a sense of confusion. The voice was a man's.

'Boris!'

He caught her as she fell forward.

Slowly sensation returned – as though infused by the tepid stream of thin sour soup Boris held to her lips. Some trickled down her chin, some down her throat.

'Quick, Nadia. Open your eyes. If a patrol sees us . . .' Boris was whispering, tipping the tin flask and shaking her at the same time. 'Drink it. Don't spill it. It's all the soup I have.'

'Boris, Boris,' she murmured, pushing away the lip of the flask.

'Just listen, don't speak,' he went on, talking in the same monotone whisper. 'I saw your mother. She told me about this arrangement to meet here. Nadia, keep awake. Now listen to me, carefully.'

'Wait, I'm better, I'm all right,' Nadia said. She tried to get to her feet, staggered. Boris offered a supporting arm and lifted her.

'There's no waiting to be done,' he insisted. 'I can't stay here. Nor can you. A man from the underground told me. About the fiasco. You have a safe house?'

'Yes. Someone told me to go there. He –'

'No, don't tell me. It's best I know nothing.' He paused. 'Who? Who told you?'

'I don't know. A man came. He just came to the shed.'

'Shed?'

'Where I was hiding.'

'So he knew.'

'He knew the Gestapo had found out – about the shed.'

Boris sighed deeply. 'You can't go on with this craziness. Nina Petrovna had already caused enough problems in the Party. No better than Ali Aziz. There must be coordination. Leadership.'

A quick flame of anger, of loyalty to Nina Petrovna, leaped up inside Nadia, but she damped it down.

'Did you see our little Dasha?' she asked, putting a cold hand to his face, turning it so she could see her husband better. 'Oh, Boris. I'm so happy you came. It has all been so frightening. But – do you know how many were killed last night? How many they captured?'

'Two nights ago, Nadia. You're losing track of time.

Control yourself. There must be no more adventures, you understand.'

'But I too, I am fighting. For the same cause. Women can be brave too, Boris.'

'Yes, brave. But you also have a duty to survive.'

'Boris, don't you remember how you used to feel about such ideas? Women at home, men going out to protect them? We both used to laugh at that. I loved you because you understood –'

Boris interrupted her. 'That's not the point, Nadia. Not now. You must stay wherever you are hiding. Soon the town will be liberated. The Germans are weakening everywhere. We are building up our strength.'

'Boris, Boris,' Nadia said urgently, tugging at the lapel of his mountain peasant coat. It was now totally dark in their recessed shelter. She couldn't see his features at all. 'Do you think of me when you are away in the hills? Do you think of us here? Do you still love me?'

'Of course. Of course. But we are at war, Nadia. At war.'

'But in war it is *more* important to love. How else can we be sure –'

'Are you still hungry? Is there soup still in the flask?'

'Yes. But it's for you.'

Boris raised the flask to his lips and drank, then wiped his mouth with his sleeve. 'This man,' he said, as if reluctant to come back to the subject, yet compelled to, 'this man who came to the shed where you and Nina Petrovna . . . describe him.'

'I hardly saw him – he was so wrapped up against the cold. Small, dark-skinned. He had a Balkar accent.'

'How did he find you? You said he knew you already?'

'I daren't go back to that room he sent me to. A blind woman is there. He paid her. Something about her – him too – the zebra!'

'What?'

'I call him – the zebra.'

Boris gave a harsh laugh. 'If you'd only got out of Pyatigorsk when I told you.'

Nadia then tried to explain what had really happened there in Pyatigorsk, but she couldn't. Sobs welled up from her chest and drowned the words before they could form in her throat. She felt a deep tenderness for Boris. She put a hand on his arm. 'Boris, please, just tell me before we leave each other, will you be returning to the mountains? Will I see you again – soon? Will you bring me news of Dasha and mother if we can find a way?'

'Yes, yes. Of course.'

He shook himself, as if coming out of a trance.

'But you must go, Nadia. Quickly.'

'Yes.' She reached up for his face. 'Kiss me, Boris. Kiss me before I go. Please. It is important.'

He seemed not to hear her. 'It will be curfew any second.'

When she looked up, Boris had gone.

*

Her last hope of protection had gone.

Despair, a miserable sense of being unfairly condemned to unknown dangers, assaulted Nadia's mind just as the gang-rapists had her body. She felt this new assault physically too. The numbness of her hours in the shed and later in the hateful room was wearing off. Pains in her stomach and the side of her head surged with each memory of the lonely misery forced on her.

Nadia longed to believe in a God against whom she could blaspheme, whom she could blame for her wretchedness.

Even the blind woman would have been a comfort. But when Nadia finally reached the house, no-one was inside. She slumped onto the floor, as if concussed.

But her dreams continued feverishly to try and unravel the confusions her waking mind left unresolved. Images of Pyatigorsk and the ward flickered like a silent movie with a hectic motion. People – unknown people – began to fall apart. Limbs and small parts of their bodies, noses and fingers, loosened and slid off, as if they had been inadequately stuck on with diluted glue. Somewhere, up in a kind of gallery, a huddle of children in Pioneer uniforms and scarves watched with appalled fascination. Nadia was with them, supposed to be giving a class on what was going on in the ward below. It was her job, but she couldn't do it, didn't know how to interpret these horrific events. The boys laughed and played the fool. The girls got bored and began plaiting each others' hair in a circle, like elephants holding each others' tails in a circus ring. Nadia screamed to them to pay attention, but they wouldn't. They started mocking her. Clusters of red-lipped mouths framed in pink cheeks and curls sang ribald pseudo-patriotic songs. A man in Red Army uniform burst in, shouting that the noise they were making endangered national security. He opened fire with a submachine gun cradled in his arms like a sleeping child. Nadia fell whimpering to the floor, trying, struggling, to remember if Dasha had been in the class, or was she home sick, she couldn't . . . she had to remember, but she couldn't . . .

Shivering like a malaria victim, Nadia fought to wake herself. Again and again dreams dragged her back into their nets of sleep, refusing to let her escape till she knew the answers. Finally another image, another riddle, began superimposing itself. She was waiting for someone. Someone was coming. She and that someone had a rendezvous together. But the person coming wasn't the person she was expecting. Who was she expecting? Whoever it was, the wrong person was coming. The meat-canning factory – she should be there already, hours ago. But her limbs were like lead. What was she doing on the floor like this, fixed to the floor as if by a great weight, when she was meant to be *there*? Of course it was Boris. Boris was coming – unexpectedly. But now she knew, of course, yes, she was expecting him, her husband. But Boris had no idea where she was, never thought of her anymore, had left her. His love for her had turned into hatred of the Germans. Why was he here then?

It was cold, terribly cold.

A shiver shook her body.

Yes, he was here, watching her. A man was watching her. The zebra! Oh, God, the zebra. She tried to open her eyes, but realized they were already open.

Was that the zebra?

Like a dying person's last surge of life and energy, the confusion of her dreaming self made one final assault on her mind. Only this time she was one of those painted children, laughing.

The dream was momentary, then died.

'Nadia,' the man standing there said. 'No, don't move. Everything I feared for you – for us – has happened. Just please, consider, if I cannot help you. I am ready to do anything you wish, my darling, anything you ask me.'

Nadia sat up. She rubbed her eyes, her face, her hair with her cold hands. Leaning forward, she pulled up her knees as a platform for her forehead.

She said nothing. But at last she was thinking clearly. The nightmares were over. She was awake now, fully.

Yet reality was even more ludicrous.

'Sit down, Colonel.' Her words were slow, slurred, her voice barely under control, only usable at all because she was trying to say something everyday, neutral.

Her head still on her knees, she smiled. She was thinking, I smell. I stink. Perhaps my Colonel will let me wash. He did before.

'I'm afraid for you,' he said at last. 'The Gestapo are on your track.'

Nadia said, 'Are you – alone?'

'Yes. No-one saw me come. The jeep is two blocks away. This whole area has been evacuated.'

'Evactuated?'

'The structures are unsafe.'

Brandt knelt down beside her and took her hand. 'Who was the man who guided you to this place?' he asked.

'I can't –'

'You must tell me. You have to trust me. And to prove it, I'll ask you a question. Was this man thin and dark-skinned? Did he have teeth which – in the front –'

'The zebra!' she gasped. 'You know this man? He told me –'

'Listen, Nadia. Nothing I did revealed to the Gestapo that you are here. It was the man who brought you here. He told them and that's how I found out. Nothing is known that connects me with you. I haven't broken my promise to you.'

'But he – the zebra – knows that you and I, that we –'

'He knows now.'

'What shall I do?'

'Nadia, I'll tell you what I think you should do, and then

you can tell me what you want. It's you who must choose. I can offer you safety. But I can't and won't force you to accept it. I have arranged to be away from my regiment on a special mission. There's a cottage near the edge of Pyatigorsk. I found it. No-one knows about it but me. If you will take the risk of coming there with me, I think we will be safe.'

'But –'

He interrupted her and rushed on. 'The invasion of the Caucasus is doomed. There can be no German victory now, thank God. I'm convinced of it. I have believed for a long time now that our whole strategy is wrong, criminal. I have learned a great deal from the Soviet resistance in the mountains. I feel the German retreat will come soon, and I can't fight again in the German army until it has turned back. Now that Stalingrad . . . we are trapped there, and the southern flank will be enclosed – but . . . Nadia, I've been a loyal soldier all my life. But you – you and your people – have shown me that there are more important things. It took me a long time to learn that, wouldn't you say?' He smiled at her, a smile full of pain and tenderness.

'You don't have a gun,' she said suddenly. She felt light-headed. What was happening to her? Everything was changing, changing too fast for her to understand.

'No,' he agreed. 'I don't have a gun.'

'If we'd succeeded, captured the guns – perhaps I would have shot you. Did you think of that?'

'You'll have the chance again.'

'Do you know what happened? What we tried to do?'

'You are in great danger, that's the only thing I know for certain now. We must hurry.' Firmly, as if trying to transmit his own strength to her, he said, 'Come. Come.'

'You must join the Soviet resistance,' she said, her voice shaking.

He lifted her in a single movement and took her in his arms.

'They mustn't know,' she whispered, tucking her face into his shoulder, clenching her eyes shut. 'My family. They mustn't know.'

*

Not a soul saw them leave. Not a soul but the one small, swarthy man who had seen the Colonel enter. The messenger.

Yusef Tsagov smiled, exposing his teeth striped with yellow and tarnished silver, like a flag the devil had designed. But not to Brandt, not to Nadia. Tsagov kept himself and his smile well hidden.

He watched the jeep drive off. It puzzled him that it continued out in a westerly direction. Except, he thought, without lights a U-turn could be dangerous. He shrugged and walked off, well satisfied, curious to see how his intrigue would develop.

SEVENTEEN

Nadia slept, warm at last.

Despite potholes and frequent security checks – which Brandt, in full-dress uniform with papers and passes in equally immaculate order, had no trouble getting through – the journey went smoothly.

Less than two hours after leaving Nalchik the jeep, its four-wheel drive engaged, began to crawl up a steep hillside. Beneath a thin wind-blown dusting of snow was a track of worn limestone rocks twisting between parallel lines of black hawthorn bushes. Night had fallen, but a narrow moon untroubled by clouds let Brandt negotiate the half-hidden track without lights.

Of course he had done it before.

One night in September. Just in case.

The place Brandt had chosen – in case – lay in an isolated fold on the lower slopes of Mount Mashuk. He first saw it during a visit to the grave where the poet Lermontov was buried immediately after his fatal duel. He had walked on up the hill through the neglected paths between the gravestones and the rough metal and wooden crosses with their extra, tilted arm in the Orthodox style, until at the top edge of this wild sweet-scented burial ground the upward slope, unexpectedly, had fallen away to a secretive hollow, itself buried in a natural grave of thick trees and shrubs. At the far end of this hidden valley was a roof, more exactly the tip of a roof whose broken tiles and bare wood beams and battens hinted at years of abandoned isolation.

He had pressed on, feeling more and more like one of those child characters in his earliest fairy tales, until he had found the cottage. As he imagined, it had not been lived in for a long time. Perhaps it had been the property of some dispossessed kulak, or of one of the millions who, since the Great War and the Revolution and the Civil War, had simply never returned.

He knew at once it was ideal.

And now, outside this same whitewashed cottage, its square outline blocked faintly against a black background of the steeply-sloping wooded Mount Mashuk, Brandt cut the engine. She had come. He slumped for a second over the wheel as the hot motor sputtered into silence and a vast cold stillness swallowed them up, wrapping them in the camouflage of night.

Brandt heaved his legs out, stretched, breathed in deeply. He walked round to the back of the jeep and lifted several layers of fur – a white fox-fur coat, two heavy skins of mountain goat, a calfskin, six or seven pelts of rabbit, miscellaneous more-or-less ragged garments that once protected the warm-blooded bodies of unnameable beasts. The Colonel's 'collection'. He smiled. Inside, like a hibernating dormouse, Nadia, curled and seemingly content, slept on soundly.

'Come on.'

He leaned in and lifted her clear like a child who had gone to sleep in the wrong bed and had to be transferred. Just like such a child, her arms encircled his neck and her head lolled sideways onto his shoulder. From her half-open lips came a peaceful sound, part sighing, part snoring.

Furs and all, he carried her to the door, holding in his free hand a heavy iron key. Bending awkwardly so Nadia almost slipped from him, annoyed with himself that he hadn't thought to do this job first, he twisted the creaking key, and pushed the door open. Then, because two months before he had gone through the same action in rehearsal, he walked confidently into the right-hand of the two rooms and laid his living bundle on the huge divan bed he knew to be inside.

He left her there. Still using the light from the crescent moon that was just beginning to dim behind swirls of high cloud, he unloaded the jeep. He brought in boxes of army rations, candles and matches, clothes, cooking pans, jerry-cans, two huge blocks of army-issue soap, his shaving kit, old newspapers, a kilogram of tea screwed up in a double page of *Kabardinian Truth*, a wooden case of Georgian champagne, several bottles of vodka, blankets, a shovel, tarpaulins and groundsheets; finally two MP 40 submachine guns with folding stocks and ten magazines each containing thirty-two 9-mm rounds. Enough, he had calculated in the jeep somewhere between Baksan and the bridge over the Malka River, enough to fire a total of 38.4 seconds of rapid fire.

But a single shot – or two – would be enough – in an emergency.

He put the jeep in the lean-to shed where in September he had found the badly-hidden key, and whose brushwood roof was now solid with frozen snow. Finally he came inside the cottage, dug out some bread and sausage and began to chew.

Through all this Nadia slept.

Brandt himself went to sleep in the left-hand room, the 'busy' room – kitchen, eating place and focus of warmth that would come. Meanwhile it was cold and damp. Still in his uniform, Brandt lay on and under such blankets, clothes and furs as Nadia had no need of.

Soon after dawn he woke. After checking Nadia was safe – still, dormouse-like, wrapped in fur – he stood outside the cottage door. As if in welcome, the sun began to throw pink and orange rays on the hillside above. The cottage was still deep in shadow. Only the late afternoon and evening sun would penetrate here. But the spectacle of brilliant sunlit snow thrilled him, filling him with a new optimism. He was reminded of that time on the roof of the sanitarium, when together they had watched the dawn sun steal over the twin peaks of 'shy Elbrus'.

Suddenly a verse of Heine came into his mind – *'Wo wird einst des Wandermüden/Letzte Ruhestätte sein? Unter Palmen in dem Süden? Unter Linden an den Rhein?'* Yes, he thought, when I am tired of wandering, where *will* my last resting-place be? Under palm-trees in the south? Under lime-trees on the Rhine? Or here, beneath the canopy of oaks and firs in the foothills of the Caucasus? But no. I came here, not to die, but to love.

If so – his practical mind took over – the precautions must be absolute. Though the cottage was isolated, hidden in a hollow, difficult of access — chosen for these very reasons — the danger of discovery was obvious.

Only at this moment did he realize he was still wearing uniform.

Turning, he ran back inside.

Here — before even he made up a fire — he stripped off every single item of clothing that bound him to the German army, his shirt and underwear too, until he stood naked in the freezing room.

He didn't feel the cold. The ecstasy of this new freedom was enough to warm him.

Still naked, in a dream-like state though concentrating carefully on what he was doing, he tore up several editions of the local *Pravda*, crumpled them, stuffed them into the simple open fireplace, laid on top of them a pattern of small twigs, then small logs from the pile in the corner of the room, and set a match to the fire. Squatting in front of it, he blew encouragement, prodding the black-edged paper with the longest of the sticks. Gradually, despite hissing protests from the residue of the sodden ashes left by the previous owners, flames began to flicker and shoot. A small warmth crept tentatively out of the fire like yeasty fragrance from a bread oven. Feeling it, Brandt held out his hands, rubbed them, and gave a soft contented chuckle.

Suddenly a loud laugh behind him made him fall back. His buttocks thumped on the ice-cold earth floor. The laugh became a shriek. He turned and saw Nadia, bent double, shaking like a leaf in a squall. Slowly, weak from the gusting paroxysm of laughter, she slid to the floor herself, clutching around her the skin of fox-fur in which she'd slept. Kneeling, he turned to face her. She put an arm over her eyes, and the laughter bubbled over again. Catching the infection, Brandt too began to laugh. At the same time the immense cold hit him like an avalanche. Scrabbling on his hands and knees, he pulled to him the nearest blanket and wrapped his nakedness in it like a shawl. Close now to Nadia, he put out a hand and touched her face, wet with the tears of her laughter.

Suddenly she pointed behind him.

'Quick! Look! The fire — it's going out.'

'Damn!'

He kissed her – a light kiss that flicked out as quick as a chameleon's tongue – then rushed to rescue the guttering flame.

*

It was on the second morning that Nadia caught sight of Brandt's uniform, folded and tucked away on the floor beneath a rickety cupboard – the only piece of kitchen furniture, just as the divan bed was the only furniture in the other room.

'Please,' she said, 'Colonel, please burn it. Here, let me.'

He held her arm. 'No. Wait. Wait until . . .'

'Until?'

He looked at her. She returned his gaze.

'Until you stop calling me Colonel,' he said.

'But I shall call you Colonel. *Polkovnik* – it suits you.'

'Then I shall keep the uniform.'

'You would keep it whatever I called you.'

He looked away, into the fire. 'Yes,' he said. 'I would have to keep it.'

'In case.'

'In case.'

'And if someone comes here, finds it?'

'If someone comes here looking, they will find it. They will find the jeep. They'll know soon enough I'm no Russian.' He stopped, started to say something, stopped again. Then said, 'Nadia, thanks to this uniform we arrived here safely. It can be used again.'

'If you change your mind.'

'If you change your mind also.'

'I hate that – that bundle here.'

'I know. Come here. Kiss me.'

But Nadia, for the first time, turned away. She regretted the action immediately. It was childish. Until now, nothing had spoiled the passionate oneness they had created. Naked – in a heap of blankets and furs. She stopped, smiled, then turned back again to show him the smile. 'Here,' she said. 'I kiss you, Colonel. I am sorry.'

'I love you.'

They slid back into the furs, made love. Their love-making blended into their whole being together; the sprinting of their heartbeats, the climbing up to the strong pulse of their love ... and the falling back into a happiness like the slow movement of a symphony endlessly replayed.

And slowly they discovered more about each other.

Brandt was constructing a bath-tub from a dilapidated rain-barrel, reinforcing it by every kind of cracked plank and beam, then carefully laying in it first a huge gray tarpaulin, then a smaller green groundsheet. Nadia said delightedly, 'I never knew you would turn out to be such a Robinson Crusoe.'

Brandt laughed. 'I was a resourceful only child. I made my own tree-houses and mountain shelters. I tried to worry my father by spending nights on end in the Black Forest or in the mountains, making sure he'd seen me set off with just a pack of food on my back. He never turned a hair. Look, it's ready.'

They boiled up whole drifts of snow, filling every container they could find that would bear being heated at the roaring fire, and tipped the water lavishly into the brand-new tub.

'Just the tiniest trickle,' Nadia said, pointing at a thin wriggling worm of water that escaped onto the earth floor over the groundsheet where it was badly secured.

Brandt jammed the sheet in tight. The slightest imperfection would have spoiled it all.

There was just room for the two of them to sit down, so long as their legs, tangling together, took up the minimum space. Neither cared now about the water splashing over onto the floor. Clutching pieces of soap, they began washing each other, peering closely as layers of grime came off.

'To think I'd been taking this body of yours on trust all along,' he said with a laugh.

'And you, Colonel, you remind me of the first boy I ever saw naked. Don't look so shocked. I was twelve and he was thirteen. We went swimming together in the Nalchik River. Just the two of us. Oh, it was cold! It must have been October. He was fair-skinned like you. He came from the Baltic somewhere. Perhaps it was Leningrad. I even forget his name. He was so beautiful! I shall never forget that. So slim and strong.' She laughed. 'I remember I told him an old Caucasian story about two lovers who ran away from their parents. Let me tell it to you now. He was the adopted son of a prince and she the daughter of ordinary people. But beautiful of course. Their parents came after them, chasing them and chasing them, until the two children were trapped. They agreed to throw themselves over the cliff. "You go first," he said. "I will spare you the sight of my mutilated corpse." She kissed him one last time and jumped. Then he looked over and thought, "Well, we can't get married now. What a waste of life if I throw myself over too." And he went back to his father! It happened near Kislovodsk, quite near here. You can visit the cliff. Shocking, isn't it?' She laughed again. 'He was so different, my friend. Different from me, I mean. You cannot imagine what it is like to live in one small town all your life, with no hope of ever going away, no real hope. He came from another world, that boy. Like you.'

'Another world,' Brandt said softly, soaping her shoulders slowly, massaging them gently, round and round. 'You are my other world. You know, I don't think I have ever had a single happy *private* relationship before you, Nadia. There was no-one in my family. The army is the same. Except there I am respected. I have an excellent professional understanding with my colleagues . . . with most of them. We are, I believe, a little special, the mountain people.'

Nadia stood up, holding her breasts and looking down at her slim figure.

'I am a mountain woman,' she said proudly. 'Years ago, young Kabardinian girls strapped their chests in leather corsets. Did you know that?'

Brandt leaned forward and held her two buttocks in his hands, rubbing them gently. He kissed the suds on her dark triangle of hair and looked up, following the very faint line of hair which, like a downy arrow, pointed up to her breasts, to the nipples visible through the gaps in her fingers, and finally to her wild, mobile, laughing face, the skin the colour of the light hot earth of the steppe in summer.

'Why did you never marry, Colonel?' she said, looking down, vertically, into his blue-gray eyes.

'I was waiting for you.'

'Too easy. Too glib.'

'But true. I didn't know your name was Nadia. But it fits the woman I was waiting for. It fits very well.'

'What was wrong with your German girls?'

'Oh, there were good girls, made to be officers' wives, plenty of them. But . . . ,' and his expression turned serious for a moment, 'I knew I'd have been tied for ever to my caste, my career, just as you were tied to your town.'

She sat down again, slopping a wave of water over the side. 'Stand up.'

Brandt stood, and she kissed him, exciting him, until he bent and lifted her out of the water and held her dripping and slippery with soap and lowered her onto him. At last they subsided, exhausted, back into the foaming water and lay back, as far as they could stretch out, their arms dangling down the rough slats of the makeshift tub.

After a while Nadia said, 'Why do you part your hair so high on your head? I think you'd look more handsome . . .' She arranged his short fair hair with her fingers, watching his face all the time. 'So regular, all your features. Not like our men. Nose so straight. Colonel, now tell me honestly, do you or do you not pluck your eyebrows?'

*

When they made love that night, a memory penetrated, like a flash of physical pain, at the very strongest surge of Nadia's orgasm, then spread all over as her body relaxed. The memory was of a bench in a dusty street. She was there with Luda, and they were making a promise together. They promised to make no exceptions. To kill the enemy. To die as bravely as the women soldiers of the Red Army. They had sworn it together, solemnly.

'Nadia! Why the tear?'

She turned aside, unwilling to let him see how far she had been away from him. How close, even now, she felt – no, not to Boris – but to Luda, to her mother, above all to little Dasha. Soon, she knew, all too soon she would have to go back. There *was* a world outside. A world at war.

*

For eight days and nights, however, this world continued to find a way only rarely into their fortress, their oubliette. The idyll that from the start they were determined to create and live with retained its integrity. Like the surface skin of a placid lake, broken only by air bubbles or the snapping of lazy fish, and then reforming whole again, their happiness remained intact. But just as a lake stays calm only when left to itself, with no wind or cresting speedboat tearing its smooth skin, so was their peace fragile, contingent. The extremes of emotion and physical exhaustion that threw them together, that led them to escape into each other's love, were at last, inevitably, calmed and healed by the love itself. The numbness wore off. For the first time, after more than a week they began to hear the distant gunfire, to see the flashes, to feel the vibrations of aeroplanes throbbing overhead. The past, their entire past lives, at first so effectively blotted out, interrupted their unthinking happiness, reminded them more and more frequently of dilemmas and obligations.

Once Nadia had asked if they could listen on a radio to news of the war's progress.

'I didn't bring a radio,' he answered her. 'I didn't want to.'

That first mention of the means to keep in touch with the outside world was no accident.

Both Nadia and Brandt – unknown to each other, though both suspected – had begun to think their own separate thoughts about the future.

Brandt's chief concern was the plausible limit of his cover story. To the German authorities he was still an active soldier. No-one would be searching for him. Not yet. He was on a 'secret mission', engaged in high-mountain reconnaissance. Officially he was now climbing the high passes with a small team of VT's, the 'trusted' local people, investigating the feasibility of a high-altitude attack to coincide with more conventional advances across the Georgian Military Highway and down the Black Sea coast. An unorthodox mission, certainly. But that was his reputation. A daring, unconventional soldier. He could get away with it. Just. For a time. He had cleared it with his Commanding Officer. Von Kreuss would back him, however bizarre the report he might submit. And yes, of course, he *could* be pinned down by storms, captured even – before making a daring escape. So many possible stories. So many reports he could make on his return. It started almost as a tantalizing game. But now . . . ?

Nadia had no comparable obsession. Hers was a more general confusion that seeped into her mind like poison gas – now, more and more, after their lovemaking.

One gray morning – the day was December 18, the Muslim feast of Kurman when, fifty miles away in Nalchik, amid elaborate ceremonies, tribesmen presented the local 'government' with the gift of a white horse to pass on to the Führer – Brandt went out for the first time to 'check on the jeep'. In the lean-to he found it damp from the snow dripping through the roughly-piled brushwood on the roof, but otherwise well-screened, well-insulated. For a moment he stood and looked at it, at its familiar scratched and dented frame, the shiny leather seats up front, the mountain-goat emblem painted white on each side of the hood.

The keys were in the ignition. Abruptly he climbed in, pulled the choke lever out, stamped four or five times, viciously, on the gas pedal – and made contact. Amazingly, the very first time, the motor roared into life like a dog sleeping on the hearth suddenly offered the chance of a day's rough shooting. Taken aback by the sudden growl, he fumbled for the key, reversed it, and the motor died away.

When he went back into the cottage, Nadia looked at him with a mixture of sadness and anger.

'That made a dreadful noise,' she said.

She meant: *Why?*

'You know why,' he said. His voice curt, soldier-like. He turned, walked to the next room and threw himself on the bed.

Nadia, busy warming bread that she had just softened with melted snow, turned back toward the fire.

That evening, in their bed of furs, she said, 'Colonel, there're only two bottles of champagne left.' She tried to smile.

For the first time they talked openly about the war.

They talked tensely, intently.

There was no lovemaking all the long while they talked, lying side by side, touching at the shoulders and the hips and the feet, as if these points, not their mouths, were the channels of their words and thoughts.

Brest, Kiev, the Crimea, Rostov, Krasnodar – the tortuous, often precipitous, journey to the Caucasus – Brandt recounted his seventeen months of combat. He gave an impersonal account, however, not daring to try and explain the extent to which he had accepted emotionally the duties of a soldier, giving no hint of the delirium he felt in the chase across the Kuban. Nadia mixed her own story with his. She spoke about Boris – breaking what had been a tacit compact to avoid mention of him – telling Brandt how she had cared at first for her wounded husband, in the summer of 1941, and later nursed her sick father, all the time watching and waiting, dreading the inevitable arrival of that bestial horde.

'The hunter running down its prey – and yet, now –'

'The wolf also shall dwell with the lamb,' he said. 'From the Bible. Is that us?'

'The lamb,' she replied with a sigh, 'would have to be insane. Best arm itself and shoot the wolf.'

'But if the wolf weren't really a wolf but a sheep in wolf's clothing?'

'Then all our fairy tales would have to be rewritten. Human history would have to be rewritten.'

'Look how small my teeth are!'

'But sharp,' she said. Twisting, as quick as an eel, she bit him on the top of his shoulder. Blood welled up into the marks. He lay there, immobile, as if he had felt nothing.

Nadia fell heavily back against the pile of furs.

'I'm sorry.'

'No,' he said gently. 'I am to blame. *Polkovnik!* Thank God you don't call me Herr Oberst!'

*

Nadia made several attempts to 'spy' on her lover. But they were half-hearted, and immediately deflected by Brandt.

The sparring emphasized a mutual acceptance that change was coming. The periods of silence grew longer. Their bodies grew used to each other.

The only piece of hard, useful information she got from him came unexpectedly. He was telling her how he first entered 'her town'.

'I was thinking of you, my darling, all the time. Nothing but you. Where did you live? Were you safe? How could I make sure nothing happened to you? Where, when, how could I see you again? I searched for records. There were none.'

'I spent four days like the biggest coward possible,' she said, wriggling deeper into the furs, 'perfectly safe with my family. We were in a cellar under our house. All the houses have them. I thought of you too.'

He turned to kiss her. 'Oh?'

'Yes. But with shame. Shame for myself, I mean. I told no-one.'

'Shame! Yet so many – unlike you – had real cause for shame.' Brandt spoke angrily, staring up at the ceiling, his hands behind his head. 'The very first citizen of Nalchik I encountered was an NKVD Captain. You know how he greeted me? "*Willkommen auf Nalchik!*" 'I remember so vividly the way he introduced himself, like an hotel manager, you know –' Brandt laughed. 'How could you know about hotel managers? I mean someone over-anxious to please. "Captain Bekirbi, at your service." And he – *Nadia*! You've gone white.'

Nadia turned away and laughed uneasily. 'It was your imitation.'

The mention of Bekirbi made Nadia impatient to return. She wanted suddenly and urgently to end this escape, this standing outside the danger and the common struggle. She wanted to go, in order to keep the memory of this time spent with her Colonel alive and happy.

'Perhaps,' she said to him hopefully, 'the Red Army is already near us.'

'No, Nadia,' he replied. 'When the German retreat comes – and that, I'm sure, is several weeks away – the noise and the destruction will be fifty times worse than the advance. Even here we would not escape it.' He sighed deeply. 'Nadia, darling, listen to me. We must not be fools – not more than we have been. We must not throw our lives away. We are not innocent children.'

She took his face in her hands. Urgently, almost violently. 'But you cannot go back and kill! You cannot. You have promised me. You know I would never have come with you if . . . if . . . Yes, I love you. You are mine. But you cannot, you must not, kill my people again. You cannot kill my husband! You must kill me first if that is your plan.'

Her fingers gripped the soft flesh of his cheeks.

'*No killing.*' The words were forced from her throat in a barely suppressed scream.

'Nadia, you must trust me.'

She turned away from him angrily.

'It is easier to love,' she said, 'than to trust.'

Brandt sighed. 'I don't see how –'

'I'm frightened. You know that. Of course I am scared. What will happen when they – when Boris and my family find out about us? They will never let me see my daughter again. Perhaps he will kill me. Perhaps that would be the best thing. What have I done? I too had such a . . . such an ordered life.'

Brandt held her tight in his arms.

*

They left as dusk fell. This time, physically refreshed and conscious, Nadia found the journey in the back of the jeep excruciating – long, painful, airless. But it was not merely the discomfort that made the two hours such a hell. It was what Brandt told her just before they left the cottage. About Ilya.

Ilya was dead! The Gestapo had killed her brother. He said they had shot him – but did the Colonel really know how Ilya had died?

At each checkpoint it was harder and harder to suppress her urge to grab one of the submachine guns in back with her and kill as many Germans as she could, much harder even than suppressing her sobs.

Why hadn't he told her before? Yes, she knew why. She understood even. Yet she should have been told. What for? To give herself this torture, to feel this horror, for longer? No, he was right. But also wrong. That was their tragedy. How could their love be anything but wrong, deeply wrong?

Yet it exists, she said to herself, over and over, our love exists.

All Nadia wanted was to sleep, but instead she was sucked down and down into a whirlpool of hopelessness.

The jeep stopped just out of view of her family house, near Kabardinskaya Street. This was the great concession he had made to her. Wrapped in fur from head to toe, without saying a word to her Colonel, she pulled herself stiffly to the ground, walked across a dark patch of snow-encrusted waste land and pulled open the iron gate into the courtyard. It clanged shut behind her.

She had an hour. Just an hour, precisely. The concession had been granted reluctantly, on that rigorous condition.

Dasha, sleepy, hardly realized her mother had been away so long, but smiled and rubbed her eyes and began telling her about how she'd seen a tank run over somebody's foot and then . . . until Nadia had to kiss her quiet and beg for time to talk to Mariana.

Nadia noticed at once how her mother had aged. She seemed old, old; suddenly a grandmother not just to Dasha but to Nadia herself. Mariana cried soundlessly on Nadia's shoulder, murmuring the name of her son. In the corner Old Rags turned away and sighed. His eyes too were filled with tears.

And then – for Nadia it was not too soon, so little did she have to offer of comfort, so little of her life and thoughts could she share – the hour passed. The jeep was there.

Hidden again, she was taken quickly the short distance, less than half a mile, to Brandt's billet.

'Welcome back, Herr Oberst,' Hans Guggenbühl said, greeting his master on the verandah with a shake of his fat rump as his heels clicked together. 'Mission accomplished?'

'Certainly, Hans. When I've taken in this roll of fur, unload the rest. Then I want a word with you.'

Hans began removing – the creases on his brow growing deeper and deeper – more and more unusual bundles from the back of the jeep. He made no comment.

But if I ever see that little weasel with the stripey teeth hanging round here again, trying it on, he muttered to himself, I'll exterminate the vermin.

EIGHTEEN

Wipe out the Fascist Barbarians!

The words on the poster – splashed in red below a crude black-and-white caricature of a pop-eyed, bullet-headed mob forming a swastika – were wrinkled against the rough stone wall of the hut. The flour and water paste was hard to keep sticky in the intense cold. Boris Surkov stepped back and admired his handiwork like a painter hanging a picture at his first one-man exhibition.

It was December 24, 1942, at the edge of the village of Bagubent. Liberated now, like Kashka Tau. The Fritzes were back in their hedgehog, the city of Nalchik. And even then, Boris said to himself, what good will it do them? Besides, I can get in and out of Nalchik as I please.

This was the last poster he had to hang up. The propaganda campaign was going well. What effect it was having, no-one knew. But the quota of posters and leaflets had been overfulfilled by a hundred and fifty percent.

'Hey you!' he yelled at the kid working with him – valuable on-the-job training, Boris called it, for the ten-year-old village boy. 'Take the brush and bucket back to headquarters. Tell Comrade Kochan I'll be there at ten hundred hours for briefing. Move!'

Boris squeezed out a plug of *makhorka*, the sickly tobacco he had found in the dead Killa's haversack. He rolled it clumsily in a piece of newspaper and struck a match on the sole of his boot. He inhaled – a new habit and he didn't like it. But it was better now, it didn't rasp his throat like it used to. He coughed. It hardly hurt.

How about 'Captain' Surkov? That sounded better. He wrapped his cloak around him, hugging the thought.

Boris had only heard the name of the master plan the day before. 'Saturn' was the name the *Stavka* gave it. Plan Saturn. The Fritzes would be rounded up like cattle. The Red Army would make an heroic dash toward Rostov and cut them off there. Every last one of the mother-rapers would die. Maybe a few would be taken prisoner – but not by him!

'This is *history*,' he said aloud, but to no-one; the kid had gone. 'History *I* am going to write.' He laughed catching himself at his own thoughts. Well – victory was sweet.

He was about to set off back to camp when an old peasant called out to him. Boris, who knew the man by sight, went over to where he stood, beside a bombed-out barn.

'Yes?'

'A message for you, Comrade.'

'Who from?'

The partisan shrugged, wiped a drop off the end of his nose. 'I reckon I got it maybe third hand.' He handed Boris a dirty brown envelope.

*

All along Kabardinskaya Street surged the soft lush sound of *Stille Nacht*. A thin tenor; a slow, rolling, deep chorus. *'Alles schläft, einsam wacht.'* The peaceful song of Christmas Eve drifted down with the snowflakes – new snow that was spreading out over the old crust like a clean white tablecloth, as if preparing the earth for Christmas dinner. A group of soldiers – mountain soldiers, Bavarians for the most part – carolled in the light of a torch. Passing civilians stopped to stare, fascinated, despite the slow alien rhythm and the alien wash of words, by the sweetness of the music.

Nadia heard it too as she slipped through the anonymous crowd.

Again he had tried to stop her going, her Colonel. But Nadia had not returned to Nalchik to be permanently immured, away from her family. Whatever they had both hoped, the town was still occupied, the retreat seemed no closer.

'I shall go tonight, your Christmas Eve you've been telling me so much about, that'll be safer for me,' she had told him.

'Tomorrow morning I'll come back. I'll dress up in the old widow's clothes.'

Brandt had begged her to stay with him over Christmas. Hans was preparing special meals – goose, chestnut stuffing, *Pfeffernüsse*, noodles, wines from Germany. But Nadia had to choose. 'You are not my prisoner,' he told her.

When she left he had kissed her lightly, asking her, yet again, to be 'careful'. She had kissed him back, saying carelessly, 'of course'.

As soon as Nadia arrived home, her disguise – far more than her mere arrival – turned misery into loud tearful laughter. Dasha began playing like a kitten with the tassels of the ancient shawl. Mariana tested the cane, making fun of her deepest despair, her sudden descent into old age. Old Rags roused himself and wheezingly reminisced of the times he had seen Ukrainian ladies dressed in such magnificent finery.

Nadia had also brought a cake – she said nothing of where it or the clothes came from – and they devoured it on the spot, yelping their delight.

Which was how Boris found them.

They didn't notice him at first, in the doorway.

Then they saw him – open-mouthed, his whole body shaking. He was dressed in ragged clothes, the uniform of rejected soldiers – the sick and parasites. And spies. In one hand, he held a crumpled piece of paper. With the other he pointed at Nadia.

Absolute silence clamped down on them all like a steel vice. Silence but for the distant strains of *Stille Nacht* drifting in through the door along with the freezing night air.

He started to say something. No words came out.

Nadia, thin and startlingly beautiful in an oversized shift of threadbare maroon velvet, as if she were the star of some amateur theatrical gala, quivering, remained by Dasha's side, her arm hooked tensely around her child.

Mariana spoke first. 'Boris, how . . . wonderful. Nadia, Nadia just . . . come along in to the warm. Nadia, darling, is a crumb of the cake left? Yes, look. No, Dasha, leave that for your father. Come in, Boris, come, come.'

'Where did you get it?' Boris asked in a hoarse voice,

coming inside at last and closing the door, locking it with ostentatious care. He coughed. 'Is there something to celebrate?' He advanced further in. 'Christmas? Like the Fritzes?'

Nadia – recovering – reddened. 'Boris, what . . . what are you doing here?'

'Why isn't the child asleep?'

'Because Dasha's with me! Boris, what is the matter?' She took a step in his direction – stopped. Then her mouth opened and she felt the words pour out. 'You are surprised to see me. I know. I am surprised to see you. Boris, after the terrible thing that happened – that night, of course after then, ever since, I've been hiding, but I had to . . . I had to come and see Dasha, to see mother, when I could. I had to risk that. My mother, my child, I had to know they are alive. They had to know that I am alive. You remember, after father died, how long I was away. And now Ilya. Did you hear, Boris, did you hear what they did to Ilya?'

Tears began to come, first Nadia, then Mariana – because in the first excitement of Nadia's coming, in their delirium, they had not yet spoken of Ilya – and finally Dasha burst into tears, clinging to her grandmother and howling loudest of all.

Boris – whose face had suddenly gone white – stood opposite Nadia, with the kitchen table between them, while she told him the little she knew – the little that was known by Brandt and passed on to her.

At the end Boris looked down at the floor. His fingers played nervously with the piece of paper he had been holding in his hand.

'I must talk with you, Nadia.'

'Mother, take Darya to bed,' Nadia said gently. 'Go with her. Old Rags, please, go too for a moment. I have to speak with Boris.' Her voice was still shaking.

As soon as the others had gone, she plunged on, dreading to hear whatever it was that Boris had to tell her, 'Boris, when will it be over? When will the Germans go?'

Boris didn't answer her but said with what seemed to Nadia an inquisitor's suspiciousness, 'Where have you been? Not here?'

'Why? What do you mean?'

'No-one has seen you. Did you return to the safe house as I told you?'

His anger gave her a kind of courage.

'Of course no-one has seen me. If they had, the Gestapo would have seen me too.'

Boris seized Nadia's hand and stared at her with the look of a madman. 'Ilya!' he said, so urgently it was obvious he had tried to dismiss the question from his mind but couldn't. 'Do you *know*, Nadia, is it true what you just told me, that they took him in Kashka Tau? Is it sure?'

'Let me go, you're hurting me.'

'You are sure it was Kashka Tau?'

'Yes,' she whispered. 'It was in Kashka Tau.'

She looked at him in fear that he would ask her how she knew, but that query seemed far from his mind. He was shuddering.

'What's that?' Nadia cried suddenly.

Outside, the faint sound of a carol – no longer *Stille Nacht*, but the livelier sound of *O Du Fröhliche* – was cut dead by a single shot.

*

Boris had even less time than he suspected.

For that single shot was aimed. It killed a man.

Outside, the action had begun the moment Boris was seen jumping over the back fence alongside the tiny house that once belonged to Hassan Pachev. Two Gestapo agents on night-watch duty, a Balkar and a Cossack, were finally rewarded for their patience. First had come an old woman, whom they ignored. Then the prize. Lieutenant Boris Surkov.

A message radio'd to headquarters reached Major Stegl. The order was given. A simple code word. The details of the operation had been planned in advance.

Two armoured troop carriers with twelve armed men sped down Kabardinskaya Street, past the carol-singers, halting in the gloomy shadow of the cinema. The commanding officer met the two agents in place, consulted briefly. Men fanned out, took up positions.

But no operation goes smoothly. Not even the snapping shut of a carefully prepared Gestapo trap.

This time an old neighbour of the Dobroliubovs was responsible.

From his window on the opposite side of the street, through the chinks in the warped shutters, he saw both figures. The woman going through the front gate was a mystery. But the old man recognized young Surkov's tall, hunched figure coming over the fence, even though he had the briefest of glimpses. He was glad to see the boy had come back again. A fighter, a young fellow doing his duty. If I were younger, the old man thought to himself . . . and was still mulling over the ways he would kill the hated Fritzes if it weren't for his arthritis, when he saw the first troop carrier arrive. It stopped out of his view. But he knew. He could guess all right.

He was moving by the time the second carrier sped by.

Ignoring the pains in his legs and back, he slung on a goatskin cloak, jammed his round fur hat down over his ears, then hobbled across the twenty yards of lumpy street between the two buildings. His boots left irregular patterns in the new snow like the footprints of a wounded bear. His bent hand grasped the handle of the iron gate.

The bullet hit him that second, without warning.

The old man's last split-second thought was to curse his filthy painful disease. Christ! What a twinge! A stronger oath had half-formed in his brain . . . when it blanked out. His body slid backward slowly, slowly, picked up momentum, fell into the snow, lay still. There was no bloodstain. The gristly leather of his cloak closed over the hole, made neatly by a single shot from a Mauser rifle.

The next moment a green light flared over the low roofs, like the magnesium flash heralding the pouncing entrance of a pantomime demon.

Steel-shod boots clattered on the street. The gate was kicked open with a clang of hobnails on iron.

Glass splintered in a window of the empty cottage next door. A man with stormtrooper's helmet and a submachine gun took up firing position inside.

Already, as soon as the flare lit up the night, Boris and

Nadia had reacted like foresters when suddenly a huge tree swivels and begins to fall toward them.

Snatching at a small pistol awkwardly wedged in his waistband, Boris, with his other hand, wrenched open the door. Nadia, pulling on her old woman's cloak, seizing the cane, yelled at him to come the other way, to the back of the house. Boris ignored her cry. He ran out onto the porch. Splinters of stone and plaster from a volley of rifle shots made blood spurt from his face. Partially blinded, he jumped the two steps out into the yard. The two Germans coming at him were knocked backward. One – helmet spinning off – slammed his bare head against a protruding gutter with a noise like a dropped garbage can. The other fell on his rifle, his finger squeezing the trigger. The bullet slapped harmlessly into the snow.

Free, Boris ran toward the gate gaping open into the dark street and safety.

But a brilliant searchlight suddenly lit the whole courtyard, the house, the gate, the street. Boris shielded his eyes, stumbled, disoriented.

Shouts in German, in Russian, yelling at him to stop, surrender, throw down his gun. Boris aimed his pistol and punched a volley at the glaring light, pumping the trigger. A pink smear of blood on his grazed eyeballs distorted his vision. The shots winged wildly out into the streets, into the bare branches above distant roofs.

Then a fierce pain erupted in his forearm. The pistol flew from his fingers as if he had obeyed the shouted command and hurled it away. In seconds two men had seized him, jumping on his back. They all fell together, struggling, wrestling. But it was sport for the Germans now. A chance to rough up a man already their prisoner.

During the fight, a Gestapo officer stepped forward and picked up a piece of paper that had fallen to the ground.

Nadia saw none of this.

Smashing the one small window in the back bedroom, where Mariana was clutching Dasha to her in horror and Old Rags was huddled in a corner, Nadia squeezed her body through the narrow frame. Jagged edges of glass scarred her hands and cut shreds off her trailing shawl. She fell sprawling out into the snow.

No-one saw her. The soldier posted at the back had run round to the courtyard as soon as Boris – the only prey they'd come for – came out that way.

Picking herself up at once, she ran across the small garden plot, scuttling like a hen knowing it's been picked out by a hungry fox, to the nearest shelter. Behind a heap of rubble she made a right angle. Another hundred yards and she was on a dark pathway that led to a mass of sheds beside the railway track.

She had gone twenty yards down the alley when she ran full-tilt into two men.

The breath shot out of her body.

The strong hands of the men seized her, preventing her from collapsing.

One was Kafarov, Boris's first contact in the resistance. The second was another worker used by the Germans to keep the railway track in repair. Again, a member of the Nalchik underground.

As soon as they found out what had happened, who Nadia was, they took her, running from shadow to shadow, back to Kafarov's house.

Their women hid her, tended her, fed and nursed her, not countenancing the idea that she should leave. Hours, days went by. She felt safe, grateful, free from pain – yet imprisoned. Imprisoned by shock and by their insistent care.

Emotionally she became numb. It was the only course, the product of instinct not choice.

By the time she was joined by her mother and her daughter in the evening of the third day, she barely reacted, barely recorded their presence. Luda came in regularly, but even she made no impression on Nadia at first.

Kafarov tried to tell her what had happened, while she stared at him blankly.

The Gestapo took Boris. After forty-eight hours, they came back and blew up the Dobroliubovs' house. Mariana and Dasha were moved out, but both were forced to watch their home explode into ruin.

'Old Rags?' Luda asked faintly, holding Nadia's hand.

Kafarov had found out what happened to the old man. They had left him inside, grumbling and cursing. One German was overheard saying, 'Old bastard's going to get a special seat in heaven. That's how they like going off, burnt to a crisp when they can still feel it.' 'Hindus, dumbbell – these guys are Mohammedans,' another said, laughing. The demolition troop, witnesses reported, kidded around the whole time they were setting the charges.

Kafarov told Luda that shock had made the old fellow's heart give out.

Nadia heard it all but took nothing in. It was doubtful if any news could have affected her. Her heart, as well as her brain, was deadened by shock. She fell into a kind of mental coma. For the first time in her life she lost contact with the sources of her youthful, unusually robust power of self-preservation.

The play was over. The curtain hung black across an empty stage.

NINETEEN

New Year brought no celebrations. For the Russians, weariness – and a superstitious dread of tempting fortune – kept their smouldering joy from exploding into flames.

The German mood was unmitigatedly grim. Nothing had gone right since early November. Brandt remembered Kashka Tau as the turning point, the moment when he himself was finally convinced of the folly of the German advance into the Caucasus. Openly now, and virulently, he argued for a complete withdrawal.

The predicament was at last recognized at Army Headquarters in Berlin. Hitler, sobered by the Stalingrad battle and the lack of success both north and south of the Caucasian crest, reluctantly authorized a phased withdrawal as far as the line of the Kuma River, a few miles west of Pyatigorsk. Over the New Year his decision was furiously argued at the highest levels at Army Headquarters and among senior officers in the field. This 'half-measure' – the professional view was unanimous – would solve nothing. The whole Army Group A in the Caucasus risked encirclement. There had to be a withdrawal far further west than the Führer had directed. It was useless for the Führer to be already planning his spring offensive, thinking only of the springboard from which he would launch it.

But Hitler heeded just one basic piece of logic: to lose the Caucasus was to lose the war.

Meanwhile, vaguely aware that the game was up though not yet informed of the top-level decisions, the ordinary German soldiers began slowly to pull back from their forward positions. Under fierce, repeated attacks from a hating enemy aroused by the smell of German blood, they abandoned strongpoint after strongpoint. Step by step, like the villain in a swashbuckling movie beaten back and back by the grinning, swordflashing hero, the German army was pushed nearer the last big centre on its easternmost flank, Nalchik.

But, unlike the movies, the hero had no false generosity; if the Fritzes dropped their sword, it wouldn't be flicked back into their hands. The Russian enemy was earnest, bloodlusting, full of cruelly earned revenge.

*

In the hectic confusion Lieutenant-General von Kreuss didn't even trouble to read Brandt's report on his special mountain mission. The military situation was changing too fast.

On January 1, 1943 – the very day news came of the Russian encirclement of the German army trapped inside Stalingrad – Brandt scrambled to plan and oversee the retreat of his 1st Battalion from its exposed position on the Cherek River. A badly mauled Romanian Division suddenly left his men vulnerable on both flanks. The Battalion Commander was killed in a sustained barrage from deadly 'Stalin organs', the 72-round Russian rocket launchers. Almost a hundred men were killed or missing before a new defensive position was taken up just three miles east of Nalchik itself.

Then there were the remaining high-mountain units. Time after time Brandt telephoned emergency orders, rescuing them from being stranded in remote valleys or ambushed in the tall gorges.

Day after day the Russians closed in on the city.

In all this there was no time to search for Nadia. No time to think of her – yet he thought of her all the time.

The night she left him to see her family again – that terrible Christmas Eve – he found out, almost at once, what happened. But not where Nadia had got to. The Gestapo didn't know she was there in the house at all, he was sure of that. How had she escaped? Could she – would she now – come back to him? Would there be time?

Brandt thanked God for the Russians' fury. Without it,

without the desperate work it gave him, he could not have remained sane.

On the night of January 2 he returned to his billet for the first time in four days and nights. Hans had no message for him. Again he felt that sagging despair inside himself.

He slept – with deep, urgent, unremembered dreams.

Early next morning he left on foot to confer with von Kreuss.

In front of him, a weak-kneed, wobbling figure was stumbling along on the piles of rubble, moving slowly but with sudden jerks of speed. Brandt recognized the man even from behind. Captain Nazir Bekirbi, formerly of the NKVD, now 'of service' to the German occupying forces.

Good, Brandt suddenly thought, let him be of service! Perhaps he knew the 'zebra'?

Catching up with Bekirbi, he put a firm hand on his shoulder and spun him round.

Bekirbi leaped like a jack-in-the-box. His bloodshot eyes swam with fear.

'Herr Oberst! Erkh . . . Oberst Brandt. *Es fr . . . es freut milr –*'

'Is Major Stegl content with your . . . collaboration, Captain?' Brandt said in Russian.

Bekirbi retreated into a shell of silence like a threatened tortoise. But Brandt too waited.

'I hope the service I rendered . . . I tried to make sure . . . the woman, it wasn't easy, Colonel,' Bekirbi stammered out at last.

'Woman? What woman, Captain?'

Icy blasts sliced down the street from off the Nogai steppe, a north wind that swirled the snow in myriads of whirlpools.

'The woman,' Bekirbi stumbled on, 'Nadia Sergeevna . . . Surkova. The Lieutenant's wife, the man who's the brother of . . . a connection, I think, with you, Herr Oberst . . .'

Brandt kept silent. His brain worked furiously to make unsuspected connections.

'Perhaps I have more information, Herr Oberst, which might be of service. I –'

'How did you know about the woman and myself?'

'Ah, Herr Stegl wondered, Herr Oberst, if –'

'Stegl! Who employed you as his spy! Ah – so it was you, Bekirbi, who sent that man to me to tell me she was there, in that half-ruined house, a place you yourself had selected?'

Bekirbi began nodding furiously, but Brandt noticed the blankness in his eyes.

'Where is she now?'

'Where is she now? The woman, Colonel? But the Gestapo took her husband, you know that surely? He came into the city, the young idiot, a week ago, there was a trap and –'

'Yes, it is excellent we have met.' Brandt held Bekirbi beneath the arm. 'Come, let's walk. It's too cold to stay here like beggars.'

He strode off. Bekirbi struggled to keep pace, half-tugged along, half-scurrying.

'Lieutenant Surkov first,' Brandt said, not turning his head. 'He is alive?'

'Yes, yes, Herr Oberst. I assure you he is alive.'

'Perhaps he would be better dead. And – the woman?'

Bekirbi nervously licked the sleeve of his German greatcoat with a tongue like a lizard's. 'I may know,' he whispered.

'What are you saying?'

'Perhaps I have the number of a certain street where she –'

Brandt spun round and seized Bekirbi by the throat.

'Have you told Stegl?'

'No!' Brandt's grip relaxed, and Bekirbi gulped in icy air. 'He . . . I can't be sure. My sources are my own.'

Brandt said, 'Is Stegl looking for her? Actively?'

Bekirbi shook his head.

'And the number?' Brandt insisted.

Bekirbi stammered out an address in the northern quarter of town, again near the Baksan Chaussee.

Brandt put out a restraining hand and brought Bekirbi to a stop beside him. They were at the corner of a wide boulevard and a narrow alley lined on both sides by high wooden fences and almost blocked by rubble and refuse. 'I can guess that Herr Sturmbannführer Stegl already has good cause to be grateful to you. Your skills and intimate knowledge must be invaluable to the Gestapo. In the ambush laid for Lieutenant Surkov, for example, your close acquaintance with the family –'

'No!' Bekirbi tried to wriggle free, but Brandt's gloved hand gripped his throat again like an eagle's talon a struggling lamb.

'– was surely of use to the authorities,' he went on icily. 'I deduce from this, Captain, that one particular faculty is lacking in you, a faculty I prize, one that seems to me to go some way to counteract the evil that is in us all. I don't mean the ability to tell the truth. No, no, to lie is human, Captain.' Brandt's grip tightened even further. 'I mean the faculty of loyalty.'

Bekirbi began stuttering nonsense syllables, pop-eyed with panic.

But as if bemused by a conjuror whose skill is to distract the audience's eye – so they see his 'business' but not his sleight of hand – Bekirbi was so distracted by the fierce pressure on his throat that he failed to notice that, slowly, they had both been edging backward down the alley, that Brandt's free hand had slipped beneath his greatcoat and fastened on the butt of a pistol.

Then suddenly Bekirbi's distraction snapped.

The strength of his panic surged into his muscles. Flinging himself at Brandt, clawing at him with his nails, he swung both of them, whirling like dervishes, back to the top of the alley. Swearing and spitting, Bekirbi tore himself free. Brandt jerked the pistol from inside his coat.

That moment, from the boulevard behind, came a blare of engines. A jeep roared out of the snowy gloom leading a line of trucks and troop carriers like a scaled-down locomotive hauling a full-sized freight train.

Bekirbi seized his chance. Spinning away from Brandt, he ran down the alley, dodging and weaving round the obstacles like a rat in a maze.

Brandt took two quick steps after the fleeing man. He raised his pistol . . . let it drop. He did an about-turn toward the jeep. As it passed, spewing out snow from its wheels and spattering him with a wet dirty slush, he stood straight and saluted. The Panzer Captain in the back of the jeep returned the salute with correct formality.

*

Brandt ran to the nearest telephone. Pleading urgent regimental business to von Kreuss's aide, he rescheduled his appointment for the afternoon. Then he ordered his own jeep to come pick him up. Twelve minutes later Corporal Klaus Beutner was rushing him to the address off the Baksan Chaussee Bekirbi had provided. 'As fast as you dare, Klaus,' Brandt said impatiently.

Time, in every sense now, was running out. Any moment Bekirbi would reach Stegl. Brandt prayed Nadia would be at the house, that he'd be able to take her away before the Gestapo came. If not . . . there were only hours, a few days at the most, before the Red Army would be back in the city. Without her, he had no choice but to retreat with the rest of his 'fellow-countrymen'. He said the word to himself with scorn, with hatred. Yet Klaus, beside him, what had he done to be the target of his hate?

Minutes later, the jeep pulled up in front of the last in a line of low wooden structures, ramshackle boxes backed against a high factory wall. Brandt sprang out and ran to the door set in a porch at right angles to the road.

He knew the danger. The danger that coming here posed to *her*. But he had no time to play safe.

The noise of his fist on the rickety door brought a scurrying inside. He rapped again, making a dull hollow sound. Inside, women's voices were raised in fright.

'Regular army!' Brandt said loudly in Russian. 'Don't be afraid. Routine. Open up.' He paused. 'Be quick – please,' he added.

After thirty seconds bolts were pulled back, and the door opened cautiously. A girl of about sixteen put her head in the crack.

Brandt pushed the door wider open and stepped inside.

It was the same poor interior he had seen in so many Caucasian houses: carpets strewn more on the walls than on the rough wood floors, large beds also covered with carpets, rather than blankets, a small tile stove, a few pots and dishes in a stone sink; the only decoration, apart from the wall carpets, were one or two metal plates crudely hammered into reliefs of mountains scenes or peasant cottages.

'Who is the head of the family?' he asked, looking round. In addition to the girl who had opened the door, stout and plain, there were three smaller children and one elderly woman, her hair tied back in a bun and covered with a black scarf. No men. Above all, so far, no Nadia.

The girl pointed at the old woman, who stared at him with hatred in her black eyes.

'Listen carefully,' Brandt said quickly. 'I am looking for a woman. I have reason to believe she is here or she may have been here recently. Now don't, please, be afraid. I am a German officer. You see that plainly enough. But –' he hesitated, then took the biggest risk of all. 'Her name is Surkova, Nadia Sergeevna.'

But there was no reaction on the face of the old woman or of the girl. Even the small children, whom he observed closest of all, stared back at him impassively. They stood or sat where he had found them, in a rough circle with himself at the centre.

'She's not here?'

The old woman shook her head.

'But she had been? She was here?'

Again the old woman's head moved from side to side. So did the girl's.

'Recently?'

'No.' The word was uttered softly by the girl, but at least it was speech. 'Never heard the name,' she added.

'You expect her here?' he insisted.

The girl shook her head silently once more.

'I will look. If I may.'

There was nothing anyone in the house could do to stop him. In three minutes it was obvious that Nadia was in no part of the small house, not even in the cramped cellar beneath the trap door in the floor. There was no way to escape out back. The rear wall of the house was the same high brick wall that formed the side of the factory. Nor was there any trace of her, no clothes, none of the things he knew her to possess, that were so intimately associated with her. Not even a lingering trace of her smell. No feeling that she had ever set foot in the miserable shack.

There was no way of persuading them to help him find her without betraying her – even if they did know, and of that he was far from sure.

He tried one more time. 'This woman is in grave danger. From the Gestapo.'

But the faces were blank. He was no more believed than if he was Adolf Hitler. There was nothing more for him to say. He turned and walked out of the house.

*

'Speed it up,' Brandt said impatiently. If Bekirbi had already seen Stegl, and perhaps given him Nadia's real address, the order might already have been given to arrest her. Perhaps he himself, too, had been finally compromised.

The jeep's rear wheels flicked from side to side on the icy surface like a duck shaking its tail. Soon Brandt was running up the low flight of steps in the Gestapo building.

Again he had to wait, however, to see Major Stegl.

Waiting, even in an upper office, brought home the real nature of the brutal place. No walls were thick enough to deaden the guttural barks of the commands, the clash of steel-shod boots on bare concrete, the distant but piercing shouts from the basement-level cells.

So far as he could, Brandt shut his ears to it all.

At last a square-headed Sergeant showed him into Stegl's office.

'Heil Hitler!'

Brandt said nothing, looked all around. There was a new disarray. The neatness of the first days, when Gestapo officers and Stegl, their SS watchdog, took over the building and the reins of power from the NKVD, had given way to a welter of paper, junk-strewn furniture, overflowing filing cabinets, dust on the desk and on the floor.

Outside, a barrage of heavy guns shook the whole building. Small pieces of plaster and a shower of fine dust sprinkled over the office.

'Well?' Stegl said impatiently. He brushed the yellowish powder off his black uniform, also less immaculate than in the first days of occupation.

Brandt felt a sudden calm.

'You have been working too hard, Herr Sturmbannführer.'

He drew up a chair and sat down before being invited; crossed his legs, folded his arms. Such was his contempt for Stegl that even his heartrate dropped.

'An agent of yours,' Brandt continued in a hard, even voice, 'not only gave me false information, he attempted to blackmail me. No doubt he has been telling you a story to back up this attempt. I shall not waste your time refuting whatever lies this man has invented. It would only give credence to someone of whom I wish only to say, Herr Sturmbannführer, that if I see him again I shall shoot him. I regret not having done so already.'

'If, Herr Oberst, you –'

'Yes, I'm referring to NKVD Captain Bekirbi. That is an end of it, however. I will not speak of him again. If you wish, you may pass on to him my warning. Even better advice, if I may offer it, is that you throw the man out on the streets,' Brandt smiled, 'for the Russians to find. And now there's something –'

This time Stegl interrupted angrily. 'I cannot deal now with such trivialities, Herr Oberst. I understand the man has been pestering my staff, but I have been far too busy. If that is all, I –'

'No, Herr Sturmbannführer, it is not all,' Brandt said, disguising his relief. So Bekirbi hadn't been allowed to spread his poison yet! He looked at Stegl coolly. 'There is a more important matter. You have here a Lieutenant Surkov.'

Stegl looked hard at Brandt through his close-set, blue-glinting eyes.

'I would like to see him,' Brandt continued.

'May I ask why?'

'You may not.'

'I insist.'

'He is here then?'

'You are mistaken, Herr Oberst. Surkov is – elsewhere. You are probably aware he was captured in civilian clothes. He will be treated like any other rebel.'

'He has already been tortured? Killed?'

'Herr Oberst.' Stegl stood up. Squat, square-shouldered, angry. 'The young man has information of vital importance to the military effort. If the war is to be won on the battlefield, our fighting soldiers need Intelligence that –'

'Thank you, Herr Sturmbannführer,' said Brandt, also rising. 'I repeat my request. Your bestial methods I prefer not to discuss. This boy – this young man is a soldier in the Red Army. His debriefing should appropriately be conducted by military –'

'I find your desire to maintain an innocent distance childlike, Herr Oberst. I suggest you repeat your fastidious objections to higher authority in the security services. Tell me something meanwhile, however,' and for the first time Stegl's lips formed a smile. He reached in a desk drawer and pulled out a dirty piece of paper. His fingers played with it, flattening it out and folding it neatly. 'Your interest in Surkov. The last time you had occasion to visit us, you saw an even younger boy. Dobroliubov, Ilya. Surkov's . . . what . . . brother-in-law. We had no occasion to discuss the matter at that time. Since you are here and occupying my attention perhaps you will clarify this question for me. Yes!' His final '*Ja!*' snapped out like a shark clamping its teeth on elusive, finally trapped, prey.

Brandt sensed Stegl's newfound confidence. His own powers of cool judgement were weakening fast. His loneliness, the terrible week of separation and worry, the overwhelming awareness of time running out, made reason and patience impossible.

'Very well, Herr Sturmbannführer, let me ask you a straight question. What *have* you heard about the woman?'

'Ah! We come to it. The point of it all. It seems the Lieutenant risked his life in order to see his wife, Colonel.' Again his fingers stroked the paper on his desk. 'You yourself, I suppose, have no theory as to why he wished to see Nadia Sergeevna?'

Brandt couldn't help his reaction, ostentatiously, invited

by Stegl's sneering utterance of the name. Brandt knew he had gone white, that the effort to restrain himself from assaulting Stegl betrayed his guilt. No, not guilt. Fury.

Stegl, who had been standing behind his desk, leaning forward, his fists clenched and knuckles pressed on the litter of files in front of him, stood straight as if to attention, flexed his fingers, then sat down hard in his creaky swivel chair. He kept his back ramrod stiff. 'If what I hear is right,' he said, making no effort to disguise his sarcasm, 'you performed an act of gallantry on behalf of the same woman.'

'She evaded your agents, did she not?'

'*Our* agents. We are fighting this war on the same side. Are we not?' Stegl's voice was triumphant. 'Your case has come to the notice of the highest authorities. The morale of the army is of the utmost concern. Whatever rank you hold, defeatists and cowards are not tolerated. Collaborationists least of all. My duty –'

'– is to remember, Herr Sturmbannführer, that your crimes, like all other crimes, will be punished. I advise you. Keep your hands off that boy. You know he's no use to you. The game's over. We're pulling out. You know that. Take your torturers and get out while there's still time.'

TWENTY

Boris Surkov's right eye was closed. Blood clotted in his nostrils. His testes and penis were swollen and throbbed with pain that suddenly, without warning, emitted agonizing spasms. When it happened he doubled up and moaned like a woman racked by violent contractions. Mostly he lay on the floor, stupefied. The stink of excrement from every surface of the tiny cell and of his own body acted like an anaesthetic. All the time he was in and out of a nauseous sleep. Above his head the bulb designed to keep him bathed in sleep-depriving light kept flickering and dimming as the main generator sputtered oil in its ice-bound shed. To Boris its random rhythms meant nothing. He noticed consciously neither light nor noise. Prisoners shouted, screamed, banged tin plates and bruised fists, guards yelled, men sobbed, choked, swore. Heavy feet tramped in corridors. Boots and fists and sticks thudded on victims' flesh and bones. A constant obliterating noise.

Thoughts lost all coherence. How he came to be in the cell, what had happened to his friends, to anyone he knew, the partisans, the war, his torturers, everyone and everything was vague, meaningless. His brain floated. Pain was all it could cope with, and then only partially. Time and again he lost consciousness. Time itself meant nothing.

When Major Stegl came into his cell, Boris's eyes were open. He saw no-one. No-one he could recognize, no-one in particular. But he was aware of a presence. A hostile presence. Nerves quivered all over his body; the visual messages were overwhelmed by a million instinctive reflexes of self-protection.

Stegl looked at him, nodded and left.

The Gestapo 'Annex' was the State Bank building on the edge of Dolinsk park, a pink-washed stone structure whose interior was subdivided on two floors into a maze of partitioned offices rapidly converted into cells. The door of the director's office, padded with horsehair inside black quilted leather, now led into the main interrogation room. Here Stegl waited until Boris could be 'prepared'. A thin Ukrainian interpreter sat on a chair in the corner of the room. No-one else. On this occasion Stegl required no 'apparatus'.

Boris appeared after five minutes, his eyes still glazed, a chemical stimulant flowing through his veins. The Sergeant sat him opposite Stegl at the former bank director's desk then, at the SS Major's command, left the room.

Stegl smiled.

'Enough is enough, eh! They tell me you are a brave young man.' He turned to the interpreter and snapped, 'Don't wait for me to finish each sentence. There's not much time.' Then to Boris again, 'As an officer in the Soviet army there is no reason why you should not receive the privileges due to you as a prisoner of war according to the Geneva conventions.'

Boris's brain started to register what the interpreter was saying. Was this German officer really conceding the point so easily? That's what Boris had been holding out for. 'I'm a soldier!' he had screamed at them. But they had just laughed, beaten him harder, wired him up and –

A stab of pain from his genitals brought him huddling over on his bare chair into the foetal position.

Stegl got up and went to a cupboard. He opened a drawer and took out a bottle of vodka and two small stemmed glasses.

'Here.'

Boris accepted the glass full to the brim with brown liquid. His arm was trembling as he took hold of it. Half of it spilled over him. The other half he tossed back. It made him choke violently. But when the spasm was over the pain in his testicles had gone, and he could sit up straight.

Stegl poured out another two glasses but left them on the desk between them. The interpreter looked longingly at the vodka.

'A change of clothes, a bath, would be welcome, no?'

Boris nodded. He cleared his throat. 'Yes.'

'Good, good. That can be arranged now. Your new status permits these little luxuries.' Stegl chuckled. 'Ah! If your wife were to see you now . . .'

Boris blinked. Had he heard right? He looked up at the interpreter, then at the SS officer. Yes, this was the senior interrogator he had seen before. He recognized him now, made the connection. Waffen SS, Sturmbannführer. Only once had he come before, as far as Boris remembered. At the beginning. Long, long ago. Why did he . . . ? It was hard to focus on the man. Was he smiling? What was that look on his face?

Stegl said again, 'If your wife is to visit you, Lieutenant, you must be respectable. If she wants to visit you, that is. Perhaps her other . . . commitments will prevent her.'

Boris had no idea what the hell this man was talking about. 'Where is she?' He tried to say it fiercely, challengingly, but the words came out like the croak of a sick frog.

'Nadia Sergeevna is fine, fine,' Stegl said. He got up and came round the desk to pat Boris's shoulder. 'We must have a chat soon. About her, about other things. Meanwhile I have other duties to attend to. A bath, yes, a change of clothes. Then a talk, eh, young man. We'll soon get your status rectified.'

Boris tried to put out a hand to stop him leaving, but instead overbalanced and fell off his chair. He felt himself lifted by strong hands under his armpits.

*

It was after midnight when Major Stegl reappeared at the Annex, but Boris had no way of knowing if it were night or day. He judged that several hours, perhaps six or seven, had gone by since that first strange interview. Though he had no base, no starting point to which he could relate it, his sense of time passing was returning. His sense of smell too. His cell revolted him now. He was constantly yawning and stretching and swallowing small jets of bile to keep from vomiting up the vodka and the bread and sausages they had fed him after his bath. They had even put a bed in his cell, a straw mattress, and the floor had been swabbed down. As far as his nose was concerned, however, the improvement was small.

He had lain on the mattress but hadn't been able to sleep. Outside somewhere there seemed to be a hell of a noise. Guns? Thunder? It was hard to picture the outside world, to have the faintest flicker of imagination about what might be happening out there.

Then they had come again.

He was taken to the interrogation room once more. But instead of frog-marching him there, kicking him every time he stumbled, he was allowed to walk, normally, between two guards, who didn't swear at him.

'Lieutenant!' Stegl advanced and shook Boris's hand. 'Sit down.'

But behind the welcome Boris sensed the officer was jumpier, less in control than before. Perhaps it was the noise all around, which he could now hear was definitely gunfire. A constant throb. Boris sat. Another interpreter was present this time, an old Balkar. An émigré, Boris wondered? What did it matter?

Stegl pushed a photograph across the table to Boris, who took it and examined the picture. A stiff, formal portrait, obviously taken from a file, the kind of head and shoulders attached to identity documents.

'Who is this man?'

Stegl waved the interpreter silent. The hush lasted a long time, before Stegl spoke. 'No, you couldn't know this man. He is a German Colonel. Your wife, however, Lieutenant Surkov, knows him well.' Stegl paused again. Boris saw him hesitate but was too confused to interpret this as uncertainty. 'The man's name is Colonel Brandt. 21st Regiment. 7th Mountain Division. An old enemy of yours in the mountains. He is also your wife's lover.'

When the Balkar, grinning, translated the final words the old, terrible pain kicked Boris like a mule. Nausea washed over him. He had to hold on to the edge of the desk.

'That's a . . . that's a . . .'

'Lie? By no means. Let me elaborate. This liaison has been continuing for as long as we have been guests in your delightful Caucasus country, Lieutenant. Oh, as long ago as

August, when your wife was first introduced to this collaborator, Colonel Brandt, in Kislovodsk.'

'Pyatigorsk!'

'Ah! So you —'

But Stegl's words were cut off by Boris falling off the chair and rolling on the floor into a corner of the room. Then suddenly his body gave a lurch, and he vomited hugely, convulsively.

The Balkar laughed.

Stegl gagged at the sight and smell of the river of half-digested mush.

'Get up!' he yelled. *'Wächter!'*

Stegl stepped over to heave Boris to his feet, but began to retch again and stopped, turning away. The guard clattered in. Stegl waved at him to pick Boris up. The interpreter, still grinning, made a comment in his own language that no-one else understood.

'Leave us. But stay close,' Stegl ordered the guard, who did an about-turn with almost mocking punctiliousness and marched out. Stegl turned towards Boris. 'So Lieutenant. You will help me punish this man, will you not? First, perhaps, you will tell me where I can find the woman he loves — your wife, Lieutenant. *Zhena – nevernaya!'* He had rehearsed the Russian adequately. Boris understood. Yes. His wife was unfaithful. He had known it all along, hadn't he? Even before he'd got the note. She was a traitor. He had called her a traitor. In the sanitarium.

A ball of vile-tasting spit formed in the corner of his mouth. Suddenly he sat up and spat.

The gobbet fell short.

Stegl smiled.

'Now, Lieutenant —' he began.

A salvo of shells screamed overhead, exploded. The bank, though solid, gave a lurch.

'Now, Lieutenant —'

The room exploded.

A shell had landed just fifty yards away.

The boarded-up windows in the interrogation cell blew in. Plaster split from the walls and crashed down in a welter of choking dust. A gust of night air followed, thick with splinters and smoke and the smell of burning. Stegl cursed and strode toward the door.

The Balkar interpreter started to follow, but the guard appeared in the open doorway, gesturing with the butt of his submachine gun. The interpreter stopped, shrugged, leaned against the shaking inner wall.

Boris meantime didn't move. He was aware of the blast and of the icy air gusting in through the gaping outer wall, but only deep inside his brain. His conscious mind was obsessed. Obsessed by the face of a German Colonel and, superimposed, the face of his wife. That time when she had come to meet her mother and their child, at home, their home, seconds before the trap sprang shut and he had been . . . no, no, that couldn't have been her, her work, her betrayal? *Her* trap? But she had left him. Yes. She had left him to fight his way out alone. Now they were saying – but it couldn't be true. No. Where had she been in the weeks before? What *was* her life in the town while he was away fighting in the mountains? Ilya had been tortured . . . killed by the Gestapo. Had they taken Nadia too, turned her? Had she paid for her life with her brother's blood . . . with his own blood?

He began sobbing. He couldn't help himself.

To hell with the war – with everything he'd believed in.

He thought with a sudden blinding clarity: I refuse to die in a Gestapo cell. There's nothing to die for any longer.

The room lit up. Outside, a flare had gone up. Boris raised his head. Where was the interrogator, the SS Major?

'I need my fucking interrogator!' he yelled suddenly. 'Where *is* the coward? Get him in here!' Stumbling to his feet he tried to crash out through the door, but again the guard raised his submachine gun. Boris ignored it, tried to push past. The guard slapped him with the butt across the chest, driving the wind out of Boris's body. Staggering back, he knocked into the table and collapsed onto the floor, tears spilling out of his eyes as he whimpered the same words, 'Get him in here.'

That moment Stegl returned.

*

Stegl was struggling to control his panic. Never before had he come so directly under fire. And it wasn't a random skirmish. It was the big counter-attack. He couldn't even step out of the building. There was firing all around. Machine guns, mortars. The perimeter had been pierced. He was trapped in his own prison.

The file! The Colonel's file – it was back at HQ. The urge to finish the business gripped him. Yes, he thought, I've got the proof. I'll finish that traitor Colonel. I'll squeeze him so tight he'll –

He noticed Boris. He had forgotten all about the kid. Suddenly he realized that Boris was talking to him. No, not talking, vomiting a stream of words, staring like a madman. Stegl turned wildly to find the interpreter, slumped indifferently in a corner.

'What's he saying? What's he trying to say?'

The Balkar mumbled in German, but Stegl couldn't catch it because of the noise Boris was making. He stepped forward and slapped the Lieutenant's face. But the words kept coming. Partisan detachments in the Kashka Tau area, liaison duties, names, contacts, weapons – answers to all those questions he had fired at this boy earlier, that he had typed up for the other interrogators, but the boy had refused to answer. Now he had the answers.

He had the proof on the Colonel too. As soon as he could get out of the damn Annex and back to HQ he would go personally to von Kreuss and –

A bullet whined in through the open window like a blind June bug and smacked into the powdery plaster of the wall. Stegl and the interpreter ducked.

Still Boris's words poured out. He didn't notice the bullet. The more he talked, the less constraint he seemed to have over his own tongue. Once over the waterfall his confessions, his secrets, spilled down in a cataract.

And all the time he cursed Nadia.

He loved her. She was a traitor. He would be like her. The thought had no clarity. Only power.

The crash of bullets, screams, wood and stone splitting into shrapnel suddenly burst out inside the prison annex itself.

That was too much for Stegl.

He turned from Boris and fled. The interpreter after him. Neither made it out, not even through the door.

Standing there, blocking their way, was the massive form of Tembot Kochan.

Tembot, whose beard had grown until it flowed like an Orthodox priest's, seized the SS officer with his left hand and slung him against the wall. A couple more partisans ran in. One picked up Boris, babbling incoherently. The other shoved the Balkar interpreter up against the wall, legs apart, frisked him.

'That's it. Let's go.' Tembot snapped. 'Open as many cells as you can get to. But fast.'

He watched Boris being pulled out of the room by a young partisan like a drunk ejected from a party. He had heard enough to guess what had been going on. But he didn't blame the kid. He just didn't want to know any more about that. The partisans had done what they set out to do, plucked Boris from the Gestapo's bloody claw. Now they had to get back outside the perimeter before the Fritzes got wise and counter-attacked.

'Fast!' he shouted again.

Boots rang on the stairs. Iron doors clanged. Gunbutts slammed against the walls of the narrow stairwell and passage. Firing suddenly sounded from below. Last time he'd been inside the building he'd had a hell of a row with some damn bureaucratic bank clerk. Now, in his memory, it seemed like a friendly chat.

'Bring that one!' he yelled, pointing at Stegl. 'Alive.'

The rest of the Fritzes he didn't give a damn about.

A new burst of firing from the basement reminded him that the bank was still full of armed Germans – though the surprise raid had driven most of them into defensive positions underground. The getaway had to be fast.

Then two German prison guards, cut off in the Collective Farms Loan department, made a dash for freedom. A partisan bullet put one of them down before he'd gone ten feet. The other suddenly turned and threw himself at the nearest Russian. The two men rolled to the floor, both letting out animal cries, guttural shrieks of fear and fury. A second partisan leaped in and kicked the German on the side of the head, then smashed his skull with the butt of his rifle. Seeing the German's submachine gun spin away, the partisan threw down his own clumsy Moisin and grabbed the German weapon. Then ran out toward the back of the bank where the others had led Boris and the prisoner.

Losing for a moment his sense of direction, the partisan who had seized the Balkar interpreter dragged him into the main hall of the bank. Two dazed prisoners, released from their cells, followed blindly, staggering. Here a Gestapo Sergeant and three armed men had a clear line of fire from behind a plinth where Lenin's statue once stood. All four men, partisan, interpreter and prisoners, were cut down like pheasants at a royal shooting party.

Tembot was the last to leave the bank – from the back of the building. Before throwing himself out through the ground-floor window he fired a heavy burst back through the offices – the cells – to keep the Fritzes penned down just a few seconds longer.

At the rendezvous point at the south-west corner of the building, he found Boris, seven partisans, five more-or-less active prisoners they had released – and the Waffen SS Major.

The other three partisans could fight their own way out, Tembot thought, not knowing they were already dead. He pulled the pin and tossed a grenade back through the shattered window.

'That's it. Make it fast. Go!'

*

The message came over the field telephone. Brandt received it in his billet at 02.14 hours in the morning of January 4. It wasn't the first alarm. The Russian attack had been building steadily. But this was the first time Russians had penetrated the perimeter in force. The 21st Regiment was defending that sector.

As soon as the cool signaller's voice over the harsh, crackling phone said the target seemed to be the State Bank, Brandt thought of Boris.

Boris . . . then Nadia.

He moved so fast that his own jeep was the first German vehicle on the scene. Three armoured cars followed. A heavy machine gun was positioned with a line of fire down the straight street that separated the bank from the park. Men were posted on rooftops and at the corners of nearby buildings.

Brandt knew he had to go through the motions.

The partisans were effectively trapped inside the Gestapo annex.

But they escaped. Colonel Brandt saw to it they escaped.

'Hold fire!' he yelled. Repeated the order into the telephone.

'There! There they are!'

A voice shouted, urgent.

Figures flitted out of the shadows.

'Hold fire!' Brandt shouted again.

The sights of his men's guns were lined up on the partisans, easy targets. Perhaps one of them was Nadia's husband.

Then he saw Stegl.

He hesitated – then yelled again, 'Hold fire!'

But was it Stegl? Hard to tell in the dark. Brandt was almost convinced he recognized the squat figure stumbling across the road on the end of a Russian rifle-barrel. Certainly that huge figure following was the white-whiskered giant he had once confronted on the very top of the Ice Wall.

He knew he had made the right decision.

*

Two other pairs of eyes watched the partisans escape. Dark, Russian eyes. Too far away to be sure of individual identities, crouched behind the torn stone wall at the north end of the park, shivering, protecting each other in their felt-wrapped arms, two alert excited women observed, first with a terrible anxiety, then with a surge of relief, the final stages of the raid.

Nadia clutched her sister-in-law tighter.

'I knew it, Luda,' she whispered. 'I knew it.'

'Yes, darling. Come away now.'

'No, wait. Perhaps that wasn't Boris I saw.'

Luda tugged Nadia's shawl. 'How can we tell from here? But we saw them go, didn't we, darling? We saw so many of them. They all went free. So wonderful, incredible. They didn't shoot. Yet we saw them come, the Fritzes. But they didn't shoot, did they? Come away, Nadia. They will find us here. We will not be so lucky.'

Reluctantly Nadia took her eyes away from the gap in the wall through which she had been staring, almost without blinking, for the last fifteen minutes.

Could it really have been *him*? Why else did they not shoot?

'I knew,' she whispered again.

Her heart skipped wildly. Her body felt suddenly warm – then she shivered. She must go. Luda was right. She was always the sensible one, and Nadia had barely recovered, was barely in fact – sane.

That moment the shelling began again.

The women scuttled back along the wall, darted across the open space to the end of Kabardinskaya Street and, hugging the walls, returned to Kafarov's house and Nadia's other, protecting women – to her mother and to her Dasha, her darling Dasha. For it was Dasha – and her young unshakeable optimism – that finally had brought Nadia back to life.

Slowly Nadia began to hear, to react.

At last, through Kafarov, she got a message through to Tembot.

Two days later a message from the old partisan leader came back to her. Boris had been located in the Gestapo building by the park, the former bank. He was alive. They were sending a party to rescue him at two o'clock in the morning of January 4, under cover of the general attack being mounted on Nalchik by the Red Army.

Yet now, the raid over, as she and Luda slipped back, black-draped and silent, cowering in dark recesses whenever exploding shells and tracer and distant flashes of fire lit the night, she thought not of her family or of those protecting her, not even of the partisans who risked their lives to rescue her husband . . . but of her Colonel.

If they were ever to see each other again; if they were ever to love each other again, fate alone would bring it about. She could do no more. If they were destined to live their futures together, so be it. Nadia felt all the deep submission to fate that ruled her ancestors' lives. The modern woman she had grown up to be bowed before the weight of this pressure. She felt it physically, as if she had a yoke across her shoulders and some invisible hand was pouring into the pails suspended at each end not milk but a stream of molten led.

'Nadia, what is it? Nadia?'

Nadia looked up into Luda's face, startled. She hadn't realized she had sunk down into the slush.

'I'm sorry,' she whispered, holding up her hands to be pulled off the road, too weak – too heavy – to haul herself upright without help, 'I was saying goodbye.'

TWENTY-ONE

Thin dark clouds, indented like the snouts of swordfish, swam low and threatening in the dawn sky. Way above curled the pink-flecked cirrus – foam on top of the stormy ocean beneath. All along the mountainside a gusty wind played with the raiding party. Some chewed on black bread. Others took sips of water spiked with a rough grain alcohol. No-one spoke. It was too cold, colder than the deepest ocean.

One man, chin on his knees, picking his patched teeth in a slow regular rhythm with the point of a double-edged knife, sat just outside the ring.

That man was Yusef Tsagov.

One other man was completely outside the ring. Shaking with the cold, his fingers red as cranberries thrust up into his armpits, his black uniform like a patch of volcanic rock in the fresh snow, SS Major Fritz Stegl watched his captors gloomily.

Tsagov, expressionless, savoured the moment.

He knew Stegl, knew all about him. But the Sturmbannführer knew nothing of Yusef Tsagov. Keeping one remove from the Germans had saved his life – as Tsagov knew it would if the fortunes of war reversed.

Tsagov contemplated the German's gray face. To him it was already the face of a corpse. Because of course there was still a risk. The name, Yusef Tsagov, if the German were to hear it, perhaps, just perhaps, it would mean something to the SS Major. Just possibly the name had come to his attention, maybe through Bekirbi, maybe through someone else. When Bekirbi denied betraying the name, he had been pleading for his life, so scared he'd have promised anything, he'd have castrated himself in front of Tsagov in order to save his life. If there'd been time, Tsagov thought, I might have made him do just that. But, on the matter of Stegl, he too would have to die. Of course the Sturmbannführer was due to die in any case. Surely not even Kochan would aim to keep this piece of *übermenschlich* pus alive. Surely . . .

Better not rely on others, Tsagov said to himself. Never rely on others.

Without moving his head he glanced across at the partisan leader, whose chewing jaws rippled that great white beard of his like surf. Kochan hadn't believed his story, of course not. But his old NKVD chief could hardly guess the active role the former Soviet 'spy' – and most recent partisan recruit – had played during the occupation. Belief, guesswork, trust – all unimportant. Only knowledge was important. Only usefulness. The point is, Tsagov thought, I made my move in time.

Four days ago he had joined the partisan band. Now, in this raid on the bank, he had risked his life, proved himself.

His last act on the other side was to send that note to Boris.

Kochan growled an order. The still figures began to move, their dark cloaks and greatcoats to sway slowly. Snowlumps toppled from their flat round fur hats and their hunched shoulders. They spat, rubbed their hands.

Only two men failed to move. One was Stegl. The other was Boris Surkov.

'You, Tsagov, help the lad.'

'Yes, yes, Comrade Kochan.'

Tsagov smiled. Was that a mark of confidence in him? Many of the others had taken their turn supporting the half-conscious young man, first in pairs, but now, since Boris began walking almost on his own, one man's shoulder was enough. In any case he had been chosen. That was good.

Even better if they got the chance to talk.

*

Boris's mind began to work some hours before his body showed any sign of recovery. He let his brain free-wheel while strong men lifted him higher and higher into the hills. Any co-ordinated physical effort on his part would have demanded total concentration as well as reserves of strength that only an imminent threat to his life could possibly have summoned. He needed to think, to know what he had done, and why, and what the consequences would be.

Because they had broken him, the Gestapo. Not by torture. By telling the truth. They smashed into his one-dimensional world and destroyed it as easily as he burnt German propaganda posters in the village squares. Was he wrong to have believed in the struggle for a better life, a Soviet life, in the struggle against those who tried to take his dream away, against the fascist enemy? He should have understood Nadia as a victim. Now the Gestapo had proved to him what he never even suspected: when he betrayed her – by failing to help her – he betrayed his country, far more than she had done. Later, soon – if only it could be soon – he would listen to her, understand everything.

And she would understand him. He felt good, in a way, knowing for the first time in his life he was no better than anyone else. Because he too had lost his innocence.

He began to plan.

The first reality was the capture of the SS Major. The mountains, the snow, the rocky trails – of these he had been only hazily aware. But the presence of his German interrogator never left his mind, every conscious moment the man was there: the one man who knew that Lieutenant Boris Surkov had squealed, had vomited his treachery on the cell floor.

Shame rose like bile in his throat as he remembered his tongue, lolling out of the side of his mouth, exhausted with trying to keep up with the torrent of words his brain was voiding. Surely Tembot too had heard – heard something, perhaps nothing clear, coherent, but enough to guess.

Now once again they were moving off, and the motion of his body began pumping more fresh blood into his head.

He was feeling stronger, much stronger.

The man supporting him now was much smaller than himself, but wiry, nimble-footed. Gradually Boris reduced his dependence on the shoulder. His legs picked up strength each step with the slow rhythm of walking. They were on a long flat path now through the forest, which made his growing independence easier.

It was becoming less of a problem, too, keeping his eyes open; he was blinking regularly instead of having to force the lids open each time they gummed shut. He began to study the face of the man on whom he was leaning, what he could see of it below the fur cap with its flaps of felt protecting the ears: a long thin dark face, in shape not unlike his own, but lined, the beard-stubble graying, pockmarks on the tip of his nose.

A tribesman, a stranger.

Boris opened his mouth to thank this partisan, and a slurred, hare-lipped sound came out.

The man recognized it, however, as an attempt at communication.

'Better, eh?' he said. 'Good. Good.' Then, with a whisper that Boris found strange since no-one was within twenty yards of them, 'Save your thanks, Boris Alexandrovich. Too quickly given, too quickly repaid.'

The words – and the intimate use of Boris's name and patronymic – made little impression at first. But as they walked on, side by side now, with Boris merely resting a hand on his companion's back, he began to reflect on who this man might be.

Finally, very slowly and deliberately, he said, 'Who?'

'Am I?' The man gave his name. He appeared to be watching Boris's reaction to it anxiously. But the name meant nothing to Boris.

Tsagov relaxed and smiled, turning his face toward the young man.

Immediately a shiver sliced through Boris's body like a cold butcher's blade through tender steak.

The zebra!

'Zebra!' he blurted out, but the word was garbled.

'What?' Tsagov snapped, making no sense of Boris's sudden exclamation.

Boris moistened his lips carefully and prepared his tongue.

'Comrade Tsagov,' he said with some precision, 'we could talk usefully together.'

They kept moving steadily, but for a long time they didn't talk, the silence broken only by Tsagov's regular, Boris's explosive, breathing. Gradually they slipped behind the others in the long file that followed the twisting forest tracks. At last Boris took the initiative.

'You know,' he asked cautiously, 'who the German prisoner is?'

'The name is Stegl. SS Major.'

'Yes, the name. I know the name. Stegl is a . . . a torturer.'

'They all are.'

Boris stared ahead silently a long time, before saying, 'Why didn't they shoot him with the rest of the Fritzes?'

'He knows more than the rest,' Tsagov answered quickly.

Again they walked on in silence. Far ahead a group of partisans had stopped at a point where the forest ended, where a vast expanse of flat white snow merged into a huge cloud that eddied, heavy with snow, turning impatiently round and round like an enormous white-fleeced ewe searching for the exact spot to give birth to the pressing weight inside.

Tsagov slowed his pace, as if anxious not to catch up too soon with the rest of the men, not before he and Boris had sealed the so far unspoken bargain. Boris felt the same impulse as he guessed existed in Tsagov.

'Stegl,' Tsagov whispered. 'A vile torturer.' He paused, but still had to prompt Boris. 'A man with many secrets.'

Boris drew in a deep breath. 'Yes, too many secrets,' he said heavily.

'*Your* secrets,' Tsagov insisted.

'Yes,' Boris whispered.

'The price,' said Tsagov very clearly, 'is friendship. Trust. A guarantee, your guarantee, Boris Alexandrovich. Total discretion. If need be, support. Do we make ourselves understood? Absolutely understood?'

Boris nodded.

Tsagov said very slowly, 'You will endorse my record as a loyal partisan . . . during the occupation? For which I will silence Stegl.'

'Yes.' Then Boris added, 'Soon.'

Tsagov smiled. 'Before he talks.'

They had almost caught up with the main body of the partisans. Tembot Kochan's bulk was visible in the centre of a knot of men, while on a rocky ledge, where the path cut through the last forest-covered ridge, a black-uniformed figure sprawled like a mortally wounded wild boar waiting for hunters to string it on a stout pole.

Boris, hardened by his own desperation, contemplated SS Major Stegl icily. This pig, he thought, must never grunt again.

*

An hour later Tembot's partisans were joined by another group. More men arrived during the afternoon, and they all moved down into the liberated village of Bagubent, beside the Cherek River. By nightfall two hundred partisans had collected, and still more kept coming. They sheltered in peasants' houses, in sheds, in the local Party building, though this had been torn apart by the Germans, in stables and pigsties.

Tembot Kochan was in continual conference. The attack on Nalchik was imminent. Fierce resistance was expected. Even if the attack worked perfectly, however, the Germans would try and destroy everything before they left the city. The assault had to be fast, accurate, well co-ordinated. Radios crackled with messages. There was no longer any need to conceal from the Germans that the attack was coming. It had already begun from the air. All day bombers and fighter planes had taken advantage of every small break in the cloud cover.

At midnight some of the active partisans, several of them women, one of the men well into his eighties, many only fifteen or sixteen years old, began to move off toward the capital.

Seventeen-year-old Marko, a bullet wound festering in his upper arm, was detailed to guard Stegl and the four prisoners brought in by other partisan detachments.

None of the Germans – except SS Major Stegl – was reckoned to have information of value. Since they arrived in Bagubent, several partisans, under Kochan's orders, had interrogated the Sturmbannführer – Stegl had remained obstinately silent. At times he seemed physically unable to talk, at other times the partisans suspected he was deliberately resisting them. Marko's frustration grew as the hours passed.

All this time Boris sweated with anxiety. Isolated in the small formal parlour of a peasant cottage, he relied on Tsagov for news of what was going on.

Stegl, Tsagov told him, was still silent. That was true, though the nails of both little fingers had been extracted, and he had been kicked, abused, threatened.

'He only knows German,' Boris said weakly.

Tsagov smiled. 'Language,' he said, 'is no problem. He knows. He could make himself understood if he wanted to.'

'Will he . . . come round?'

Tsagov shrugged.

But Boris was still curious.

He plucked Tsagov by the sleeve and said, 'How will I know? How will I know when the bastard's dead?'

Tsagov shook off Boris's clawing hand. 'You'll know.' A minute later he said, 'You saw his eyes, you must have seen his eyes, eh, Boris Alexandrovich? I thought so. You will remember the look in his cold Hunnish eyes.'

But the door flung open. Tembot Kochan, ducking low, came in, filling the small space, in complete contrast to the way Boris and Tsagov between them seemed almost invisible there in the parlour, Boris flat on the single couch, Tsagov nervously hunched in a corner.

'A bed!' Tembot bellowed. 'You'll be getting too soft for war, young fellow.'

'I have to thank you, Tembot Batazarovich. I –'

'Not now, not now.' Tembot turned to Tsagov. The old partisan seemed puzzled to see him with Boris, slow to place the man. 'Ah, Tsagov Yusef. Which detachment did I –?'

'Marko's,' Tsagov said quickly.

'He helped me today,' Boris interjected, not looking, however, at Tembot, 'Comrade Tsagov was an excellent support.'

'That's good. That's good.'

Tsagov got up immediately and went out, without glancing at either of the other two men.

As soon as the door squeezed shut behind him, Boris said,

'I though you'd gone down into the city already. I thought the assault party had left.'

Tembot shook his head. He sat on the end of the couch and yawned hugely. 'Damn it, I'm tired,' he growled. 'No, lad. I'm going higher. The Red Army will do the main job. They don't need me. No, half go down. The other half go up. Back up there.' He tossed the mane of hair up and behind him. 'The Fritzes are still crawling around in some of the passes. We'll cut 'em off. That's a proper partisan job.'

Boris shut his eyes and longed to tell Tembot the truth. He wanted to ask him: Is it ever possible – is it ever right – to forgive your enemies?

But he kept silent.

Tembot leaned back, so that Boris's shins felt the huge weight of the man.

The long silence continued, and Boris thought that Tembot must have gone to sleep. He was almost asleep himself, and all that was keeping him awake was the memory of what his torturer had said to him. It was a burden he couldn't get rid of.

He looked over at Tembot. The old man's eyes were open now, and he looked at Boris almost expectantly, with great calm.

Boris hadn't intended to speak. But at that look, so full of solace, he said abruptly, 'Tembot Batazarovich, why did you never marry?'

The old man laughed. 'My boy, what makes you think I never married? You think you're the only one who ever suffered?'

'I –'

'Yes, I know. When you love, you suffer. And you think nobody else knows. It's bad enough in peacetime, when all you have to worry about is getting along. But in war – being separated – anything can happen. Yes, I know all about it.'

'Nadia and I –'

'– love each other. She's a good girl, and you are a good boy. You have nothing to worry about. When I think – I'll tell you a story. Many many years ago, this country had a civil war. Even if your father hadn't died in it, you'd have known about it. They still teach it in school. Well, in this civil war there were two sides – let's call them, just to give them names, Red and White.' He grinned. 'Now, I was on the Red side. My girl was too, or so I thought. But her family wasn't. We thought, what difference does that make? The future is ours, history is on our side. No doubt they taught you that in school, too. What they didn't teach you was that you can't expect to be the custodian of the only truth in the world. There are other truths, lots of them. There's the biggest truth of all – death. In a war no-one escapes that, not even the young. Why dwell on that? In life there is enough uncertainty, too many everyday truths to choose between. Let me tell you some of them. There's the truth of loyalty, not to society, but to your parents, your family. There's the truth of the past, which this country has tried so nobly to get rid of. But it's there, somewhere, with all its priests and troikas and cherry trees and old servants and beautiful young girls in white dresses. You don't know how loyal people can be to a past like that, but twenty years ago we still knew. And there's the truth of the rest of the world. It's still out there, somewhere, as we know from these – representatives of it who have showed up here. Now, you and Nadia have never been there. Neither have I. I can't tell you whether Paris and London and New York and Rome and Monte Carlo deserve any kind of loyalty. But when you add all that up – the father and mother, and the white dresses, and the art and the champagne – maybe you have almost enough on that side to balance against the future. I don't believe it myself. But I can see, when I think of it that way, why Irina didn't stay behind with me.'

Boris said, 'If she had come back, would you have forgiven her?'

Tembot said quietly, 'My dear boy, I am a man who has lived all his life without a woman, without a family. The days and months and years that you live with a wife – what idea, what false pride, can hold out against all that time together? What can't it swallow up? It wraps around all the wounds like an oyster round its grain of sand, eh? Forgive her? I can think of nothing, no, nothing at all, that I couldn't forgive her.'

*

Boris fell into a nervous sleep. At two in the morning he was woken by a clattering of carts, shouts, catcalls. Tembot had gone. The top of the blanket was cold. Pulling himself to his feet, Boris looked out through a window from which he could see a corner of the main street. The clouds had vanished. The moon made a brilliant central motif in a Persian carpet of stars. Taking advantage of the light, a troop train with ammunition, food supplies, hay, medicines and prostitutes, which earlier had crossed the high pass from Georgia and negotiated the fearsome track high along the side of the Cherek gorge, was filing past, mules and scrawny horses pulling carts crammed with boxes and people packed on top of each other, like some medieval baggage train crawling to Poltava or Agincourt. Boris watched for twenty minutes as the slow cortege passed through Bagubent. Then the icy night air compelled him to return to the coarse blankets on the couch.

On the point of sleep again, Nadia's face came into his mind, clearer than ever he remembered. It was the day of their wedding... when they had stood side by side in front of the massive Soviet official with the red sash across her bulging bosom.

He fell at once into a deep dreamless sleep.

*

As soon as Tsagov left Boris with Tembot Kochan, he made his way to the stable where Marko the Chechen was guarding the prisoners. Marko was asleep in one stall. The prisoners were asleep, or pretending to be, locked in the other stall. Tsagov shook Marko's shoulder. He came awake with a start, saw who it was and shut his eyes again. 'What's it this time?' he mumbled. 'Never give up, do you?' The pain in his arm came back, and he cursed the man who'd woken him with a native anger that quickly, however, dissolved into sleep again. Tsagov kicked him on the thigh.

'The key,' he hissed. 'Orders.'

Marko cursed again, flung Tsagov the key to the stall, a rusty iron rod with a big, unindented bit. Tsagov caught it despite the dark. Opening the wooden door, he found Stegl ready. Even so, taking the dagger from his belt, he made a show of prodding the German out, then locked the door again and tossed the key back to Marko who, three quarters asleep, shoved it beneath his right buttock. 'Beat the shit out of the bastard,' he murmured, 'for all I care. Ayyyy!' He clutched his wounded arm and slipped gratefully back into full unconsciousness.

Stegl – primed with Tsagov's earlier promises of freedom in exchange for large quantities of roubles – co-operated eagerly to make his escape, flitting from shadow to shadow, cover to cover. But with Tsagov's felt cape round his shoulders, and in the noisy confusion caused by the mule train clanking down from the Cherek gorge, not even the moonlight created the slightest risk of discovery.

Within minutes the two men were in wooded country, able to look down through the trees on the village below. At first glance it was all peaceful, but peering more closely they could see it pulsing like an anthill whose static outline belies the throbbing activity inside.

Tsagov had thought hard about the danger of taking Stegl alone. But the danger of companions would be greater, he decided. Yes, he knew some of the partisans, like himself, would enjoy the sport. His own blood was tingling with anticipated pleasure. But better always to trust no-one, to have no witnesses.

On a small ridge Stegl stumbled and fell.

Tsagov, directly behind him, let him lie, looking down coldly at the SS officer. Neither so far had said a word. They had little vocabulary in common, though even in Russian and Balkar Tsagov had got the message through that he would help the SS Major escape in return for large sums of money – all this under cover of an 'interrogation'.

Then Tsagov noticed a glow in the sky back toward the north, back across the branch of the Cherek which, many miles higher, would join the base of the great Bezengi glacier. His first reaction was dawn had come; he had miscalculated the time. But he understood quickly the real cause. Nalchik was burning. From the direction of the city were coming long low series of explosions, merging into a steady roar like the regular thump of pistons in a combustion engine. Nalchik was burning. Tonight many of the losers, the believers in the New Order, the émigré 'traitors' and their spies and their mullahs and their gangsters would die in the fires and the battle. Tsagov knew many of them. It might be a long time, he accepted, before he would dare return to the city. But out here, in the mountains, his tracks were covered. Later he would seek out Boris, would demand his protection, the payment for this job.

Meanwhile he would live. There was always a way for the prudent to live, even in war.

'Up!' he barked, seeing Stegl still lying there in the snow, panting with exhaustion – and relief.

The German's face screwed up as he looked at Tsagov, puzzled, suddenly afraid again. He raised himself up onto one elbow.

Tsagov had spoken in Balkar, but the harsh tone of his voice meant more than the word itself.

Tsagov smiled, took the dagger from its sheath, bent down and, so suddenly that Stegl didn't even try to avoid it, slashed the blade across Stegl's face. Blood spurted from a long shallow cut from cheekbone to chin. Both lips split like plums pecked by the beak of a hungry bullfinch.

Stegl tried to scream but couldn't. That single slash was a message of death when he had expected rescue.

'Up!' Tsagov repeated, this time just gesturing with his dagger.

Slowly Stegl got to his feet. He put his hands to his face, then held them in front of his eyes and watched, with the same appalled, puzzled, hopeless expression, as the blood turned them black in the pale moonlight.

'*Marsch!*' commanded Tsagov, imitating the sound that, since August, had become as familiar in the Caucasus as the whoop of peasants goading their creaking carts. 'No, no, no. Left.' And because he'd reverted to his own language he turned Stegl, as a mahout would an elephant, with the point of his dagger in the German's shoulder blades.

Tsagov had a precise destination in mind. A uniquely suitable spot, a natural grave where no trace of Stegl's body would ever be seen again. Tserek-Kel, the sulphurous 'stinking lake'.

But first he had to walk his victim there. Not far, an hour's march, no more. Not by the easy route, the road the mule train took, but up over a thickly wooded hill.

Every time Stegl fell, more and more frequently, Tsagov found some new place on the German's body to pierce or slash with his dagger. Only twice did Stegl try, feebly, to resist. Each time Tsagov's sudden, vicious counter-attack sent him spinning, blood-soaked, into the snow.

They stumbled on, prodding and falling, till finally the lake came into view.

In the middle of a vast bowl of forest and steep snow-covered meadows, in the freezing pre-dawn night, a kind of miracle, a mirage appeared. A round lake, entirely surrounded by trees with white-rimmed branches, steaming, its whole surface trembling with tendrils of mist rising and quickly evaporating. No water could be seen, though beneath the steam was a deep, deep body of water that had never received nature's icy touch, water which through all four seasons remained at a constant nine degrees.

Stegl gasped, as if he had come face to face with some mystical Nordic burying-ground of his ancestors, as if he had died unknowingly and been condemned to boil for eternity in a huge open-air cauldron. In other circumstances – another life – he might have imagined himself at the ballet, enchanted by this Swan Lake that the most romantic set designer would never succeed in re-creating. But this was not in theatre. That steaming, apparently boiling, lake was real. Barely conscious from the loss of so much blood, he collapsed onto the ground, close to oblivion, in fact to death.

Tsagov hauled the inert body down to the water's edge, and slung it on the snowy bank, almost into the lake itself. Stegl's boots were licked by the tongues of steam.

Sticking out of the water like the bones of long-drowned giants were the grotesquely twisted shapes of bare white branches. Careful not to fall in – for the lake bottom fell away so sharply from the bank that, only fifty yards from where he stood, the water spiralled down to a depth of three hundred yards – he wrenched one of these half-sodden, half-frozen branches out. Then he unwrapped from around his waist a coil of coarse rope. Bending down and working carefully, methodically, he tied Stegl to the branch; by his neck, his chest, his thighs, one final time round his ankles. He stood up and surveyed the German, trussed like a goat on a spit, and he laughed.

For the first time, though he had wanted to many times in the last hour, Tsagov pulled out the flask of brandy. But he didn't put it to his own lips – little was left in it, and he needed every drop for a purpose much more pleasureable than merely drinking. Instead, he put the neck of the flask to Stegl's blood-clotted mouth. The dark beneath the trees made it hard to see, but with the dagger held in his left hand Tsagov felt for the hard enamel of the German's teeth, then used the point to pry open the lips. Tipping the flask, he forced a shot of brandy down into his throat. Stegl, choking and retching, opened his eyes.

'Herr Sturmbannführer,' said Tsagov mockingly. '*Sehr gut!* You are awake. Good. Now you can see.'

And then, as Stegl stared up at him, Tsagov suddenly plunged his dagger into the corner of the German's right eye. He twisted the point, ran it down, along and round. He flicked the blade, and the eye sprang out of its gouged socket. Two more deft strokes and the stringy membranes that still attached it to the face fell away. The eye slipped into the blood-flecked snow.

'For Boris Alexandrovich,' Tsagov murmured, and sighed deeply.

He looked down again at the German, whose mouth was now distorted in a rictus of horror and pain. Tsagov shrugged. Dead or alive, who could tell? What did it matter?

He waited till his own heartbeats subsided and the strength came back into his muscles. The supreme thrill relaxed into a glow of pleasure, in his body no less than his mind.

But it was cold, even by this warm water. Quickly he plunged both hands into the lake and washed them, splashing water also onto his face. Then he rinsed the point of the dagger and slipped it back into the sheath. Finally he took from one of Stegl's pockets a handkerchief, stained and rumpled. In it he wrapped the eye, putting it, with the rapid surreptitious movement of a thief, into an inside pocket.

That done, he wrenched round the branch to which Stegl was tied and plunged the end by the German's head into the lake. The mist hid the ripples. Scooping up stones from the very rim of the lake, he filled the pockets of the SS uniform. Then he took hold of the branch again and pushed hard. At first the body remained on top, the wood beneath the water's surface, but as they slipped further in, the branch suddenly span in Tsagov's hands, and the body disappeared below. Just before he let go, he gave one final heave, like a boy launching his toy boat as far as he could into the middle of a round pond.

The craft sailed out. At first its course was straight. Then, slowly, slowly, for Tsagov had known exactly where to point it, it began to turn. He watched its progress, slicing through the steam, sinking very slowly as it circled round, with a smile of deep satisfaction. It took several minutes more for him to be sure. But gradually the craft made a full wide arc, then, little by little, pulled in toward the centre of the lake in an ever-narrowing spiral.

Faster and faster Stegl's sodden body was sucked into the lake's deadly whirlpool, down into underground caverns through which the waters of Tserek-Kel for ever breathed in and out, in and out, in and out.

TWENTY-TWO

During the night of January 4–5, after two months of German occupation, Red Army and partisan forces entered Nalchik. Many of the same Russian commanders and men who had been thrown out of Nalchik and battered against the final bastion of the Caucasian mountains streamed back now into the Kabardinian-Balkar capital.

But still there was no sense of triumph.

Civilians came out into the streets. They cheered and waved. They said to each other, 'The tide has turned.' But the debris left at high-water mark was so horrifying a sight that few had the heart to celebrate. The city was burning.

Everything that could possibly have been used by the Russians was destroyed – buildings, weapons, stores, records . . . people.

Among the last to leave the burning town, in midmorning, on January 5, was Colonel Brandt.

His men noticed with alarm his more and more desperate behaviour. They wondered if his single obsession – to save lives – had turned to madness. He gave the order to counter-attack only when he saw the alternative was the annihilation of his own men, or when retreat was cut off. 'Pin them down, fire in the air, then get out fast!' What kind of an order was that? Brandt's jeep traced zigzags from unit to unit, from strong-point to strong-point, skirting the rubble and the flames and the smoke. The radio voices in his headphones were never silent. The transmitter in his hands crackled with his orders, all with the same sense. 'Take cover, get back, make it out fast!' Finally, with most of the German forces streaming from the town in headlong retreat, his own men, who had made that retreat possible, got out themselves.

Crammed in the back of Brandt's jeep was a box, a small cheap case made of Russian wood the thickness and quality of Bavarian cardboard. In it were clothes, Kabardinian clothes, taken from the truck that Hans had finally succeeded in prising open. Why? Brandt had no idea if it was just another gesture, a symbol. Or if, after all, he would tear off his field-gray uniform and put on these magnificent, traditional garments of the Caucasian tribesmen, the felt *burka*, the sheepskin *papakha* hat, the quilted *beshmet* jacket. Fancy dress! He knew that. And yet . . .

He rubbed his chin with the back of his bare hand. The stubble was coarse and sharp. There had been good reasons for neglecting to shave these last forty-eight hours. All the same, it hadn't happened before. Again he stroked his beard. It was comforting, the prickling sensation. He imagined it growing long and white.

Brandt looked up ahead and saw the tail of an armoured troop carrier, second to last in the column formed by his retreating Regiment. The last vehicle was his own jeep.

That instant the jeep lurched, and Brandt clutched desperately at the metal bar screwed into the dashboard. The front offside tyre, striking a rock, compressed like a punched cushion, slewed, re-expanded – but the jeep, knocked sideways, slithered on the gritty ice. Klaus Beutner, the driver, cursed, spun the wheel. Neither action prevented the jeep from skidding, sideways, into the back of a 3-ton Mercedes L3000 truck, abandoned in the littered gutter of the Baksan road.

'*Scheisse!*'

The impact flung Klaus, still cursing, onto the roadside. Brandt, doubled up, bounced back and forward from seat to dashboard like the vibrating arm of an alarm clock. He ended up back in his seat, intact but bruised.

Corporal Beutner, who had been with Brandt since the beginning of the Caucasus campaign, lay on the ground with his head half-hidden beneath the huge rear mudguard of the Mercedes truck.

Brandt pulled himself painfully out of the jeep and limped over to his driver. Dragging him clear of the truck, he examined him quickly. Klaus was alive, beginning to stir, to moan. From the dirty patch on the crown of his head Brandt saw he had been concussed on the icy surface of the road.

Brandt returned the few paces to the jeep, straddling the centre of the road after bouncing off the truck. One look was enough. It would never run on a wheel so grotesquely twisted. He noticed, in the back, the box of Kabardinian clothes. For several seconds he stood, immobilized, not seeing or hearing the trio of YAK 1 fighters that screamed overhead, diving to machine-gun the main body of German forces retreating further to the west. He didn't see the leading Russian T 34 tank nose out into the long straight avenue, lined with wrecks and stunted trees, less than a mile back toward town.

It was his last chance. His last chance to break free. Now — for ever. How many Germans were behind him? Perhaps none, maybe just a handful. He could take the clothes, disguise himself, run, run into the high mountains, the mountains he had always loved. When it was all over he would come down again to Nalchik, find Nadia . . .

A motorcycle with sidecar caught his eye, snapped him out of his dream. It was German, a big 751-cc Zündapp, a dispatch rider's machine, with sidecar. He could hear its engine racing, coughing on the cheap petrol as if it had blood in its diseased lungs.

Over by the truck, Klaus groaned.

The dispatch rider on his machine was, surely, the last retreating German.

'Klaus!'

Corporal Beutner gave another groan, pulled himself up to his knees, then pitched forward.

The sputtering engine of the motorcycle came nearer and nearer. Bullets began whistling in the air. Brandt had no feeling they were aimed at him. It seemed merely as if someone had tossed a huge quantity of ammunition into the burning pile of Nalchik, and the town was spitting them out at random as they ignited.

'Klaus!' he shouted again.

The motorcycle was fifty yards away, weaving from side to side of the avenue, avoiding potholes and debris. He saw the driver's face, hunched inside the wavy-brimmed helmet, white with fear.

Suddenly, determinedly, Brandt took the box out of the back of the jeep, clutched it to his chest. Then, straining every bruised muscle in his shoulders, he hurled it from him. The box flew across the Baksan road, fell tumbling into the ditch, split and ejected in all directions the bundles of Kabardinian cloaks and hats and jackets.

Brandt ran into the middle of the road. Holding his arms wide, making himself as huge and formidable as possible, he forced the motorcycle to come slithering to a halt in front of him, inches from his sleek-booted legs.

Brandt barked an order to wait right there. Moving quickly to where Klaus lay, he picked him up in his arms, then returned and half-fell, half-squeezed himself into the sidecar's oblong cavity. He held Klaus across the body of the sidecar like a baby.

'Move. Go!' he yelled.

The dispatch rider broke out of his trance, roared the motor, engaged the lowest gear and jerked the overweighted machine into motion.

*

Six hours later, with darkness falling outside and the tent illuminated by two flickering oil lamps, Brandt had his first face-to-face meeting with his Divisional Commander since the retreat.

'Rough,' agreed von Kreuss, having listened to Brandt's brief report. 'Casualties?'

'Less than other units.'

'Good man. Drink up. Probably have to ditch what we don't get through tonight. Now. Ott. What a mess. You know what's happened?'

'Nothing recent, Herr General. The last I heard Major Ott was in the mountains with units of his 3rd Battalion.'

'He's still there. In a spot of trouble. Remember that report of yours? One you did after that special mission?' Brandt flushed but said nothing, and von Kreuss went on.

'Village with odd sort of name. Valley of the Narzans. Whatever Narzans –'

'Giants. There's a myth that –'

'Just south of there Ott's got himself trapped. Moved up smartish, the Ivans. Big guns as well as their raggle-taggle chaps. Weather's not good. Avalanches, blizzards, that kind of thing. Of course the Russkies move a bit faster in the foothills than Ott up high. Anyway, whatever the reason, the chap's got himself cut off.'

'Where precisely?'

'Here, let's look at this map. You know this part, of course. Well, better see about getting him out, eh? Yes . . . here somewhere.'

They talked over the possible ways of extracting Major Ott's detachment.

'Good men up there,' von Kreuss said at the end, wagging an arthritic finger. 'Couple of the chaps who put the flag on Elbrus. Damn silly idea. But showed what we could do. Quality men. Better send a good team. Who'd you suggest?'

'Myself.'

'Nonsense. Just a small number of chaps needed.'

'I'm the only one who's been in that part before, Herr General. As you read in my . . . report.'

'Hmmm. Drink up. We must get some kip. Nonsense, old fellow. Send young Dibelius, someone like that. Young, keen, fast. Up to you, of course.'

But Brandt knew he would go himself. When he had thrown away that box of Kabardinian clothes, he had thrown away his last tempting possibility of personal freedom. His death-wish was galloping now, pulling him on, as if he were tied to a sledge behind a wild horse.

'You feeling all right?'

'Yes. I –'

'Know what? I'll be glad to get away from these damn mountains.' The gruff old officer laughed. 'Never should have commanded a Mountain Division! That's what you're saying. Ridiculous! Maybe you're right. Expect you'll miss them, Colonel. Still, no beating your head against a granite wall. Now, when're you going to let me have that lad of yours?'

'Lad? Ah, Hans.' Brandt drank off the last two fingers of scotch in his glass. 'I'll transfer him tomorrow.'

'What? Now, I didn't –'

'He's due for a change, Herr General. I'll see to it myself.' Brandt stood up. His legs were wobbling. He was desperately tired.

Von Kreuss pointed at the glass he had just half-filled with neat scotch.

'Don't,' he went on, adopting the fatherly tone that Brandt had often heard him use to more junior officers and men, 'don't lose the taste for life. Don't make complications for yourself. I've seen it happen. Life's quite simple. Whatever's on your mind will go away soon enough. Deal with the practical problems. God knows there're enough of them. It all comes down to honour in the end. Be honourable. Be loyal. You can't go far wrong.'

'Quite so, Herr General.'

'Ah, incidentally. Stegl. Gestapo chap. Can't think what he was on about. Attached to us at one time, wasn't he?'

Brandt nodded, anxious.

'Some file. Got a message. Ungodly hour in the night. Whatever date it was. Said he would send me a copy. What file? Never mind. Not now. All smashed up, Gestapo HQ.' Von Kreuss gave a hoarse chuckle. 'No idea what it was all about. Have you?'

'Yes. But it no longer matters.'

'Doubt if it ever mattered. Always believed in trusting my officers. Good night, Colonel.'

Part Four

LIBERATION

TWENTY-THREE

'Da da duuummm!' Darya hummed enthusiastically, off-key but catching the mood. The family was clustered round their radio. All the faces were excited. For the first time in the whole dreadful bloodstained course of the Great Patriotic War the *Internationale* – still the Soviet anthem – was being played to celebrate a Soviet victory. Through the smashed side of the radio set the big valves glowed like fat red cheeks.

'Even in Moscow,' Mariana said, 'they've got to believe that now, at last, the tide has turned.'

Nadia clutched Darya to her and laughed.

'You remember the tune, darling! So long ago!'

'Da da duuummm!'!' went Darya, though the music had ended and an announcer was already giving the latest details of the liberation of Mozdok and the German retreat all along the 'southern front' in that pompous, exhortatory tone of Moscow announcers which irritated everyone because the speaker seemed to be taking all the credit for himself, but which nevertheless left the most sceptical listeners brimming with pride and patriotic sentiment.

There were altogether too many people crammed into the small room in Hassan Pachev's 'house' opposite the Dobroliubov's blown-up ruin.

Only hours after the last German had left the city they had all said goodbye to the Kafarovs, falling on each others' necks with tears of gratitude and good wishes. Now they were installed, if not in their old home, at least next door.

Nadia came first, leaning on Luda's arm. Everyone cosseted her, knowing that constant love and care and attention on their part were needed to bring her 'back to normal'. Only Nadia knew that the causes of her 'insanity' went deeper than anyone around her ever suspected.

'He'll come, any day now. You must give him time to recover. They'll be looking after him well in the mountains, don't worry, darling,' Luda endlessly said, fussing over her sister-in-law. But Nadia hoped, prayed indeed, every moment of the day, that when Boris did come back, he would not, as she secretly feared, be already destroyed, one of the many – everybody had heard about them – whom the Gestapo turned into cripples. Like Ilya, only worse. The boy had died, was peaceful now, but they ... they made a mockery of living, these wretched, undead victims. It was not Boris's body she feared for. The women could tend that. It was his mind. What *had* the Gestapo done to him in the long, long week they held him in their vicious cells?

Mariana meanwhile had become obsessed with Old Rags. Nadia believed it was partly in order not to think about Ilya. Indeed, her mother's tired brain was filled with the image of her exploding house ... of the old man blown to shreds inside.

In many respects Mariana was assuming the passive, ignored role of Old Rags. She didn't take up a position on the floor, in the corner, or invent stories or complain of a wheezing chest. But she had grown so old so suddenly she seemed incapable of action anymore. Even Darya couldn't lift the heavy weight off her. The sadness of it all – Ilya above all, her husband, the many many others – overwhelmed her. 'I might as well,' she told Nadia, 'be dead.'

'Soon,' she would whisper to no-one and to everyone, to herself, 'soon, soon.'

'Why soon, Granny?' Darya asked sometimes, if she heard the whispering. 'What's soon?'

Mariana would look at her granddaughter, puzzled.

'Come on, little one,' her mother or Luda would say. 'Leave Granny alone. Come and play.'

'What's there to play?'

It was true there was nothing to do. Nothing but wait.

*

Luda came running into the room and tugged at Nadia's sleeve. 'There's someone looking for you, darling,' she gasped. 'She seems angry about something. She said she wants to . . . check up something. Perhaps she's mad. She was saying something about spies being everywhere, having to ferret them out.'

Nadia's face went white. 'Who? Who?'

'A woman,' said Luda. 'An old Kabardinian.'

'Blind? Is she blind?'

'No, darling. What makes you –?'

'Have you ever seen her before?'

'No.'

'Is she alone.'

'There's a young girl with her.'

'Where are they?'

'Outside. Shall I –?'

'No,' Nadia said quickly. 'Tell them to wait. Tell them I'll come out and see them.'

'But it's snowing, darling. You shouldn't.'

'Luda, please, please.' Nadia barely suppressed a scream. 'Do as I ask.'

Luda went outside and told the woman what Nadia said, that she'd be out very soon. The old woman grumbled, but there was nothing she could do except wait.

Luda stayed with the old woman and the stout young girl. But when Nadia finally came out she sent her sister-in-law back inside. The peremptory tone of Nadia's voice left Luda no choice.

'Yes? What is it?'

Nadia spoke in Russian. The woman replied in Kabardinian, staring at Nadia as if provoking her to confess dark secrets. Her hair was tied severely with a black scarf, and her black, patched coat trailed in the dirty snow. Her mouth was sucked into a crinkled frill of taut flesh.

'Strange visit we had. Someone was looking for you if Surkova's your name.'

Nadia nodded. 'I don't know you, granny. What's your name?'

'You know any Germans?'

Nadia flushed. Her heart, already pounding, fluttered wildly. 'What do you mean? What are you asking me these questions for?'

'Don't be so hasty, young woman,' the old one replied.

'Who's the girl? Who are you both?'

'Officer,' said the old woman, silkily, 'You know any German officers? Important ones with boots.'

'Get to the point or go away.'

'One came looking for you. I said I'd never seen you, never heard of you. And that was true enough. But afterward I found out. It's a small town, ours. People know you.'

'Then they could tell you I wouldn't know any German officers.'

'That's what they told me,' the old woman agreed.

'They told you the truth. Now, is that enough?'

'No. He asked for you. By name. Tell me.' She started screaming: 'He knew you. He must have known you.'

'What gives you the right, granny, to accuse people?' Nadia shouted back. 'What did you do during the occupation? The Gestapo killed my brother. My father was killed by German soldiers in Pyatigorsk. My husband . . . my husband, he . . . maybe he too is dead.' She blinked away a clot of snowflakes that fell on her eyelash and said with angry desperation, 'It was you the German officer came to see, not me. What's your name? If Nina Petrovna were alive, I'd tell her what you're doing. She'd soon check up and –'

The old woman put out a hand and grasped Nadia's arm.

'Eh? Nina Petrovna? Which Nina Petrovna?'

Nadia calmed down. She was being a fool. The occupation was over. Even if the Women's Resistance Group still existed, it no longer needed to be a secret.

'We all heard about Nina Petrovna,' the old woman said. Her hand still held Nadia's arm, and the emotion flowed along it and into Nadia as if they were joined by a single nerve. But suddenly, she turned to Nadia and said sharply, 'Then why did the Fritzy behave so nice, eh?'

'Nice?'

'The officer. Most often they came with guns, with whips, kicked the furniture to pieces . . .' her voice fell to a whisper, 'did things to girls.'

Nadia turned and looked at the plain girl following them like a plump donkey. A laugh bubbled up and escaped through her lips. No, he wouldn't have 'done things' to her!

To Nadia's relief the old woman also gave a chuckle.

'God only knows the ways of the Fritzes,' she said. 'I'm sorry. I trust you. I was wrong to suspect you. You know how it is. So many people saying things – and I'm a Kabardinian. The authorities, they say us Kabardinians – you know how it was. The Balkars too. Bad blood, bad blood. I didn't mean to pry. But the neighbours. They saw the German officer come. They . . . wonder, see.'

'But why to you? And why did he ask you about me?'

The old woman shrugged. How could she know of Bekirbi's random choice?

'Well, my dear,' the woman said, stopping and looking at Nadia full in the face for the first time. 'I'm glad the Fritzy didn't find you, eh! As well, eh? As well.'

Nadia looked squarely back at her. 'Yes, granny,' she said with a catch in her voice. 'As well.'

Nadia shook the elderly woman's hand, and the girl's too, then turned and walked quickly back to where her family waited.

*

Next day, under pretext of seeking out friends for news of her former colleagues in the Resistance Group, Nadia turned her steps toward the Nalchik River, and the square whitewashed house on its bank. Brandt's billet.

There still hung over the town a haze, but it was the residue of burning. Years of effort wasted, senselessly destroyed. The acrid smell caught in her throat, was enough to make one cry.

In ten minutes she reached the billet – or rather the place where it had been, the shell of the house, like a picture of a monastery chapel sacked by the French revolutionaries which figured on the cover of one of her textbooks. Burnt in places down to the ground, the walls rose, almost gracefully, to about six to ten feet high, then tumbled down again. All that was lacking was an encrusting of ivy and trailing vines. The roof had fallen in, charred timbers and heaps of once-red tiles smashed to blackened rubble. The snow was gray with debris and spiked by fallen spars and stones, but was marked with no footprints. Only now did she realize how quiet everything had become since the liberation, since the end of the days and nights of bombardment and firing and flames and huddling in cellars.

For a long time Nadia just stood and stared. The image of his battered corpse inside the ruin hovered in her brain like a mirage. Before the old woman came she had never seriously imagined him dead. Now she thought of nothing else.

Then, down by the river bank, she noticed a small boy.

She called to him but, though he heard her, he didn't move. So she picked her way through snow up to her knees to where he was standing, leaning his back against the trunk of a tall bare poplar. He was about ten years old, dressed in a woman's overcoat and a Soviet tankman's leather helmet. He looked cold and shrunk and miserable.

So like Ilya! At first the thought appalled her, but then it made her smile; the boy seeing that smile, the strong white teeth and the auburn curl escaping from the tight wool scarf, acknowledged the right of a beautiful woman to a greeting.

Nadia returned the greeting and asked him if he'd known the house. She pointed behind her. He nodded.

'I live in that one.' He indicated with his head what was little more than a wooden shed.

'Alone?'

'No.'

'With your mother?'

'No,' he said, sighing this time. Then, after a pause, reluctantly, 'With my grandmother.'

Nadia sighed with relief. 'Is she there now?'

'No.'

'Will she be back?'

The boy nodded. 'Some time.'

'Doesn't anybody live in the other house?'

'Sometimes.'

'When was it hit?'

Nadia trembled with impatience as the boy tried to connect all the events he'd witnesses one to another, on a scale of time. 'The morning the fat German left.'

'The fat one?'

'You know, they had servants, their officers. He was a servant. He used to give me things sometimes. He –'

Suddenly the boy realized what he was saying. Savagely he turned his face away and began running back up toward his house.

Nadia plunged through the snow after him, snatched at his arm. He swore, hit at her wrist, but she clung on.

'Please, please. I only want to know one thing more. I don't mind if . . . I understand.'

'Let me go!'

'Wait, *please*!'

Her desperate voice got through to him, and he turned to face her.

Nadia let his arm go.

'Just tell me one thing. The officer there. Was he inside?'

His eyes pierced hers. 'Why?'

Nadia took a deep breath. 'Because . . . because . . .' But there was nothing she could say. To lie, to say she wanted this particular vile Fritz to die because he had tortured her own little daughter, any such horrible lie to serve her purpose, to prompt the boy to give her the information, was impossible. The words would not come out, would not even form. To confess, to tell this boy about their love, that too was impossible. Again, there was no way either one could enquire about the other without the most terrible risks. Her Colonel had known that. Though once he had asked for her by name.

There was nothing she could say.

Nadia watched the boy go, turned and walked slowly back up through the snow to the ruined billet. She stood a moment more, looking at it through tear-smudged eyes.

Then, suddenly, coming toward her was a figure Nadia recognized immediately. A dumpy, sexless figure in a ragged greatcoat and a huge rabbit-fur hat with outsize flaps hanging down over the ears and dangling on the broad sloping shoulders, shuffling unsteadily.

'Auntie!'

The figure looked up. Ahead, then to left and right. Came nearer, weaving uncertainly from side to side, as if drunk but not quite like that . . .

Only when they were a few feet apart did Nadia realize that Auntie was blind.

'Auntie!' she cried again, the word caught on the lump in her throat so she had to repeat it. 'Auntie! what did they – what happened? It's me, Nadia Sergeevna.'

'Ah!' Auntie let out a long sigh. 'I thought the voice was yours. So one of you is still alive. Yes, yes, it seems to me I heard that already somewhere, that Nadia Sergeevna survived. That's good. But all of us others, we weren't so bloody lucky.'

Nadia clasped the old blind woman in her arms. 'All? All except me? It's true, then, what I was so afraid of?'

'So, it is. Me, I'm old. Acid. They did it with bloody acid. Not the Fritzes. Bloody traitors working for 'em.'

Auntie pushed Nadia from her and turned her head away. Her face was so hidden in the cap and the earflaps that Nadia could only guess at the disfigurement she must have suffered.

'What are you doing here, Auntie? Can you see at all, I mean, enough to find your way? Where are you going?'

'Going?' Auntie repeated helplessly. 'Why should I be going anywhere? Nowhere fucking well to go.'

'Have you nowhere to live?'

'Live?'

'You must stay with me, with us. We have room. Let me take you there, right now.'

Auntie protested, but feebly.

Nadia led her back to the small house. There was almost nowhere to put Auntie, but they found her a place all the same, in the corner. To Nadia's amazement – she had expected protests, even if silent protests at first – Mariana welcomed Auntie ecstatically; she hugged and patted her, speaking to her almost as if she were a baby – or Old Rags, Nadia suddenly realized.

Yes, Nadia said to herself. There *will* be a future. A future that isn't altogether separated from the life we knew.

TWENTY-FOUR

Boris came limping at last out of the hills, alone and ragged. He was no longer lean, but scarecrow thin. His narrow lips were scarred with chaps and blisters. Dirty brown stubble smeared his face, and his eyes were dull.

He saw Nadia before she saw him.

She was in the courtyard, piling snow into a metal bucket with ungloved hands.

She seemed beautiful – as beautiful as the very first time, so long ago.

He hadn't prepared this moment. He had tried, but he couldn't. His mind refused to picture it, refused to allow him to make plans, to calculate. When he saw her, he staggered in the road, like a drunk. He fell hard against the plank fencing and avoided falling onto his face only by clutching with his hands at the rough wood, taking the dead weight of his body on his knees, as if kneeling in prayer.

Nadia, hearing the noise, came quickly out into the street. Kneeling, too, she put her arms round him and pressed his battered face to hers. She recalled the time when, outside the canning factory, she had fallen, exhausted, at his feet.

They stayed like that until, almost a minute later, he fainted.

With Mariana's help she dragged her husband into the tiny room. Even Auntie, even Darya, were shooed outside so the women, Nadia and her mother, could undress him, wrap him in blankets and, as soon as he began to stir, feed him spoons of the hot broth already simmering over a fire of damp sizzling wood.

Boris looked only at Nadia.

Every time she moved his eyes flickered.

The first time he tried to speak, it was to her. But the effort was premature. Words could not yet be formed in his mouth. Physically he was in even worse shape than when the partisans rescued him from the Gestapo cell. The cold in that cottage in Bagubent, the lack of food, anything at all to eat let alone the hot food he needed, the long crises of fever and dry retching that followed, all this so weakened him that, literally, he used up his last physical resources in his long trek home.

For eventually, in Bagubent, he had found himself completely alone. The partisans had long since set off on their missions. Some of the villagers were left, a few old folk, women and children. But they had their own problems of survival. Boris, a stranger to them, a last anonymous locust bequeathed by the partisan leader, unable to make himself understood, was a burden no-one wanted to assume. And since he was about to die, there was no use wasting scarce food on him.

For several days he lay in a state of utter neglect. Then the villagers saw a man arrive, go inside the cottage and stay ten minutes – before leaving at a run, his cloak hiding his head.

Only a group of small children saw what happened next.

A weird, tall, desperately thin young man pushed his way out through the solid iron gate that guarded 'Old Misha's' cottage. His right hand brandished a dirty, dark-stained rag shaped like a small flour-bag. Out in the street he hurled the bag away from him. It skidded on the ice, burst open and landed in a messy heap at the edge of the drainage ditch. While the man-monster staggered off in the direction of Kashka Tau and Nalchik, the children swooped on the mystery package. It took several seconds before they made out that the contents consisted simply of – an eye!

Screaming their disgust they kicked at it, covering it with grit and snow, not daring to touch it even with their felt boots. In the middle of the game a mangy dog appeared, gaunt with hunger. Daring their flailing feet and their shouts, he snapped his jaws on the putrid but edible object and scuttled off to eat it out of range.

The children went back to their original game of stamping crazy patterns in the puddles of ice.

The memory of that cold blood-streaked eye still made Boris convulse, waking and in his dreams.

Yet the German officer's face – so vivid before – never came into his sleep now. More and more he dreamed of Nadia as they knew each other years before, almost children; of Dasha as a baby, with her mass of dark-copper curls and he constantly mobile, puckering, laughing, bemusedly blinking face; of himself a small boy with the red Pioneer scarf like a flag around his neck.

*

In twenty-four hours Boris was able to sit, to take soup by himself, to smile a little and, in short bursts, to talk.

When that first happened Nadia had a terrible fear her husband's brain was damaged, so blurred was his speech. This was what Luda had warned her about. But each time he tried he improved. Normal clarity returned.

From the beginning, he made no complaints. He never referred to his own pain. Instead he asked tenderly after the family and after the strange blind person whom, when Nadia told him, he begged to come over to the bed and hold hands with him and talk about how, now the Fritzes had gone, they would all begin to live again . . .

At last he was strong enough to get up.

This was the moment Nadia most feared, when they would have a chance to be alone together, when she would have to face up to what she had done. And yet some strange instinct mollified her fears. Somehow, during the long hours she spent watching him, she had read forgiveness in his eyes.

The very first thing Boris insisted on doing was to cross the courtyard and see the ruin of their own house. Nadia took his arm.

'The devil,' said Boris softly. 'Or as Auntie would put it, "fucking hell!"'

Nadia laughed nervously. 'That's unfair. She hardly says those things anymore.'

'Not when Dasha's there.'

'Or mother.'

'You did well to bring her to us. She has been wonderfully brave. You too, Nadia.'

She flushed. 'Let's look inside. I haven't dared yet. Mother went in – well, looked in.' A lump caught in her throat. A queasy feeling fluttered round the walls of her stomach like a butterfly trying to escape.

'Do you really want to? There's no need.'

'Let's go in. Together.'

They climbed, helping each other, over the lowest part of the outer wall, since the door presented the most formidable barrier, a stockade of splintered planks. Charges had been laid in the cellar as well as the two main rooms. Everything was destroyed. As Nadia looked around at the little pieces of recognizable things, at bent saucepans, shattered tiles from the big stove, splinters of furniture, shreds of material, all black from burning or gray with the dirty snow, the tears began to flow. Subtly, the roles changed, and Boris began to support her. He also was too close to tears to speak.

Nadia leaned her head on his shoulder. At last, through her tears, she said, 'Boris, there are things I must tell you.'

He stiffened, just perceptibly. 'No,' he said firmly. 'No, no. One day perhaps. Not now. Not now, darling.'

Boris bent down and poked around in the debris, though not quickly enough to prevent Nadia seeing the tears in his eyes. He picked up a few things, trying to identify objects that were still of value. 'Look, a copper pan. Just a dent. Let's find what we can.' He gave a deep sigh. 'Never mind the rest. After the war, Nadia, we'll rebuild it all. Start again from the foundations.'

They began making plans about how they would improve on the old one. Boris talked about seeing the Party street warden, about getting together a committee, about working to rebuild the whole town. 'When,' he added, 'I get back from the war.'

Nadia froze. Again a sick feeling clutched her stomach.

With the noise of the war gone, with the days passed in nursing her husband among the family again, she had almost succeeded in believing what she most fervently wished, that the war would suddenly finish; that she would go back to her classes again; that Boris, a Red Army hero, medals on his broadening chest, would stay with her, and together . . .

But the struggle wasn't over. It was too early for selfish dreams.

Suddenly a piercing shriek made them gasp and clutch at each other.

But it was a shriek of pure happiness.

'My candle! My little pink candle! Look, I found it!'

They turned to see Dasha, who had crept in behind them, holding up a big pre-Revolution box decorated with Armenian candied fruits, but blackened and dented. She tried to open it but couldn't with her small fingers. Boris took it and pulled the lid up. Inside was a tin that once contained preserved meat. Dasha peered in impatiently. 'More,' she said. Boris laughed and pulled out a matchbox. 'There, in there! Luda gave it to me.'

Dasha snatched the matchbox and pushed it open. At once her face crumpled.

'Oh! It's melted.'

'Quick!' said Boris. 'Come with me, little one.'

He dragged Dasha by the hand across the yard.

'Look.' He put the blob of pink wax on top of the stove and rolled his palm across it, keeping the wick, with its blackened tip, in the middle. In seconds he had reformed the candle.

Dasha clutched it, ecstatic. She ran back to Nadia in the ruin, leaving her father to follow at his own pace.

*

Early next morning, in the usual bustle of finding things they could face eating and heating water and rousing Darya, they almost forgot to turn on the radio. But Mariana remembered just in time to hear the latest news bulletin.

The very first item announced the re-capture of Pyatigorsk.

'Those fu . . . fun-loving Fritzes are on the run sure enough,' Auntie said from her corner.

Darya said in the middle of the silence that followed, 'So we'll see grandfather again, won't we?'

A confusion of shushing and pots being banged on the table greeted the child's remark. Mariana remained standing over the tiny stove, facing away from the room, and began stirring furiously some sticky porridge.

Boris ate his bowl of polenta and sour milk silently. He was watching Nadia. Something was cooking inside her brain, he could see that. He was not surprised when later in the morning, with Mariana and Darya out, trying to find something more interesting to eat, and Auntie busy in the yard learning again where everything was and trying to get a glimmer of light through into her brain now that the sun had burst through and there was almost a feel of spring in the air, he was not surprised when she came and sat on his bed, that same determined look on her face he was slowly coming to accept – perhaps admire.

'Boris.'

'Hmmm?'

'I have to – no, don't stop me, it's not the past I want to talk about. It's the future.'

Boris knew, however, it wasn't going to be one of those hopeful, optimistic talks they'd been having about all the things they would do when the war was over.

'Well?'

'You remember . . . you remember, in Pyatigorsk, when I was with father, and the Germans were coming?'

'That's hardly the future.'

'And we had that argument. You didn't want me to stay.'

'I didn't want you to risk your life. I didn't want to lose you.'

She smiled. 'I must go back.'

Yes, he knew it was coming. He knew he must control his reaction.

'Father might be alive. I was responsible for him. Mother has a right to know what happened.' She began to talk in a rush. 'I must know too. There was such confusion. Maybe he was taken somewhere. Maybe somebody has been looking after him all this time. And now –'

'Then they'll get a message back to us here. There's nothing to stop them.'

'I know it's unlikely. I know. But I left him there. I want to *know*. I need to know. I need to go there myself.'

Boris looked at her in silence.

She was hiding something. She wasn't telling him the whole truth, he could feel it. But had he told her the whole truth, his own whole truth? Would he ever? Didn't there have to be secrets now between them?

He took her hand.

'Yes, you must go,' he whispered.

She bent down and put her face against his.

And when finally she kissed him goodbye, saying again she would come back to him quickly, he remembered to whisper that he loved her.

*

The bridge over the railway track bent the Baksan road sharply to the right. Nadia walked steadily up its gentle incline until she could see the gangs of women clearing the debris from the marshalling yard below. Soon, she thought with a thrill of happiness, she herself would be at work again. Classes would start. But if they couldn't be organized soon, she would volunteer to help these women.

Down the other side of the bridge was a particularly hard-hit part of town. The few trees on each side of the long road that stood at all were bent or mutilated. Houses, factories, workshops, all were crushed into one enormous flat damp expanse of rubble, a man-made, grassless steppe.

At first Nadia felt simply the warmth, the unexpected, hopeful warmth, of the January sun. Soon she would be surrounded by sunflowers and wild fruit trees and bobbing corn. Meanwhile the hot sun was releasing the putrid fumes suppressed by the frost, and the smells of war were overpowering.

The noise of hammers and shovels and clattering stones came from behind her now. Ahead there was no movement, no noise at all. A few curls of smoke – from chimneys or still smouldering ruins, she couldn't tell – rose into the pale blue-gray sky.

Nadia had hoped already to have found a lift. Maybe a cart, preferably a supply truck that could get her most, even all, of the way before darkness fell. One or two trucks had driven the other way into Nalchik, and a donkey or two ridden by small boys had kept pace with her for a while before turning off down side-streets. But nothing passed her that she could signal to.

She was about to rest on a pile of stones when something caught her eye.

On the far side of the road – she was now on the very edge of the city – was a corpse. It attracted her attention because it was oddly festooned with ribbons, no, with crudely torn strips of cloth. And messages scrawled on in something dark – mud, perhaps . . . or dried blood. Most of the letters had run into each other. Curious to read them, she moved tentatively to the middle of the road. Most of the words were in Kabardinian – she could tell by the tall 'I', for instance, mixed with the Cyrillic letters – but she couldn't decipher them. Coming closer, wrapping even tighter around herself the old rug she wore over her shoulders like a cape she peered down. They were obscenities, she slowly began to realize, those words on the strips of cloth. But one Russian word was clear. The word TRAITOR wrapped around the corpse's neck. Then she noticed something she hadn't before, the uniform – the breeches, jackboots, brown shirt, black tie and black armband of a Nazi secret policeman; and, clutched in the dead arms, the folded, muddy bundle of an NKVD officer's jacket.

Her stomach was getting rapidly less steady.

Nadia wanted to stop looking, to get away. But just as she had felt compelled to leave the house, so now she was compelled to stay staring at this disgusting detritus flung into a ditch, already turning muddy in the warm sun.

Then, only then, did she see, really see, the face.

Narrow, hollow-cheeked, as if toothless; and hair, though matted, still crinkled and healthy-looking. But the eyes! Or rather the sockets – the gouged-out sockets. Through them threaded a kind of narrow ribbon, a mottled gray or khaki ribbon of the sort that went round officers' peaked caps. This ribbon was woven through the eyeless sockets, one end trapped behind the corpse's head, the other attached to a broader strip of cloth. But the message written on this filthy stained banner was crumpled into a ball and impossible to read.

Nadia stared at it a good minute before she dared lean down to touch it.

As she did so, her stomach heaved.

She straightened up, took in a deep breath, forced herself to yawn.

That moment a chill puff of wind eddied down the long road. The end of the banner flapped, unrolling the ball just a little. With her toe she helped it open the rest of the way.

The message consisted simply of a name. A name scrawled in dried blood.

Nazir Kerimovich Bekirbi.

As she read it, finally, her stomach rebelled against every restraint. Bending over, she vomited into the ditch, turning her head away just in time from the vile, defiled corpse of Captain Bekirbi.

Immediately she felt strong again.

When she looked back at the corpse – she couldn't help herself – there was no recurring spasm.

She crossed back across the road, walked on fifty yards, sat on some rubble. Her legs felt trembly.

No, she thought, it isn't that horrible sight, that reminder. Not altogether.

She remembered how odd she had been feeling that morning and off and on for the last few days. Bekirbi's corpse was just the trigger.

Was there another cause? Could there be?

She got up quickly and walked on.

*

When she heard the sound of a heavy truck behind her, she turned and, stepping out as far as she dared into its path, waved her hand.

The truck squealed, ponderously to a stop. A young soldier put his head out of the window and whistled appreciatively.

'Moscow any good to you, my beauty? Berlin? Paris?'

The older soldier in the cab with him laughed. Nadia could only just hear them above the unhealthy clatter of the motor.

She liked the look of them both. 'Just along this road'll do.'

'Hop up, my lovely. Don't mind him. That's it. Give her a hand, Volodya.'

She scrambled up and found a nest between the two soldiers who introduced themselves and told her at once what they were doing and where they were going, taking a supply of tyres and gasoline to Pyatigorsk.

'Me too?' asked Nadia. 'All the way?'

'Darling,' said the young driver, 'as I said, Berlin, Paris, wherever you want. It's just a matter of hanging around with us a bit longer, that's all.'

'All the way to Deutschland!'

The words reminded the soldiers of a song. They launched in, softly at first, but when Nadia picked up the chorus, loudly and happily. In the third verse they began putting back the dirty bits, with a nervous glance or two.

By the time they lumbered into Pyatigorsk, in the last dim light of dusk, they'd exhausted their whole repertoire, proposed, but gallantly, to Nadia ten times each and toasted victory with the brackish water of their water-bottles until they could rattle not a single drop more out of either.

For the whole three hours Nadia wallowed in a bath of happiness. And as she kissed the soldiers goodbye, confidence burst into her – like sunlight through a chink rubbed in a grimy, frost-caked window-pane.

TWENTY-FIVE

Brandt looked all around him, a vast panorama. For two days the atmospheric pressure had been rising. The snowline seemed to be visibly rising too, though like the hour-hand of a watch it was impossible to catch in motion. Elbrus itself was shyly swathed in cloud, but peaks scarcely less massive, scarcely less imposing, had begun to glisten in a big half-circle to the south. Smaller black-forested, black-rocked hills surrounded him completely in the 'first circle' of his mountain world.

And over there, in line with that tall fir-tree but many hours' march beyond and up, was the trapped Major Ott.

The desperate situation of those men from the 3rd Battalion had now become critical. Frantic radio messages revealed that the one pass by which they could escape, through the sheer-sided gorge of a tributary of the upper Malka River, was cut off by advance Russian units. Then the radio went dead.

Early that morning a rescue party led by Brandt had reached the last settlement to the south, Valley of the Narzans. Now they were midway between the romantic-sounding village and the grim reality of an almost impossible battle to free their colleagues.

They advanced in two parallel files, never more than a mile apart. Brandt led one column, Lieutenant Dibelius the other. Two columns of ten, all volunteers, with submachine guns slung across their backs – their only weapons apart from small pistols and knives. They were dressed in windproof but lightweight climbing gear and forage caps. Communication was by flag, Navy style. In each column were two men expert enough to signal quick, intelligible messages.

In action again – mountain action – with his men, Brandt felt an immense relief. It mattered to him not at all that this time he was attempting the impossible. After the carnage in Nalchik and the whole hideous retreat along the plain – the torment of leaving Nadia as near fatal to him as the enemy fire – this mountain mission was a liberation. He was among his own men.

Nor did he feel pain. The twisted ankle, the bruising from the jeep accident, all the grazes and scrapes of the retreat, none of these had the slightest physical effect. None registered, that's to say, in his brain.

He felt free.

He felt like a boy again.

The first objective, a narrow valley, came abruptly into view. Brandt raised his right hand. The men behind him stopped. His signaller contacted the second column, who confirmed they too were ready for the next stage. So far they'd met no opposition.

Just before midday, advancing again, each column keeping to its side of the small precipitous stream already gurgling with the premature spring, Brandt's men walked, cautious but confident, into the ambush.

'Halt!'
'Hände hoch!'
'Ruki verkh!'
'Halt!'
'Fritzi! Sie sind umgegeben. Kaputt!'

Voices, like shots, fired from every direction – even from behind. Shouts. Demonic laughter.

Brandt threw himself to the ground, then peered cautiously through the undergrowth.

Did they expect the Germans to surrender without a fight? He assumed not. Their tactic was to sow confusion. In the forest, voices always hit their mark; bullets were less sure.

But almost at once, from the other side of the stream, came the first shots – a raggle-taggle of fire, Russian rifles, shotguns, pistols.

Partisans!

The ambush was well sited. At this point a bend in the stream made the two columns invisible one to another.

Brandt saw where the Russians must be, above and to the sides. Straight ahead was the neck of the narrow valley, a natural funnel . . . and deadly to attempt. Below was the most obvious way out – but presenting a dangerously exposed field of fire where the trees gave way to almost flat rocky scrub two hundred yards back. Could the columns rejoin? No, the stream the tumbling, slippery, icy torrent, was a death-trap.

'Lieutenant!' he shouted, as the rifle fire broke off for an instant. 'Contingency – *Gentian!*'

Dibelius's voice came back like an echo. 'Gentian, Herr Oberst!'

Behind him, Brandt's nine men huddled behind cover, their fingers half-pressed on the triggers of their guns.

Just loud enough so they could all hear, he said, 'Go!'

They charged. Two from each column noisily down and away. The other eight back up at right angles to the stream – the feint retreat and the direct top-speed ascent.

They took each obstacle straight, the rocks like lizards, the trees like squirrels, landing like cats on all fours, jinking like deer from cover to cover, everywhere imitating their emblem, the mountain goat.

But the enemy was waiting too.

In the first seconds, three of Brandt's men – and two of Dibelius's, who had the best cover, the more accessible slope – fell to the partisans' bullets. That was their most vulnerable moment. In less than a minute, the four who had feinted downhill opened rapid fire. The main groups scrambled for the nearest firing positions as soon as they heard it. The shots below stopped. Immediately the main groups sent their first volley at the closest partisan positions, seen or guessed.

Then they took off, at forty-five degrees now, left and right, to the angle of their first line of retreat. Then more shots from below. Then more fire from above. Diversion, attack, diversion, attack. Turn, run, zigzag back onto the original line, stop, fire.

Several of the partisans were hit, not many, but enough to keep the others' heads down.

Just as he was thinking he had burst free, Brandt and two men at his side ran straight into four of the enemy. Firing from the hip the three Germans made cover beneath the rock, the vantage point of the four partisans. Speed! Don't give them time to plan! Brandt vaulted straight up at the four of them. They fired wildly, missed, turned and ran. Brandt led the others over the rock and away:

Dibelius's column was not so successful, or so lucky.

After charging in the rehearsed fashion up the steep incline, zigzagging, firing, darting on, suddenly they found the ground fall away under their feet. The trees and bushes ended in a thin bare gully. Their momentum carried all of them – all except the two who had gone downstream and the two who had already been hit – into this deadly hollow.

The partisans were waiting, right above.

Their rifles and submachine guns sprayed the German soldiers as if they were poisonous snakes writhing in a pit. All six were killed. It took less seconds than there were men.

The roar of this volley carried across the valley to Brandt, now over half a mile away.

Then came the yells of triumph, yells in Russian and what he now recognized as Kabardinian and Balkar.

He didn't stop. All his surviving group were with him now. They met no more resistance. Once over the top of the valley's ridge, they knew they had penetrated the outer ring of the partisans.

Finally they stopped in heavy cover. Brandt, two privates and Sergeant Kallfass.

'What d'you think, Sergeant? The others make it?'

Kallfass, a small, square Bavarian, looked grim.

The four men sat in a semi-circle. In a natural bower of honeysuckle interlaced with a tangle of saplings of birch and chestnut, their hot breath and sweat quickly created a comfortable foggy atmosphere. Droplets of blood and slashes of black and red scarred their faces and hands.

Brandt stood up.

'We'll post the flags. Let's go.'

Carefully he stuck the first, red, flag between two rocks on a prominent mound. From here he surveyed where he would put the second. Selecting a spot a quarter of a mile away, he went quickly to it and posted the blue flag. If any of the scattered soldiers saw either flag, then located the second – there was a clear view from one to the other – he could work out an imaginary line ninety degrees west from the mid-point between them. That was the line to follow.

On the other hand, if the partisans saw the flags first – well, they would remove them. But the signal would mean nothing.

Brandt's group now moved in a south-westerly direction, hurrying away from the ambush site and the posted flags. Only when a couple of miles had been covered did they slow down, save their energy, advance more cautiously.

With his compass, map and binoculars Brandt took more bearings. He chose a place with a good all-round view and stopped there.

'We rest an hour. Eat, drink. If no-one catches up with us we push on.'

The fifth – and last – man was lucky. Sergeant Kollfass spotted him moving through sparse trees with five minutes to spare.

The Corporal from Dibelius's column, one of the two who had tried to set up a diversion below the ambush, was out of breath and scared – though incredulously relieved he had seen the flags, taken the right course and linked up.

He was shaking as he stammered out to Brandt what happened, how both pairs had met up, but then been surrounded. 'Fifty at least. Some of them women. They were that close I could see. Blazing away. They hit all the others. We were running like hell. I guess I was lucky.'

'And fast,' said Brandt. It was true. The Corporal was divisional sprint champion.

Brandt pored over his damp map. The ambush, he decided, would not deflect him from his main purpose, his mission to rescue Ott and the men of the 3rd Battalion.

There might be a way over that ridge. There might.

But the partisans knew from experience which paths he could take, which ridges he could cross, which valleys and gullies offered the best chance of ambush and attack.

Someone out there seems to have my measure, Brandt thought, seems to understand me, read my mind. They were waiting for me. They'll try again.

The only answer was the same one he always gave: go for the impossible.

Look for a vertical cliff. Look for a glacier pitted with crevasses. Find the deepest gorge and sling ropes across.

But ultimately he had to engage the enemy, clear a path through the ring round Ott, and reach that point, six miles away, by the shortest route. It wasn't a time for fantastic exploits.

His finger traced a line on the map. The main access route was the Malka valley itself – the front gate.

'Ready? Single file. Absolute silence. Sergeant, take up the rear. Any opposition, shoot and keep moving. Okay. Go!'

*

Fifty minutes later they stopped below a ridge that separated their position from a steep though not vertical cliff down to the frozen Malka. There had been no sign of the enemy.

'Wait here.'

Brandt crawled forward, put his head over the ridge and focussed his field glasses.

Four hundred yards away was a huge pile of snow; the result of an avalanche, a fall that took place a week, perhaps two, before. At first it seemed to block the way forward. Then Brandt thought of it maybe as an opportunity. Did the partisans see it as a natural obstacle? One they didn't have to defend? Could he use it? Were Ott's men right behind it? If so, he could sling ropes down to them. His map showed a mass of tight contours.

He signalled for his men to come up and join him. Together they surveyed the massive heap of snow.

'We'll go line abreast. Sergeant, on the right flank. I'll take the centre. The others – one between myself and Sergeant Kollfass, two on my left. Get across and we'll regroup, take things from there.'

They set off at a run.

Brandt, however, had an uncomfortable feeling in the pit of his stomach. Where were the partisans? Had they been observing the five Germans all along?

Maybe not. For the last couple of hours the mist had been

thickening appreciably. Now they were virtually in thin cloud, though visibility, in patches, was up to half a mile.

They reached the base of the avalanche, where thousands of tons of snow had rolled downhill like a gigantic truck and smashed head-on into a solid rock wall – the wreckage grotesquely twisted and misshapen.

Their boots sank deep into the soft snow. Sometimes there was a deceptive crust. Then their legs plummeted down, and the snow grabbed them up to their waists. But slithering and hauling themselves along, using their submachine guns and torn-off branches as anchors and every firm object as footholds and handholds, they climbed up, eventually, onto the very top of the summit.

Brandt relaxed for a second, looked left and right.

It seemed, in the stillness, he could hear the Malka River, melting and trickling down underground chambers that all the while it was hollowing out, way beneath him, through thirty yards or so of snow. A soft, Alpine sound.

Then, that instant – partisans!

Again, partisans, right there – right in front! Jumping up out of the snow, yelling and firing, like Ali Baba's thieves popping out of huge curly-handled jugs.

Flinging themselves flat the five Germans crawled for cover.

But there was only snow.

Brandt lost sight of his four companions. It was every man for himself. He struggled to get out his flare pistol. Perhaps, if Ott's men were near, they could make a run for it now. Perhaps he could hold enough heads down in this damn snow . . . A black-stubbled face half-hidden in a sheepskin hat suddenly appeared in front of him. A huge hunting rifle snapped up to a shoulder. Brandt had only the flare pistol. He pressed the trigger. The fat cartridge caught the partisan on the right side of his chest, knocking him sideways, then ricocheted up into the air, where it exploded in a blaze of red. Even before the flash Brandt dived onto the tribesman. They rolled in the soft snow, almost burying themselves. Brandt grabbed hold of the rifle and sent it slithering into a gully. Unable to reach his own weapons, even his knife, he twisted his legs beneath him, felt the flailing, grunting partisan on top and kicked out with both feet. The man shot away like a human cannonball, tumbling down the snow slope, then ramming the stump of an uprooted tree. Not even his thick hat saved him from instant knockout.

Brandt looked quickly around. Where the hell was his submachine gun? Buried!

He fumbled for his Walther pistol, drew it out of its holster.

He looked up again.

Christ – him!

There, just six feet away, a man he recognized. That huge, magnificent, patriarchal partisan.

Kochan had the same instant recognition.

'Ahhh!' he roared. 'The man who climbed Mishirgi!'

*

Physical sensations seeped slowly back into Brandt's body like droplets of red blood staining a laboratory beaker of pure water. At first he believed himself in a train, looking out of the window at a forest flashing past. Then on deck, in a lounge chair on a transatlantic liner. Then in the back of his jeep, sightless under a pile of heavy, so heavy, furs . . .

'Herr Oberst?'

Who was –? Ott's voice.

'Nearly safe, Herr Oberst. We'll get you there.'

'Where?'

Though Brandt mouthed the word, no sound came out. He opened his eyes stickily – and saw his Battalion commander's face.

Major Ott began to tell Brandt how they were having to keep well west of Kislovodsk. The spa towns were in Soviet hands. Partisans, Red Army units.

Fragments of an earlier story came back to Brandt.

'Not so fast, Major. I was wounded?' The words came now, if slowly. 'I'm not a – let me think. I'm on a stretcher.'

'Can you see all right, Herr Oberst? Your eyes – the right eye –'

'Hit? I see something. What happened? Yes, the partisans.

Him! Him again.' Brandt began to laugh, his eyes to leak cold drops of tears.

Ott, puzzled, related to his commanding officer as simply as possible what had happened, though it wasn't easy to get near enough to talk. The terrain was rough. Major Ott, tall and thin, had himself to hold the ropes of the makeshift stretcher at the heavy, head, end.

The battle had been over quickly. The thirty trapped men of the 3rd Battalion had stormed up the bare open slope out of the forest as soon as they heard the shooting on top of the snowdrift. The partisans, attacked from front and rear, first counter-attacked. But too many of Ott's men made the climb. After three or four minutes the partisans bolted, melted into the snow and the trees. They left behind five dead.

'The big one too?'

'Their leader? No, he survived. We got him though. Winged.'

'He's *here*?'

'We lost six men. Four of your men died. We couldn't find more.'

'Four?' Brandt registered the news. 'All four dead?'

'You are the only one to – I must thank you, Herr Oberst. We could never have –'

'Sergeant Kollfass? Those three kids.' Brandt's mind began to picture the faces of all the men who had come with him on the mission. And just himself, he alone alive. When he was so sure . . . 'Major Ott!'

'Herr Oberst!'

'Get me up off this goddamn thing. Stop a moment.' His voice scarcely carried as far as the Major.

'We must push on. And you can't . . . you can't by yourself, Herr Oberst,' Ott said, almost as softly.

'Let's see.'

Brandt tried to move. Nothing. Not a muscle obeyed. Not even his neck, to get a look. He could just see Ott, above him, jerkily. Gray sky, branches, the Major's head. A raven, gliding overhead across his field of vision like a Heinkel flitting across a movie screen. But no, he couldn't even twist around.

'Bad as that?'

'We'll have to see, Herr Oberst. When we catch up. You'll be okay.'

But suddenly the conviction, the *happy* conviction, came to Brandt that he too wouldn't survive.

'Eh, *Polkovnik*!'

A deep Russian voice.

'They told me you'd waked up.'

'Where? Where are you?'

'On your right. Kochan, Tembot Batazarovich. Ha! I knew, up on Mishirgi, we'd meet again. I had a picture of you, Colonel. It lived with me. That square-jawed German in your forage cap, parka hood thrown back, looking at me like you knew who I was all along. How could I forget?'

Brandt felt a deep sense of contentment. So the feeling up there had been mutual. He whispered, 'So they got you.'

'They? *You* got me.'

Brandt was appalled. 'Me? I –?'

'No, you bloody fool Colonel. Your soldiers. You know what *you* did. Pointed that pea-shooter pistol right at my guts. Then you chucked the damn thing in the snow. Now, what made you do a thing like that, eh?'

'I did? Then how –?'

'Someone got me in the pinkie! The littlest bit of me. Made me so mad I forgot to run away with the rest of 'em. What was up with you then, eh, Colonel? Lost the taste for killing Ivans?'

'Ott! Major Ott!'

'Herr Oberst!'

'Still there? Yes, I see, I think I see you. Give the ropes to the partisan.'

'But he –'

'He can do it.' Then in Russian, 'Tembot Batazarovich, take the ropes, damn it. I didn't shoot, is that right? That's it. You don't need more than nine fingers. Who's got the other end?'

'A German lad,' Tembot said, shouldering the stretcher ropes as if they were the reins of a donkey cart. 'He won't drop you, no more than I will. That bullet only bent my finger. I already bent it back again. Little throb it makes, good as a cup of black coffee for keeping me awake and lively.'

Brandt felt his body sway, then steady.

'So, Colonel,' Tembot said, 'you have our language too.'

But Brandt's mind had lost track of the sounds and sights around him, was somewhere in Pyatigorsk . . . a cottage . . .

Tembot's voice was like a distant echo.

'Bad timing, such bad timing,' the old partisan was saying. 'We Russians spend enough years destroying ourselves. We were just starting to build again.'

Brandt, concentrating now, replied, 'That's what the Nazis feared.'

Tembot adjusted his hold. 'Ha! So, Colonel, you're not one of them.'

'I fought for them. Maybe that is worse.'

Brandt's thin voice was drowned by Tembot's deep laugh. 'Finally I get a Fritz in my power, can tip him over any precipice I like, and he tells me he's not a Nazi! I should have killed you on Mishirgi. A man like you gives people ideas. Maybe all Fritzes aren't Nazis, people start thinking, hey, wasn't Karl Marx a German, Rosa Luxemburg, what did those books say happened in 1919? Then they aim crooked. Oh, yes. I should've been quicker on the trigger. But you're lucky, Colonel. You are dying now.'

'Ah!'

Brandt was relieved to hear it so bluntly.

A smile almost succeeded in overcoming the paralysis of his muscles. Should I tell him, he wondered? It's my last chance to tell someone, and this old man will understand. But, no. He would understand, but he would not, could not, approve. Some secrets are too precious to tell. Too precious and too dangerous. Yet if I could get a message through . . . I'd tell her: it's *all right*. I am dying. It's all right.

'What happened,' he asked softly – the rhythm of the bobbing stretcher was a comfort now – 'at the end of the battle?'

Tembot shook his head, and the ropes that passed over his shoulders and crossed behind his back tautened like mooring ropes tied to a rocking boat.

'Ahhh! You sprung the trap, Colonel. Damn it, we had

'em. They were surrounded, cut off completely. But they'd have had to break out before long, suicide though it would have been. Fact was, we wanted 'em to as well. We couldn't hang around for ever, there were other jobs to do. We dug in the snowdrift, where the avalanche had come down. Calculated they'd try and slip out that way if we kept our heads down long enough. All goes according to plan, then, bugger me, if you don't come scrambling up the other side. Up we jump – and shambles! You had us looking the wrong way, Colonel. Still, I wouldn't have stood there staring and got a bullet in my pinkie if you hadn't gone berserk.'

'Berserk?'

'Crazy as a frog in a puddle. Happy crazy. Chucked your pistol in the snow, threw up your arms and shouted something in German. Then you laughed. Still laughing when the bullets got you, Colonel. What the hell was so funny, I don't know. My finger didn't get blasted till afterward!'

'Laughing,' Brandt whispered.

'Down on my fat old ass I fell,' Tembot went on, growling to himself, seeing Brandt's eyes close and a wave of pain sweep over his pinched features, 'Fritzes jumping on me from all sides. Still, I shook 'em off. Till one of 'em knocked me on the head with his pistol butt. Too bloody old to waste a bullet on, I guess.' He walked a few paces in silence, then began muttering again, 'Second bloody time. Mishirgi – then on top of the avalanche. Twice he could've knocked me off.'

'Three times,' came Brandt's voice faintly.

'Eh?'

'Outside the State Bank that night.'

Tembot's reply was a roar of laughter. Then, deep in thought, shaking his massive head from side to side, he trudged on, still uttering from time to time a low chuckle.

The Colonel seemed to have dropped off to sleep, but suddenly he spoke.

Brandt's voice had no power left in it, and Tembot amplified the order with his own voice. 'Major!'

Ott came and bent down beside the wounded Colonel's head.

'Major Ott. Get one of your men over. Have him take these ropes. Are there any other prisoners?'

'Two, Herr Oberst.'

'Let them go. Let all three of them go.'

Ott flushed. 'Impossible, Herr Oberst. Our prisoners –'

'*Gefangener!*' broke in Tembot. 'Another German word I had to learn. What's all this about?'

'Go!' said Brandt with as much force as he could. 'Go back to your mountains!'

'Mountains!' roared Tembot. 'Hell, the battle's on the plain now, Colonel, on the steppe. I have to go with it. No, don't you let me go, Colonel. There's Fritzes yet for me to kill.'

'Ott, let them go.'

Major Ott protested again. 'Herr Oberst, we are in enemy-held territory. If we let them go, they will reveal our presence immediately. You have rescued us. You cannot want us to be killed now.'

Brandt remained silent for a few moments. His breathing seemed to flutter in his chest. He felt his body beginning to get cold already, cold and stiff.

'Tembot Batazarovich. Give me your word. Neither you nor the two prisoners with you will reveal the presence of this unit.'

'Colonel! Your mind is going. Think. These men of yours, what will happen? They will reach Kislovodsk, if the town is still in German hands. If not, they'll push on till they link up with their Battalion. They'll rejoin the fight. They'll kill Russians. How can I allow that? Now, how can I?'

Brandt sighed. He felt too tired. Too tired to argue.

'Major Ott. You are in command. Do as you think right. Just tell me. What was it I . . . what were my words when . . . at the end back there? Did you hear what I said?'

Ott, who had been bending to hear his Colonel's ever more feeble words, straightened up, turned his head away.

'Well?' Brandt insisted.

'You said, Herr Oberst, you shouted, I think, "I promised her!" Several times.'

'Ah!'

Brandt stared silently up at the sky, which was darkening

fast. The north star was like the last faint orange spark in a heap of dead ashes. He closed his eyes. A tiny bright spot remained.

'Major Ott.'

'Herr Oberst?'

'You will obey one final order.'

'Yes, Herr Oberst.'

'Leave those words out of your ... your operational report.'

Ott paused only fractionally before saying, '*Jawohl*, Herr Oberst.'

*

At 19.15 hours Major Ott's twelve remaining men, his wounded commanding officer and three prisoners were two and a half miles due west of Kislovodsk. From the city came sounds of sniper fire. The big guns were booming far further to the north. To Major Ott it sounded as though the shellfire was rolling across an endless plain, that already the German army was back in the terrible emptiness of the Ukraine. Brandt had lost consciousness. At 19.20 hours the Major and his senior NCO finished a discussion about how best to rejoin the retreating German forces.

They had stopped in a sheltered spot with their backs against a long low outcrop of limestone rock. The ground at their feet was clear of snow but tacky with a film of black mud. The evening air, out of the wind, was surprisingly mild. The men were in good spirits despite being tired.

The Red Army patrol that surprised them was a mounted reconnaissance platoon from the 63rd Cavalry Division.

The battle was frenzied. But brief.

Major Ott was wounded in the leg. Three of his men were killed. The rest surrendered.

Colonel Brandt, his sleep deepening into coma, had no awareness of the battle.

Tembot Batazarovich Kochan was killed in the first seconds. A Siberian Red Army Private, frightened by a fierce apparition at his reins, mistook the partisan leader for a Cossack mercenary – in the evil of which he was well indoctrinated. He fired the shot at point-blank range. The bullet split the bearded head like an explosive charge in a block of granite.

The Siberian was riding a Shaloukh stallion. Much later, the cavalryman understood that the bellow erupting from the giant Kabardinian's throat the second before he died was not of rage or hatred or fear. It was a cry of joy – of recognition!

Meanwhile, next morning, in the early hours of January 13, 1943, all the wounded, Russian and German, were transferred in a captured Opel ambulance to the nearest 'safe' town. That town was Pyatigorsk.

TWENTY-SIX

'Colonel . . . Colonel . . . Colonel!'

Slowly, slowly, it seemed to Nadia her words were getting through to him. Gradually he was understanding how close she was to him. At last his eyes flickered open.

'Colonel!' her voice repeated. In the same word she put always a different message for him – hope, concern, encouragement, love.

He stirred.

'Don't try to speak yet,' she said. 'I'll stay with you.' Despite the bandages which wrapped the top of his head and the strapping round his eyes, enough of the lower part of his face was visible for Nadia to observe the effort he was making to communicate.

She sat by the bedside, quietly watching.

Nadia couldn't believe her own composure. Even if he couldn't hear her, she had been blessed with the chance to say goodbye. It was so easy to be here beside him.

The doctors said he was sure to die. Not only did he have extensive head wounds, there was internal bleeding and damage to several organs which the overworked medical staff had no time yet to inspect.

Nevertheless, a bottle of blood was suspended above his head by leather straps, and a plastic tube wound down from it across his body and entered an artery in his right arm through a needle invisible beneath more bandages. The minimum gesture was being made. Here in the hospital, where even in the extreme pressure of the moment, with war tracking its gory course back through the city, no-one, not even the enemy, was left to bleed to death.

She saw he was whispering something, and bent nearer.

'Hand.'

Brandt was strapped into the bed as if in swaddling clothes, but Nadia pulled the ends of the coarse goat's wool blanket out from under the mattress and reached for his left hand. It was icy cold. She took it and rested it in her own hand on top of the bed, in the hollow beside the rigid bolster of his stretched-out legs.

From his expression, the small part of it she could see, Nadia knew what the touch recalled. The cottage – only a few hundred yards, maybe a mile, from this ward in the half-ruined sanitarium where they had first seen each other, where he had saved her life. Now she was unable to save his. For the first time a tear danced behind her eyes like a bubble of champagne.

She waited till his face began to relax and said, 'It's all so simple. So sad. So wonderful. I came to find my father. I must still look for him. So far there's no trace. I've been to hospitals and mortuaries, and I've tried to see people who might remember. But no-one remembers. I was here, looking for father, when the ambulance brought you. You – but I didn't know at first it was you. It was Tembot Batazarovich I recognized, even though his face . . .'

The memory of that old man's terribly mutilated though still magnificent head made Nadia's tears finally overflow. They fell in a steady trickle down her cheek and onto their joined hands.

Brandt stirred.

His lips, painfully, formed words.

But Nadia heard only confused sounds. She went on softly, 'Then I saw you! You were on a stretcher beside him, alive. But he is dead.'

His lips moved again.

'Boris . . . . Nadia, is he . . . he . . . ?'

Nadia suddenly saw what his fear was. 'No, Colonel, no, Boris is well. He is in Nalchik. He was wounded, terribly treated by the Gestapo, but –'

'I know. I am glad he . . . was saved.'

Nadia had to suppress a sudden desire to shout. 'It *was* you! Colonel, it was your men! Outside the bank – I knew it.'

She bent forward and kissed the smile that half-formed on his dry lips.

'I saw,' she whispered. 'I thank you.'

They held hands in silence. His skin felt like the petals of a flower.

At last he said, 'You must go . . . Nadia. The people here will . . . be curious.'

'They're too busy. Don't worry, Colonel. You are one among many here. German, Russian, Caucasian – it's the same for everyone.'

And, in fact, in the big L-shaped room crammed with beds and straw mattresses, crowded with wounded soldiers and families and doctors and nurses in blood-stained coats, there was no curiosity about the bandaged figure in a corner bed and the young woman holding his hand. Nadia had hardly noticed the others. They paid no attention to her or the dying man she tended.

Again she squeezed his hand. And as if the energy that flowed from her into one arm had combined with the blood dripping down into his other arm, amalgamating into a life-giving force, a kind of shudder shook his body.

'Colonel,' she said. 'I have your child. It is growing inside me.'

The pressure of their hands suddenly became too great for her to bear. Yet it was her own pressure, entirely hers. And as she relaxed it, she felt him too slip back into a more peaceful state of exhaustion. His lips moved, and she leaned forward.

'Bring me . . . a glass of wine,' he whispered. She thought this was what he asked.

Intent on receiving this almost inaudible message, Nadia failed to hear the commotion growing behind the foot of the bed, footsteps, people protesting as they were pushed aside.

Then she heard her name.

She turned – and saw him.

'Boris!'

For a second they both looked at each other, then Boris's eyes turned slowly to the German Colonel.

She leaped to her feet.

'I –'

Instinctively she stepped back. Overbalancing against the side of the low hospital bed, she thrust out an arm to stop herself falling. Her hand which, seconds ago, had been holding her lover's, struck the plastic tubing attached to the heavy bottle of blood. The fixture sprang loose. Desperately she tried to stop the flow. Boris jumped forward to help, but struck the bottle clumsily with the back of his hand. It swayed in its leather straps, spilling from the open top. A nurse seized it, held it steady, clutched for the tube, a dark snake pulsing on the pillow. Another nurse ran up and put strong arms round Nadia and Boris. 'Out. Quick. Both of you. Misha, have you got it safe? Okay, okay. Now. You two. Out!'

The large gray-haired woman hustled them into the long stone corridor like a couple of drunks out onto the sidewalk.

*

At first they stood, not looking at each other, staring at the cold flagstones, stunned. Slowly waking to the danger of obstructing stretchers and crutches, Nadia pushed Boris into a narrow recess by a locked door.

Boris took her hand. Drawing in a deep breath, he said, 'The Gestapo, yes, they told me. They showed me a picture of him. I don't know if there's anything to forgive, but I forgive you. I trust you. I didn't come to . . . to spy. I –'

'Then I must tell you *why*. Boris, I thank you so. Thank you for your trust. Now, listen, listen to me.'

She talked and talked, holding nothing back.

Boris drew her into his arms and held her tight and he himself began to talk. There were tears in his eyes.

All the time, right beside them, the physical horror of the hospital, the bandaged, flapping, shrouded figures, the stink of blood and infection and ether, raged along the corridor like a mountain stream after a storm, swirling along the uprooted debris, jagged and dirty. Boris and Nadia clutched each other for safety in their shallow backwater at the edge of the torrent.

A stretcher like all the others, a frame of thin dented tubular metal with squeaking wheels covered with a gray shroud, was thrust along the corridor by a shouting orderly against the current of the arriving wounded.

If either had lifted the end of this plain sheet they would have seen, stiff and pale, the lightly-bearded cheeks and chin of Colonel Brandt. Had they followed the stretcher down the stone-flagged passage, out into the sloping street, they would have seen the body lifted unceremoniously into a waiting truck, where in the back, it was stacked among a dozen others.

Later, if they had followed this makeshift hearse, they would have seen the body of the Colonel, hard to distinguish among so many others, manhandled into a grave, one of many in a long line dug in a snowy field on the eastern edge of the city.

There was no sign on the grave, no cross or tombstone, nothing to mark it out from any other in the field.

Boris put his arm round Nadia's shoulders. They walked together slowly, following in the wake of yet another shrouded stretcher, to the big main door of the sanitarium.

Outside, the snow had begun to fall.

Nadia pulled back into the shelter of the pillared porch and stared out at the fat flakes tumbling through the low gray afternoon sky.

Trees, roof-tops, gardens, the galleries and grottoes where the poet Lermontov flirted and gossiped and quarrelled his way into a senseless, fatal duel, all were spread with a pure white shroud of fresh snow.

As she watched, she felt the soft trembling wings of a butterfly trapped deep inside her. It is too soon, she thought, this tiny sign of life. Yet I feel it. A spasm of sickness shook her body.

She waited a moment until she felt recovered.

A low growl came out of the sky.

High over their heads, invisible above the snowclouds, a squadron of Stormovik assault bombers of the Soviet Air Force droned steadily toward the west.

All this while Boris and Nadia spoke long and honestly to each other. Only when they both lapsed finally into an exhausted silence did the old gray-haired nurse see them, and take pity on them, and fight her way across the corridor to tell them it was not their fault, but the German was dead.

EPILOGUE

The retreat of the German armies turned at the Caucasus front and at Stalingrad continued for two years and four months.

One year and two months after the liberation of Nalchik, in March 1944, Red Army and NKVD trucks brought into the city every man, woman and child of Balkar origin found in the mountain villages. Together with their compatriots already living in Nalchik, they were assembled at the railway station and herded into cattle trucks. The survivors were dumped in towns and villages in Central Asia. The Kabardinians were not exiled as a race. Many thousands, however, were executed as war criminals and traitors.

The Balkars returned in 1957, their exile officially admitted to have been 'a mistake'.

Yusef Tsagov escaped the round-up in 1944. Four years later he was apprehended on suspicion of murder in Alma Ata. Identified, he returned for trial as a traitor and Nazi agent in Nalchik. He was executed in January 1949.

'Auntie' and Mariana died within weeks of each other in the autumn of 1960, the first of viral pneumonia and the second of a stroke.

Luda Alexandrovna married a Georgian boot factory chairman, Georgi Rustaveli. She still lives in Tbilisi, where she moved immediately after her marriage in 1947. She is now a widow.

Captain Boris Surkov was killed in a German bombing raid behind the lines near the Polish border in October 1944, just one of twenty million Russian dead in the Great Patriotic War.

Boris knew about Vanya from his frequent, sometimes

difficult, often warm, correspondence with his wife. He never saw the little boy.

Nadia continued to live with her two children in Nalchik after Vanya was born on September 19, 1943. She taught in her old school from 1946 until soon after her mother died. In the spring of 1954 she moved to Moscow where she married Vladimir Dozorov, an aeronautical engineer and widower. Nadia Dozorova died of cancer in Moscow in July 1980. Her second husband survived her by six months, also dying of cancer.

Nadia's daughter, Darya Borisova, married a movie actor in 1957, divorced him after two years, remarried a young professor of linguistics in 1963, had two boys in quick succession, and followed her professor to Kiev, where both have remained, happily, ever since.

Vanya grew up spoiled and bright, dropped out of Moscow University, travelled with actors, working with them on stage and behind, returned to his studies and qualified as a doctor in 1973. He is now a neuro-surgeon in a Moscow polyclinic, unmarried, showing the first signs of acquiring a reputation for seducing nurses.

Hans Guggenbühl became the batman of Lieutenant-General von Kreuss. Both survived the war. Hans cooked noodles for several more years at his own Austrian inn, sometimes playing host to a gathering of veterans. He died of a heart attack in 1961.